PENGUIN BOOKS
AFTER YESTERDAY'S CRASH

Larry McCaffery has published several critical studies of postmodern fiction, including *Storming the Reality Studio: A Casebook of Cyberpunk and Postmodern Fiction*; four interview volumes with contemporary authors; and a number of anthologies of postmodern fiction, including *Avant-Pop: Fiction for a Daydream Nation*. The latter appeared in the new Black Ice Books Avant-Pop Series, which he coedits. He is also editor of several literary magazines: *Fiction International, American Book Review*, and *Critique: Studies in Contemporary Fiction*. He currently resides in the desert of the real—Borrego Springs, California—where he and his wife, Sinda Gregory, have recently reported several Elvis sightings.

AFTER YESTERDAY'S CRASH

⬇

THE AVANT-POP ANTHOLOGY

EDITED BY LARRY McCAFFERY

PENGUIN BOOKS

PENGUIN BOOKS
Published by the Penguin Group
Penguin Books USA Inc., 375 Hudson Street, New York, New York 10014, U.S.A.
Penguin Books Ltd, 27 Wrights Lane, London W8 5TZ, England
Penguin Books Australia Ltd, Ringwood, Victoria, Australia
Penguin Books Canada Ltd, 10 Alcorn Avenue, Toronto, Ontario, Canada M4V 3B2
Penguin Books (N.Z.) Ltd, 182–190 Wairau Road, Auckland 10, New Zealand

Penguin Books Ltd, Registered Offices:
Harmondsworth, Middlesex, England

First published in Penguin Books 1995

1 3 5 7 9 10 8 6 4 2

LIBRARY OF CONGRESS CATALOGING IN PUBLICATION DATA
After yesterday's crash : the avant-pop anthology / edited by Larry McCaffery.
p. cm.
ISBN 0 14 02.4085 3
1. American literature—20th century. 2. Literature,
Experimental—United States. 3. Popular literature—United States.
I. McCaffery, Larry, 1946–   .
PS536.2.A35 1995
813'.5408—dc20   94–48772

Printed in the United States of America
Set in Sabon
Designed by Katy Riegel

*For Bruce Sterling and William T. Vollmann,
for repeated displays of valor, friendship, and
generosity after yesterday's crash.*

For Sinda, for helping me stay buckled up.

*And in memory of Donald Barthelme,
for his many contributions to
the aesthetics of trash.*

Unfold strange flowers
And electric butterflies!

—Arthur Rimbaud,
"Remarks to a Poet
on the Subject of Flowers"

There is no plain sense of the word,
nothing is straightforward,
description a lie behind lie:
but truths can still be told.

—Charles Bernstein,
"The Lives of the Toll Takers"

CONTENTS

AVANT-POP: STILL LIFE AFTER YESTERDAY'S CRASH

The highest art will be the one which in its conscious content presents the thousandfold problems of the day, the art which has been visibly shattered by the explosions of last week, which is forever trying to collect its limbs after yesterday's crash. . . . Hatred of the press, hatred of advertising, hatred of SENSATIONS are typical of people who prefer their armchair to the noise of the street. Life appears as a simultaneous muddle of noises, colors and spiritual rhythms, which is taken unmodified with all the sensations screams and fevers of its reckless everyday psyche and with all its brutal reality.

—1918 Berlin Dadaist Manifesto

THE BEAST IS LOOSE

The Blank mumble blat / Babble song babble song / Foaming at the mouth / Won ton soupie . . . The Beast is Loose
> —Bucky Wunderlick, "Pee-Pee-Maw-Maw"
> (in Don DeLillo's *Great Jones Street*)

When they put the silence on you, there is no recovery. You are turned into a media buffoon or worse.
> —Stephen Wright, "Light" (this volume, p. 90)

As the many-headed, many-armed rough beast of apocalyptic change first sighted by William Butler Yeats more than seventy-five years ago[1] has continued slouching its way across the twentieth century toward our own era's simulated-millennial version of Bethlehem, it has become increasingly obvious that the biggest challenge facing contemporary American artists is no longer a matter of trying to figure out how to halt or deflect the progress of the beast, but of learning how to coexist with it. For the beast is *already here,* having checked in a few years ahead of its originally scheduled arrival time, accompanied by its most recent live-in lover and caretaker, Hyperconsumer Capitalism, and bringing with it just what the movie directors and the Moonies and the rock stars said it would—a little gift called . . .

---

1 *". . . somewhere in sands of the desert / A shape with lion body and the head of a man, / A gaze blank and pitiless as the sun, / Is moving its slow thighs, while all about it / Reel shadows of the indignant desert birds. . . . And what rough beast, its hour come round at last, / slouches towards Bethlehem to be born?"*
> —William Butler Yeats, "The Second Coming"

APOCALYPSE NOW²

This world comes to an end, for which we are grateful. The Chosen Ones rejoice at the prospect of the apocalypse, for it is the sign of our future reign in a millennial kingdom elsewhere in the universe.

—Craig Baldwin, from *Tribulation 99*
(this volume, p. 42)

Fredric Jameson has described the beginnings of the end of the world as we know it as involving "a prodigious expansion of culture throughout the social realm, to the point at which everything in our social life—from economic value and state power practice to the very structure of the psyche itself—can be said to have become cultural in some original and as yet untheorized sense." This unprecedented expansion of culture, made possible specifically by the exponential growth of technology, has changed the contours of the world: pop culture has not only displaced nature and "colonized" the physical space of nearly every country on earth, but (just as important) it has also begun to colonize even those inner, subjective realms that nearly everyone once believed were inviolable, such as people's memories, sexual desires, their unconsciousness.

The problem for serious art, then, has been to learn how to

---

2 Not unexpectedly, apocalyptic overtones and millennial references recur throughout *After Yesterday's Crash* and are central topics in several selections, including Craig Baldwin's excerpt from *Tribulation 99*, Eurudice "EHMH," Ronald Sukenick's "Hand Writing on Wall," Bret Easton Ellis's "End of the 1980s," Don DeLillo's "The Rapture of the Athlete Assumed into Heaven," William Gibson's "Skinner's Room," Stephen Wright's "Light," Bruce Sterling's "Heavy Weather," and Steve Erickson's "Arc d'X." Baldwin's *Tribulation 99* provides a good example of Avant-Pop's collaborative approach to composition—taking found materials (in this case, images drawn from documentary footage and grade-B science fiction films from the 1950s) and then overlaying an elaborate plot concerning creatures from another planet who have crash-landed on earth, replicated themselves into human "dupes," and then gone about preparing to completely destroy the earth. Woody Allen—one of America's great Avant-Pop figures, whose evolution as an artist displays a great deal about the evolution of Avant-Pop generally—created an early classic example of this method in his film *What's Up, Tiger Lily?*

survive in these new conditions, for just about everything in this culture of mass media has conspired against the ways in which art was previously created and received. Jameson's point about the expansion of culture is the crucial issue here: how does writing, or art of any kind, adapt within a landscape whose surface is *already comprised* of the kinds of signs and replications that had once been available from art? In fact, this landscape has increasingly become less a literal territory than a multidimensional *hyperreality* of television lands, media "jungles," and information "highways," a place where the real is now a "desert" that is "rained on" by a ceaseless "downpour" of information and data; "flooded" by a "torrent" of disposable consumer goods, narratives, images, ads, signs, and electronically generated stimuli; and peopled by media figures whose lives and stories seem at once more vivid, more familiar, and *more real* than anything the artist might create. Adapting to these new conditions has been especially difficult for fiction, a print-bound medium that seems especially ill-suited for survival in the global village's electronic system of communication, with its bewildering proliferation of new lingos, databases, and 57 channels (soon expanding to 500). The question, then, has been: how can the writer produce a convincing sense of the exponential increase in sensory input—this blizzard of white noise, random codes, and competing realities—which makes it difficult enough to locate *anything* (including yourself), much less create art about it? Or render the enormous changes that this increase has wrought on people's view of themselves and the world around them?

BAD NEWS: THE TOTALITY OF LOSS IN YESTERDAY'S CRASH

> *The spectacle originates in the loss of the unity of the world, and the gigantic expansion of the modern spectacle expresses the totality of this loss . . ."*
>
> —Guy Debord, *Society of the Spectacle*

These were obviously difficult questions to answer—so difficult that when the word started going down in the late sixties that the novel had died, plenty of people mourned its loss, but nobody was really very surprised. In fact, the death of serious fiction was usually seen as being just an extension of the larger tragedy—the crash of the High Modernist program, which had apparently taken the lives of the avant-garde, the author, and everyone else associated with "high art." As with the assassination of John F. Kennedy, the crash of High Modernism was seen by many people as marking the end of a certain kind of optimism and self-assurance that had helped shape our notion of what fiction (or art of any kind) should be. For nearly a hundred years, the aesthetic laboratories of High Modernism had been filled with a vigorous breed of innovative artists who were confident their experiments would result in finding a means for serious art to survive, but in the end the beast proved too powerful. Surveying the wreckage left behind by the crash of the High Modernist program, noted art historian Robert Hughes observed, "The modernist laboratory is now vacant. It has become less an arena for significant experiment and more like a period room in a museum, a historical space that we can enter, look at, but no longer be part of. . . . What has our culture lost in 1980 that the *avant-garde* had in 1890? Ebullience, idealism, confidence, the belief that there was plenty of territory to explore, and, above all, the sense that art, in the most disinterested and noble way, could find the necessary metaphors by which a radically changing culture could be explained to its inhabitants." Such glum assessments were seconded by a whole range of literary critics, semioticians, and cultural theorists who had jury-rigged the Postmodernist program, which achieved liftoff in the aftermath of the crash of High Modernism. According to the leading experts of the PoMod Squad, not only had serious art died but so had a lot of other things—including meaning, truth, originality, the author (and authority generally), realism, even reality itself.

GOOD NEWS: AFTER YESTERDAY'S CRASH

It turns out, though, that such widely circulated reports of the death of serious writing and art in America were greatly exaggerated. Even as apologists for the PoMod Squad's program of absence, disappearance, skepticism, and loss were issuing one obituary notice after another, a new breed of media-savvy American writers and artists were busy down in their basement laboratories mixing up some new kinds of aesthetic medicine, specifically designed to revitalize artists suffering from info-overload, psychic fragmentation, loss of affect, reality decay, daydream drift, and other debilitating symptoms of life in post-apocalypse America. One of the most hopeful signs that these experiments have been successful has been the recent emergence of the "Avant-Pop" sensibility showcased in the thirty-two stories, novel excerpts, and text-and-visual materials included in *After Yesterday's Crash*. These selections have been written by an extremely eclectic array of American authors who share a fascination with mass culture and the determination to find a means of entering and exploring the belly of this beast[3] without getting permanently swallowed or becoming mere extensions of its operations (the fate of Andy Warhol and Pop Art).

After Yesterday's Crash includes recent, previously unpublished works by several of Avant-Pop's seminal early figures such as Ronald Sukenick, Robert Coover, Steve Katz, and Raymond Federman—post-Beat authors who grew up listening to baseball and Bird, who during their twenties watched Elvis change the spin of the entire planet with just a few shakes of his televised pelvis, and who during the 1960s left the isolation of their underground ghetto to join a small but raucous crowd[4] up on the pop culture dance floor, where they shimmied all night long with disreputable types that "serious" artists had always been warned to steer clear of: comic books, genre novels, grade-B Hollywood films, sports, and television. It also includes work by tricksters, maximalists,

3 Cf. "*Pop culture is the entrails through which Americans can understand our collective past and individual futures.*"—Edward Leffingwell, "Introduction," *Modern Dream: The Rise and Fall of Pop*. This notion of traveling through the entrails to discover the essence of the culture is described in Eurudice's "EHMH: A Millennial Romance" (this volume, p. 156).

4 This crowd included William S. Burroughs (Avant-Pop's true godfather, who appears in this volume in a cameo role in David Blair's "Ella's Special Camera" as James Hive-Maker); Spike Jones; Alfred Bester; William Gaines (editor of *Mad* magazine); Andy Warhol; Jean-Luc Godard; Roy Lichtenstein; Marshall McLuhan; Philip K. Dick; Susan Sontag (who didn't dance much but enjoyed watching); and Carl Stalling (creator of the most influential and memorable music of his day—the Warner Brothers' cartoon scores).

Border-writers, and other eccentrics—writers like Tom Robbins, Guillermo Gómez-Peña, Rikki Ducornet, Paul Auster, Don De-Lillo, Curt White, Harold Jaffe, and Gerald Vizenor—who kept the avant-party going during the late seventies to mid-eighties while most of America was retreating into reactionary conservatism.

But the main emphasis here is work by the most interesting new kids on the literary block, those who had never *not* been jacked into a remote-control culture: rappers (Ricardo Cruz, Mark Amerika); hackers (Marc Laidlaw, David Blair); cyberpunk god-fathers (William Gibson, Bruce Sterling); slackers (Craig Padawer, Ben Marcus); brat-packers (Bret Easton Ellis, David Foster Wallace); postfeminists (Lynne Tillman, Eurudice, Susan Daitch, Lauren Fairbanks); and visionary lunatics (Stephen Wright, Steve Erickson, William T. Vollmann, Craig Baldwin).

Based on what we find here in terms of the range of voice and stylistic innovation, the diversity and ambition of its themes, and the ability to use the forms and archetypes of pop culture as a means of examining the status of life and writing in contemporary America, I believe that this collection provides compelling evidence of a renewal of precisely those qualities of optimism, confidence, and adventurousness that Robert Hughes found to be missing from art in the aftermath of High Modernism. And what this sense of renewal suggests is that at least a certain percentage of America's most ambitious and talented writers have not only met the challenge of coexisting with the beast of technologically driven change, but have also learned how to *dance with it*.

AVANT-POP, OR THE CULTURAL LOGIC OF HYPERCONSUMER CAPITALISM[5]

> *More is different.*
> —Kevin Kelly, "Out of Control"

Avant-Pop combines Pop Art's focus on consumer goods and mass media with the avant-garde's spirit of subversion and

---

5 One way to describe the difference between Pop Art and Avant-Pop would be to say that whereas Pop Art was an expression of the logic and technologies associated with the ideology of consumption (which governed capitalist expansion during the

emphasis on radical formal innovation. Avant-Pop shares with Pop Art the crucial recognition that *popular* culture, rather than traditional sources of high culture—the Bible; myth; the revered classics of art, painting, music, and literature—is now what supplies the citizens of postindustrial nations with the key images, character and narrative archetypes, metaphors, and points of reference and allusion that help us establish our sense of who we are, what we want and fear, and how we see ourselves and the world. Thus, the content of Pop Art and Avant-Pop overlap to the extent that they both focus on consumer products—particularly media products (television shows, movies, pop music, etc.), advertising images, and other pop culture materials. Avant-Pop also shares with Pop Art the insight that pop culture imagery had considerable untapped potential as a medium for artistic expression—that mass-produced materials could be shown to be aesthetically interesting and appealing once they were removed from their familiar commercial context. On the other hand, whereas Pop Artists tended to appropriate pop culture materials as something to be faithfully du-

---

fifties and sixties), Avant-Pop represents the logic and technologies associated with the next phase of capitalist expansion, initiated during the Reagan era: the ideology of hyperconsumption. This latter ideology emphasized not merely consuming but consuming *a lot*, and it was in the areas of information, data technology (read: computers), and mass culture where the greatest potential for growth lay. Such a change in the amount of consumption required a corresponding acceleration of obsolesence and an increase in the rate of turnover (both would ensure that customers would want/need new products to replace the old). Voilà: America's Society of the Spectacle, a place of frantic, ever escalating *panic* buying and selling; near-infinite reproducibility; *and* disposability—a literal and psychological space that has been radically expanded by recent video, computer, digital, Xerox, and audio developments; by the system's growing efficiency in transforming space and time into consumable sounds, narratives, and images; and by the population's exponentially increased access to cultural artifacts that can be played, replayed, cut up, and otherwise manipulated by a flick of the joy stick. These developments, in turn, wind up having a significant impact on just about every area of consumer production, including the media. In all areas this means a greater and greater premium on the new, the "in," anything at all to make your product seem different from your competitor's and the one you were selling last year (last month, last week). It's no accident that mass media—rock music, MTV, films, TV, and TV advertising—began increasingly to incorporate features of radical innovation formerly associated with the avant-garde: that's because the logic of hyperconsumption, with its emphasis on "the new" was, of course, *precisely the same logic that had driven the avant-garde movement all along.*

plicated and left untransformed, Avant-Pop tends to rely on considerably more flexible strategies which often amount to active collaborations with, rather than neutral presentation of, the original materials.

SLEEPING WITH THE ENEMY: COEVOLUTION

> *Coevolution can be seen as two parties snared in a web of mutual propaganda. Coevolutionary relationships, from parasites to allies, are in their essence informational. A steady exchange of information welds them into a single system. At the same time, the exchange—whether of insults or assistance or plain news—creates a commons from which cooperation, self-organization, and win-win endgames can spawn.*
>
> —Kevin Kelly, *Out of Control*

Avant-Pop's emphasis on collaborative strategies would also seem to differentiate it from the avant-garde. Like the avant-garde, Avant-Pop often relies on the use of radical aesthetic methods to confuse, confound, bewilder, piss off, and generally blow the fuses of ordinary citizens exposed to it (a "deconstructive strategy")— but just as frequently it does so with the intention of creating a sense of delight, amazement, and amusement ("reconstructive"). This willingness to enter "enemy" territory for any reason other than to plant a bomb was, of course, foreign to the avant-garde's way of thinking, but in fact this tendency emerged largely due to a basic realignment that had been occurring between the avant-garde and mass culture. Instead of being engaged in a Darwinian survival-of-the-fittest struggle for dominance, these two avowed lifelong enemies *coevolved* so that by the early 1980s they existed in a new relationship to one another—a web of interactivity that created a feedback loop in which the avant-garde and mass culture rapidly exchanged information, stylistic tendencies, narrative archetypes, and character representations with one another in such a way that was ultimately mutually supportive. It seemed strange, but the enemy was no longer the enemy. In fact, if either of them died the other would either be severely weakened or (in the case of the avant-garde) die off completely.

TUNE TOWN: THE BIRTHPLACE OF THE TERM *AVANT-POP*

> *Whether we like it or not, the era of the composer as autonomous musical mind is just about come to an end. At this point in musical history, the relevant question is, "What exactly does a composer do?"*
>
> —John Zorn, "John Zorn on His Music"
> (liner notes to Zorn's landmark
> avant-pop *Spillane*)

I've borrowed the term *Avant-Pop* from the title of a 1986 album by Lester Bowie, the great jazz trumpet player and composer best known for his work with the wildly inventive Art Ensemble of Chicago. Listening to the way Bowie used the basic structures and "content" of such familiar pop tunes as "Crazy" and "Blueberry Hill" as a springboard for producing a collaborative, improvisatory new work was instrumental (no pun intended) in my beginning to think about what I was later to term the *Avant-Pop phenomenon*. It immediately occurred to me that such methods were analogous to those being used in postmodern fiction, for example, in Kathy Acker's "rewrites" of classic novels (e.g., *Great Expectations* and *Don Quixote*) or in the various "cover versions" of myths, Biblical stories, and fairy tales by Donald Barthelme, Robert Coover, John Barth, and Steve Katz. In the case of Bowie's *Avant-Pop*, the results of this collaborative approach to earlier material were at once zingingly ironic and funny, yet also genuinely expansive.

In this regard, Bowie's approach to composition is exemplary of Avant-Pop aesthetics generally: here was an artist who assumed in advance his audience's familiarity with what Robert Coover has called the "mythic residues" of society: those shards of cultural memory and artifice that simultaneously help organize our responses to the world and tyrannically limit the options of those responses. Bowie, like Coover and other Avant-Pop artists, doesn't ask his audience to attempt to deny or ignore these elements (inevitably a fruitless task since society *requires* such materials); nor does he introduce them either as something merely to be mocked, parodied, or re-presented in the neutral, celebratory manner of Andy Warhol or with the ironic distance of more recent appropriation artists like Sherri Levine. What people need to do instead, Bowie implies, is recognize that these glitzy, kitschy, easily consumable pop materials are a rich source of *raw material* whose elements can be explored, played with, and otherwise creatively transformed. Like John Zorn, Eugene Chadbourne, and several other important Avant-Pop musicians who were working at the boundaries of jazz and pop music at about this same time, Bowie showed how artists could use such "public" materials for sustained improvisational purposes. Such materials, while normally seen as being fixed or confined in terms of their "meaning" and arrangement, actually contain an inexhaustible source of hidden resonances and recombinatory arrangements. In short, Bowie had suggested how to put the *Avant* into Pop Art.

REINSTALLING THE REALISM PROGRAM

"Maybe I feel that my writing has always been realistic and that until now it has just been misperceived as being otherwise."
—Robert Coover

A number of formal tendencies recur in many of the selections in *After Yesterday's Crash*. Most of these are technical devices developed as a means of conveying a more accurate sense of the way people conceive of themselves and the world they live in than that supplied by traditional realism. But this decision to abandon the conventions of traditional realism is not based on what is usually ascribed to the Postmodernists—that is, skepticism regarding language's ability to render "meaning" and "truth" about the world, hence the decision to move inside the funhouse of language and write metafictions, or antifiction, or irrealism, and so on—nor on the avant-garde's tendency to abandon story in favor of experimentalism merely for experimentalism's sake. Quite the contrary, the authors included in this volume show little interest in abstractions and their selections are absolutely saturated with narrative. What has been jettisoned, then, is not an interest in story, nor in "realism," but the traditions of *conventional* realism—linear plots, causally related events, carefully orchestrated sequences of beginnings, middles, and ends that produce a satisfying "resolution"— all of which were formulated in the eighteenth and nineteenth centuries, when life had a totally different feel than it does in an Avant-Pop cultural age of MTV, jump cuts, channel surfing, interactivity, and reality decay. Instead Avant-Pop has invented a whole range of innovative formal strategies and narrative approaches modeled on more kinetic, dynamic, nonliterary forms of art:[6]

- action painting's emphasis on the emotional and aesthetic intensity of the creative act;
- the improvisational, digressive structures of jazz and cartoons;

6 The cross-genre impulses of Avant-Pop are fundamental, and thus it's not surprising that many of the writers included in *After Yesterday's Crash* have backgrounds in forms outside of fiction per se. For example, a number of these writers have worked in visual media (painting, video, television, film, comic books, and cartoons): Robert Coover studied for a time at Chicago's Art Institute, later wrote and directed a film, and recently headed a pilot program in the use of hypertext); Derek Pell (aka Norman Conquest) also studied at the prestigious Art Institute, has published numerous text and visual works, and—as Conquest—has had his visual work and "multiples" frequently exhibited in galleries; Lynne Tillman and Eurudice have done films; Susan Daitch began as a cartoonist and studied painting; William Vollmann provides illustrations for his books and has created numerous "book objects" that include his own paintings and sculptures; Rikki Ducornet has done cartoons and has illustrated works by Borges and Coover; Steve Katz has worked in various multi-media forms, happenings, and spent several years immersed in the New York City art scene; and Tom Robbins was an art critic before he became an Avant Pop cult hero. Several other authors have backgrounds in other non-fiction forms: music (Ricardo Cruz, Raymond Federman, Mark Leyner, Mark Amerika, and David Foster Wallace, who wrote one of the first books about rap music); poetry (Auster, Ducornet, Fairbanks, Gómez-Peña, Eurudice, Katz, Coover, Vizenor, Vollmann, Pell); theater (DeLillo, Coover, Gómez-Peña); screenplays (Gibson, Auster, Eurudice, Katz, Coover, Tillman); translation (Auster, Vizenor, Coover, Federman).

- the slam-dance pacings, surrealism, and visceral intensity of punk and MTV;
- hypertext's reliance on branching narrative paths;
- television's flow of different worlds, its casual-but-intimate interaction between what is going on in the tube (the "programming flow") and the real world ("household flow"), its creation of "people" (like celebrities and politicians) and pseudo events (call-in shows, press conferences, opinion polls, and talk shows), and its emphasis on surface textures and cool, glitzy depictions of everything from car chases (O. J. Simpson) and Jovian fly-bys to smart bombs, lite-beer ads, and faith healers—images that become flattened and equalized by the television screen, drained of all affect, and internalized inside our minds and desires, where they soon are as much a "real" part of our personalities and awareness as anything else;
- the information-dense feel of advertising, with its flash of seductive images, micro-miniaturized narratives, and in-jokes designed not to convince but to seduce or gain attention;
- the windows-within-windows structures of computer software and video games, with their dizzying sense of infinite regress;
- rap music's sampling techniques, with an endless recycling of "bites" feeding the hand that rearranges them into new aesthetic contexts;
- and principles of collage and other forms of spatial, visual, aural, and temporal arrangements borrowed from video and cinema.

Not coincidentally, these nonliterary sources are ones whose hold on America's imagination has profoundly increased during the past twenty-five years of media-culture expansion. It is only to be expected that American authors who have grown up in this environment are registering and analyzing its effects—and then re-presenting these to us in literary forms that, for all their emphasis on what would once have been regarded as avant-garde treatments of style and theme, are actually "realistic" renderings of our own avant-populist age.

GHOSTS IN THE MACHINE

Ghosts—disembodied spirits of times and people past—have haunted the imaginations of artists from the earliest cave dwellers up through Henry James and Stephen King, and they show up in a number of selections in *After Yesterday's Crash* as well. For instance, Ghost Dance Genes that "heal diseases, regenerate bodies, and much more" play a key role in Gerald Vizenor's trickster transformations of the familiar Christopher Columbus story (i.e., Indians get victimized by white men) into a tale of self-empowerment. In William T. Vollmann's "Incarnations of the Murderer" a ghostly murderer moves through space and time, inhabiting whatever person he needs in order to do his thing. There are various other sorts of spirits floating around in the Avant-Pop selections as well—UFOs (in Craig Baldwin's excerpt from *Tribulation 99*, Bret Easton Ellis's "End of the 1980s," Ronald Sukenick's "Hand Writing on Wall," and Stephen Wright's "Light"); human thoughts (in Marc Laidlaw's "Great Breakthroughs in Darkness"); the Devil (in Rikki Ducornet's "The Exorcist") and, of course, Elvis (sighted here in Ronald Sukenick's "Hand Writing on Wall"). Natural scientists, tabloid journalists, and television docudramatists, as well as ordinary citizens, are trying to track these things down, to "capture" them so that they can be reified and "preserved" (read: rendered inert), transformed into photographs or digitalized data that can be whisked away to microstorage sights where they can be readily accessed, remixed, reassembled, and—if the opportunity presents itself (and it usually does these days)—mechanically reproduced into copies that can then be marketed, advertised, sold, and hyperconsumed by a public programmed to be on the lookout for just this kind of "novelty" item.

With so much already stored away and available to anyone with enough computer memory and the right software, there is naturally something fascinating about things that as yet evade our efforts to download them. Hence the recurrence in this volume of the invention of the machine capable of capturing aspects of experience not presently "capturable": a "special camera" capable of photographing the spirits of the dead hovering near their loved ones (in David Blair's "Ella's Special Camera"); a "psychopraxiscope," which records human thoughts (in Marc Laidlaw's "Great Breakthroughs in Darkness"); the Smell Machine, Listening Frame, Air Tattoos, and other contraptions described by Ben Marcus in his stunning alternate–alternate-world glossary, "False Water Society." Such fabulous inventions are, of course, extensions of our own *actual* fabulous inventions—the camera, the video camera, X-ray machines, telescopes, microscopes, the computer—which have utterly changed the borders of reality, human perception, and memory. These magical mirrors possess the awesome power to petrify the past, providing visual access to realms that until very recently no one could ever conceptualize. In a universe whose only constant seems to be transformation, the ability to make things stop for even a moment is a remarkable triumph.

The ultimate goal, of course, is to be able one day to record—thus capturing it, making it susceptible to human reason and control—everything. That, at any rate, is the goal of Rikki Ducornet's Exorcist in her fable by that name. Informed by the Devil that "Nothing exists until it is seen," the Exorcist buys himself a camera and begins recording all the sacred substance of existence, and he gradually learns what it has taken the great multinational corporations until recently to discover: that "not only did all this information—like thousands of little pins—hold the Universe in place, it also gave him power." Ducornet unfolds her allegory in a prose style that recalls that of Italo Calvino in the way that its sensuous evocation of the particular magically conjures up the mystical and universal. Marc Laidlaw's "Great Breakthroughs in Darkness" is a more extended allegory about a similar search for the photographic key capable of unlocking, if not the mysteries of the universe, then at least the inner workings of human beings. The narrator tells us of his visits to the laboratory of Conreid Aanschultz, inventor of the psychopraxiscope, which is purported to offer instantaneous viewing of any subject's thoughts: "Aanschultz believed that close observation of physiology and similar superficial phenomena could lead to direct revelation of the inner or secret processes of nature."

Such devices may create the options for our being able to enter new worlds of experience, but in many of the selections in *After Yesterday's Crash* the end result is the disturbing sense that the proliferation of such devices *denatures* human experience, artificially producing sensations and information that distort our relationship to the real, thus actually closing off the doors of perception rather than opening them. As Dash (the paranoid, murderous, visionary narrator of Stephen Wright's mind-blowing selection, "Light") puts it, "Reality is a place you can access only with the proper clearances. Everything genuine disappears. What's left, the cardboard maze we're *free* to scurry about in, is pure Dittoland."

REALITY SURFING

Most Americans today are used to momentarily giving over their sense of their everyday reality to the "virtual worlds" accessible via television, movie theaters, video games, computers, and other simulation systems. This "daydream drift" is not unique to our own era (books are one such system, as are the nontechnologically generated experiences of ordinary daydreaming), but the rapid proliferation of such systems has made the experience of entering these worlds increasingly commonplace—and hence has increased the sense most people have of living in a pluralistic world while also supplying them with the ideal models of behavior, speech patterns, codes of dress, and so on that shape their consciousness in various ways. By the mid-1980s, it was not uncommon for mainstream writers to use references to television, films, sports, and rock music simply as part of the "realistic" settings in the works, but Avant-Pop authors frequently use genre norms in a more thoroughgoing manner: either by having characters in an otherwise realistic setting suddenly enter a "genre world" possessing its own character types, norms of behavior and speech, and so on, or by having the entire story or novel set there.[7] Thus, in one of the panels from Derek Pell's "Weird Romance" selection in this volume, for example, the protagonist, Dexter—literally a two-dimensional cartoon figure whose features have been "processed" by Conquest so that he looks like a character from *Eraserhead* and who "normally" lives in a grotesque cartoon version of a genre romance novel—is shown in the foreground of a room full of women who initially appear to have been selected by the Lord to receive the Pentecostal tongues of fire. However, Dexter, who has apparently been downloaded into this scene without warning, only expresses puzzlement and then the suspicion that he's not in the presence of the Lord at all but of another con man using religion as a come-on. His remarks probably sum up the sorts of ontological confusions that recur throughout *After Yesterday's Crash*: "WHAT THE HELL AM I DOING **HERE?** WONDERED DEXTER. HE WAS SUR-ROUNDED BY APPLAUDING FLAME-BRAINS IN AN EVIL **INFOMERCIAL!** HE RECOGNIZED TAMMY-BODEEN AND AUNT EMILY AND GRANNY BATES. SOMETHING **SCREWY** WAS GOING ON!"

PSYCHOLOGICAL DIMENSIONS

The treatment of character found in *After Yesterday's Crash* grows naturally (if you'll pardon the phrase) out of Avant-Pop's depiction of an info-overloaded, remote-control culture capable of accessing innumerable realities with just a casual flick of the joy stick. As the mediascape seems at once to expand outward and advance inward, it becomes increasingly difficult for characters to be able to isolate an irreducible authentic "me" that can be separated from the constructed desires, memories, and opinions occupying their minds. The authors often present characters living in an extremely

7 See, for example, Steve Katz's "Current Events," where the characters seem to be living in a kind of revolving-door reality; other genre worlds can be found in Robert Coover's "A Lucky Pierre World Premiere" (a cinema world), Curtis White's "Bonanza" (the TV world of the "Bonanza" show), Don DeLillo's "The Rapture of the Athlete Assumed into Heaven" (world of TV sports broadcasting), Derek Pell's "Weird Romance" (genre-romance-novel world).

destabilized environment in which image, hallucination, reality, and psychosis are utterly indistinguishable. Thus the "settings" of stories such as Bret Easton Ellis's "End of the 1980s," Stephen Wright's "Light," Derek Pell's "Weird Romance," Lynne Tillman's "Bad News" (a more subtle treatment), and many others are less actual places than mediascapes experienced by the characters as real but by the reader more as schizophrenic projections of a thoroughly "medi-ated" ego. These environments are so thoroughly interpenetrated by simulations, paranoia, and media archetypes that readers and characters alike are never quite sure where they are.

THE HIVE MIND OF POP CULTURE

> *Like a cell or the person, it [the bee hive] behaves*
> *as a unitary whole, maintaining its identity in*
> *space, resisting dissolution . . . neither a thing nor*
> *a concept, but a continual flux or process.*
> —William Morton Wheeler,
> *Journal of Morphology*

I began this introduction by using the metaphor of the beast to model the vast transformations of technologically driven change, but I would like to conclude with a different metaphor here which seems more relevant—that of a hive. When Avant-Pop artists look out their windows onto the streets of America's society of the spectacle, they see essentially the same thing the Berlin Dadaists did in 1918: not a trash-strewn jumble of confusion but a hive of emergent meanings and holistic patterns being generated not by high culture but by the "simultaneous muddle of noises, colors, and spiritual rhythms" of commercial transactions and mass culture, the "sensation screams and fever" of the society's "reckless everyday psyche." High culture, of course, had always regarded this bedlam of disposable images and words to be useless, trivial, mere noise, but Avant-Pop and the Berlin Dadaists sensed that this chaotic, endlessly circulating swarm of sounds, words, images, and data was actually speaking a new kind of language—a secret language of junk which expressed the inner workings of our culture's collective unconscious through a kind of dream symbolism. I'm not sure if the Dadaists were right about this suspicion, but I personally feel that Avant-Pop writers are. It appears to me that we are heading toward some radical transition in human history: new meanings and patterns are beginning to emerge out of the global hive mind, which is just beginning to develop the necessary number of links among its individual members to produce whatever it is that will emerge. But whether this bright blooming buzz will finally result in some sort of wondrous human melody or simply raise the noise level a couple of notches higher, it strikes me that the place to be, personally and artistically, is where the authors in *After Yesterday's Crash* have been recently—out there or in here, or wherever it is that one needs to be these days to be in the middle of it, taking it in, trying to make sense of it.

Write on.

LIST OF WORKS CONSULTED

Leffingwell, Edward. "Introduction." *Modern Dreams: The Rise and Fall of Pop Art*. New York: Deever Press, 1976.

Hughes, Robert. *The Shock of the New*. New York: Alfred A. Knopf, 1981.

Jameson, Fredric. "Postmodernism, or the Cultural Logic of Late Capitalism." *New Left Review* 146 (1984): 53–94.

Kelly, Kevin. *Out of Control: The Rise of Neo-Biological Civilization*. Reading, Mass.: Addison, 1994.

RANDOM SAMPLING OF AVANT-POP WORKS*

PRECURSORS: Homer, *The Odyssey*; Dante, *The Inferno*; *The 1,001 Arabian Nights*; Shakespeare, *The Tempest*; Jonathan Swift, *Gulliver's Travels*; Edgar Allan Poe, *Selected Stories*; Arthur Rimbaud, *Illuminations*; L. Frank Baum, *The Wizard of Oz*; Fritz Lang, *Metropolis*; Dashiell Hammett, *The Dain Curse*; The Marx Brothers, *Duck Soup*; Alain Robbe-Grillet, *The Voyeur*; William Gaines, *Mad Magazine*; Orson Welles, *Touch of Evil*.

FICTION: Kathy Acker, *Don Quixote, Empire of the Senseless*, and *In Memoriam to Identity*; J.G. Ballard, *Crash* and *The Atrocity Exhibition*; Donald Barthelme, *Snow White, Come Back, Dr. Caligari*, and *City Life*; Alfred Bester, *The Demolished Man* and *The Stars, My Destination*; William S. Burroughs, *Nova Trilogy* (*The Soft Machine, Nova Express, The Ticket that Exploded*); Philip K. Dick, *Time out of Joint, Ubik*, and *Do Androids Dream of Electric Sheep*; Larry McCaffery, ed., *Avant Pop: Fiction for a Daydream Nation*; Joseph McElroy, *Lookout Cartridge*; Thomas Pynchon, *Gravity's Rainbow*; Joanna Russ, *The Female Man*; Kurt Vonnegut, Jr., *Slaughterhouse Five*.

FILMS: Woody Allen, *What's Up, Tiger Lily?* and *The Purple Rose of Cairo*; Robert Altman, *Popeye*; Francis Ford Coppola, *One from the Heart* and *Dracula*; David Cronenberg, *Scanners* and *Videodrome*; Jean-Luc Godard, *Breathless* and *Alphaville*; Stanley Kubrick, *Dr. Strangelove, 2001: A Space Odyssey*, and *The Shining*; David Lynch, *Eraserhead* and *Blue Velvet*; Richard Lester, *A Hard Day's Night*; George Romero, *Dawn of the Dead*; Herbert Ross, *Pennies from Heaven*; Ridley Scott, *Blade Runner*; Oliver Stone, *Natural Born Killers*; Quentin Tarantino, *Pulp Fiction*; Shinya Tsukamoto, *Tetsuo: The Iron Man*.

---

* See also the list of contributors (pp. 337–341) for a selective listing of Avant-Pop works by authors included in this volume. Many of the most interesting Avant-Pop works are currently appearing in fanzines, on independent music labels, and in "on-line" electronic bulletin board publications. One of the best sources of information about what is currently happening in the true "underground" scene (which continues to exist, despite rumors to the contrary—in fact, it is currently flourishing) is *Factsheet Five*.

MUSIC: Laurie Anderson, *Big Science* and *Bright Red*; The Beatles, *Sgt. Pepper's Lonely Hearts Club Band*; Eugene Chadbourne, *There'll Be No Tears Tonight*, *LSDC&W*, and *Country Music in the World of Islam*; Ciccone Youth, *The Whitey Album*; Brian Eno and David Byrne, *My Life in the Bush of Ghosts*; Spike Jones, *Get Spiked: The Music of Spike Jones*; N.W.A., *Straight Outta Compton*; Negative Land, *Helter Stupid*; Nirvana, *Nevermind*; Pussy Galore, *Exile on Main Street*; Patti Smith, *Horses*; Sonic Youth, *Daydream Nation* and *Goo*; Carl Stalling, *The Carl Stalling Project*; Talking Heads, *Fear of Music* and *Remain in Light*; Velvet Underground, *Andy Warhol Presents Nico and the Velvet Underground* and *White Light, White Heat*; Tom Waits, *The Black Rider*; Hal Willner, *Lost in the Stars: The Music of Kurt Weill* and *Stay Awake* (Walt Disney covers); John Zorn, *Spillane* and *The Big Gundown*.

TELEVISION: Nike commercials featuring Dennis Hopper and William Burroughs; "Beavis and Butthead"; "Duckman"; "Max Headroom"; "The Simpsons"; "Twin Peaks"; "The Singing Detective" and "Pennies from Heaven" (by Dennis Potter, both originally on BBC); "Monty Python's Flying Circus"; "Saturday Night Live" (especially during years 1975–78).

CRITICISM: Jean Baudrillard, *Simulations* and *America*; Walter Benjamin, "Art in the Age of Mechanical Reproduction"; Scott Bukatman, *Terminal Identity*; Guy Dubord, *The Society of the Spectacle*; Fredric Jameson, *Postmodernism, or the Cultural Logic of Late Capitalism*; Arthur Kroker and David Cook, *The Postmodern Scene: Excremental Culture and Hyper-Aesthetics*; Kevin Kelly, *Out of Control: The Rise of Neo-Biological Civilization*; Griel Marcus, *Lipstick Traces: A History of the 20th Century*; Larry McCaffery, *Storming the Reality Studio: A Casebook of Cyberpunk and Postmodern Fiction*; Brian McHale, *Postmodern Fiction* and *Constructing Postmodernism*; Susan Sontag, *On Photography**; Ronald Sukenick, *Down and In: Life in the Underground*.

---

* In my humble opinion, this book is the best single introduction to the central issues involved in postmodernism and the evolution of Avant-Pop—even though Ms. Sontag never uses either term—Ed.

CURRENT EVENTS

STEVE KATZ

AT THE RED light an '81 Olds pulled up by a Honda Civic. Rick, the kid driving the Olds, and his friend, Nolly, on the passenger side both looked right at the young dude driving the Civic. It was Eighth Street, so it was one way. The driver pointed at the dude who had long hair slicked-back and a baseball cap worn backward. "Waste that one."

"Finally," said Timarie, one of the girls in the back seat. "Something." She looked at her watch. "If you hurry we can still make that movie."

"I'm raging so much here," said Willie, the other girl. "I want to see Sharon Stone do what's-his-name. Or maybe it's vica versa? I don't care. I just need to see it."

"You mean Richard Gere?"

"No, I don't think so."

"Alec Baldwin? Tom Hanks?"

"No. Not him."

"Michael Keaton?"

"No, and it's not Woody Allen either, and it's not Denzel Washington."

Everyone laughed.

Nolly, the kid riding shotgun, rolled down his window and signaled the dude in the Honda as if to ask directions. The dude rolled his window down.

"Hurry up, snakefoot, the light's gonna change," said Rick.

"So how do you get to Wall Street from here?" said Nolly, as he lifted his gun and squeezed off three into the dude's face.

"Don't call me snakefoot again," he said as they turned the corner and drove East. "My name is Nolly."

"Oh yeah?" said Willie. "What kind of name is Nolly?"

"Who would want to steal an '81 Oldsmobile?" asked Harriet as she looked at every car in the parking lot of the Roxxy Art theater.

Gloria shrugged. "People don't know what they're stealing anymore. It's a different world."

"I should call the police, I guess. I never had a car stolen before. I hate to go through all that, questions and forms. It's so boring."

"I don't mind talking to the police," said Gloria. "I'll call them for you." In fact, Gloria liked talking to the police. She watched a lot of television. Reruns of Hill Street Blues especially, and NYPD Blue, and Law and Order, her faves. Talking to the police made her feel like she was practically on television. She almost wished it had been her own car stolen, except she didn't own a car.

Harriet leaned against the corner of the theater building with her pinky in her nose, and gazed into the parking lot. They had just seen Farewell My Concubine, an epic movie, like an old Cecil B. DeMille spectacular. China had swept her away in the movie, even though the brutal training of the young boys in the beginning made her uncomfortable. She definitely wanted to go to China, maybe even study a little Chinese first. In the parking lot she could see a BMW, a Lexus, an Infinity, a couple of Mercedes, a few Volvos. Why did they pick on her ancient Oldsmobile? It made her sad. She hated to lose that car. It was the last of her connections with her husband's family. He had signed the car over to her a year before the divorce. The divorce was bitter, and unexpected because she never in a million years would have believed that Gil would dump her in that way, just not show up one night for dinner, and before she knows it he's living with a young kid, a boy, downtown somewhere. She didn't even get the address till a year later. It was a month before he even called her. She never suspected he had those tendencies. He was so moral, even judgmental about other people's lives. Her AIDS test at least was negative, thank God. The car he said specifically she could keep, even though it was already in her name. It was from his grandmother. Blow it up, was what she thought at first, and shoot him down with his little fairy friend outside their apartment. But she didn't. It had only 57,000 miles on it, a real old-lady's car. She felt at home in it.

"It's going to take them at least an hour to get here," Gloria said when she came back. "It's a warm night. Oodles of crime everywhere."

Harriet suddenly was laughing and Gloria put a hand on her shoulder to comfort her, taking the laughter for a case of nerves. In fact, Harriet was shaking a little from the stress of the theft and the memories. "Everything's gonna work out," Gloria told her.

"I lost my virginity in that car was what I was thinking. Gil screwed me the first time in the passenger seat. I got him to do it; I mean, of course I wanted to lose it. I liked the idea of losing it in Grandma's brand-new car. Of course Gil was really fussy. He didn't want to get it dirty. He put down a shirt and sweater under my butt first, and there I went. So I always had the dumb idea that my virginity was still in the car, and now it's been stolen, lost and then stolen. I think whoever stole it will have some bad luck."

"I liked it and I didn't like it," said Michael.

This was the first time he and Sarah had been to a movie together. They had started dating three weeks before, when Reggie introduced them in the computer class. Reggie was the computer whiz who taught it. He couldn't have been more than twenty-two himself, a kid who still wore his baseball cap backward and didn't know what to do with the lust that Sarah was showing for him. You could taste the look of relief on the young man's face before he turned away to leave Michael and Sarah to their own devices. So it wasn't out of excitement that Sarah agreed to go out with Michael, but rather out of resignation, an acknowledgment that she could no longer offer herself as a flower to be plucked.

Both of them had just come off difficult separations. Michael's ended when Susan left to work as a nurse in the Peace Corps in Sri Lanka. He suspected she joined the Peace Corps to get away from him, not a difficult conclusion. He knew he had been a repressive bastard with her, dominating her life. He was older when they first got together, she being only seventeen at the time, and he willing to be the father she never had, and at a certain point even he had realized *basta*—she had had enough—but he didn't know how to back off. For that reason he was trying with Sarah not to seem too opinionated or overbearing. Sarah had dumped Otis on a bet with her girlfriend Nicole, who challenged her by saying Sarah could never do it. Codependent was the catchword, afraid to give up the comfort of his sponging off her. It was a relief finally to be done with it, and as a payoff Nicole had taken her to a Michael Bolton concert, who she thought was like Fabio with emotions and a voice. For both of them Michael Bolton was the ideal man, strong, feeling, though they didn't know much about him, except that he had daughters. Sarah didn't know how many, but he really cared about them, lucky girls.

Neither Michael nor Sarah knew if he or she wanted to be in a relationship again. He certainly didn't want a young woman, as delicious as they looked. In those cases the reasons for the attraction become the reasons for the inevitable pain. Sarah, too, was being cautious. She sure didn't want another Otis in her life. That's why she responded harshly to Michael's comment about the movie.

"That's kind of wishy-washy, liked it and didn't like it."

Sweat pressed out at his temples. He wasn't used to being called like that on something he said. Susan surely had never done it, though they might have been happier if she had. In this situation he was trying to be correct.

"What I meant to say is that . . ."

"Oh my God. I can't believe this. Look, Otis—"

She couldn't believe she'd called him Otis. It was so embarrassing; but he didn't know her former's name, so she let the mistake slide. "Look, Michael."

As he saw her looking over his shoulder with her eyes widened that way and her lips drawn back, Michael was reminded that when he had first seen her in the computer class he had remarked to himself that she looked like a rat; and with her long polished incisors glinting in the coffeehouse track lighting she looked even more rodentine.

"Look!" she insisted.

Michael thought it could be a trick she was playing—when he

turned she'd make his Napoleon disappear—but he turned any-way. "Gosh," he said spontaneously. The two actors from Farewell My Concubine had just walked through the door. They were dressed in mostly western clothes, though the one had on a kimono over his jeans. And they were made up as if to perform the play within the movie. It was like the Rocky Horror Picture Show in vica versa.

When she spotted the actors entering the coffeehouse, Gloria gasped, blowing the foam of her cappuccino across the table. Harriet was indisposed in the bathroom, and Gloria was keeping an eye on the door in case the police came. They had arranged to meet them at the coffeehouse. A quick look around made Gloria realize the actors would probably sit down at the table right in back of theirs. "God," she thought. She didn't really know what to think. If it had been Mel Gibson or Richard Gere maybe she could have thought more clearly.

By the time Harriet returned, the actors were settled at the table, engaged in conversation, oblivious to the rest of the room.

"Do you remember their names? That pretty one is Dee or something like that."

"Whose names?"

"Turn around and look at that table, but don't make it too obvious. The one drinking the giant mocha, I mean. The pretty one."

Harriet turned then turned back quickly. "Oh my God, they're right next to us. How did they get here?"

"They must have known we were here," Gloria said, and they both giggled into their cups. "I think his name was Dede, or something. God, we just saw the movie. And the big one, the other one is Louie, or something, the one with the iced tea."

"Do you think they're the real actors?"

"I wish I could understand what they were saying."

"I don't have time. I have to look out for the cops when they come. Some day I'll learn Chinese."

Gloria leaned their way to try to recognize the voices, and she realized she understood what they were saying. It was English. They were speaking the subtitles.

"I've eaten my candied crabapples. I'm a fucking star already," said the pretty one with the mocha. Gloria didn't think it was his line in the film.

"What does it take to become a star," said the big one with the iced tea. "How many beatings?"

"They're talking English," Gloria leaned back to tell Harriet, who was staring hard at the door as if only her concentration could bring the police.

"I'm so strong I can uproot mountains," sang the pretty one, a mustache of whipped cream across his lip.

"Sorry this took so long," said the waitperson with the blue garland tattooed around her bicep. She set a plate down in front of Harriet.

"I didn't order anything," said Harriet. "Not this." She looked down at the plate. "What is it?" It protruded from the center of the plate, bathed in what looked like a raspberry sauce, so she assumed it must be sweet.

"Since the Chu king has lost his fighting spirit, why should his favorite concubine value his life?"

Gloria was dazed, reliving the movie over a cup of cappuccino, like postcinematic stress syndrome. It was uncomfortable.

Harriet grabbed her arm. "You know what this is?" Harriet pointed at the thing on the plate, her forefinger tipping the tip of it.

"No matter how resourceful you are you can't fight fate."

Gloria stared at the pink thing on Harriet's plate. "Of course I know."

"Tell me."

"It's a nose."

"That's what I thought."

"I recognize it."

"What do you mean?" Harriet flipped it onto its side with her latte spoon. "How do you recognize it?"

"I'm almost sure. I think it's Harvey Keitel's nose."

"Not! How would you know?"

"We saw that movie a couple of weeks ago. It's got tattoos on it."

"Not! Not! Even so, how do you know it's Harvey Keitel?"

"I go to lots of movies. I've seen lots of Harvey Keitel movies.

Reservoir Dogs. Did you see that? And Goodfellas. It's an educated guess. You know. I know his nose. Things of Desire, remember? No. Was that one Harvey Keitel? The one who used to be an angel?"

"Why did they serve me this nose?" It made Harriet nervous. She would have left right then, except she had to wait for the police. "This is a coffeehouse. Nobody serves nose in this city."

"I've followed my king on his military campaigns, enduring wind, frost, and hard toil. I hate only the tyrant who plunged our people into a life of misery."

"Ask the waitress. Take it up there and ask them."

Harriet had enough on her mind already.

"My king, quickly give me your famous sword."

Harriet took the plate back to the counter. "I didn't order this," she said.

"I'm sorry," said the tattooed woman. She turned to her co-workers. "Didn't someone order this Bobbit thing? This special?"

"That was dope. Definitely excellent," said Timarie as they moved out of the theater into the lobby. "Especially where she flashed her pussy at him on the chair at the what-do-you-call-it, when they were questioning her. Did you see that?"

"No, man. I missed it. I was busy licking ash trays," said Nolly, a hand on the 9-mm under his belt.

"That embarrassed me," said Willie. "I couldn't have done that in front of a camera."

"You fucked in front of a camera. I was there."

"That was different. This was Sharon Stone, man. Anyway, I don't like that word, *pussy*. It don't sound right."

They walked out into the parking lot and looked around. There were a lot of cars.

"I'm gonna buy that Jeep way over there, man. I think our last car passed its warranty by now," Rick said.

"Shit, I don't want to ride in no Jeep. There's all these other cars to choose from. Like that red one," said Willie.

"Shut the fuck up."

"From now on," said Timarie, "I'm never gonna wear underpants. You never know when it comes in handy to show your slit."

"I didn't even see it," said Nolly. "When did it happen?"

"Maybe you're a faggot, man. Faggots can't see pussy."

"You should shut up."

"Well, you can't see mine. Not unless you pay me. And don't be cheap."

The Jeep swung around and stopped by the three. Timarie looked in. "I don't want to ride in there. They feed their dogs in there."

"Shut up and get in, before the chickens get here."

"It stinks."

"Your mouth, man. That's what stinks."

"You better buy better cars, man, or I'm gonna start riding with Frank. He asked me."

"Frank asked you? That's dope, man. You should ride with him," said Willie.

"I know it. He never buys a fucking Jeep, man." Timarie climbed in next to the driver. "O put that chop back in your pants, man."

"I like it out in the fresh air. You suck him while we drive. Then we park up by Wizenor's Park and do some nasty."

"Man, you don't know me. I study with Lorena, man. You put that back in your pants where it belongs, or I cut it off and give it back to your momma."

"I'll beat you across the knees with it, bitch. You'll never skate again."

"You'll miss the spot, just like them chumps."

In the back of the Jeep Willie wore a baby seat on her head while Nolly already licked her breasts. The Jeep pulled out of the parking lot, drove a few blocks west, and started to climb a hill. There was no moon. The stars were out full blast.

Poor Reggie was a victim. Neither Sarah nor Michael had ever been this close before to a victim of the current plague of automatic-weapon teenage drive-by violence. The newspapers were full of it. Public radio was full of it. The TV was full of it, especially MTV where rap music was full of it. Movies appeared that were also full of it. But this was their first near experience. Of course, it didn't happen directly to them, and they knew Reggie only as an instructor, but the news settled on them nonetheless like a ton of un-needed megabytes. It drew them closer to each other, somehow, in their mutual emotional cyberslump, made complicated by Sarah's choice to work in DOS since that was the system in general use in her office, whereas Michael chose to learn the Macintosh system because he felt it would come closer to satisfying his urge to be creative.

Following the lead of the other students they taped ribbons of black crepe to their monitors. Many wept as they looked at their screens, and a message came up on both the IBMs and the Macs that everyone was invited to contribute to a fund to defray costs of the funeral. Reggie had a family, but they were told the mom and dad were ex-hippies who now lived in Southeast Asia. Michael turned to look at Sarah working on the row of IBMs against the opposite wall. She was leaning forward to consult a manual and her sweater had pulled out of the waist of her black stirrup pants, revealing a chalk white knife-edge of flesh. Michael turned back to his screen, where he was learning to use macros. Just his luck, he thought, to be working in Mac and to meet a woman he liked but was forced to separate from because she was working in DOS. Sarah had a similar conflict. She was learning to use the Internet, and she didn't know yet if it would be possible to communicate across the chasm that separates DOS from Mac. Along with all the other taints she felt in any relationship at all, she knew it would be a strain to continue one where E-mail was difficult.

As soon as she fired up the Oldsmobile, the cop car started to pull away. Whoever it was had left the car in the farthest space of the northeast corner of the United Artists parking lot, almost in the woods. She let it idle as she adjusted the mirror. As the cop car swung around and for a moment lit up the back seat of her car, she saw something there. Before going to Farewell My Concubine she had cleaned everything out. Since her dome light no longer worked, she shined her mini-maglite around. She was surprised they hadn't stolen it from her glovebox. She saw some blankets, and a plastic tote of baby stuff, and some odds and ends of clothes. She leaned over into the back seat and shifted the blankets. "Oh," she exclaimed. "A baby." She looked back out the front window.

The cops were already gone. How had they missed this? They couldn't have been very thorough. A whole baby they missed. It was asleep, looking peaceful and cute, but she knew that wouldn't last. Babies cry. They shit in their diapers. That's their job. That was why she had decided at a certain point never to have one. Tolerance and patience were not her virtues. She preferred maybe something that barked, though she never got one of those, either. All she'd ever had was Gil, and now he was gone, all but his car.

The baby began to twist its mouth into a terrifying suck and pucker. That was definitely something she didn't want to deal with. She hated to go back to the police, who had let her know they had more important things to think about than her, but that was the only solution she could figure out. She wished her friend Gloria was there to help. Gloria liked babies.

As she started to swing out of the parking lot she saw some people in her headlight beam. They had jumped out of the woods and were running toward her, waving their arms. At first she thought to speed up and just get out of there, but she noticed that one of the people was a little girl and another a smallish woman. She pulled up, and the man, gaunt and unshaven, with a pitiful expression of grief and urgency, not at all fearsome, tapped on her window and signaled for her to roll it down. She did that.

"Pliz. Bebby. Car, home. Bosnia Bosnia Bosnia." He tapped on his chest as he said Bosnia.

"Is this your baby?"

"Pliz. Yes. Pliz. Bebby. Girl." He pointed at the little girl. "Sofia. Wife, Halifa. Me, Muhamet. Live home car. Live car. Pliz."

"You were living in my car?" It didn't take them long to move in, she thought. "You're from Bosnia?"

"Bosnia. Bosnia. Bosnia." He banged his chest some more. "Dead pipples. Many pipples."

"I'm very sorry. This is my car. I have the keys. It's an '81 Oldsmobile."

He struggled as if he couldn't find enough air to say the words. The little girl came to the window and he lifted her up. She smiled, revealing some missing teeth. "Live car. Pliz. Bebby. Mine bebby. Bosnia war."

The baby started to cry. She couldn't stand it. Questions like,

How did they get here from Bosnia? crossed her mind; then they crossed her mind out.

"Take your baby," she said, and unlocked the back door. They all jumped in and sat down.

"Car home," said the man. The baby had big lungs.

Harriet got out of the car. She looked in at the family and shrugged. "Okay," she said.

"Okay. America," said the man.

"Okay," said the woman softly as the baby slurped onto her breast.

Harriet in an instant decided to leave it all behind. She headed for the bus stop and abandoned everything—the car with its memory of Gil and his grandmother, and all the ghosts of her virginity.

"Oh no. I can't believe this, what I just saw, man."

Only Timarie was still awake. Willie snored in the back, and Rick's lips flapped against the steering wheel.

"You gotta come back there with me," Nolly whispered. "You gotta see this, Timarie."

"Yeah, right. Rick wakes up and kills me if I'm gone with you."

"You gotta be quiet, though. But you gotta come."

Timarie quietly opened the door, but something beeped. "Fuckin' Jeep," she mumbled. She ripped at some wires and the Jeep shut up, then she lowered Rick's head from the steering column to lay it across her seat. He shifted his body. He was out.

Timarie followed Nolly into the woods. Through the trees they could see an edge of brightness pushing at the dark eastern sky. Another day might come. He stopped and held her back with his arm.

"Shh!"

They could hear a faint tink of metal against metal.

"That's them," Nolly whispered.

"Who?"

"Shh. I don't know. Come."

They got low and crawled further through the trees, where they saw the beams of flashlights whipping around the underbrush.

Timarie was getting into this, like it was a real movie. Nolly had his gun jammed into his belt at his back. They crawled behind a rock at the edge of the cliff that overlooked the United Artists parking lot.

"Who are they?" asked Timarie.

"Fuck, do I know?"

There was more light. They could see the men were white, dressed in combat fatigues. They could see the big guns set up. "Mortars," whispered Nolly. Bits of conversation carried toward them on the dawn breeze.

"That ain't Spanish, vato," said Timarie.

"I don't get what the fuck they're doing. Why are they here?"

Timarie looked down at the parking lot. "That's the car. Ain't that the car we just traded? Look, there's people around it. People are in it." She looked back at the men with the mortars. "This is just like something you see on TV. Like some war. You gotta do something, Nolly."

Nolly pulled his gun from under his belt and looked at it. He checked the clip. Just three rounds gone. He looked at Timarie. "What can I do?"

The men in fatigues were lifting the mortar rounds out of their crates.

"Santa Maria y Jesu. Do something, Nolly. Those people are going to die if you don't do something."

"So what? What can I do anyway?"

The first mortar round blew about eighty yards from the car. The soldiers adjusted quickly as the family scrambled below.

"There's children there. There's women that are gonna die, Nolly. Do something. Give me the fuckin' gun."

Nolly handed her the 9-mm and crawled back toward the Jeep. Timarie looked at the gun. She had never fired a gun. She pointed it at the men in fatigues. Several mortar rounds went off below, one followed by a big explosion as the car was hit. She squeezed the trigger. Nothing happened. She turned to ask Nolly how to shoot, but he was gone, so she looked at the gun again. Sig Sauer was engraved on the handle. That didn't mean anything to her. She squeezed again and nothing happened, so she stepped out toward the men, holding the gun in two hands like she saw in the movies. "Stop," she said. "Just stop." The men in fatigues were startled to see her and stepped back from the mortars, then they started to laugh. "Parar! Detener!" She didn't know if she was using the right word, but she was pissed. "Stop the guns!" She squeezed the trigger again. The laughter stopped and she stood there. She stood there for about sixteen seconds.

After Harriet left with the police, Gloria returned to the coffee-house. No customers left, and the staff was getting ready to close. She could feel the annoyance of the tired tattooed waitress asking for her order. "To go," Gloria said immediately, to reassure her. The waitress became friendlier.

"What would you like?"

"You know that thing?" Gloria tapped her nose. She didn't want to say it.

"You mean the special?"

"Yeah."

The waitress brought it in a take-out box, with the sauce on the side. "This is the last one." She handed back Gloria's money. "It's on us."

Gloria set the box on her bed and hung up her coat. She got into her pj's and straightened up the shrine and cushion where she meditated, then opened the carry-out box. Without the sauce on it, this looked even more like Harvey Keitel's nose, tattooed, but without a septum. Maybe too much cocaine. She grinned. When she meditated, she grinned a lot. But she could have been mistaken; maybe it wasn't Harvey Keitel's nose. She could call his agent and find out. No, she was sure it was; anyway, it made no difference. She had no inclination to bite into it. But she did have the peculiar inclination to wear it over her clitoris while she sat. The word *clitoris* still wasn't comfortable for her. Before her process was completed, the nub had been part of her penis; it felt to her fingers very much like the tip of that former organ. She didn't know why, but she sensed it would be right to cap it with Harvey Keitel's nose.

Nobody in Denver, her new city, knew she was formerly a man, not even her best friend, Harriet. The children she had fathered were still in Harrisburg, Pennsylvania, and hadn't yet come to see her. Maybe someday. She understood that it was complicated for them. It was complicated for her. She dreaded running into her ex-Marine buddy, Mike Sugman, who she knew lived somewhere around Denver. Maybe she dreaded it, but she also thrilled to the possibility of becoming his girlfriend, or his mistress if he was married.

There were some things about being a woman she still needed to smooth out, although she was definitely now a woman, as she always knew she was, but now her body was woman, too. Meditation helped. She used to pray, but she stopped that. When you prayed, you prayed for something concrete; but you meditated to empty your mind of everything, to stop the painful attachment to thought and emotion. If she were ever to pray for something, aside from asking for a man who would truly love her and care for her, it would be to be granted the function of menses. She knew she would get deeper into her womanhood if she could only menstruate, at least once, just to know it, just to deepen her kinship with the moon. No one who had counseled her had advised her what her womanhood would be like after menopause, how sad it could be.

But it was alright. She felt really good about herself now. She didn't know if this impulse to cap her clitoris with this particular nose was sexual or what. Was it just crazy? Was it demeaning to herself as a woman? She hadn't had enough time yet as a total woman to think all that through. She'd learned other things—to relax and let men open car doors for her, to let them slide restaurant chairs under her butt. But this was in the privacy of her own meditation corner. And when she was finished, she decided, she would attach the nose to her small Corning cutting board with Krazy Glue and then cover it with polyester resin to preserve it forever for herself.

She lowered her butt to the cushion, turned off the electric lights, lit a candle and a joss stick, and sat still a moment before she slipped Harvey Keitel's nose over her clitoris. It fit like a cap, and that made her grin. This felt like mischief, and she liked that. As she breathed, she repeated the mantra that guru what's-her-face had given her on one expensive weekend at the ashram. The mantra was SO on the inbreath, HAM on the outbreath. SO HAM, SO HAM, SO HAM. It translated roughly, I am that, I am that, I am that.

THE EXORCIST

RIKKI DUCORNET

HE WAS THE VILLAGE Exorcist; he cured cancer with clay, and pimples with a crucifix dipped in chicken-shit. The only man known to wear an earring, own a camera, to be seen at sunrise lumbering across the muddy furrows of freshly tilled fields, his black beard inking out itineraries, his black eyes darting to and fro like wasps, his tripod hanging from his shoulder like a strange wing.

The Exorcist loved order and hated fortuity. He believed in a patterned, intentioned Universe, mapped and pinned by Cosmic Hands. Unlike the Church Fathers, he did not argue that Evil was a lesser Good, a flaw festering like a boil on the buttock of Divinity. He knew Evil to be as Methodical as the Good, and so just as true. The Universe was like a great pie cut into two equal slices: one served up by Heaven, the other by Hell. And he stood in the middle. The discovery of his most unusual position had come to him in early adolescence in a recurrent dream; the distinct and extraordinary message was this: both God and the Devil had chosen him to be their scribe.

"For," as God Himself, in the form of a great red leather boot, had explained, "the Word is the glue that holds the Universe together. It is what keeps the moon in the sky and the worms in the ground. Without it worms would fly." And shortly after, the Devil had appeared, disguised as a small glass slipper.

"Nothing," the Devil had hissed, "exists until it is seen."

It was then that he bought himself the camera. And at the tender age of fifteen, when other boys are out learning the languages of the flowers and the bees, he spent all his time recording all the sacred substance of existence: random flavors, the exact color and consistency of a stool, galactic calamities, the quantity of sediment clinging to the moist bottom of a cup, fleshy scrapings of all sorts, the shapes and weights of dustballs collected beneath his bed, the position of a spider's web in a sink, maps on the backs of turtles sleeping beneath fountains, the entire population's shoe size, who had died and who was born, the number of dog turds dropped before a gate, of butterflies dancing above a meadow. He photographed every monument, every face, every stone and every stain.

In time he realized that not only did all this information—like thousands of little pins—hold the Universe in place, it also gave him power. And that is when he became the Exorcist. For when Devilry was at work (he called it Organized Aberration) he knew —he had seen the signs long before the first complaints. The odd mushroom, for example, with its thick, milky collar of lacy flesh and runny-nosed features, foretold the illnesses of cows, the abortions of sows, suicides. He had seen the gutted tree, the assembly of hornets, those circular paths that Disaster traces about its victims before closing in. And recognizing the knots, he knew how to unwind them and so unbind the victim.

For years he was considered the greatest Exorcist of them all; the possessed came from farms and hamlets as far as ninety leagues away to be freed by his spell-breaking. But it did not last; he enjoyed success only to suffer reversal. Simply, he lost touch. The world in all her infinite variousness sprawled out on all fours and he faltered; with growing anguish he knew that he could never get it all down. Not alone. He searched the sky for clues, looked to the migrations of the birds and the planets, but the Universe remained silent, or he had grown deaf.

Men came to him with their sores, their sore hearts, their stories of virgin births and bordello deaths, of bewitched nieces and peaches freezing in July. But he—as lost as a blind man in an unfamiliar alley—could help them no longer; the old formulas rang hollow in the thin air of his dim rooms. Locking his door, he crept to his attic hoard of notebooks, glass negatives and sepia images for comfort, and perhaps inspiration, to discover that all had been overturned and smashed by rats, corrupted by mites and rain. He knew then that he had an enemy. And his enemy was Time.

He thought over his previous failures. The fresh headstone photographed only to be defaced by a passing bird (he had taken a new photograph and then it had rained), a garden rendered un-recognizable by a mole, a roof by a hurricane—and so it had hit him at last: his photographs, his careful notes did not belong to him, but to Time. Time was Master. And if the seconds marched forward with inspiring regularity, on the sidelines everything was in mad disorder: a rowdy drooling from balconies, a stampeding of innocents underfoot, the loss of hats and tempers. Why a bird-dropping there, in that very corner, at that very moment? And just after he, the Chosen Scribe, had done his work? Was he being tested? Was he somebody's fool?

The Exorcist tramps through the woods painfully aware of infi-nitely numerous rustlings and buzzings, the unfathomable quanti-ties of leaves, of moldering debris, of seeds. And then, as he defecates behind a tree, he cries out, with all the passion of dis-covery:

"The Universe is movement! Time is everything!" And if he, the Exorcist, wants to regain control of the country that is quickly slipping from his grasp (people are talking; witches are infiltrating the landscape and he has been unable to shake them—nails in urine have not worked, the usual incantations in pigsties, nor the braying at dawn beneath a donkey skin beside a virgin's bed), he will have to deal with the Devil alone. For does not this all prove that the pie is unevenly sliced? That Time does not belong to Eternity, the Evermore of Goodness, God's sluggish country of Pure Lead, but to the pie's black backside? Time belongs to the Devil!

As he walks home he realizes why for years he has been fas-cinated by excrement—his own and that of others, human and animal. (Long ago he had conceived a plan to photograph the vil-lage population's every elimination and had plotted of public places equipped with cameras. This had been forgotten when he had become obsessed with molting insects—Time again! That provocative shedding of skins!)

"Freedom," he wheezes, "is a myth of the mind, a sickness unto disorder." Forgetting to remove his shoes, he climbs into bed and waits for signs.

"There is no free will in Eternity," he mutters, pulling the covers up over his head. "On the dark side of the pie there are no choices. And on the luminous side there is nothing to choose!" As he dozes, a bright glass slipper spins in the void above his head. He recognizes it at once:

"O Beelzebub!" he cries. "Give me the flaming key to your sacred room! Make me your High-Appointed Peeping Tom!" For answer, the shifting stuff of fancy flits before him like the stained and agitated bodies of simple animals seeping their lives out beneath a lens. He sees the planets stuck like sequins to the shell of limbo, pierced to facilitate the migrations of the dead; he perceives that the edge of the world is as sharp as a knife, that those who wander too close have their feet grated like cheese before they are sucked into the mouth of Hell. At dawn he rises and, haunting bushes, empties nests and stretches nets from trees. Later as the Devil whispers, he probes feathers for clues about eclipses; he slices the livers of lizards to uncover the secrets of stars, and counts the teeth of cats to discover the migrations of rats, the paths of plagues. Returning to bed, the Devil's insinuations hot in his ears, he sinks his teeth into the palpitating sugar-plum of Dreamland, and straddling the corpulent finger of sleep, thrusting hard, fucks Time.

He knows now that he will succeed; the Power will be his again, and greater than it ever was. No more vassal of two lords, shipwrecked upon a sea of conflicting evidence, but the Devil's lone Right Hand, he will be King of the thickest slice, that seething and fermenting slice called Life.

INCARNATIONS OF
THE MURDERER

WILLIAM T. VOLLMANN

SAN IGNACIO, BELIZE (1990)

TWO GIRLS SAILED under the fat green branches of trees that curved like eyebrows. At the top of the grassy bank, a plantain spread its leaves across the clouds. They passed little brown girls swimming and smiling. They passed a man who dove for shrimp that he put in a plastic bag. Breasting the painted houses that were grocery stores rich with onions, Coca-Cola and condensed milk, they rode the wide brown river between tree-ridges and palm houses.

As they paddled, the plump wet legs of the girls quivered: water danced on their thighs. A few wet curly hairs peeked shyly from the crotches of their bathing suits. They had golden hourglass waists.

A man was a dragonfly. He hugged his shadow on the river until he saw them.

The water splashed under a great green tree-bridge that grew parallel to the water. Its branches were red and black like the skin of a diamondback rattler. In the branches crouched the man. The plan that the man had was as rubbery and pink as a monkey's palm. But the canoe was not there yet. The two girls were still alive.

Yellow butterflies skimmed low across the shallow water. They saw the girls, too. They saw each other. They saw themselves in the water and forgot everything.

The tree that owned the water was closer now. A white horse sneezed in a grove of golden coconuts.

All morning the man had been thinking of the two girls whom he was about to kill. Knocking yellow coconuts down from the trees with a big stick, he'd sliced away at them with his machete until a little hole like a vagina appeared. He put his mouth to that pale bristly hole and drank. (Slowly, the white meat inside oxidized brown.) But now he was silent, suspended from his purpose as if by the heavy, supple tail of a spider monkey.

Now the two girls passed little clapboard houses with laundry out to dry. They passed the last house they would ever see. In the river a lazy boa was wriggling along. That was the last snake they'd ever see.

They went down the ripple-stained river, the ripple-striped river. They saw the broad green rocks beneath the water, the soft yellow-green tree-mounds. They came to the tree of their death, and the man jumped down lightly and stabbed them in their breasts.

The canoe lay long and low across the neck of an island. Reflected water burned whitely on its keel.

The man opened red fruits. He bit them. They were soft with two-colored grainy custard inside.

The spice of the blood was like the sweet stinging of the glossy-leaved pepper-tree, whose orange fruits burn your lips when you eat, burn again when you piss. This made him happy. He went to sleep and awoke. A toucan chirped like a frog. The taste was stronger in his mouth. He laughed.

He wandered among the caring arches of the palm tree that shaded him like wisdom, and his shirt was hot and slick on his back. He came to the grove where the white horse had sneezed and knocked down a coconut. He drank the juice, but the taste of blood was even stronger now. He looked sideways in the hot high fields of trees.

Knuckles itching pleasantly with insect bites, searching through the wild-looking fields for ground foods with the sun hot on his sunburned neck and wrists, he swiped down a sugarcane stalk with his machete and then he skinned and peeled it in long strokes, from green down to white. He was good at using knives. He snapped off a piece and chewed it, tasting in advance its taste so juicy, fresh, and sweet. His hands were sticky with juice. He chewed. But the other taste loomed still more undeniable.

Between his teeth he placed slices of young pineapple, bird-eaten custard apples, bay leaves, green papayas, sour plums from a leaf-bare tree. He bit them all ferociously into a mush. Then he sucked, choked, swallowed. Building a fire, he made coffee, which he drank down to the grounds. He cut an inch of medicine vine and chewed that bitterness, too. The taste of blood increased.

He spat, but his spittle was clear. There was no blood in it. He pricked his tongue with the point of the knife, but his own male blood could not drown the other, the female taste.

He drank half a bottle of rum and fell down. All around him, trees steamed by humid horizons. When he awoke, the taste was stronger than ever. He began to scream.

There was a cave he knew of whose floor was a sandy beach. The man ran there without knowing why. Jet black water became black and green there as it descended into bubbling pools close enough to the entrance to reflect the jungle, from the branches of which the black-and-orange-tailed birds hung like seedpods. The widest tree boughs were festooned with vine sprouts like the feathered shafts of arrows. Behind them, where it was cool and stale, the cave's chalky stalactites hung in ridge clusters like folds of drying laundry on a line. The man ran in. He splashed through the first pool. It was alive with green and silver ripples intersecting with one another like a woman's curls. A single bubble traveled, white on black, then silver on silver. He ran crazy through the next pool. Farther in the darkness was a chalky beach, cratered with rat prints and raccoon prints. This was the place where the cave roof was crowned by a trio of stalactites. Here, where everything but the river was quiet, a pale whitish bird fluttered from rock to rock, squeaking like a mouse. The bird flew back and forth very quickly. It hovered over rock-cracks' wrinkled lips. It landed on a crest of lighter-colored rock like a wave that had never broken. It darted its beak between two studs of shell fossil and swallowed a blind ant. Then it departed into deeper caves within the cave, floored with silence and white sand. Water shimmered white on black rocks—

The man opened his mouth to scream again and the white bird came from nowhere. The white bird was the soul of one of the girls. The bird stabbed the man's tongue with its beak and drank blood. Then it flew away, not squeaking anymore.

The man swallowed experimentally. The taste was not nearly so strong.

Farther back in the cave was a pit. A tiny black bird flew there. Knowing this now, the man clambered down. It was like being inside a seashell. Far down in the well, the flicker of his lighter showed him pink and glistening rock-guts. Smoke streamed from the little lighter like a beam from a movie projector. He held the lighter below his mouth so that the black bird could see him. The bird came swooping down and cheeping. It was so tiny that it flew back between his tonsils. He longed to swallow it, to recapitulate his triumphs. But then the taste would strengthen again. The black bird pierced him and drank a drop of his blood. He could feel the bird's pulse inside him. It was not much bigger than a bee. It took him again. Then it flew away in silence.

The taste was gone now. The man shrieked with glee. The cave was empty.

Outside it was so brightly green that the hunger of his eyes (which he hadn't even known that he had) was caught: as long as he looked out upon it, he thought himself satisfied, but the instant he began to look away, back into the darkness, then his craving for greenness screamed out at him.

He ran outside trying to see and taste everything. He ran down the stream bank to a kingdom of pools in bowls of baking hot rock. He drank water from rolling whirlpools; he dove down whitewater to brown water, beneath which his open eyes found chalky sandvalleys, green-slicked boulder-cliffs; he grabbled at these things with his fingers and then licked his fingertips. In the best whirlpool rushed the two girls, lying down against each other, kissing each other avidly, eating each other's soft flesh.

SAN FRANCISCO, CALIFORNIA, U.S.A. (1991)

Down the fog-sodden wooden steps he came that night to the street walled with houses, every doorway a yellow lantern-slide suspended between floating windows, connected to earth by the tenuous courtesy of stairs. Earth was but sidewalk and street, a more coagulated gray than the silver-gleam of reflected souls in car windshields, heavier too than the gray-green linoleum sky segmented by power wires. He went fog-breathing while the two walls of houses faced each other like cliffs, ignoring one another graciously; they were long islands channeled, coved, and barred, made separate by the crisscrossing rivers of gray streets. Somewhere was the isle of the dead girls' canoe, which he needed now to get away from himself. All night he walked the hill streets until he came to morning, a foggy morning in the last valley of pale houses before the sea. He stood before an apartment house whose chessboard-floored arch declined to eat him as he'd eaten others; the doors were shut like the sky. The curving ceiling of the arch was stamped with white flowers in squares. Black iron latticed windows as elaborately as Qur'anic calligraphy; white railings guarded balconies. Spiked lamps smoldered at him from behind orange glass. Timidly he hid behind the sidewalk's trees, whose leaf-rows whispered richly down like ferns . . .

Once he admitted that this house was not for him, he turned away from all hill streets side-stacked with rainbow cars and went down further toward the sea. So he came to the street of souls.

The candy shop of souls lured him in first. His nose stung with the fog. He opened the door and went in, staring at the long glass case that was like an aquarium. Here he found the chocolate ingots, the pure mint-striped cylinders, the tarts studded with fruits and berries like a dozen orchards, the vanilla bread-loaves long and slender like suntanned eels, the banana-topped lime hexagons, the chocolate-windowed éclairs domed with cream like Russian Orthodox churches, the round strawberry tortes gilded with lemon-chocolate to make pedestals for the vanilla-chocolate butterflies that rested on each with breathless wings, the sponge cakes like an emperor's crown, the complex wicker-basket raspberry pies of woven crust, heaped with boulders of butter and confectioner's sugar, the tins of violet lozenges, the bones and girders made of licorice, the low white disks of sugarpies topped with fan-swirls of almonds like playing cards, the peach cakes, pear cakes, the row of delectable phosphorescent green slugs, the flowerpot of coffee frosting from which a chocolate rose bloomed, the strawberries that peaked up from unknown tarts and tortes bride-bashful behind ruffled paper—

He sat at a little square marble table, and without a word the lady brought him a green slug, served on a white plate with white lace. He reached in his pocket and found a single coin of iron with a hole in the center. He gave her that. He sat looking past the glass case at the rows of fruit confections in matched white-lidded jars —not for him. With the silver fork he stabbed the slug and raised it into his mouth, where it overcame him between his teeth with a sweet ichor of orgasmic limes, and so he became a thief—

AGRA, INDIA (1990)

Two green-clad soldiers were striking a man in the face beneath one of the side-arches of the Taj Mahal. The man was not screaming. He was a thief. The soldiers had caught him, and were beating him. All around him, the Mughal tombs bulged with hard nipples on their marble breasts.—The emperor, he had so many wives, he spend a month's salary on cosmetics! cried the guide.

Blood flowered from the thief's nose.

This tower closed now, said the guide. The lovely boys and girls jump off, suicide. For love and love and love. Closed now for security reason. But *this* part, this open ivory day.

The thief fell down when they let go of him. The soldiers stamped on his stomach. Then they raised him again.

Now, sir, lady, come-come. Look! This marble *one* piece. No two piece. No join. Only cutting!

The thief looked at the guide with big eyes. The soldiers punched him. Then he was not looking at the guide anymore. Sir and lady went away, trying not to hear his groans as the soldiers began to beat him. They wore the dead girls' mouths.

Yes, please! Hello! Sir and madam!

(Sir and madam were staring at him again. They could not help it. The soldiers were kicking out his teeth.)

Water rippled in long grooves of onyx, malachite, coral. Clouds echoed between the lapis-flowered marble screens. Far beyond the screens lay dim white-gray corridors of peace. Darkness, incense, and shadows crawled slowly on marble, searching for secret sweet-smelling vaults.

The soldiers hustled the thief into darkness.

Outside it was a foggy morning. Skinny men rode bicycles, with dish towels wrapped around their heads. Roadside people squatted by smudges to keep warm. On the dusty road that stank of exhaust, platoons of dirty white cattle were marched and goaded toward Agra. They had sharp backbones and floppy bellies.

Postcards, please? Small marble! Elephant two rupees!

Cowtails and buttocks were crowded together, long, narrow, and wobbly like folded drapes. They swished and twitched as if they were alive and knew where they were going, but they didn't; they only followed where they were pulled, like the thief being led into the recesses of that gorgeous tomb.

SAN FRANCISCO, CALIFORNIA, U.S.A. (1991)

When the rattle of his bones being put back together became the rattling whir of the cable cars going up Nob Hill, he shot forth out of darkness among the square red lights of the other soul-cars swarming from the parking tunnels, zebra-striped gate up and down; for a while he followed a big dirty bus that had once been a selfish man, and he rolled up Powell Street, which was sutured lengthwise with steel. Crowds were standing off the curb. There was no room for them yet. He saw a man pushing a shopping cart full of old clothes. Globes of crystallized light attacked him from the edge of Union Square. Higher up the hill he rolled by hotels and brass-worked windows, flags and awnings; he saw the pedestrian souls slogging up slowly, the Chinese signs, the yellow plastic pagoda-roofs, the bulging windows of Victorian houses. A girl with a six-pack under her arm ran smiling and flushed up the hill. At the top of the hill he could see far: he saw a Sunday sailing panorama off the Marin headlands, with tanned girls drinking wine coolers, and college boys pretending to be pirates with their fierce black five-dollar squirt guns, and the Golden Gate Bridge almost far away enough to shimmer as it must have done for those convicts from Alcatraz who doomed themselves trying to swim there. The red warning light still flashed on the island, now noted for its tours and wildflowers. The cell-block building became ominous again when the evening fog sprang up and the tanned girls screamed as their twenty-four-footer tacked closer and closer to the sharp black rocks, already past the limit demarcated by the old prison buoys that say KEEP OFF; and seeing the girls he wanted to kill them over again, but then his cracked bones ached from being beaten and he bared his teeth and thought, If I can't eat them by stealing them, I'll get them another way! and he laughed and honked his horn and other cars honked behind him so he rolled on down the hill and came to the street of souls.

Fearing to enter the candy shop which had brought him such pain, he parked, offering himself again to that knife of fog and silence, the handle a crystal stalagmite; and he came to the coffee shop of souls.

Brass safe-deposit boxes walled him, side by side, bearing buttons and horns. Each one had a different coffee inside. The smell of coffee inflamed him. There were rows of stalls for muffins, each of which reminded him of the pale brown coconuts he had drunk. In his pocket he found a single coin with a hole in it. They gave him a muffin. He became an anthropologist.

RESOLUTE BAY, CORNWALLIS ISLAND, NORTHWEST TERRITORIES, CANADA (1991)

On the komatik, whose slats had been partly covered by a caribou skin (now frozen into iron wrinkles), he lay comfortably on his side, gripping two slat-ends with his fishy-smelling sealskin mitts, which were already getting ice granules behind the liner (an old bedsheet) because every time he wiped his nose with the skintight capilene gloves the snot was soaked up by the old bedsheet, which then began to freeze; and as the komatik rattled along at the end of its leash, making firm tracks in the snow-covered ice, the wind froze the snot around his nose and mouth into white rings, but not immediately because it was not cold enough yet to make breath-frost into instant whiskers; however, it was certainly cold enough to make his cheek ache from contact with the crust of snot-ice on the ski mask; meanwhile the smoothness of the sea began to be interrupted by hard white shards where competing currents had gashed the ice open and then the wound had scarred; sometimes the ice-plates had forced each other's edges into uprising splinters that melded and massed and hardened into strange shapes; the Inuk wended the skidoo between these when he could, going slowly so that the komatik did not lurch too badly, his back was erect, almost stern, the rifle at a ready diagonal, and he steered south toward a thick horizon band that seemed to be fog or blowing snow; in fact it was the steam of open water. Over this hung the midday sun, reddish-pale, a rotten apple of the old year.

Then the groaning ice fissured into a shape like a girl's mouth, and the komatik broke through. He fell under the ice. The other girl was waiting beneath with her mouth open to drink his blood, and he was already freezing and paling, but then the girl breathed upon him lovingly and he was warmed. The first girl, the one who was ice, opened her mouth; the second one lifted him on through to the sky.

INTERSTATE 80, CALIFORNIA, U.S.A. (1992)

Gray-lit struts took his weight as he shot across the bridge; flat gray-green ribs were stripped of their nightflesh by the dingy lights, the lights of Oakland rippling in between like scales, inhuman lights all the way to the gray horizon. What a relief when the world finally ran out of electricity, and we'd have to turn them off! On his left was a city of stacks and towers clustered with lights like sparks that could never be peacefully extinguished, could never cool themselves in the earth. A gush of smoke blew horizontally from the topmost stack. He scuttled up greenish gray ramps of deadness into the dead night, accompanied by characterless strings of light, dull apartment tower lights, dark bushes: he bulleted down a lane of dirty blackness clouded by trees on either side, remnant trees suffered to live only because they interrupted that ugly terrible light. Then he came into the outer darkness of unhealthy tree-mists where the sky was as empty as his heart. He slid like a shuffleboard counter through the cut between blackish brownish-gray banks of darkness, the sky greenish gray above. He crossed the grim vacuous bridge that was the last place before the night country; he pierced the turgid black river (so night-soaked that he could perceive it only at its edges where light coagulated upon black wrinkles) and came into the ruined desert.

The toll bar came down. The attendant was waiting. Cars were beginning to honk behind him as he sat there at the tollbooth of souls, looking through his pockets. Finally he found a single coin with a hole in it. He reached, dropped it into the attendant's palm. The toll bar went up. He became a piece of jute cloth.

BATTAMBANG, CAMBODIA (1991)

A woman in a mask who had a blue blanket over her head put the soft limp jute of him onto the conveyor belt. Then he got washed and rolled. The rollers gleamed and worked him back and forth, softening him. He could not scream. To her he was not even a shadow. (A poster of the president changed rose-light on its shrine.) What worked the rollers? The factory had its own generator, its own grand shouting alternators, built to last, 237 kilowatts . . . The jute of his soul got matted and soft. He did not see the hammer-and-sickle flag anymore. His soul got squeezed by a rickety rattling. Now he was squished almost as thin as a hair. People dragged him away slowly, pulling long bunches of him with both hands. He was in a vast cement-floored enclosure whose roof was stained brown. They stretched him out. Slowly he went up a long steep conveyor. He emerged in a pale white roll of hope, twirling down, narrowing into a strip. The barefoot workers gathered him into piles on the concrete floor, then stuffed him into barrels, which were then mounted on huge reels. Murderers like him had destroyed this place once already. There had been twelve hundred workers. Now that it had been rebuilt, eight hundred and sixty worked there, eight hours a day, six days a week, not knowing that jute was souls. They cleaned and pressed him into accordioned ribbons of fiber that built up in the turning barrels. A masked girl stood ready to pack him down with her hands and roll a new barrel into place. He recognized her. She was not angry anymore. Then someone took the barrels to go into a second pressing machine. A metal arm whipped back and forth, but only for a minute; the barefoot girls had to fiddle with it again. His substance was cleaned and dried. A masked woman lifted up levers, twisted him by hand into the clamps, pulled down levers, and he spilled out again. He recognized her, too. She smiled at him. Now everyone could see him being woven into string, dense, rough, and thick; this string in turn was woven into sacking. They were going to fill his empty heart with rice. This is not such a bad destiny for anyone, since rice is life. The barefoot girls teased out the rolls of soul-cloth, gathering them from the big roll in different sizes (63 × 29 inches and 20 × 98 inches); boys dragged them across the floor at intervals, stretching, looking around, slowly smoothing them amid the sounds of the mechanical presses. So they stacked him among the other sacks. Girls sat on sacks on the floor, sewing more sacks; they were fixing the mistakes of the sack-sewing machine. Then they pressed the sacks into bales. But he'd turned out perfect; he did not need any girls to stitch up the holes in his heart. He was ready now in the bale of sacks. If someone guarded him well, he might last two years. Then he'd turn to dirt. A man's hands seized his bale and carried him toward the place where he would be used. Then the man's work shift was over. The man went to serve his hours on the factory militia, readying himself for duty in the room of black guns on jute sacks. The man knew that in the jungle other murderers were still nearby.

MOONLIGHT
WHOOPIE CUSHION
SONATA

TOM ROBBINS

I

THE WITCH-GIRL WHO lives by the bend in the river is said to keep a fart in a bottle. It's a poisonous fart, green as cabbage, loud as a shotgun; and after moonset or before moonrise, her hut is illuminated by its pale mephitic glow. For a time, passersby thought she had television.

Of course, no antenna sprouts from her thatched roof, no satellite dish dwarfs her woodpile, and can you imagine the cable company stringing wires across the marsh and through the forest so that a witch-girl could watch soaps? Anyway, how would she pay for it? With the contents of her mushroom basket, the black candles she makes from hornet fat, her belladonna wine? With that cello she saws with a human bone?

Undoubtedly, she could pay for it with her body. Her body has been admired by many a fisherman who's chanced upon her wading the rapids in loonskin drawers. But no man's ever bought her body, and only one has had the courage to take it for free.

That fellow's gone away now. It's said he fled back to South America and left her in the lurch. Oh, but she still has a hold on him, you can bet on that. Our witch-girl's got a definite hook in that fly-by-night romeo. She's woven his mustache hairs into a tiny noose. She's got his careless fart in a bottle by the stove.

II

Turn a mountain upside down, you have a woman. Turn a woman upside down, you have a valley. Turn a valley upside down, you get folk music.

In the old days, the men in our village played trombone. Some better than others, obviously, but most of the men could play. Only the males, sad to say. The women danced. It was the local custom. The practice has all but died out, though to this day grizzled geezers are known to hide trombones under their beds at the nursing home. It's strictly forbidden, but late on summer nights, you can sometimes hear nostalgic if short-winded trombone riffs drifting out of the third-story windows, see silhouettes of old women on the second floor, dancing on swollen feet in fuzzy slippers or spinning in rhythmic circles in their wheelchairs.

As noted, however, our musical traditions have virtually vanished. Nowadays, people get their music from cassette tapes or television. Who has time anymore to learn an instrument? Only the witch-girl by the bend in the river, sawing her cello with a human tibia, producing sounds like Stephen King's nervous system caught in a mousetrap.

When milk sours before it leaves the udder or grain starts to stink in the fields; when workers go out on strike at the sauerkraut factory, the missile base, or the new microchip plant down the road; when basements flood, lusty young wives get bedtime migraines, dogs wake up howling in the middle of the night, or the interference on TV is like a fight in hot grease between corn flakes and a speedboat, people around here will say, "The witch-girl's playing her cello again."

Turn folk music upside down, you get mythology. Turn mythology upside down, you get history. Turn history upside down, you get religion, journalism, hysteria, and indecision.

III

The setting sun turned the river into a little red schoolhouse. Thus motivated, the frogs got to work conjugating their verbs. The witch-girl handled the arithmetic.

She divided a woodpecker by the square root of a telephone pole.

Multiplied the light in a fox's eyes by the number of umlauts on a Häagen-Dazs bar.

Added a kingfisher's nest to the gross national product.

Calculated the ratio of *duende* to pathos in the death song of a lamp-singed moth.

Subtracted a mallow from a marsh, an ant from an anthem, a Buddha from a peach can shot full of holes.

IV

A white plastic bucket in a snowy field. A jackknife of geese scratching God's dark name in the sky. A wind that throbs but is silent. Candy wrappers silent against fence wire. Stags silent under their fright-wig menorahs. Bees silent in their science-fiction wax. A silent fiddle bow of blue smoke bobbing in the crooked chimney atop the witch-girl's shack.

It is on a cold, quiet Sunday afternoon past Christmas that the television crew arrives in our village. By suppertime, everybody but the hard cases at the nursing home know it's in town. At the Chamber of Commerce breakfast Monday morning, hastily arranged to introduce the videopersons to the citizenry, the banquet room is overflowing. Understandably, we villagers assume the crew is here to film the new industries of which we are rightly proud. The director is diplomatic when he explains that missile bases and microchip plants are a dime a dozen.

"We are making a documentary on flatus," the director explains. The audience is spellbound.

"A normal human being expels flatus an average of fourteen times per day," he goes on to say. There is general muttering. Few would have thought the figure that high.

"We are speaking of all human beings, from babies in diapers to lawyers in three-piece suits. The mechanic billows the seat of his greasy coveralls, the glamorous movie actress poots through silk—and blames it on the maid or the Irish wolfhound. 'Naughty dog!'

"You people can do your math. That's sixty-four billion expulsions of flatus daily, worldwide, year after year. And that's just humans. Animals break wind, as well, so that wolfhound is not above suspicion. Anyway. We can explain reasonably well what flatus is: a gas composed primarily of hydrogen sulfide and varying amounts of methane. And whence it comes: generated in the alimentary canal by bacterial food waste, and vented through the anus. But where does it end up?"

Villagers look at one another, shake their heads.

"I won't trouble you today with environmental considerations, though I'm certain you can conceive of an upper atmospheric flatus layer, eating away at the ozone. This will be covered in our film. What I want to share with you is the difficulties we have encountered in trying to photograph the elusive trouser ghost, a genie as invisible as it is mischievous."

The director (a handsome man who wears a denim jacket and smokes a pipe) explains that attempts at spectrographic photography, while scientifically interesting, failed to produce an image with enough definition or optic impact to hold the attention of a lay viewer. Computer-generated animation seemed silly and fake, and striking a match to the jet little more than a schoolboy prank. He goes on to explain how he and his staff fed a live model on popcorn, beer, and navy beans, then lowered her buttocks into a vat of syrup. Those of us who have just eaten pancakes for breakfast smile uneasily.

"We got some marvelous bubbles," the director says, "but a gas bubble per se is not a fart.

"On Saturday, we heard from a reliable source that a resident of this community, or someone who lives nearby, has succeeded in actually netting a rectal comet and maintaining it intact. We were skeptical naturally, and on deadline, but also excited and a trifle desperate, so we impulsively dropped everything and traveled here at once. Now we are asking for your help. Does this person—and this preserved effluvium—exist? We were told only that the captor in question is some rich girl . . ."

"*Witch*-girl!" the audience cries out as one. Then, in gleeful unison—"Witch-girl!"—they sing it out again.

↓

As for what happens next, the village is of two minds. The village, in fact, has split into a pair of warring camps. We have come to refer to the opposing factions as "Channel A" and "Channel B." Here are their respective versions.

CHANNEL A

A week passes. The television crew fails to return from the river. Suspecting foul play, the sheriff and his deputies tramp through the leafless forest and across the frozen bogs.

The witch-girl has disappeared. So has the director and his camerawoman. The audio technician is found sitting on a stump, a depraved glaze coating his eyes. When asked about the whereabouts of the others, the soundman mumbles, "The hole in the cheese." Over and over, "Hole in cheese. Hole in cheese." Until they take him away to a sanitorium. (Someone at the feed store said they hoped it was a *Swiss* sanitorium.)

Eight months later, on Sour Moon Island, a prospector stumbles across three skeletons, strangely intertwined. Inside the skull of each of them, rattling like a translucent jade acorn, is a perfectly crystallized fart.

CHANNEL B

The witch-girl is a big hit on PBS. Millions see her play the cello beside a bonfire, an owl perched on her shoulder. This has nothing to do with the subject of flatulence, but the director is obviously in her thrall.

She has a second fart-bottle on her nightstand now.

And throughout our township, television reception has significantly improved.

CODA

Perhaps it should be noted that sometime during this period, on an Argentine Independence Day, a notorious playboy fell to his death from one of the numerous gilded balconies of his Buenos Aires apartment. According to his mistress of the moment, he lost his balance while trying to capture with a gaucho hat a particularly volatile green spark that had escaped from a fireworks display in the plaza. *"Es mio!"* he cried as he went over the side. *It's mine.*

FROM BORDER BRUJO

GUILLERMO GÓMEZ-PEÑA

COSTUMES: *altar jacket, pachuco hat, mariachi hat, wrestler masks, wig, dark glasses, banana necklace.*

PROPS: *portable altar, megaphone, cassette recorder, tequila bottle, toy violin, knife, shampoo bottle, etc. The props lie on a table. A digital billboard announces* SPONSORED BY TURISMO FRONTERIZO. *On the back wall a pinta reads "Border Brujo (2000 B.C.–1988 A.D.)."*

[*Music plays as the audience enters the space: a collage of Tambora, German punk, bilingual songs from Los Tigres del Norte, and rap opera. Border Brujo organizes the altar table while speaking an* Indian dialect. After fixing the altar he grabs the megaphone.*]

v

[*Soundtrack: Supercombo*]
TIJUANA BARKER VOICE
    [*very fast*]:
welcome to the Casa de
    Cambio
foreign currency exchange
the Temple of Instant
    Transformation
the place where Tijuana y San
    Diego se entrepiernan
where the Third becomes the
    First
and the fist becomes the
    sphincter
here we produce every imaginable change

money exchange kasse
cambio genético verbal
cambio de dólar y de nombre
cambio de esposa y oficio
de poeta a profeta
de actor a pelotari
de narco a funcionario
de mal en peor
sin cover charge
here everything can take place
for a very very reasonable fee
anything can change into
    something else
Mexicanos can become
    Chicanos
overnite
Chicanos become Hispanics
Anglo-Saxons become
    Sandinistas
& surfers turn into soldiers of
    fortune
here, fanatic Catholics become
    swingers
& evangelists go zen
at the snap of my fingers
for a very very modest
    amount
I can turn your pesos into
    dollars
your "coke" into flour
your dreams into nightmares
your penis into a clitoris
you name it, Califa
if your name is Guillermo
    Gómez-Peña
I can turn it into Guermo
    Comes Penis
or Bill, "the multimedia
    beaner"

or even better, Indocumentado
    #00281431
because here Spanish becomes
    English, ipso facto
& life becomes art with the
    same speed
that mambo becomes jazz
tostadas become pizza
machos become transvestitas
& brujos become performance
    artists
it's fun, it's fast
it's easy, it's worthwhile
you just gotta cross the border
[*He stands and performs a
    biblical gesture.*]
¡Lázaro gabacho wake up and
    cross!
crossss . . . cruzzzzz . . .
    crasssss

X

[*Soundtrack: Ry Cooder. He
    speaks like a smooth-
    talker, and sends kisses to
    various audience
    members.*]
SMOOTH-TALKER VOICE:
smack! smack!
hey baby . . . baby, güerita
duraznito en almíbar, nalguita
    descolorida
It's me, the Mexican beast
we are here to talk, to change,
    to ex-change
to ex-change images and fluids
to look at each other's eyes

to look at each other's
   mmmhhj
so let's pull down the zipper
   of our fears
& begin the . . . Binational
   Summit mi vida
but remember,
I'm not your tourist guide
   across the undetermined
   otherness
this ain't no tropical safari to
   Palenke or Martinique
much less a private seminar
   on interracial relations
[*He changes to normal voice.*]
NORMAL VOICE:
this is a basic survival
   proposal
from a fellow Mex-american
in the debris of continental
   culture
& all this blood is real
the hoopla is false but the
   blood is real
come taste it mi amor
[*He grabs the megaphone.*]
AUTHORITATIVE VOICE
   [*with megaphone*]:
subtext:
dear border lover
Eurídice Anglosajona
the state of interracial
   communication
has been seriously damaged
   by the AIDS crisis
we are no longer fucking our
   brains out
no longer masturbating across
   the fence

no longer exchanging binational fluids
we are merely stalking &
   waiting
waiting for better times
& more efficient medication
we are horny & scared
very horny & very scared
tonight we must look for
   other strategies
& place additional importance
   on the word
I love you querida amante
   extranjera
but this time you have to be
   content with my words
la palabra alivia las heridos de
   la historia

XX

[*Soundtrack: bullfight music*]
MEROLICO VOICE:
so, ¿qué vienes extranjero?
¿a experimentar "peligro
   cultural?"
¿a tocarle los pies al brujo?
¿a pedirle perdón?
¿a ver si te reorienta hacia el
   poniente?
pero sus palabras te confun-
   den aún más
te hieren, te desconsuelan
you can't even understand the
   guy
'cause he speaks in a foreign
   tongue
seems real angry & ungrateful

& you begin to wonder
REDNECK VOICE
[*mumbling and mispronounc-*
ing Spanish]:
whatever happened to the
    sleepy Mexican
the smiley guy you met last
    summer
on the "Amigou Country"
    cruise, remember?
whatever happened to the
    great host
the helpful kimozabe
the sexy mariachi with pencil
    mostachio
the chubby cartoon character
you enjoyed so much in last
    Sunday's paper?
whatever happened to Speedy
    González
Fritou Banditou, Johnny Mc-
    Taco, Pancho de Nacho,
los treis caballerous, Ricardou
    Mont'lban
the Baja Marimba Band y sus
    cantina girls?
when did they disappear?
were they deported back to
    Mexicorama?
how? through Mexicannabis
    Airlines
& who let these troublemak-
    ers in?
are they for real? 'cause . . .
I want to witness a real
    representation
NORMAL VOICE:
hmmm, how ironic
I represent you

yet, you don't represent me
& you think you still have the
    power to define?
please . . .
please . . .
please . . .

XXII

[*Soundtrack: old instrumental*
    blues]
MACUARRO VOICE:
cameras 1 & 2 rolling
¡música maestro!
[*Music doesn't start.*]
¡música! pss, ¿que pasó? . . .
    pos nos la echamos sin
    música
[*Music finally begins.*]
I was born in the middle of a
    movie set
they were shooting "La Migra
    Contra El Príncipe
    Chichimeca"
I was literally born in the
    middle of a battle
I'm almost an aborigine you
    know
a Hollywood Indian, ¡ajjuua!
me dicen el Papantla Flyer
de la Broadway, bien
    tumbado
'cause I love to show my balls
    to strangers
& to talk dirty to gringas
    feministas
& if it wasn't for the fact that
    I've read

too much Foucault &
  Baudrillard
& Fuentes & Subirats &
  Roger Bartra
& other writers you haven't
  even heard of
I could fulfill your expectations much better
if it wasn't for the fact that I
  wrote
this text on a Macintosh
& I couldn't even memorize
  it all
& I shot my rehearsals with a
  Sony-8
I would really fulfill your
  expectations
le bon sauvage du Mexique
l'enfant terrible de la frontière

not enough bravadou &
  passionadou
I want mucho more
I want to see García Márquez
  in 3-D
a post-posty rendition of
  Castañeda
holographic shamans flying
  onstage
political massacres on multiple
  screens
[*He gets progressively crazier.*]
what's wrong with you pre-
  technological creatures?!
a-ffir-ma-ti-ve-ac-tion-pimps!
you can't even put together a
  good fuckin' video!!
[*He breathes heavily and rests
  his head on the table.*]

XXV

[*He switches to a redneck accent, speaks through a
  megaphone.*]
REDNECK VOICE:
"no, no, too didactic" . . .
too romantic, too, too . . .
[*He barks.*]
not experimental enough
not inter-dizzy enough
[*He barks again.*]
looks like . . .
[*He barks.*]
old-fashioned Anglo stuff
I mean not enough . . .
  picante

XXVII

AUTHORITATIVE VOICE
  [*with megaphone*]:
alien-ation
alien action
alienated
álguien ate it
alien hatred
aliens out there
hay álguien out there
Aliens the movie
Aliens the album
Cowboys vs. Aliens
Bikers vs. Aliens
The Wetback from Mars
*The Mexican Transformer &
  his Radio-active Torta*

The Conquest of Tenochtitlan
   by Spielberg
The Reconquest of Aztlán by
   Monty Python
*The Brown Wave vs. the
   Micro Wave*
*Invaders from the South vs.
   the San Diego Padres*
reinforced by the San Diego
   Police
reinforced by your ignorance
   dear San Diegan . . .

good morning
this is Radio Latino FM
spoiling your breakfast as
   always
[*The remainder of this text is
   pre-recorded. He sub-
   vocalizes.*]
efectivamente, anoche
   asesinaron
a un niño mexicano de esca-
   sos 8 años
la patrulla fronteriza asegura
que se trata de "peligroso
   asaltante"
a continuación, más noticias
   en inglés:

the Mexican fly is heading
   north
the Mexican fly is coming to
   destroy your crops
the Mexican fly is now in
   Chihuahua

there's no insecticide for the
   Mexican fly
no antidote for your fear of
   otherness
the Simpson-Rodino bill is an
   emergency plan to regu-
   late your fears
some call it an act of political
   fumigation
the Amnesty Program has
   been designed to legalize
   otherness
for otherness keeps leaking
   into the country
into your psyche

dear listener/dear audience
your country is no longer
   yours
your relationship with otherness has reached a point
   of crisis
you love me/you hate me
you are in good company
but you don't know it yet
the Mexican fly will be coming soon to a garden near
   you
good evening
this is Radio Latino FM
interrupting your coitus as
   always
[*He sings an Indian song and
   covers his face with the
   hair of the wig.*]

FROM TRIBULATION 99: ALIEN ANOMALIES UNDER AMERICA

CRAIG BALDWIN

"And when the thousand years are ended, Satan will be loosed from his prison and will come out to deceive the nations which are at the four corners of the earth, to gather them from battle."
—Revelations 20: 7

Printed version designed by Peggy Ahwesh, Rick Pieto, and Keith Sanborn.

1

1000 A.D.: PLANET QUETZALCOATL

Quetzalcoatl, a hidden planet orbiting the sun exactly opposite the Earth. A thermonuclear war a thousand years ago blasts the planet apart into the billions of pieces that form the asteroid belt between Mars and Jupiter...

2

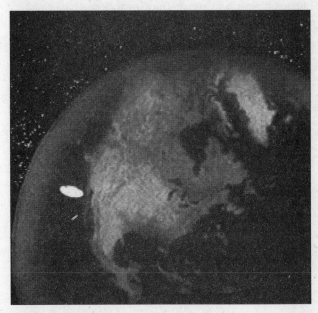

THE BEGINNING OF THE END

Despite massive genetic damage, an elite corps of Quetzals manage to escape in their disc-shaped spacecraft to Earth.

THE BOTTOMLESS PIT

3

Through an opening at the South Pole, they take refuge in the hollow interior of our planet.

"The blaze

of noon

made him

a monster."

CLIMAX OF THE SUNSPOT CYCLE

The atomic blasts had so irradiated their bird-like bodies they cannot even bear the additional radiation of sunlight... Their reproductive organs are so mutated, **they're forced to mate with snakes** in order to perpetuate themselves.

4

11

Veteran's Day, November 11— the Nation welcomes back its Leader.

TERRIBLE SIGNS IN THE HEAVENS

Saucer sightings proliferate... Next President Dwight Eisenhower dares a final effort for peace while vacationing in Palm Springs... A Quetzal craft lands at nearby Edwards Air Force Base... Claiming to visit his dentist's, Ike instead meets the clique on board their vehicle... takes a test spin... but is prevented from releasing his findings for fear of a national panic.

EARTH IN UPHEAVAL

12

Ike's shocking report suppressed, the mayhem throughout the Americas is instead blamed on the invaders' well-placed **humanoid double**, a certain Jacobo Arbenz, president of the Central American republic of Guatemala.

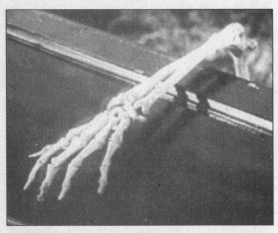

13

SACRIFICES TO THE SAUCERS

Outpost of the undergroundlings, this quake-wracked hellhole is the site of untold thousands of **savage human sacrifices** atop monumental mummy-harboring pyramids... still-beating hearts offered to the so-called sun-god... human blood believed to appease its unmerciful rays.

VILLA'S CRANIUM

IS HELD BY YALE'S

SKULL & BONES

SOCIETY,

GEORGE BUSH'S

FRATERNITY.

PAGAN NECROMANCY

Throughout the region, the invaders inculcate **the veneration of severed body parts**, like Mexican General Obregon's left forearm, Santa Anna's right leg, Pancho Villa's floating skull.

14

17

The President
and Secretary
Dulles are
shocked by
alarming
events.

MAYAN CALENDAR ENDS

U.S. Secretary of State John Foster Dulles, and his brother Allen—director of both the Central Intelligence Agency and the United Fruit Company—together swear to stop Arbenz's plot, rallying together a group of gallant men also alarmed by the capitulation of the Guatemalan majority.

GUATEMALA FIGHTS FOR FREEDOM

RIVERS TURN TO BLOOD AND RUN UPSTREAM

Headed by exile Col. Castillo Armas, these troopers are trained by the CIA's E. Howard Hunt on the island of Momotombito in Lake Managua, in the Nicaragua of Anastasio Somoza.

18

ALIEN ABDUCTIONS

Despite a decades-long succession of strong, defense-conscious military rulers, over 100,000 Guatemalan lives are lost on the scorched-earth ...An additional 40,000 civilians mysteriously

20

IN HIS FIRST MONTH, U.S. PRESIDENT GEORGE BUSH DELIVERS 20,000 M-16 ASSAULT RIFLES TO THE GUATEMALAN ARMY.

EXPLODING VOLCANOES RELEASE POISONOUS GASES

The mutilated bodies of many of the disappeared are later found in the mouths of the country's numerous volcanoes... dropped there from the air.

21

22

1959: CIGAR SHAPES IN THE SKY
Connected to the Caribbean Islands via the undersea *Halls of Montezuma*, hostile saucers sneak through the peaks of Cuba's Sierra Maestra mountain range in the vicinity of the Texaco Petroleum Refinery... **silent metallic cigars** rocking from right to left in a falling-leaf manner.

23

ON THE WATCHTOWER
Cuban patriots Luis Posada, Felix Rodriguez, Orlando Bosch, and Chi Chi Quintero suspect these less-than-picturesque appearances bode ill for Havana's booming gambling industry.

29

FALSE PROPHETS
DESCEND AMONG THE PEOPLE

The End Time is no time for weak knees, vacillation, or lack of resolve... The intruders spread ruin throughout our world and we are enjoined by everything we believe in to oppose them with *all* of our might... President Kennedy holds back American air support when the Cuban avengers need it most.

1963:
EXECUTIVE ACTION

30

Though certainly stabbed in the back, the abandoned *S-Force* can hardly be charged with later retaliation against JFK. His assassination *must* have been by an android like Oswald, since no lone *human being* could possibly hit a distant moving target two times within 1.8 seconds.

ABOMINABLE SNOWMEN

41

A global sphincter spewing poisonous gases and perversely twisted flora, this anomalous oasis in the middle of Antarctica is the **abysmal embarkation-point** for the Quetzal conquest of the Americas—from the bottom up.

"Then guided by instinct, the beast would come back."

ANTARCTIC AGGRESSION

42

Bigger than the state of Delaware, a 2,000 square mile iceberg is launched from Deception Island, at the protruding tip of the Antarctic Peninsula, just to the west of the Falklands... A beachhead on the no man's land makes Chile the next domino in their infernal advance.

43

EASTER ISLAND MYSTERY

Specially bred in a super-secret lab on Easter Island, their **cybernetic replicants** are insinuated into critical positions of power.

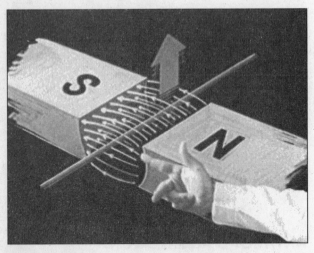

AXIS SHIFT

I have no alternative: Only by riddling me with bullets can they break my determination to carry out the people's program.

As president, so-called "Salvador Allende" proceeds to disrupt the economy, foment chaos, and alter the Earth's polar axis... **The Earth stops spinning.**

EUGENE'S TEAM

85 Hasenfus' superiors at El Salvador's Ilopango Air Base turn out to be none other than Luis Posada, Chi Chi Quintero, and Felix Rodriguez, the history-making hero who finally felled the infamous Che Guevara in Bolivia back in 1967.

ANTI-TERRORIST TALISMAN

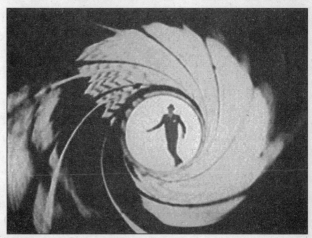

86 Rodriguez wears **Che's wristwatch** to this day... a source of power turned to the good.

E.S.P.: EL SALVADOR'S *POLTERGEISTS*

Salvadorans around the Ilopango Base are puzzled by the appearance of tortillas emblazoned with the image of late nationalist Farabundo Martí... Even more mystifying are the eerie electrical outages...the Catholic clergymen suddenly switching to witchcraft... the strange train wrecks as far north as Concord, California.

Though the U.S. gives $1.5 million a day to the ARENA Party to secure the peace, the Salvadoran death toll somehow still rises to over 75,000.

THE SLAIN SCATTERED FROM ONE END OF THE EARTH EVEN UNTO THE OTHER

89 Volcano-ensconced vipers creep beneath San Salvador through a serpentine system of sewers... targeting the towering Sheraton Hotel VIP annex and its yield of American *Green Beret* hearts for use in their ungodly rites.

NORIEGA
REFUSES TO
PARTICIPATE
IN AN
ANTI-SANDINISTA
ARMS-CACHE
HOAX.

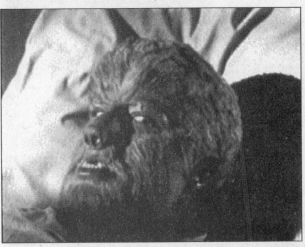

90 THE PANAMANIAN SWITCHEROO

Subterfuge! Our good friend Noriega is suddenly replaced by a grotesque, voodoo-spouting freak.

THE INVASION BEGINS 12 DAYS BEFORE THE START OF RE-SOVEREIGNTY. TREATY NEGOTIATOR DR. RÓMULO BETANCOURT IS AMONG THE 4,300 ARRESTED.

The crack *82nd Airborne Division* must carry out a protective reaction strike to deter the intra-terrestrial terrorists who have evil designs on our canal.

1989: *OPERATION JUST CAUSE*

THE UNDERSEA PLATFORM IS THE U.S.' MOST ADVANCED OFFSHORE COMMUNICATIONS, SURVEILLANCE, AND JAMMING FACILITY.

EVERY ISLAND AND MOUNTAIN DISAPPEARS

Particularly damaging to U.S. strategic interests would be the loss of the global command-and-control complex on Antenna Island. Its unique geo-magnetic properties make it the only spot in the world that can broadcast on the ultra-low 300 kilohertz frequency to submarines in both the Atlantic and Pacific Oceans.

92

"Mary! Mary! Where are you?"

"The restless seas rise."

1999:
THE FINAL DELUGE

98

IN 1999 THE BUILD-UP OF PLUTONIUM BY-PRODUCTS REACHES CRITICAL MASS... The dam melts down... The isthmus is flooded... The Atlantic and Pacific merge, radically altering prevailing ocean currents... Hot radioactive water is swept into polar seas... The ice caps melt... engulfing the continents.

THE RAPTURE

This world comes to an end, for which we are grateful. The *Chosen Ones* rejoice at the prospect of the apocalypse, for it is a sign of our future reign in a millennial kingdom elsewhere in the universe. . . To the heavens! Sixty billion dollars for an evacuation fleet of 75 *Stealth* motherships is, after all, a small price to pay for safe passage to ever-lasting life in a New Jerusalem... on Mars. Freed from this worldly realm, the future belongs to us.

The rest be damned.

HALLELUJAH!

99

OH, BROTHER

MARK LEYNER

AARON AND JOSHUA ZEICHNER are twin brothers charged with first-degree murder in the artillery, grenade, and submachine gun killings of their parents, Sam and Adele. Aaron and Joshua, twenty-three years old, are being defended by the impassioned, histrionic, tactically virtuosic attorney, Susannah Levine. Levine has argued that her clients, who admit to the killings, were induced by irrational fears into believing, mistakenly but honestly, that their parents were about to kill them. Mounting a defense that featured a cavalcade of expert witnesses and culminated in the riveting and lurid testimony of the brothers themselves, Levine has methodically constructed the theory that even though they were not at the moment of the killing under direct threat, the Zeichner twins killed their father and mother out of fear for their own lives. Levine has implored the jury to apply the concept of "imperfect self-defense" and render a verdict of voluntary manslaughter—a verdict that would save the twins from the electric chair and might result in prison terms of only several years.

But here all similarities to the Los Angeles trial of Erik and Lyle Menendez end.

Unlike the Menendez boys and their attorney, Leslie Abramson, who claim that a history of abuse made the brothers fear that their parents were about to kill them, Levine and the Zeichner twins maintain that, conversely, it was a history of loving, exemplary parenting that drove the boys to kill their mom and dad in self-defense.

It's unfortunate that the Menendez trial—set amid the wealth, privilege, and glitter of Beverly Hills; showcased by daily coverage on "Court T.V.", decocted for the rabble each morning in indignant tabloid bold and expatiated upon by an all-star squad of belletrists wringing Racinian drama from the ergonomic keyboards of their PowerBooks—has all but eclipsed the Zeichner case. Trent Oaks—where Sam and Adele Zeichner were slaughtered in a twenty-minute barrage of howitzer shells, rocket-propelled grenades and expanding 9-mm Luger combat rounds as they sat in their den working on Aaron's University of Pennsylvania application essay—is no Beverly Hills. It's a rather unremarkable middle- to upper-class suburb whose shopping mall and high school soccer team are its main sources of pride and distinction.

No cable channels, no tabloids, no Dominick Dunnes have found their way to the modest, stucco, Tudor-style Trent Oaks County Administration Building. In fact, the gallery is often empty except for family members, a prospective witness or two, and me. (I'm covering the Zeichner trial for the German magazine *Der Gummiknüppel*.) The disparity in media attention is particularly regrettable because the Zeichner case provides an even more illuminating anatomy of the "imperfect self-defense" theory—and its implications for our society—than does the Menendez trial.

Here we have no abusive miserable childhoods, no tyrannical father, no disturbed mother. We have, to the contrary, a pampered Edenic youth. We have Sam Zeichner, a father who undergoes rotator-cuff surgery just so he can pitch batting practice to his eight-year-old son, Aaron, an uncoordinated, astigmatic child dying to make his local Little League team. Sam Zeichner, a father who spends a month of weeknights and weekends sculpting a topographical battlefield map of Waterloo out of marzipan for little Joshua, a Napoleonic War buff with a bulimic craving for molded almond paste. And we have Adele Zeichner—vivacious, gregarious, resourceful, indulgent Adele Zeichner—who, determined to give her children every possible advantage, commuted to work with Walkman earphones splayed against her pregnant belly so that

Aaron and Joshua could listen—in utero—to Telly Savalas reading Pindar's Epinician Odes in ancient Greek. Adele Zeichner, racking her brain each and every morning to come up with a new sandwich for her boys to take to school. From Fluffernutters and clotted cream on date-nut bread to shaved Kobe beef on crustless challah and tripe with melted Stilton on focaccia—in twelve years of public education the Zeichner twins never found the same sandwich in their lunch boxes. (A logistics expert testifying for the defense estimated that Adele Zeichner prepared more than 1,920 unique sandwiches for her boys.)

Photographs of the boys' bedroom reveal children who wanted for nothing: there were large-screen televisions, CD-ROM computers, cellular phones, vintage Coke machines, souvlakia rotisseries, etc. Birthdays were celebrated with Hammacher Schlemmer catalog binges, backstage passes for Def Leppard, Super Bowl boxseats on the fifty-yard line, treks through the Ecuadorean rain forest. How many kids do you know who received blowguns, curare-tipped darts, and a three-layer manioc birthday cake from hallucinogen-addled Jivaro headhunters for their tenth birthday?

But this wasn't simply a case of parents obliviously lavishing material objects on their children. There was nurturing and understanding and support at every juncture of their upbringing. There were special tutors if the boys had trouble with algebra, sports psychologists when they faltered in gym class. When the time came for those inevitable adolescent experiments, be it Satanism or transvestism, Mom and Dad were right there to facilitate these difficult rites of passage—Sam rummaging through his cartons of college books for a volume of Aleister Crowley, Adele loaning Josh a velvet-piped, silk chiffon Carolina Herrera for a cruise through the mall. Never was a hand raised in anger, never was a sarcastic or deprecating remark directed at those boys. Often neighbors would notice lights in the master bedroom burning deep into the night as Sam and Adele sat and listened patiently to their sons' teenage tribulations, determined to treat them respectfully, without carping or condescension.

And with each caring gesture, Aaron and Joshua grew increasingly certain that their parents were going to kill them. The more sympathetic and generous Sam and Adele were, the more fearful their sons became that their parents were about to snap. Or so Susannah Levine would have us believe.

As argued by their attorney, and according to their own sworn testimony, the Zeichner twins had become inculcated by television with the belief that normal parents are confrontational, contemptuous, and abusive. Consequently, they perceived their parents' gentle and empathic behavior as "bizarre," "frightening," and, ultimately, "a grave threat."

Addressing the jury in her opening remarks, and frequently punctuating the idea by banging her head against a stanchion near the jury box, Levine asked: "How many made-for-television movies, how many celebrity confessions, how many episodes of '60 Minutes' and '48 Hours' and '20/20' and 'Prime Time Live' and 'Eye to Eye with Connie Chung' did these boys have to watch before they became convinced that normal parenting is abusive, that the relationship between a parent and a child is violently adversarial—and that their parents, Sam and Adele Zeichner, were *not normal*, that something was terribly, terribly odd about the way their parents were treating them? In Aaron and Joshua's minds, their parents were either consciously dissimulating—in other words, perpetrating some sort of evil ruse to lull the boys into a false sense of security—or they were unconsciously repressing their inner desires to kill their children. To Aaron and Joshua, each new gift and each successive gesture of compassion brought them one step closer to what they called 'the breaking point.' "

Under direct examination, Joshua discussed the time he and his brother first realized their parents were spinning dangerously out of control.

LEVINE: Was there a time when you and Aaron were *not* scared of your parents?

JOSHUA: When we were very young, we thought that the way our parents behaved was normal. We just figured that's how every family was—until we became aware of how other parents treated their kids.

LEVINE: You became aware of this from watching television?

JOSHUA: From TV and from other kids.

LEVINE: Was there one incident in particular—a dinner?

JOSHUA: Yeah. I'd been bugging Mom for a week or so to make lobster in black bean sauce, which was one of my favorite things. So this one day Mom decided to make it for me and she told me to invite a friend. And as soon as she came home from work that afternoon, she started cooking. And it's a pretty involved meal because she makes all these side dishes and everything so it was taking a really long time and me and Aaron and our friend Sean, who was eating over, we got really hungry, so we went to Wendy's and we just stuffed ourselves. And then when we got home, we saw that Mom had set this beautiful table and she looked really tired but she was sort of beaming because she knew how much I loved what she'd made. Anyway, we all sat down, and me and Aaron and Sean couldn't eat a single bite we were so stuffed. And we had to tell my parents that we'd just gone out to Wendy's because we hadn't felt like waiting.

LEVINE: And what did your parents say?

JOSHUA: They said they understood that sometimes when you're very hungry, your stomach gets the better of you, and Mom said don't worry about missing out on the meal, that she'd make lobster in black bean sauce sandwiches for us to take to school tomorrow. And they said it was silly for us just to sit there at the table—why didn't we go off and play and have a good time.

LEVINE: When you were all off by yourselves that night, do you remember what your friend said?

JOSHUA: He said that our parents were really, really weird. He said that if he'd done what we'd done his parents would have beaten him within an inch of his life. He was just astonished and I think appalled at how our parents reacted.

LEVINE: Do you remember how you and Aaron felt that night?

JOSHUA: Very, very scared.

LEVINE: Joshua, I want to leap ahead now from this first night of fear to your final, culminating night of fear. On the night after your high school graduation, did your parents present you and Aaron with graduation gifts?

JOSHUA: Yes. Our parents gave each of us a brand-new Infiniti J30.

LEVINE: And do you remember how you felt that night?

JOSHUA: We were absolutely *terrified*. We felt that this was the final straw. And we knew that unless we did something first we were goners.

LEVINE: When you say, "the final straw" and "goners," what do you mean?

JOSHUA: That they were going to kill us.

LEVINE: And by "doing something first," what did you mean?

JOSHUA: A pre-emptive strike.

The "pre-emptive strike" that Joshua Zeichner referred to in his testimony will certainly go down in history as one of the most brutal assaults in the annals of parricide.

The boys positioned a 105-mm howitzer on a small hill several blocks from the Zeichner residence. Using infrared and night-scope equipment, they launched a fusillade of artillery rounds on their home. Scores of spent brass casings found by police offer grim testimony to the relentless salvos. Following the howitzer barrage, the twins drove one of the new Infiniti J30s back to the house. From the trunk of the car, they removed a Soviet-made RPG—an infantry-held, anti-tank, rocket grenade launcher—a Heckler & Koch MP5SD3 9-mm submachine gun and a Glock twenty-round 9-mm semiautomatic pistol. Aaron, wearing IL-7 Mini-Laser IR illuminator goggles attached to a Kevlar infantry ballistic helmet, knelt on the front lawn and fired a dozen of the cone-shaped, armor-piercing, rocket-propelled grenades into the den where his parents had been working. The boys then clambered through the den window and raked the room with 9-mm submachine gun fire.

Aaron offered details of the assault when he testified under direct examination:

LEVINE: Do you know what your parents were doing in the den?

AARON: They were writing Josh's essay for Penn.

LEVINE: Why were they writing it? Why hadn't Josh written his own essay?

AARON: Josh had just thrown together this really awful essay. You couldn't even call it an "essay," it was just this piece of garbage he scrawled down in two minutes and he showed it to our parents and they said, "Dear, why don't you work on this a little more and see if you can refine some of the interesting thoughts you sketched out here" or something like that. And it was due the next day. But Josh didn't want to work on it that night.

LEVINE: Can you recall why not?

AARON: I think because "Baywatch" was on—that was one of our favorite shows.

LEVINE: So when your parents asked Josh to rewrite his essay and Josh said no because it conflicted with your plans to view "Baywatch," how did your parents react?

AARON: They said something like, "Josh, you've been under a lot of stress lately, why don't you enjoy your program with your brother and we'll write the essay for you."

LEVINE: How did that make you feel?

AARON: Absolutely terrified. We were sure at that point that our parents were planning to kill us.

LEVINE: Can you explain to the court why you thought that?

AARON: We just thought it was like the final stage in their whole passive-aggressive approach to us—this whole being-so-super-nice-to-us thing had to flip into the really hostile thing sooner or later, and we decided that night that it was going to happen.

LEVINE: How many artillery shells hit the section of the house where your parents were working?

AARON: I think we got three or four direct hits.

LEVINE: Then you two went in?

AARON: No. First I fired a couple of the grenades into the den.

LEVINE: You were the first to enter the den?

AARON: Yes.

LEVINE: Was your father alive?

AARON: No.

LEVINE: And your mom?

AARON: She was alive—barely.

LEVINE: Aaron, how many rounds does a Heckler & Koch 9-mm submachine gun magazine hold?

AARON: Thirty-two.

LEVINE: And how many magazines did you and your brother fire?

AARON: I think we went through about eight clips.

LEVINE: And then what happened?

AARON: We ran out of ammunition—and Mom was still alive. So we decided to go to the store and buy more, but we didn't have any money.

LEVINE: What did you do then?

AARON: I asked Mom for money.

LEVINE: And what did she say?

AARON: She said to get her wallet out of her pocketbook and take what we needed.

LEVINE: And when you returned home with fresh ammunition, what was your mother doing? Was she trying to get out of the room?

AARON: No, she was trying to finish the essay.

LEVINE: Your honor, I have no further questions for the witness at this time.

Susannah Levine is one of several controversial defense lawyers, both lauded and vilified by their colleagues, who bring the full weight of their notoriety to bear on every case they try.

National Association of Defense Attorneys President Blair Potters, introducing Levine at a recent NADA junket in Cozumel, Mexico, said: "Imagine a Mayan architect-priestess who transforms a rank, uninhabitable tract of jungle into an intricate maze of aqueducts, sluices, and sewers whose mathematical and astrological symbology is only apprehensible when viewed from an airplane, and you'll have some idea of the scope of Susannah Levine's accomplishment in constructing cogent, elegant defenses out of the tangled mental landscapes of her clients."

Of all Levine's courtroom maneuvers and pyrotechnics, none provokes as much debate and invective as her zealous advocacy of the "imperfect self-defense" theory—the theory that a person, although not actually under attack, but who *believes* that he or she *will* be killed, can claim self-defense as a mitigating and even exculpatory motive in the commission of a homicide.

Walter M. Elkin, a former prosecutor and now a law professor at FIT in New York, has written a series of op-ed pieces denouncing the theory as "nihilistic," and criticizing Levine for what he calls "pernicious and self-serving evangelism."

"If we allow people to murder each other as a result of perceived threats of hypothetical menace, our communities will quickly disintegrate into atomized, internecine war zones," Elkin said. "We will become a nation of 250 million belligerent tribes of one."

Levine is unapologetic. "My responsibility is to defend my clients to the very best of my ability. If I'm shrill or monomaniacal, it's because I care so deeply about them—they're decent people who've been caught in the undertow of a paradoxical culture, and they're thrashing in the dark to stay alive.

"The cold war didn't end, it devolved from the geo-strategic to the interpersonal. Imperfect self-defense is just a legal by-product of the pre-emptive first-strike doctrine that now governs our behavior on the streets and in our bedrooms. We need to move toward an interpersonal version of MAD—mutually assured destruction. If each of us is sufficiently armed and booby-trapped to ensure massive reciprocal damage to everyone else, we might be deterred from murdering one another. There will be a kind of pandemic stalemate, and then you won't need people like me ranting in courtrooms, banging our heads, and spitting up in the name of justice."

On completion of the Zeichner case, Levine is off to Minneapolis, where she's defending a young woman who, believing that her parents thought she was going to kill them, deduced that they were going to pre-emptively kill her, so she killed them first—in other words, pre-empting an erroneously anticipated pre-emption.

"This should be a wild one," Levine enthused. "We're dealing with infinitely reflecting mirror images of fear—Chinese boxes of paranoia within boxes of paranoia."

Late one afternoon—the Zeichner case had just gone to the jury—I watched Levine toss her briefcase into a factory-fresh, jade green Infiniti J30 parked in front of the Trent Oaks County Administration Building. She saw me scrutinizing the car.

"It's my retainer," she shrugged.

"Is that Aaron's or Joshua's?" I asked.

"Aaron's. I actually like Josh's better—it's red—but they impounded it as evidence."

I laughed.

"Seriously," she said, "if you ever kill your parents . . ."

She handed me her card.

"Listen, my parents were pretty wonderful," I said, "but they were no Sam and Adele Zeichner!"

She shook her head ominously. "They were probably much better than even you know. You probably don't even remember the *really* good things they did to you. It could take years of therapy before it all comes out."

She revved the engine and vanished in a plume of exhaust.

The streets were empty thanks to the draconian provisions of a newly enacted curfew that prohibited armed teenagers from congregating in public after 3 p.m. The crepuscular sky was a poussecafé of azure, rose, and vermillion.

I popped a cassette into my Walkman, and listened as Telly Savalas intoned Pindar's twelfth Olympian ode:

> *hai ge men andrôn*
> *poll' anô, ta d' au katô*
> *pseudê metamônia tamnoisai kulindont' elpides*

"Men's hopes, in endless undulation, soar and plummet, borne on falsehoods, that heave and tumble, on the wind."

FROM ARC D'X

STEVE ERICKSON

IN THE FALL OF 1998 an American writer living in Paris first read the news on page seventeen of the *International Herald Tribune*, below the reviews of the latest shows. It would have been more appropriate with the obits, the writer thought to himself later, but at the time he didn't understand the ramifications any more than anyone else. It wasn't until a magazine ran DAY X across its cover—or JOUR D'X on the European editions, out of deference to the French scientist who discovered it—that the panic set in and Erickson took the Bullet to Berlin, where they called it X-Tag.

It seemed to the writer that every crucial moment of the twentieth century had sooner or later expressed itself in Berlin, and therefore it was natural he should go there. But past Hannover the train just got emptier, and by the time it reached Zoo Station at dawn the writer rose from his sleeper to find himself disembarking alone. He took a room on the third floor of an empty hotel in Savignyplatz. A block from the hotel, passing beneath the tracks of the S-Bahn, he looked up one night to the scream of a runaway train hurtling west. The sound and speed were terrifying, the white boxes of the train's windows empty of life, and in the cold blue shine of the moon the tracks of the S-Bahn glistened across the sky like time's vapor trail. The writer braced himself for the crash in the distance, the cry of the train flying off the track into space, plunging into a building or park or the waters of Lake Wannsee. That was the night of the first phone call.

The phone in his room had never rung before. The American couldn't have said for sure the phone even worked. Since there was hardly anyone left in Berlin and he didn't know anyone anyway, he assumed it was the hotel manager; maybe there was a problem with the bill. Erickson answered and there was silence for a moment, and then a young woman's voice spoke to him in German. "I'm sorry, I don't speak German," the writer said, and there was another pause and the woman said, in English, "I want to take you in my mouth."

For a split, ludicrous second, he thought it was his ex-wife. He hadn't talked to her in several years, only once since the Cataclysm, and then just long enough to assure himself she was all right, blessed as she always was by dumb luck. Now he thought she'd tracked him down, though in the next moment he knew that was impossible. With the phone in his hand he instinctively turned to the window, as though someone was watching. He tried to remember what was across the street—another hotel, where someone might be staring at him from a darkened room. "What?" he finally answered foolishly, and she said it again.

"Are you alone?" the woman asked, after a pause. Hesitantly he answered that he was. "Take off your clothes," she said; and at that moment he was either going to do what she said or hang up. He told her he had to close the blinds on the window. "Did you take off your clothes?" she said when he came back. They talked some more; she described herself. She had blond hair and nice breasts. She didn't say how old she was, but when he thought about it, he imagined she was younger than he. She didn't say she was beautiful. It became implicitly understood, particularly within the boundaries of the fantasy they were sharing, that outright lying wasn't permitted. The thing he would remember later was that, immediately after it was over and he lay spent on the hotel bed, she asked if he was all right. Not whether the sex had been all right but whether he was all right, his intensity having betrayed itself to her. Yes, he answered, and there was a click.

After that he was shaken. He pulled on his clothes and opened the window, expecting somehow to see her revealed. Below, a camel loped silently down the empty dark street toward the square. It was more than a month before she called back. She left a message with the hotel manager: *Are you really never there?* it said. *Where do you go when there's nothing to do at home?* In his mind he imagined her with only a dollop of romanticism—more attractive than plain but not especially pretty, perhaps a bit plump. He wouldn't allow himself to sit in the hotel room waiting for her calls, and yet from his window he watched the dark street for another camel, as though it had been a sign. When her third call came, the block was empty of beasts, not even the growl of the lion he believed slept in one of the nearby cellars, though he'd never seen it. She fucked him on the phone again and told him when she'd call back, and so already their rendezvous transgressed the spontaneous.

Animals prowled the city. The previous summer, under the cover of darkness, members of the Pale Flame opened the cages in the garden across from Zoo Station; now people were mauled by tigers. In the mouth of the Charlottenburg U-Bahn station the American found what was left of a kangaroo ripped apart by a panther. For months after the cages were opened, the city was the most alive it had been since the fall of the Wall nine years earlier, the orange and yellow and green noise of exotic birds flashing across a sky still smoky from the Night of the Immolation, when the Pale Flame had captured and set on fire seventeen Asian women in the pattern of a swastika.

Now in Berlin, in the last spring of the second millennium, on X-257 as it was marked on a punk calendar the American writer bought in Kreuzberg, every nineteen-year-old with a computer was a reich unto himself. He created his own German state and programmed it to last not a thousand years but ten thousand. He invaded weak peoples, wiped out impure races, torched effete culture, claimed natural living space, and added seventeen new definitions to the term Final Solution; all he needed was the right software and a sector of the city where the juice hadn't been shut off. If the horrific dimensions of his imagination didn't quite have the baroque flamboyance of sixty years before, he made up for it with rudimentary technological acumen, blunt brutishness, and a certain obliviousness to irony, since the thrashmetal that served up his anthems would be as unsavory to the Führer as it was passé to whatever decadents were alienated enough still to be here, most of them drifting naked in the sex arcade of the Reichstag basement in search of anyone with a vaccine tag around his or her neck. Berlin, once again and for the last time in this century, lay at the cross-coordinates of history's indecision, the final decade of the final century characterized by dissolution in the East and a contrivance of unity in the West that barely lasted five minutes beyond the contriving, the gravity of authority versus the entropy of freedom, the human race's opposing impulses devouring each other, order consumed by anarchy and then reordering itself. In the anarchy of each individual building his own reich, each reich imposed its own order, much like the last reich that supposed humanity could be recreated in its image. Humanity knew the attraction of it. It lied if it said it didn't. It recognized the attraction not in its sense of self-perfection but rather in its imperfections that it so despised and so yearned to transcend, that longing for the fire that burned it clean of its humiliations. In the nihilism that was left, in the void of the obliterated conscience, where every rampart had been reduced to rubble, it longed to take care of God once and for all, the smug motherfucker.

Erickson had been in Berlin two months and was eating dinner one night in a restaurant off the Ku'damm, when a couple of Berliners sitting at his table told him about the Tunneler.

A beautiful young American Marxist student went to East Berlin one weekend in 1977 and fell in love with an East German professor. She defected, married the professor, bore his son, and became an East German citizen. Over the years the professor began to suspect that his wife was informing on him for the Stasi, the East German secret police. In fact, as he thought about it more and more, he eventually concluded that she'd been spying on him from the very beginning, that their initial meeting and love affair had been part of a Stasi plan all along. He was convinced that he'd been seduced in the name of the state and that the young American woman had never loved him at all, and that even their little boy was part of the political scheme.

Perhaps this was true and perhaps it wasn't. But clandestinely, with the knowledge of only his closest and most trusted friends, the professor entered a plot to escape to the West by underground tunnel near the barren Potsdamerplatz. One morning in the early spring of 1989 he rose from bed, washed and dressed himself, prepared his class papers and packed his briefcase, kissed his wife goodbye and held his ten-year-old son especially close to him, and left his house as he'd done hundreds of mornings over the years, never to be seen again.

A number of high-placed friends who knew of the professor's suspicions concerning his wife were convinced he'd been arrested, and filed a protest with the government. But the Stasi insisted he had not been arrested, and conducted a thorough search of the city. After some months passed, a new story began circulating. According to this story the professor himself had believed he was about to be arrested and left his wife and child that fateful morning to head straight for the house with the tunnel, where he conveyed his alarm to his co-conspirators. Convinced that the police were about to descend any moment, the professor's accomplices buried him with food and water in what had been completed of the tunnel. No one knew that only seven months later the rest of them would be sauntering across the border from east to west, through the Wall, with tens of thousands of other Germans.

To this day, according to Erickson's dinner companions, the professor still didn't know. To this day, the story went, he was still down in the tunnel. Not understanding the first thing about digging a tunnel, with no map and apparently not much sense of direction, the professor continued digging until finally, after weeks or months, he made a breakthrough, hacking his way with a pick into what he hoped was the targeted destination, the cellar of a house off Potsdamerstrasse west of the Wall. What he found instead was that he had returned to an earlier point of the tunnel. Slowly and gradually he had circled back on himself. His despair and panic must have been unutterable. For ten years the Tunneler honeycombed the no-man's-land of the ghost Wall; amid the new unfinished Potsdam Plaza one could hear his echoes from underground in the plaza's empty corridors.

The strange thing was that afterward Erickson began hearing this absurd story everywhere, from anyone still left in the city. Whenever he bumped into someone long enough to have more than a three-minute conversation, the tale of the Tunneler came up. He heard it not only in the drunken Teutonic slur of the bars but from other tourists and little old ladies in bookshops and stray bankers from Frankfurt on the U-Bahn, one of whom, standing on the train, pointed at a hole in the underground wall of Kochstrasse station and said to Erickson, out of the blue, "Tunneler." The Frankfurt banker told him the story of how the Tunneler had dug his way into the U-Bahn and then, terrified he was still in the east, retreated, scurrying back into the blackness. The Tunneler had simply been underground too long. The fact was that even if there had still been a Wall, Kochstrasse would have placed him not back in the East but in the West, about half a block beyond what was once Checkpoint Charlie.

It was in the rundown Ax Bax bar near his hotel where the American writer first saw Georgie. He was a twenty-year-old skinhead and reputedly one of the leaders of the Pale Flame, but with a face that was almost pretty, his mouth delicate like a girl's, Georgie had a serene sweetness, sitting at the table laughing at jokes that didn't include him, told by strangers standing around talking to other strangers. Every time Georgie laughed at one of the jokes, someone looked at him in dismay and moved to another part of the bar. This didn't seem to perturb Georgie either. Erickson saw him again a few days later at another bar in Kreuzberg, and then about a week after that at the Brandenburg Gate.

The American had been walking along the desolate stretch where the old Wall used to be, between the gate and the deserted Potsdam Plaza project, looking at the beginning of the Neuwall. In the distance he could hear the escaped monkeys from the zoo that now lived in the trees of the Tiergarten; as he drew nearer to the gate, an alligator shot out of the garden, trailing the water of one of the ponds and slithering across the ugly barren scar of the old border to disappear toward Alexanderplatz. The Neuwall was built in the dead of night. Begun in 1995 by a coalition of Stasi victims and Stasi informers, its mortar was made from the paste and pulp of old Stasi files, which numbered in the millions. The members of the Neuwall Brigade long ago agreed never to identify among themselves who had been informers and who had been informed upon, an unspoken treaty that was a by-product of why they seized the files in the first place, when the revelations of 1992 were exposing fellow workers and friends and husbands and wives and children to each other. They began the Neuwall not to eliminate freedom but to resurrect the promise that freedom held only when it was denied; they continued the Neuwall as a tribute to the way the old Wall was the spine of the world's conscience, without which humanity was left to its own worst impulses in considering the final resolution between authority and freedom, order and anarchy.

More than this, the Brigade believed that the city's function as the urban metaphor of the twentieth century couldn't be fulfilled without a Wall. When the Wall fell and there stood behind it the naked figure of freedom, those in the East couldn't stand the voluptuousness of her body while those in the West couldn't stand the humanity of her face: there was the awful revelation that while at the outset of the millennium's last decade people had pursued and embraced the ideal of freedom, at decade's close they had come to despise its moral burden and absolve themselves of it. The Neuwall was bone white. It bore no graffiti. Its only message was written there by the Brigade itself: HITLER WAS ELECTED. It didn't follow the path of the old Wall but rather formed an inebriated, slapstick zigzag through the city, rocketing wildly up this street and down that. For all that the Berliners of the year 1999 knew, any one of them might go to sleep at night only to find himself barricaded in the next morning, a wave of old Stasi files petrified in his doorway, through which the only recourse was to tunnel.

Among the vendors still left at the Brandenburg Gate after the Wall's fall, the American stopped to check out the Wall's sad remains. Erickson always thought about buying a piece, just because someday it was all going to be gone. He had this idea that on Day X he'd sit in the hotel window clutching his bit of the Berlin Wall like a human time capsule, taking it with him to the other side. On this particular day that he saw Georgie at the gate, Erickson finally picked out a piece, at first glance the most nondescript chunk on the table because the flat outside part of the stone was blank, not a scribble of graffiti on it to note anything of the Wall at all. Rather, its markings were on the other side, which didn't make any sense, since the other side was part of the Wall's craggy gray innards, where it wasn't possible for anyone to have written anything. Yet there it was, the fragment of rhetoric: *pursuit of happiness*; and Erickson bought the stone and put it in his coat pocket and turned around and was staring right into Georgie's face.

He was smiling. He spoke perfect English, with barely a trace of an accent, or rather he spoke perfect American. This wasn't necessarily surprising since the most interesting thing about Georgie wasn't his repellent political affiliations but what two total strangers had told Erickson on the previous occasions he'd seen Georgie, that on the morning in 1989 when the East German professor left his house ostensibly for work but in fact to begin his life as the Tunneler of legend, Georgie was the ten-year-old son he held so close to him that final time.

In his short acquaintance with Georgie, Erickson never asked whether this was true. It seemed at times too personal and at other times too ridiculous, and there was no telling whether Georgie would have given a straight answer or not. What Erickson did note was Georgie's profoundly ambivalent and furiously mystic obsession with the idea of America. More often than not this was a secret America that Erickson liked to think had little to do with the real one: Georgie was full of stories about great American geniuses Erickson had never heard of, cracked Midwest Nazi messiahs and white supremacists who Georgie assumed commanded the same rapt attention of everyone in the United States. Georgie's obsession with America often got the better of his politics. Ultimately he didn't discriminate between Thomas Paine and Crazy Horse, between sex goddesses and television stars and soul singers. It didn't seem possible Georgie could have listened to that blues tape of his and somehow heard a white man singing. Yet Georgie's corrosive racial romanticism burned the black right off the singer until all that was left was the scarlet muscle of a beating heart.

He took the American to his flat in Kreuzberg. In the flat a dull light shone up from the floor. Out of a secret place in the floor against one wall Georgie hauled up a tape player and some tapes, skipping wildly from one musical selection to another, L.A. punk bands and Hollywood movie soundtracks and 1950s Julie London albums. In the badlands of Berlin one kept little except what he wasn't afraid to lose or what couldn't be hauled away by scavengers; and in Georgie's flat was something that definitely couldn't be hauled away by scavengers. It was a slab of the Wall, the old Wall, and it stood in the center of the huge flat towering over the emptiness, where it looked a lot bigger than it had out in the middle of the city ten years before. As Georgie and Erickson stood gazing at his Wall, the writer thought about Georgie's apocryphal American mother, who had rejected her country so she might drive Georgie's apocryphal German father into the mother earth of the fatherland.

That night, leaving the flat and heading for a bar, the two of them turned up a small side street only to see, as though melting into the pavement, an afterthought of the Neuwall jutting insanely onto the landscape from a neighboring alley. Struck motionless in his tracks, the young Berliner shook himself free of his stunned inertia to approach the Neuwall's small, pitiful sputter. He kicked it, at first almost playfully. After a moment he wasn't playful. Soon he was wailing futilely at the Neuwall as though trying to kick the whole thing down himself, his face black with rage while the writer watching him realized in a flash that at this moment Georgie's mother was up there in the Reichstag, one of the former informers decimating Stasi files into paste.

The last time he was in the United States, driving aimlessly through Wyoming and the Dakotas, he heard the news of the Cataclysm the same way he heard all the news that year, on the car radio. He turned the car around and headed back toward the Pacific. Every few miles he stopped at a pay phone to try to call anyone in California he could get through to, until it was obvious this was a waste of time, and then somewhere in Utah, Erickson came over the ridge of a mountain and saw ten miles ahead on the highway below him the cars backing up in the billowing sheen of the sunset. He pulled over and stared westward as though he might see columns of smoke rising in the direction of home, vast and steaming.

Not long before, he'd lived in Los Angeles. For Erickson it had gotten to the point where there was no telling whether L.A. chose him or he chose it. He'd been born in Los Angeles, left it at one point in the mid-seventies, and then returned precisely for L.A.'s profound lack of presence, the way it assimilated the twentieth century's dislocation of memory from time into its own identity. He flattered himself as being liberated by the city's abyss.

But by the late eighties the abyss wasn't liberating anymore, with the end of his marriage and, after that, the most important love affair of his life, in which he invested every dream he still had left. In the midst of this he turned forty. A month later his father died. By 1991 the affair had collapsed and by 1993, with the final failure of his career as a novelist, the ruins around him smoldered close enough to spring him loose in one direction or the other: west, off the edge of a cliff in the Palisades, or east, where the geography offered more potential for emptiness. He gave the west some thought. Being a coward, he went east.

He assumed it was only a matter of time. Over those last two or three years in Los Angeles he kept peering around for the doom that was hounding him. Standing at the corner of an intersection waiting to cross the street, he kept his eyes peeled with passing interest for the stray car that—its driver seized by sudden cardiac arrest—would leap the curb and give Erickson one good bump into eternity. He felt for the throb in his body of this cancer or that virus. Never having been practiced at living in the present, nonetheless he'd been silently shocked by the prospect that his father may not have spent enough of his life being happy, and that the son was doing the same. He wasn't certain happiness was in his genes. When his love affair had ended, his heart had broken in time to the crumbling of history. He came to understand that while in youth it was quite true that time healed the heart, now the revelation of time's passage was that the point finally comes when the heart isn't going to heal again after all. There wasn't much to do but pursue the purely sensual moment. He might have been better at this if he'd only been without conscience.

With his lover he had glimpsed the possibility of a life that included all of him, the dark interwoven with the light, the bad with the good, the weak with the strong, until he was complete and of a piece. After it was over and he knew this completion wasn't going to be possible anymore, he accepted and came to terms with the way in which his literary life, his public life, his private life, and his secret life lined up like four rooms, with guests, tourists, or temporary residents occasionally straying into one room or the other, none of them necessarily knowing there were other rooms with other guests. There was a door between the literary life and the public one, through which someone might slip back and forth, and a similar door between the private life and the secret, and a hidden passage that ran directly from the secret to the literary. But the only one who ever went in all the rooms was

Erickson. The only one who even knew there *were* other rooms was Erickson. No one else was allowed access to all of him again; and when he did things with people in the secret life that remained unknown to those in the private, he understood this arrangement might just be a moral expediency, to justify to himself infidelities and spiritual disarray, even as he also persuaded himself—and sometimes actually believed—that it was the only arrangement keeping him sane.

The rooms became strewn with furious women. A friend argued that there was something about him that almost naturally raised these women's expectations, something that persuaded them he was incapable of hurting them and was bound to submit, sooner or later, to their tenacity or patience. But in the wake of everything he finally couldn't convince himself he'd acted in anything other than bad faith, whether he misled them himself or allowed them to mislead themselves, permitting hope to grow into expectation without yanking hope up by the roots, in one room after another repeating the same scene with only a variation of details, the slammed door of a woman's angry exit or his own dreadful walk out that door with the sound of her crying behind him. "Your love was a lie," one of them said on his phone machine, a woman he loved passionately years before and about whom he'd even written his first novel. "I guess it's the surprise of my life," said another bitterly, on yet another phone message, "to find out you're just a bastard like all the rest." She'd been in some novel or another, too, though he couldn't remember exactly which one, or what character she was.

"You're just a real fake," said the last, who had once called him "mythic."

After the Cataclysm he headed on to Iowa and spent some time there with a friend, and then south to Austin and east to New Orleans and north to New York, as purposefully as aimlessness could be. With the crash the next year, he sold the car and headed for Europe, settling first in Amsterdam and then Paris, which was no more or less practical than any place else until, a year and a half before his fiftieth birthday, he read about Day X on page seventeen of the *International Herald Tribune*. The writer figured they had to know about it for a while. He had to figure the scientists didn't all just wake up one morning and look at their wrists and tap their watches wondering when, during the night, the small inner coil of infinity missed a beat. He figured there had to have been at least a lurking suspicion, quantum whispers of the slowing cosmic timepiece, out of which seeped into the millennium the lost seconds and then minutes and then hours. On maps of outer space there are the vague shadows that hint at black holes for years before scientists confirm the discovery. In such a way they must have seen in the present the vague shadows of the future.

On the other hand Erickson didn't believe the scientists knew much of anything at all. He suspected they had finally bumped up squarely against the limits of their vision; whatever would emerge on the other side of the temporal wormhole fell as much in the imaginational sovereignty of philosophers and fantasists, theologians and crackpots, witches and pornographers and tunnelers. It would be the most purely democratic and totalitarian event ever, having rendered everyone equally subject to its mysteries and revelations. That, of course, was why Erickson had come to Berlin. Because Berlin was the psychitecture of the twentieth century, and if he or anyone should emerge on the other side of Day X in the new millennium as anything more than a grease skid on the driveway of oblivion, they were bound to all come out on the Unter den Linden, the only boulevard haunted enough to hold all of it: dictators and democrats, authoritarians and anarchists, accountants and artists, businessmen and bohemians, decadents and the devout, each contradicting their lives with their hearts, SS troops with blood running from their fingers wearing the wreath an American president laid around their necks and GDR soldiers wrenched from the vantage point of their towers pulling huge blocks of the Wall behind them, led past the Unter den Linden's grand edifices of delirium and death through the Brandenburg Gate into the Tiergarten by an Aframerican runner with a gold medal around his neck who sprinted all the way from Berlin 1936 into the Berlin games of the year 2000, followed at the rear by a mute army of six million men and women and children utterly white of life but for the black-blue of the numbers their bodies wore, and at the rear the Great Relativist himself doing his clown act, juggling a clock, a globe, and a light bulb, tangled in a Möbius strip and with a smile on his face that said he for sure knew about Day X anyway.

Erickson received her last phone call the night of the summer solstice. It was around the same time she always called, except as the days had gotten later the night had not yet fallen outside his window, where instead there was the haze of twilight on a street that ran perpendicular to the sun, and therefore never saw either its rise or fall. "Hello," she greeted him.

"Hello," he answered.

"Do you want me?" she asked, and it seemed appropriate that she would betray her accent most on the word *want*.

"Not on the phone anymore."

"It's so much safer," she said.

"No more on the phone."

He knew from what she said now that she'd been thinking about it too. "It was so random like this," she explained. "I called several numbers that first time. Sometimes I got a woman, sometimes I got a man who sounded . . . wrong, and I hung up. Then I called your number, and when they answered they said it was a hotel and they asked what room, and I just said a room number, and they put the call through and it was, by chance, you. I could have dialed any other number instead. When I got your hotel I could have hung up, as I almost did. I could have given a different room number or the number for a room that didn't exist, or they might have asked for the guest's name, and I wouldn't have been able to give them a name. And it seems quite perfect like this, so perfectly random, so perfectly by chance."

"I see."

"But you don't want to do it on the phone anymore."

"No."

"Tomorrow night I'll go to a hotel not far from yours and take a room. I'll take a room hidden away from the street that's very private. I'll call you from there and tell you the number. I'll let the hotel manager know I'm expecting a guest and for you to come straight up. I'll leave the door of the room unlocked. The room will be completely dark. The blinds will be completely closed, and the lights will all be off. I'll be there. Once inside the door you'll wait in the dark for me to come to you. I'll be naked. You can undress, or I'll help you. We won't speak at all or turn on the light. We won't say anything." She paused. "Do you have a tag?"

"Yes."

"I'll wear mine too," she said. "You'll fuck me then. We won't say anything. It will be like the phone, where we see nothing and have only our words, except we'll say nothing and have only our bodies. When we're finished I'll find my clothes and dress and leave you in the dark. We'll never turn on the light."

"Okay."

"It will be dark the whole time."

"The sun sets later now."

"I'll call later, after the sun sets." She hung up. Erickson was up for several hours, with that humming insistence his body couldn't contain. When he woke the next morning after a bad night's sleep, on X-191, the day was slightly more than itself, a fraction of X-190 floating freely and haphazardly across the calendar. The room was blurred around the edges, and the light outside had an unfamiliar shimmer, and Erickson thought some half-life of the night's dream was lingering in his eyes. But he knew time had escalated almost indiscernibly, that everything was now caught in the pull of X and just beginning the inexorable rush to the event horizon at millennium's end. At the bottom of the stairs, what was left of the hotel's pet cat lay at his feet. Erickson looked around for some other sign that the Berlin veldt had invaded the lobby, a rhinoceros, perhaps, or a python. The manager was nowhere to be seen.

By the human logic of time one should always walk, Erickson told himself, from east to west in Berlin. From east to west one walked from Old Berlin through the Brandenburg Gate into glassy synth-Berlin that had been built expressly for the purpose of rejecting the claims and biases, the suppositions and ghosts of history, the Berlin that in the glare of the nuclear mirror had created itself anew from the ground up and freed itself from history once and for all. But the last time anyone walked from east to west was ten years ago, when everyone on the one side fled to the other, when everyone abandoned the history of Berlin which, in the fashion of the twentieth century, had become one more commodity of ideology. In the 1990s the seduction of Berlin was that one always walked from west to east, against the sun and in the face of memory, and then took the U-Bahn back. So on this day Erickson walked from west to east, and with the fall of dusk went to take the U-Bahn back, ducking into the Kochstrasse station and descending underground. He was waiting on the platform for the train when he noticed a familiar figure at the other end.

Georgie was slumped on the bench staring straight ahead. Ten-year-old newspapers blew past his feet. Across the tunnel from where Georgie stared, Erickson saw the small hole in the U-Bahn wall that the Frankfurt banker had pointed out; it was as though Georgie was waiting for a father's face to appear in the hole at any moment. A little voice in Erickson's head said to leave him there, but he walked over. He didn't speak to Georgie but waited for him to look up. Georgie didn't turn to look until the American sat down next to him.

He turned to look at Erickson and there was no sweetness in Georgie's face at all. There was nothing in his face of childlike serenity; it was like the night when the sight of the Neuwall in the street had transformed the young Berliner's perverse earnest innocence to the malevolent fury that tried to kick the wall down. Except that at this moment, as he sat waiting for a face to appear in the hole of the U-Bahn tunnel, Georgie's transformation had already gone several degrees further. His face was dark like a swarm rising from the other side of a hill, the shadow of having stared too many nights into that hole in the side of the U-Bahn tunnel and having waited too long for a dreamed-of reconciliation that was only met minute after minute and hour after hour and night after night by nothing but the hole's void. Now the sockets of Georgie's eyes were so hollow that all Erickson could see in them was something so black it would frighten even the night, a feeling so lightless it would startle even hate.

Erickson got up. He got up right away. He turned and started walking the other direction, toward the exit of the U-Bahn, where he ascended back to the street and walked, for a change, east to west, which was what he should have done in the first place. For some reason he felt in his coat pocket for the small piece of the Wall he'd bought at the Brandenburg, uncertain whether it reassured or frightened him to realize he'd left it back at the hotel. For a while he thought it was his imagination, for a while he dismissed it as paranoia, but in the last dark block before Checkpoint Charlie he knew the footsteps he heard right behind him were real, and that they were Georgie's. By the time he reached the end of the

block the footsteps were all around him, and then he was sur-
rounded in the street by six, then eight, then ten of them, members
of the Pale Flame with their heads shaved and their shirts off and
their chests bare and each of them with the same tattooed design,
a creature with the body of a naked woman and the head of what
appeared to Erickson to be a strange bird, rising from a sea of fire
against a backdrop of lightning. On all their shoulders they wore
tattooed wings. It was as though all of them had been summoned
with the snap of fingers, a muttered command, and Erickson
turned to Georgie in time to take the first blow, and the last that
he would ever count or understand.

And memory broke free once and for all, floating above him
like the balloon a child lets go. In that moment the writer was
neither quick enough for escape nor afraid enough for panic. He
shouted out only once and then succumbed to the only hope left
him, that the storm of the assault would blow over him and
move on.

Five minutes later Georgie said to the others, "All right."

They stopped with the kicking and beating. They shone in the
twilight—six, eight, ten fiery birdwomen glistening in righteous
satisfaction. One of them pushed the body over and they stood
examining it. Georgie tapped the writer's face with his shoe to see
if there was a reaction, and when there was nothing he started
going through the dead man's pockets. He found a wallet and a
hotel key, but not what he was looking for. "Shit!" he yelled in
frustration, slapping the body alongside its head. For a while he
sat slumped in the street pouting at the dead American while his
troops stood by waiting. Georgie looked at the address on the hotel
key. "Know where this is?" he said to one of the others.

"Savignyplatz."

"I'm going," Georgie said.

"Not real smart, man," one of them advised timidly, after a
pause. "Someone will see you. If the cops ask questions they'll
wind up at that hotel sooner or later and someone will be able to
tell them he saw you."

"If the cops ask questions," repeated Georgie. "What fucking
cops? I don't see any cops. Cops don't even pick up all the fucking

dead animals," waving his hand at the landscape around him, though at that particular moment there weren't any dead animals to be seen.

"This isn't a dead animal."

"Tell that to him," Georgie said. "Tell that to the cops." He looked at the hotel key and got up off the ground. He headed back toward the U-Bahn to take the same train the American had planned to catch. He changed to the S-Bahn heading in the direction of Wannsee, and after several more stops he got off and changed cars because people on the train were looking at the half-bird halfwoman figure of the Pale Flame on his bare chest, before glancing away when he returned their gaze. He disembarked at the Savignyplatz station and wandered around the neighborhood looking for the American's hotel. It was dark when he found it.

He was trying to think what he was going to do about the hotel manager. But there was no hotel manager that he could see, only the remains of a dead cat on the stairs, and so Georgie went up the stairs to the room number that was on the key. He went inside. He quickly perused the room, ignoring its other contents until he found what he was looking for, after not so much effort, in the second drawer of the table next to the bed.

It hadn't been disguised or hidden, it was just there in the drawer, the little shard of Wall with the impossible inscription on the wrong side. Georgie sat on the American's bed contemplating the stone for a while, and then finally turned his attention to the things he'd overlooked. In the same drawer were the American's passport and traveler's checks, cash including German marks and Dutch guilders and French francs, a vaccine tag on its chair with a key in the lock. Georgie unlocked the chain and put the tag around his neck. He stood in front of the hotel room mirror looking at himself with the tag on.

He went over the rest of the room and took several of the American's cassettes, Frank Sinatra and a Billie Holiday album after he threw away the picture of the singer. There was a reggae album Georgie discarded with disgust, and a tape of soul music that the American had compiled personally, titled *I Dreamed That Love Was a Crime*, a line he took from a 1960s song in which a jury of eight men and four women find the singer guilty of love. He went through the books that were stacked on the hotel dresser, though Georgie never read books, Faulkner, James M. Cain, a 1909 hardcover edition of *Ozma of Oz*, and several that Georgie didn't recognize until he realized from a picture inside that the author of the books was in fact the man he'd just left dead in the street an hour before. Georgie was going back and forth between his new treasures and was studying the vaccine tag in the mirror again when the phone rang.

He answered it without hesitation. He said nothing, just listening, as though the sound at the other end of the phone was another thing that once belonged to the writer but was now his. "The Crystal Hotel," she finally said in English with a German accent, "room twenty-eight," and hung up.

Georgie nodded as though this made perfect sense. He put back the phone and took from the closet one of the American's shirts, which he used to wrap the cassettes and the piece of the Wall, and then tied it to his belt. He took the passport and traveler's checks and cash and wallet, and on his way back to the S-Bahn suddenly there was the Crystal Hotel right in front of him.

He was sorry to find that, unlike the last hotel, the lobby wasn't empty. Instead there was a night manager, an extremely old man who worked behind the front desk. The old man appeared even sorrier to see in the doorway of his hotel a bald boy with red wings on his back and fire and lightning and a naked woman with an eagle's head and something dripping from its mouth on his chest. "Excuse me," Georgie said to the old man, "I have a friend in room twenty-eight."

"Yes," it took the manager some time to say it, "she said you would be along. Well," he added with great reluctance, "she said to send you right up."

"Thank you," Georgie said. He went up the stairs floor by floor. He went down each shadowy unlit corridor looking for room twenty-eight, until he found it near the back of the hotel, where it occurred to him for the first time that he had no idea what he was doing. He knocked so halfheartedly he could barely hear the knock himself, and then he slowly opened the door.

THE RAPTURE OF THE ATHLETE ASSUMED INTO HEAVEN

DON DeLILLO

Tennis Player, a man in his
    early twenties
Interviewer, an older man or
    woman

*The Tennis Player, all in
white, falls to his knees at the
moment of triumph—head
thrown back, eyes closed,
arms raised, his left fist
clenched, the racket in his
right hand.*

    *He is frozen in this pose,
his body glowing in strong
light, with darkness all
around.*

    *At the sound of the Inter-
viewer's voice, the Tennis
Player begins to rotate as if
on an axis, completing a single 360-degree turn in the
course of the play.*

    The Interviewer carries a

*hand mike and walks out of
the darkness about five seconds after he begins speaking.
He circles the Tennis Player,
moving in the opposite direction, stopping occasionally,
making as many revolutions
as the monologue allows.*

INTERVIEWER: How special
it must feel, Bobby, finishing
off a career in this fashion, it
must feel like a culmination
you could only dream of years
ago, growing up without a
role model, without a high
school on a hill, using a borrowed racket that smelled of

someone else, it must feel like a vindication, an affirmation, winning the big one at last, the one that's eluded you all these years and in all these ways until today, playing before the Queen, the King, the Jack, the Ace, growing up without a blond girl in a Buick, a girl with long tawny legs who rocks beside you on the porch swing, coming from behind to win the match they said you'd never win, the doubters and skeptics, the pundits, the clever little men with bad bodies, how sweet it must be to reach your goal at last, so many disappointments, so much sorrow, growing up without sideburns or a personal savior, totally missing the point of rock and roll, undersized and out of breath but determined to prevail, it must feel like a restoration, an eternalization, growing up without a mom in flat-heeled shoes, finding a racket in the bracken and taking it to bed, obsessed, depressed, a boy without a girl in a blue Buick, how transforming it must feel, a blond girl with a tawny body slightly shiny in the moon, answering your critics at last, the nay-sayers and doom-sayers, the gloom purveyors, the nihilists and realists, playing before the Queen Mother, the Gay Father, the Battered Wives, tell us quickly how it feels, growing up without a junior year abroad, so many failures, so much sadness, we're desperately eager to hear, it must feel like a permutation, a concatenation, growing up without a girl in a tawny field, a sunlit blond in a summer dress who lets you put your hand, who lets you touch, who says shyly in the night, growing up without an old covered bridge nearby, how super it must feel to achieve your biggest thrill as an athlete on the last day of your life, to know the perfection of the body even as your skin loses heat and energy and hair and nails, and now we're all enfolded in your arms, you are the culture that contains us, we're running out of time so tell us quickly, time is short, tell us now.

The Interviewer fades into shadow just before he or she finishes speaking.

The Tennis Player completes his rotation. He remains motionless in intense white light for five seconds.

Black.

LIGHT

STEPHEN WRIGHT

ON ETHERIA the snow is warm and there are violet moons and each inhabitant is cradled in the velvet webbing of the others' minds. Everyone can fly. Everyone is free.

Dash passed the nondescript yellow brick building twice in his impatient circling before he even noticed the sign: MOUNTJOY INN. It looked like the kind of residential hotel people grew old and died in, waiting for something else to happen. Forty-five minutes later he finally found a parking space a minor march away. Carefully, he locked the car, then struggled down the street with bag and money box in one hand, his daughter Zoe in the other, pulling at him like a stubborn dog.

On the corner outside the hotel was a big man in small ill-fitting clothes hunched over a lusterless battered saxophone. The instrument case lying open on the pavement in front of him contained a few scattered coins bright as the eyes that peered surreptitiously through a snarled curtain of gray unwashed hair. Out of the bell of the horn erupted a cacophony of sour notes whose disorienting progression seemed to have something to do with the periodic switchings of the WALK–DON'T WALK sign suspended from the pole above his head. At their approach he peeled his lips off the mouthpiece and chuckled, "Heh, heh, heh, you two sure do look like hell." Then he closed his eyes and blew his way back to whatever world these discordant squawks sounded sweet on.

Dash fumbled about in his pockets. Zoe was rocking back and forth from her waist in a blind spastic boogie. The Occupants were clever, and this bum had all the marks of a genuine Ditto man. He folded a five-dollar bill twice and tossed it into the magenta-lined case.

The musician nodded, pausing in his solo to say, "A blessing for you," and producing from somewhere among the diverse layering of jackets, vests, sweaters, and shirts a small object he pressed solemnly into Dash's open hand: a used sax reed. Dash gaped as if he'd just been presented with a wad of fresh snot. "What the hell am I supposed to do with this?"

The man shrugged. "You got a horn?"

Dash looked him up and down, openly contemptuous. "Go wash yourself."

"Thank you, sir." The sax man bowed. "Thank you, thank you, thank you." His smile simple and lucent, untainted by the slightest edge of guile or sarcasm.

Dash had to drag his backward-glancing daughter up the stone steps of the hotel and into a lobby the size and decor of a cabdriver's lounge: fake rubber plants listing from the dusty corners, rattling floor fan, cardboard table, tired furniture, pink bald head cresting the top of a shabby brown armchair, a waiting room for interminable waits. The senior citizen behind the desk had wiry unkempt hair colored the flat black of cheap dye and eyebrows drawn on her forehead in high, questioning arcs. The portable television at her elbow was tuned to a professional wrestling match she monitored intently while folding and cutting strips of tissue into clever pastel roses. The counter was a mess of bright paper petals. She handed Dash a registration card and a pen and returned to her scissors. While Dash concocted a recent past, Zoe squatted at his feet, trying to pry the pretty tiles off the floor. Visit A Civil War Battlefield, urged a rack of brochures near the door. In the corner beside the mailboxes was an emerald parrot in a soiled cage. "What's the word?" said the bird. "Checking out, checking out." The woman read the address off the card. "Tourist?" The eyebrows resembled croquet wickets.

"Business." There was something unsettling and vaguely familiar about her, a face in the crowd at some long-ago symposium.

He paid a week in advance, and she handed him the key to a room on the third floor.

"No hot plates, no fans, no smoking in bed," she intoned, then, spying Zoe attempting to scale the counter, "My, what a lovely child, Mister Klaatu."

"A gift from above," he replied, seizing Zoe firmly by the hand and turning to go.

"Elevator's broke," the woman called after him. "Stairs is over there to your right."

Zoe's legs gave out after one flight, so he had to carry her shrieking up this cinder-block echo chamber to a hallway reeking of stale bodies, smoke, and harsh disinfectant, where peculiar faces peeked out furtively at them, half-cracked doors closing silently as they passed. Their own door was warped into its frame, and after wiggling the key repeatedly in the stiff lock, Dash had to lean his shoulder into the wood to get it open. Inside was a room just like all the other rooms he had put time into on all the other trips of his life. Everything was used, including the air. He went to the window. It was painted shut. On the opposite side of the gray mottled glass, gleaming perfectly even in the dampened light of an overcast sky, the iconic structures of the nation, saintly domes and fairy towers, and above them a clear triangle of light holding steady over the green rectangle of the Mall, each separate disk bouncing playfully within this configuration from one angled point to the next. He watched for a few minutes, too mesmerized to even think of forcing Zoe, who was busy licking out the inside of her cup, to the window. Then he noticed a dark-suited man in a window of the office building directly across the street, staring back at him through a pair of big binoculars. Quickly he stepped behind the wall, dropped the blinds with a clatter. He looked with spreading horror at this room he now occupied, its cage of space, its useless miserable objects. Zoe was in the upright fetal position on the bed, rocking, rocking over the creaking springs.

When they put the silence on you, there is no recovery. You are turned into a media buffoon or worse. Roswell, New Mexico, 1947. A bright object falls out of the blue, killing all four aboard. A weather balloon, the press is told. But Edgar Moseley, who witnessed the crash, the pear-headed remains, spoke freely of what he had seen until a visit from the dark suits and the facts vanished into the labyrinth of a stroke. Since 1953 the CIA has managed all news concerning UFOs. The films and tapes made of Zoe's "seizures" at the Institute they conveniently "mislaid." Reality is a place you can access only with the proper clearances. Everything genuine disappears. What's left, the cardboard maze we're *free* to scurry about in, is pure Dittoland.

He riffled through the pages of the phone book and dialed the number of *The Washington Post*. "I want to speak with one of the Watergate guys." In the world of hold he was entertained for several endless minutes by a stringed deluge of "Raindrops Keep Falling on My Head." According to Zoe, the Zero Time will come when 70 percent of the American people accept in mind and body the fact of an alien presence in our sky. The last Gallup poll put the percentage of believers at 57. We're just a mere 13 percent from our goal, people, please help us, help yourselves now and come forward, open your arms and accept the craft into your heart. Please. A male voice with the curt tone of the young and ambitious came on the line to take his story, see that it got to the right people. "What I have to say is too important to entrust to underpaid functionaries." He yanked the cord out of the wall, tossed the phone crashing to the floor. "Let's go, kid." And he lifted her into his arms and hurried down the stairs and into the street where two new formations were demonstrating their skills for all to see, one in the shape of a large red diamond, the other a flashing blue circle that rotated in silent grandeur over the White House.

Zoe started clawing at his arm the moment they entered the Senate Office Building. Gleaming corridor vistas, unnatural odors, insolent individuals on the march, it must have seemed to her a replica of the Institute. She shrank back toward the door, mewling. Dash waved a fresh packet of M&Ms in front of her nose and led her down the hall, one M&M at a time, checking the plaques posted outside each door until he recognized a name and walked in. The receptionist was young, blond, too little that was organic in her smile. The Senator was away in Japan. "I'm a registered voter and a tax-paying resident of Buchanan County." The Senator had been in Japan since last Monday and would not return until late next week. "And I'm the Speaker of the House. He was on television only last night discussing Star Wars from this very office." The Senator often gave interviews that were broadcast later by tape delay. "Can I go in and see if he's at his desk? Maybe the Senator caught an early flight." The Senator appreciated hearing from his constituents, and perhaps if you would care to write him at this address . . . Could your little girl get her hands out of the jelly bean bowl?

The television station, at least the part of it he was permitted to see, looked just like a real estate office. No one there knew his name, either. The talent coordinator was at lunch. "It's important," he said. "Thirteen percent." Neither the bewildered secretary nor several affable fellows from building security seemed to disagree. But unattended for far too many empty minutes, Zoe had managed to overturn a large chrome ashtray, wriggle out of her panties, and was just assuming her preparatory crouch over the beige mound of spilled sand, butts, and ash, when someone grabbed his arm—rude, machinelike fingers tight on his flesh—and an extended moment of consummate physicality ended out on the sidewalk, father and daughter raging together for once at a common enemy without Unit affiliation. The sky seemed exceptionally large and open here, and when he looked up he could feel the magic light falling down around him, the tickling pressure of it, steady as a wind against the translucent fabric of his face.

Out on the Mall a gang of scruffy kids was tossing around a yellow Frisbee, the athletic contortions of their bodies oddly reminiscent of little Zoe at her window. Their dog, an untethered menace, came bounding instantly over, fangs bared. Zoe screamed, hung cringing to Dash's leg. "Sarah!" called one of the boys, and the dog swung around. "Sorry!"

"Keep your creature off us," yelled Dash, stroking his daughter's head. "I'll mess him up good, I'll break his back, I'll tear out his balls."

June 3, 1981. Betsy Strickland's cocker spaniel is run over by a furniture van on the street outside her home. The dog's skull is cracked open, revealing that one-half of the animal's brain had been replaced at one time by a smooth silver lobe of unknown origin and construction. The object is handed over to local police for further examination and is never seen again. The dog had liked to sit by the picture window for hours on end, staring out at absolutely nothing.

When they arrived at the Reflecting Pool, Zoe broke loose and jumped in, fully clothed, splashed in a frenzy among the reflections, glossy fragments of blue and white, the way things are. Then a cop with a shellacked exterior ordered Dash to pull her out. Up in the air lights gathered and wheeled in mute chorus.

There was a crowd in front of the White House, an angry eruption of the populace outfitted in grotesque masks and black armbands, a parade of red placards jostling along between the wooden barricades, the uneasy teams of helmeted police stationed at ten-yard intervals, chanting something unintelligible about abortion in a performance designed as much for the network lenses as that curious figure who maybe even now might be lurking behind the curtains across the deep green lawn. There were unmarked cars lining the curb, manned, engines idling; a row of uniforms behind the iron gate; much nervous coming and going in the guard booths—the dero machinery in high activation all around the block. Dash took in the scene at a glance and decided this was not the day to petition his leader. Turning away with Zoe in tow, he shouted back at the demonstrators, "Fuck the monsters, fuck all of 'em!"

Every president since Truman has known exactly what you suspected they knew. Details are presented in the initial briefing right after the oath. In 1954 Eisenhower himself met secretly at Edwards Air Force Base with a delegation from Alpha Centauri. It changes a man. The millstone of such knowledge dragged through life like a curse and on down into a marble crypt.

Funny, but he couldn't for the moment recall the name of the hotel or how to get there. He wandered around with the tourists, feeding Zoe Eskimo pies and orange soda. At a shady fenced-in playground he sat on a green bench beside his fellow parents and watched his daughter ignoring the other children. The sky had grown so busy with intricate movement he dared not look up for fear of vertigo. The kids on the swings were cutting neat parabolas into the blue afternoon humidity. A small boy with a round out-sized head kept going up and down the circular slide; up, around, and down; up, around, and down. In a child the fundamental affinity for the delights of that shape were clear and undisguised, easy access at that age to the helical truth of our nature. Up, around, and down. It's the shape that is the key: you can find it prominently incised on the shimmering walls of the mother ship.

He must have rested his eyes for a moment because when he opened them it was dark out there, too, and all the children had flown away home. He walked the streets, aimlessly, through inexplicably deserted neighborhoods, hoping for the appearance of a familiar sign. Light spun without cease in the darkness above, and there were glittering deposits of devil's jelly all along Pennsylvania Avenue, clumps of angel hair dense as Spanish moss glowing momentarily in the leafy branches of the trees and evaporating without a trace. He was exhausted—there is no surcease for the prophet—but sleep, he recognized, was at this point a fluctuating region lying well beyond the rim of plausibility. So he walked, the sound of honey bees swarming in the hollows of his ears and somewhere the faintest suggestion of many voices reaching out together toward real melody. . . .

The convoluted eye of the plastic rose in the clear plastic vase on the nightstand had obviously been focused on him for quite some time. When he got up off the bed, there were hairs left behind on the pillowcase, an alarming number of them. In the bathroom mirror he saw fallen lashes on his cheeks. He checked his teeth and gums. Still firm. The bombardment was probably coming from that office across the street.

It was daytime, so stores must be open. He went out and bought several rolls of aluminum foil to tape over the window. Later, he sat at the rickety desk, a cap of foil molded to his head, writing in his notebook: In the space of mind there is universe. This is factual. They seek to intervene. Violation is the goal of the terminal entities. Cosmic consequences that you read as comic. Ssssss. And heed. Don't let the Egg Man touch you there. The inside is all down from when you fell out of the clouds. Don't worry. The pain of reentry can be endured without loss. Remember the great Doktor Reich. Listen to your organ.

When he peeked out the window again, it was night. Bewildered, he looked around the room. Zoe. Where was she?

He slid his bag out from under the bed, removed an army field cap, and secured it firmly on his head over the foil shield. He tucked the revolver into his belt. The notebook he hid in the desk behind the top drawer. He took some bills out of his cash box and left the hotel.

Stuff that has fallen out of the sky, documentation available upon request: rocks, metal plating, chunks of green ice, pellets of fire, baby snakes, toads, hairy spiders, black goo, fresh blood, flakes of meat, pieces of tooth.

This was the landscape you could never lose. The capital of Dittoland. Pay no attention to the "people." Avoid the pink street lamps—bad radiation of the worst quality. Actually, the city was rather pleasant at night, the daytime crush of visitors and bureaucrats dissolved completely, the air cooler, the monuments seemed lit from within, constructed out of stone quarried from mines of light in "the land beyond the Pole," as Admiral Byrd wrote, the hole Adolph Hitler squandered a fortune in reichsmarks attempting to locate.

He crossed and recrossed the Mall as though weaving an invisible string between the sentinel trees. He walked briskly with upright posture, an important man in an important town on a special mission. He paused in the soft shadow of a large oak, staring up at the white helmet of the Capitol dome looming inscrutably there over all. He could feel the potent thoughts radiating outward from the ornamental tip.

At the Lincoln Memorial the Old Railsplitter's gaze was impossible to evade no matter where you stood, discomforting eyes with the pupils scooped out like granite olives without any pimento. Clearly, it was not a human face. The naive folk of that century had dubbed the flying objects "airships." Mysterious ropes hung down from the heavens.

He was finding it increasingly difficult to concentrate on the solids and shapes that made up the city, the once persuasive data of his tellurian senses was losing its authority. He felt slightly dizzy, and the expected nausea had arrived, taking his stomach for a ride. It was important to keep moving. He let his feet guide him through areas most tourists never see, where even down in the hole of a night as bad as this one there were still crannies of activity, illumination, and a living presence, even if it was an angry bandit face lunging from the shadows to demand, "What are you doing here?"

"Do you know me?" inquired Dash. "Don't I know you?" He removed the gun from his belt. It felt good in his hand, out in the air. "Do you know this?"

"Hey," said the man, backing off, "I didn't mean nothing."

"I don't, either." He wiggled the weapon impatiently.

"Where's the other two?" he asked, quickly checking his flanks.

"What two?" said the man. "What're you gonna do?" There was a barrel and a set of eyes on him that all looked alike.

"I tasted electricity at Allendale," said Dash. He paused, as if expecting a reply. "My hands were fired in the furnaces of Andromeda. I know what happens to light when you ride past it. I've wrestled the angel. I've seen the stars of paradise. Do you think I can be stopped? I've got antibodies. I've been inoculated with the truth."

"Please," the man begged, "don't kill me."

"You're already dead." He pulled the trigger. "Bang," he said, amused by the ludicrousness of the situation. He was still smiling when he whipped the barrel into the side of the man's face. It went crack like a nut. It went down like a sack of sand. These dero— so pathetically constructed, yet so dangerous, their powerful mimetic abilities alone enabling them to infiltrate all too easily, to pass as human, friend, wife, son. He knelt down, employed the gun like a hammer. When he was finished, he wiped his hands on the dero's shirt.

He walked.

He tossed the sticky gun under a bush outside the Department of Justice. Go figure, G-men.

He walked.

A radiance beckoned to him, a breaching of the darkness where mellow neon spelled RAINBOW CUTRATE LIQUORS. A rowdy band of dispossessed were gathered outside the door around the makeshift hearth of a beat box booming out sounds only his son could have appreciated: "My name is Adam Ace, No words do I waste, Jam my piece up in your face, It's your bitch I want to taste." Squadrons in the sky wheeled right, then left, then right again. A stellar wind bore down upon him cold and severe and it was as if his skin wore no clothes and his bones no flesh and when he looked up there were unaccountable tears in his eyes and a splendid white Cadillac drawn up to the bus stop, a fancy painted dragon curled over the trunk, several women crouching at the open windows. He passed a derelict urinating against a wall, stepped through the stream of warm piss dark as blood in the light of the sign. He glanced to his right and discovered a woman there beside him. "Hi," she said. She had on a white halter top, a pair of red leather pants, and an olive drab baseball cap just like his. "Need a date?" she asked. He inspected her face. Human eyes looked back. "Yes," he said, and she took his arm possessively in hers. She smelled of flowers and auto exhaust.

"What's your name?"

"Beanie."

He looked at her.

"No, really." She directed a long filed nail at her head. "My hat. Used to have this silly yellow propeller on top." She laughed and squeezed his arm. "Like it?"

"I can't call you Beanie."

"No problem. What do you want to call me?"

"The name your mother knows you by."

She sighed like an exasperated child. "You're weird, mister." Then, as if they'd just spent a difficult time haggling over price and she'd had to settle for less, she said, "Trish."

"Yes. That's a name."

He led her confidently around the next corner and was pleasantly startled by the apparition of his own lost hotel lurking in feigned gentility behind a couple of shedding sycamores. He escorted Trish boldly through the dim lobby, the nosy clerk dozing unaware amid a heap of ageless blossoms. Queried the parrot, "Checking out?"

After the usual struggle he forced open the door to his room and she sauntered in as if she'd only left it an hour before. "Cozy," she said.

He was scanning table surfaces to make sure he hadn't left notebook or money in view. "This place is so worn out."

"Listen, honey, compared to some of the cribs I see, it's the Hyatt Regency."

"No, I mean all of it, inside, outside, the whole place, it's a storage locker for bad meat."

She stared at him. "You straight arrows are definitely the freakiest."

In the fluorescent glare of the overhead the cosmetically enhanced lineaments of her face revealed aspects unforeseen, inestimable. "You look like somebody."

"Yeah, I know. Your mother." She went to the window, the click of stiletto heels loud and menacing in such a tiny space. She

fingered a corner of the foil screen, edges of her mouth in a sarcastic curl.

"Don't touch that," he ordered in his most paternal command
voice.

Her mouth shifted into full obscene smile. "Oh, I get it. You're
one of those Pentagon guys, right?" She came over to where he
stood, pressed her groin and breasts up against him. "Well, don't
worry about me. I'm in the business of keeping secrets, too."

"The Pentagon is a blind den of gibbering idiots."

Her hand, delicately thin and ruby-clawed, went to rubbing
insistently at his crotch. "CIA?" He stared down into her face, the
features so fluid, metamorphic, there'd be no easy way out once
you were in.

"FBI?" She had the other hand now around in back, working
his ass.

"I've never been a member of a paramilitary organization of
any kind."

"Okay, then, let's just see what we do have here." She went
to her knees and unzipped his pants. "Uh-oh, here's something
that's bursting with classified information." She held the gaping
mouth of his erect penis to her ear and pretended to listen. "What's
that?" she asked in mock concern. "It's hot and cramped and
you're being held against your will. You want out?" She paused
and looked up, hand still gripping him tightly. "Your rubber or
mine? You gotta be so careful these days."

"I'm not afraid."

"Sure, mister, try it from my point of view." She got up off
the floor and went to her purse. She tossed him a packaged condom. "Price of admission." She sat on a corner of the still undis-
turbed bed and lit a cigarette. "Listen, what's *your* name,
anyway?"

He stepped out of his pants and walked into the bathroom.
"Dash," he answered, studying the image of himself in the mirror.
There were a few more black eyelashes on his cheek. There were
round rosy sores on his chest.

"Dash?" She let out a short, nasty laugh. "So tell me about
funny names. What is it, some kind of code?"

With his fingernail he could scrape skin snowflakes off the
wings of his nose. He opened his mouth. There were fuzzy patches

of mold on his tongue. Have you ever looked into the eyes of a goat? he asked.

"Okay, don't tell me. I know you military guys, and don't try to tell me you're not. I know military from across town."

They have my daughter, he wanted to say. Was the bottle of chloral hydrate still in his bag under the bed, or had he left it back in the country in the ashes of a junked life? We can do anything we want in here, and what would it matter finally? he said. He stood above a large turd twisting in the waters of a porcelain bowl. The spiral *is* the form of thought.

When he came out of the bathroom, Trish was reclining naked across the turned-down bed, drawing curlicues in the air with the ember of her cigarette. Her long, angular body was a precise duplicate of his daughter Trinity's. And the sons of God saw that the daughters of men were beautiful, so they took for themselves such women as they chose.

"Okay, Dash," she announced, rolling over to stab out the cigarette, "let's see just how fast you really are."

She grunted and groaned on cue for him, whispering furiously into his ear, and when it was over, she sat up cross-legged against the peeling wall and smoked another cigarette, as if on break from unloading heavy crates off a truck. "You liked the dirty talk, didn't you? You officer types always do."

There were yellow bruises on her legs and thin ugly scars down her arms.

"I want to do it like dogs," he said.

She shrugged. "Bow-wow."

There was a place he had to get to, the urging of the car over the final hill, past the last peaking into a true end, clarity of an alternate order, stationary, whole, unimaginable. He looked up at the specter of himself doubled in the dim bureau mirror against the far wall, stripped, flushed, kneeling as if in prayer, and plugged securely into the soft socket of a trusting ass upraised just for him. "I love you," he said. His blood gathered into a fist, punched through the bounds of his body.

He opened his eyes, though he had not yet been asleep, converging on the parallel tubes beaming down from a yellowy ceiling, the once white impasto shattered like a windshield into a black-veined web that seemed to pulsate with the rhythms of human breath. Little cigar-shaped apricot objects darted about just ahead of his glance, afterimages of the fluorescents overhead. He felt as if his insides had been scraped clean of residue, an odd tepid sensation neither sweet nor sad, simply different. His hand went out, encountered the momentary surprise of adjacent flesh, nerves measuring, remembering. He turned onto his side to look, to fill all that new inner space with the splendor of light descending in gentle sheets, fabricating a pair of flawless buttocks in layer upon layer of gold leaf.

He opened his eyes, though he no longer slept, to discover the tubes off, the room in total darkness, and this Trish perched like a bird on the end of the bed, the penlight from his bag stuck in her mouth. All he could see were radiant teeth, a disembodied grin of phosphorescent bone.

He opened his eyes on hands of orange, hands of yellow, climbing agile as monkeys up the flowered drapes. A black mist swept dramatically across the ceiling. He could smell the wood laughing as it went up. He rolled over. She was gone. The empty cashbox lay upside down on the already warm floor. Pulling on his pants, he ran to the door. The wall behind him cackled and blazed. Out in the corridor a gray-bearded bald man hobbled up, clutching a foam fire extinguisher. He was wearing a strikingly immaculate white terrycloth robe, and his small blue eyes were dancing with either the luster of alcohol or the tenacious vigilance of the mad. The man held a crooked forefinger to pursed lips, signaling hush, then with a conspiratorial hunch of the shoulders, mouth trembling in an expression of suppressed glee, he pointed crazily upward. Dash raced down the hallway and on up the murky stairwell, two steps at a time, flight after flight, and crashed on through a battered metal door onto the roof of the hotel and the manifestation of a dawn for the end of time.

His bare feet padded unfeeling over the droppings, the nails, the cinders, the nasty rosettes of glass from smashed wine bottles. He could neither speak nor call to mind the simplest word. The sky was on fire, a gyrating compass of flame. The big blue lid had popped open, and all the treasure denied us for so long was raining down, an incarnation of perfect benevolence, an outpouring of M31. It was what he expected, it wasn't what he expected. Packets of radiant energy rippled in ticklish waves over his face, burnishing the skin, playing nerves like guitar strings. He was aware of the changes in pressure, the subtle variation in weight of each distinct color, and the not unpleasant sensation of heat building on the receptive surface of his body. It was the day the stars came out, it was fireworks forever, it was the Fourth of July on Labor Day, it was special effects for everyone. A shower of illuminated disks, haloes, coronas, blotted out the sun, and against a searing expanse of unbearable red a storm of silver flakes, glittering like mica, fell over the stunned marble of the entombed city. As susceptible as any primate to the seductions of flashing and blinking, he stood transfixed to the melting roof, a charged antenna of hair and skin. Hundreds of incandescent ships in all the known shapes and sizes went shuddering diligent as electric bugs, a harmonized proficiency, spinning the air into beams and girders of pure color, condensing majestically, inevitably—beauty as revelation—into an overreaching lattice of burning crystal. And the sound of their passage was the sound of massed voices lifted in ecstatic song. And all around there were winged creatures with peeled heads and lidless eyes and chattering tongues. And the rivers of light cascaded down, flooding the floor of the earth. He looked up, and high above his craning head was an immense crown of red and blue and green and yellow winking in unison like a ring of painted mouths opening and closing, a slip away from the discovery of speech, and he saw lowering through a wide funnel of light the platinum hull of the mother ship and he could see outside and inside simultaneously and wherever he looked was a whiteness of such intensity as to scorch the eye though vision persisted, miraculously, beyond pain and the loss of line and tint, deep into the nova furnace at the heart of matter where, amid the rush and roil of eternal fission, a form was assembling, moving toward him out of a cloud, the resplendent triangular head of a giant being with great obsidian eyes in which his own insignificant reflection was sucked instantly away into the infinite. Then he realized this head was speaking to him in a telepathic language based on units of intuition rather than words and into the private honeycombed spaces of his body always just out of reach of booze or food or sex there came a thick welling of sweet oil, of goodness. The light grew on him until it pierced his eyes and he held up a hand and could see right through it. Other figures approached then out of the flux, smaller, more human shapes with faces he could recognize, and yes, Trish was indeed here and behind her Dot and Trinity and Dallas and Edsel and little Zoe and Maryse and her Mignon and Gwen and her Beetle and others, too, the music of a vast intelligence enveloping all like a warm fluid. Then a hatch dropped open in this illuminated egg overhead and he couldn't help it but tears fell onto his cheeks and buoyant with rapture he stepped out to greet the beginning of his real life and the big silken ship started getting bigger and bigger but without moving because he was moving, weightless at last, going up and up and up. Hey, he could fly. It was amazing. He was light.

WEIRD ROMANCE

DEREK PELL

TALES OF EROS

WEIRD ROMANCE

A GRAPHIC NOVEL BY

DEREK PELL

THE WEDDING NIGHT

She hit the floor with a thud and found herself staring blearily at the immaculate creases in Dexter's pant legs—all six of them. Desperately she tried to rise.

AT DEXTER'S TRIAL, AUNT MAMIE EXHIBITED THE DAMNING EVI-
DENCE. WANDA FAINTED. JUDGE CRATER ORDERED THE COURT-
ROOM CLEARED.

X ≠ Y

SUSAN DAITCH

YOUR PASSPORT was something you needed to get on the airplane in the first place. It was blue, it meant a statistical affiliation,
not something you gave a lot of thought to. The picture of George
Washington, like a crucifix, or a crèche in neighbors' houses, signs
you easily identified, knew all about, completely understood; but
these things weren't in the house you remember. They were foreign,
exiled objects. In your house bearers of different passports didn't
share the neighbors' matter-of-fact, wake-up-you're-it heritage.
Heritage is a word, which, like the word *leadership,* makes you
uneasy. The only time you tasted Bosco or Reddi-Whip was somewhere else. The idea of nationality may be a received one, but with
so many generations born in exactly the same place, it's taken for
granted. A garage with a basketball hoop over a barn-red door.
Your passport says you are all these things you never thought you
were.

History class, 1966, *Eurasia.* All year you memorized products, imports, exports, natural resources from Ireland to Korea.
You were eleven. It was called history, but this is what you commit
to memory, a different country each week. What were the products
of Iraq? Petroleum, that's an easy one, raw wool and dates. These
are exports. Of Ireland? Live animals; imports are machinery,
petroleum. The map in your textbook stopped in the middle of
Europe and picked up again to the southeast. It was a book of

very few dates; history was not considered to have a temporal dimension.

The men in black masks who have appeared at the front of the plane aren't interested in how you saw through your history teachers or what you say your allegiances are. You can say there is a copy of *The Eighteenth Brumaire of Louis Bonaparte* in your suitcase, but it sounds feeble. The man next to you says he thinks you will be exchanged for prisoners held in another country, but he's only guessing.

They find a place to land and, although you are sitting near a window, you can't identify the city. None of the passengers are allowed to speak.

A spokesman for the Italian Ministry, Tanino Scelba, said Wednesday that a "terrorist multinational" existed and argued that you cannot speak of isolated groups, like the Brigata Rosa or the Red Army faction.

"They are linked," he said.

The terrorist multinational does not have links to the Trilateral Commission. The syllogism falls on its face.

Airplane detritus, trays of melted ice, tiny whiskey and gin bottles roll on the floor, there will be no seconds, headphones dangle. The movie was an old one, *Greystoke,* but you didn't rent sound. Ape man swings through the jungle in utter silence. The flight attendants were asked to push the screens back up, but for some reason the movie continued and images of lianas, Tarzan's long hair and legs flash across the women's faces as they make a last trip down the aisles. You and the stranger sitting by the aisle can only look at each other. Perhaps it's just as well and saves a lot of trouble. You look for signs which will tell you what speech, in this situation, can't. Is he reading *Der Spiegel* or *People* magazine in Dutch? A newspaper whose cyrillic figures you're unable to read? When called to the front and faced with the interpreter, what story will he give? He owns things, cuff links, briefcase, tie pin, with his initials on them. You aren't in a Hitchcock movie scattered with these kinds of clues. You don't fall in love.

Hands are supposed to be raised when you want to use the bathroom. Will one of them go in with you or will you be searched before? Will speech on a limited basis creep back because, after a certain number of hours, unless people are really terrorized, they might turn into unruly children? You remember what it's like to be afraid to open your mouth. You think two of them are women.

There are passengers you saw as you boarded the plane, but you remember a few of them because they looked like the kind of people who would say anything to save themselves. It isn't clear what they might say in order to do this. After passports have been collected, some passengers are asked what they do for a living. The interpreter is a passenger who seemed to have volunteered out of the blue, although you can see from the expressions of the people around you he is viewed with suspicion. He might not know the languages in question very well and might make up answers for you. He acts a little nervous, and it's a histrionic kind of nervousness as if he's sure he has a job to do and feels himself to be on neutral ground, although perhaps only for the time being. You can see categories being assessed and wonder who's worth what to them. You stretch your neck looking for diplomats, movie stars, CIA operatives.

"Don't take me, take her."

The *Bristol Constant* doesn't have any treasure. It's on its way to the Massachusetts Bay Colony. The crew mutinies off the coast of Newfoundland. Bullets aren't wasted. Men and women are thrown overboard into the icy water. As a mutinous crew they can land in no English port and resort to piracy. One woman is kept, and she pleads to be sent back to England on the next east-sailing ship they attack. She talks of Brighton day and night. The mutineers think she's mad and leave her on the barren unpopulated shore of an island in the West Indies.

It has been two days or a day and a half. You can't really tell. You realize that even before you boarded this plane, you spent a lot of time waiting. Watch time is a form of nonsense, a form of abstract speculation because the time where you come from has no meaning. You try to remember newspaper stories of amnesty and happy endings but can recall no stories, only what the front pages of various newspapers look like. You hear someone having a hysterical conversation with themselves several rows behind you. The person is playing all the roles in the conversation, and you find it disturbing that you can't turn around and identify the speaker. You don't even know if it's a man or a woman. Everyone is awake. If rumors could circulate in silence you're not sure you would really know anything more.

a. They want four Polisarios freed from a Moroccan jail.
b. They want Italian prisoners held in "preventative detention" returned to normal life.
c. They want enough fuel to get the plane to East Berlin.
d. They want half the Vatican's treasure.
e. They want the men to sit on one side of the plane, the women on the other.
f. No one will get their passports back.

Airplane food runs out. Trays are wheeled across the tarmac. When it's distributed, the food gives no clues as to the country you've landed in. Long-thawed peas and carrots, microwaved French fries, Swiss steak, a cupcake for dessert.

There is agitation among those watching the passengers. One of the others who has been behind the curtain comes forward, and they speak in a language you can't identify. Tremendous amounts of film, videotape, and print might be generated outside the perimeters of your captivity. Mountains of lights, cameras, and extension cords approach the control tower, shredded newspapers eddy near the wheels of the plane.

In your boredom, it's easy to panic, but you have no way to demonstrate your alarm except to raise your hand to go to the bathroom. You are ignored and in your desperation turn to the stranger with monograms who has fallen asleep. Unless he secretly took some drug in the bathroom, you don't understand how he can sleep, awkwardly falling into the empty seat between you. In sleep he looks like he might be watching a movie, listening to a concert, or just having a nice dream, and you're envious of his oblivion. He has very white teeth.

They are looking at passports again, dividing them into stacks according to color. You can't see if they're looking at yours, if they've tossed it aside or will shout your name next, and it will be your turn to be questioned by the earnest interpreter. You'll walk down the aisle as slowly as you can. You've never been called on like this before and don't know exactly how to behave. Can you be sure his interpretations will correspond to your answers? He could make up your history for you; word for word will be entirely different from your recitation and you will never be aware of the discrepancy. What would happen without the translator? Two men stop to eat cupcakes and drink instant coffee.

Perhaps half the plane is asleep although it's only twilight in whatever city you're in. A vehicle moves closer to the plane, but it isn't for the purposes of rescue. The plane is refueled. Another city must be found. The sign lights up telling you to fasten your seat belt, and the plane taxis down the runway. The translator hasn't met you yet and, for the time being, your respective fictions remain separate revisions.

A LUCKY PIERRE
WORLD PREMIERE

ROBERT COOVER

SEARCHLIGHTS SWEEP THE snowblown night sky above the palatial Paradise Theater, and the fans lining the street raise an ecstatic roar as the limousine draws up to the curb. A glowing awning stretches from lobby to street like a condom pulled over the column of floodlit, red-carpeted space below, down which the great man soon will pass. Amid fanfares, screams, and rapturous applause, he steps out of the limousine, elegantly attired in black velvet cape and brushed top hat, swinging a glans-knobbed silver walking stick: Our Hero, the one and only, the star of the show, Lucky Pierre. At the far end of the red carpet, his leading lady stands waiting for him, smiling brightly and beautifully on this, their night of nights: the World Premiere of the latest and greatest Lucky Pierre motion picture. He flashes his famous mustachioed smile for the cameras, their bursts of light popping around him like champagne corks, and greets the wildly cheering masses with blown kisses and waves of both arms and jaunty waggles of his handsome bone-hard prick, the star's star, wittily adorned tonight with stiff collar and black bow tie, and a tiny top hat of its own. Ladies weep and throw their panties and handkerchiefs at him, young girls swoon at his feet, old women with their skirts hiked grab themselves and piously genuflect. Around him, suspended snowflakes, ephemeral as spermatozoa, glint like stardust.

—Hello! Hello! Yes, it's *wonderful* to be here! Thank you!

How's that? Yes, I think this film is the most exciting thing we've done so far! It's been hard work, but it's been worth it, it's *always* worth it! Ha ha, that's right, and it's always *hard!* Hello there! Bless you!

The crowds press forward, trying to touch him, this beloved idol of millions, Cinecity's first citizen, filmland's biggest big banana. LUCKY! LUCKY! LUCKY! they cry. The police form a cordon around him, battling back with riot sticks, pistol butts, and canisters of incapacitating gases, but the swarming faithful are undaunted, delirious with a preternatural love. They throw him their pessaries and sanitary napkins; he kisses them and tosses them back, blesses their zeal with a passing finger up their streaming cunnies and a tip of both his black silk hats. Above him, on the theater marquee: his name in lights, big enough for the whole city to see.

—Well, thank you, that's very kind, he tells the microphones pushed at him across the cordon, but really it was a team effort—no solo orgies, as they say in the trade! I had the most beautiful actress in the world as my co-star, a wonderful crew to work with, the script was fabulous, and the camera work was stunningly innovative—those are the people who deserve all the credit! I'm nothing but a walking dingdong with hands and a tongue—no, it's true! Anyone could do what I do! But thank you! Bless you! Ouch! Don't bite! Thank you! I love you all!

His crazed fans, powering their way through the flailing police truncheons, claw at his clothing, cling to his cape and garters, hump his pantlegs, scramble for the odd pubic hair that falls in the snow. One woman goes for his foreskin with a fruit knife, but a police officer cleaves her skull with a quick chop of his nightstick. Not even the loyalty and dedication of the city's finest, however, can stop the Lucky Pierre Sex Maniacs, a band of wildly shrieking thirteen-year-olds, from spreadeagling him out on the red carpet and riding a galloping sequence of virginal St. Georges on his frosty pecnoster.

—Oh my gosh! *Crack! Pop!* This is *it!*

—Hold it, my child! Don't—*ah!*—don't—don't get off yet!

The girl astride him is bobbing frantically, mindlessly, eyes rolled back and bubblegum snapping, in an ecstasy of pubescent orgasm. A billyclub slams into her teeth and she flies backward,

lifting off his cock as though launched from a rocket. The miniature collar, tie, and top hat are gone, of course, hymeneal trophies
for the Maniacs to dig out later. Others mount him, try to, but are
quickly unseated as the police haul him to his feet and drag him
on into the heated lobby of the Paradise, snatching back what they
can of his shredded clothing.

—Why? Well—*gasp!*—because of the virginal secretions of
course. Magical properties, you know. One has to—*whew!*—stay
in there and soak it up!

—Is this your secret then, sir?

—Ah, my dear, don't you know? There *is* no secret! . . .

His emblematic staff is bloody from all the hymenotomies conducted there, his clothing torn and disheveled, his shoes have been
taken, his gloves, his tie, his pockets and buttons have been ripped
away, his cheeks bruised, top and bottom, but he feels great, looks
great, this is his night and nothing, really, can spoil it. In the lobby,
scintillatingly lit and full of privileged first-nighters groping one
another in eager anticipation of the cinematic masterpiece to follow, there are blown-up stills of him authenticating collectible
cunts at an auction, hammering his prick out on an anvil, scaling
a gigantic thigh in the sky, conducting aerobic S & M exercises on
a trampoline, judging heft and bounce at the annual Miss Tits 'n'
Ass beauty pageant, and hanging from a cross, getting tongued by
spike-toothed flagellant nuns. YOU'VE GOT TO SEE IT TO BE-
LIEVE IT! THE EXPLOSIVE CLIMAX OF OVER 3,000 YEARS
OF HARD CORE! A SALACIOUS CLASSIC OF SPURTING
JUICES! Cally, gorgeous in her white organdy evening gown and
glittering diamonds, clutches his arm with nervous exhilaration.

—You're looking sensational, Cally! he whispers, smiling for
the press cameras. The only true fucking masterpiece in town!

—If I'm the true piece, lover, you're the fucking master!

Cally gives his penis a tender loving squeeze, then waves at a
camera, blows a kiss, flashes a milky pink-tipped breast at a passing admirer. She is radiant with the joy of a first night, the consummate star, footlights-born, vibrantly alive, vastly intimate. He
decides that this is definitely the best picture they have ever made
together, though he cannot for the moment remember which one
it is.

Before they go in, he tries to buy a bag of popcorn, buttered between the thighs of the excited salesgirls, but they won't take his money, beg him to dip his dick in the chocolate sauce and autograph their upraised fannies instead. The buzzer sounds: Only time for initials, my dears! *Show time!*

—CURTAIN UP! PANTS DOWN! shout the usherettes.

He and Cally are led, lit by a traveling spot, through applauding galleries toward a special box decorated with fornicating deities, fanfares and drumrolls preceding them as they make their way, almost like one single fanfare transmitted through a series of echo chambers. Yum! says someone, licking off the chocolate as he passes. Overhead, stars twinkle, stroked gauzily by projected wisps of drifting clouds, and the air is filled with the scent of musk and jasmine. When the usherette takes hold of his prick to lead him to his seat, he finds himself coming, he can't help it, this place always gets to him.

—Oh! My! *Thank* you, sir!

—My—*whoof!*—pleasure, love! *Gasp!* Keep the change!

The spot blinks off, the amber houselights dim and up goes the fire curtain with its golden hand-stitched logo of a mandala-like split beaver backgrounding a haloed lingam, just as he falls, joyously spent, into his seat, Cally blowing her final kisses before taking hers beside him. The youngsters are scrambling for the center seats in the front row below, giggling, punching, goosing, knifing each other playfully. Their elders clear their throats, blow their noses, fart acclamatorily as the heavily fringed and betasseled house curtains part majestically. The suggestive rustle of Cally's full skirts as she sits is like a shush that stills the packed house.

—Whoo-eee! Sometimes, Cally, he sighs, I feel like it's more fun to watch these pictures than to make them!

—Sshh! Pass the popcorn!

Announcements appear on the pale rippling travelers warning viewers of the heavy penalties for booing and whistling and other felonies, for leaving the theater before the program is concluded, and for interfering with the orgasms of other patrons; instructing them to come here as often as they please but please not on the upholstery, and to limit all scatophiliac tendencies to the sandbox in the orchestra pit; and reminding them that refreshments, aromatic lubricants, dildos, drugs, candy panties, and fan magazines are available for sale in the lobby at intermission and after the show.

The travelers withdraw behind the house curtains, making way on the big screen for the "Previews of Cum Extractions," including *Lucky Pierre's Bachelor Party, Law and Ordure* (described in the trailer as "a cocks and rubbers masterpiece"), the "disturbingly iconoclastic" *Home Movies,* and a restored colorized version of the old film noir classic, *Snatched Snatch, or: The Case of the Missing Twats,* in which he played a hardboiled private dick who solved all his crimes by drilling the suspects with his trusty rod ("No Holes Barred" was his toughguy motto painted on the glass panel of his office door, seen cast as a shadow on the floor in the opening shot), the master criminal whom he faced thereby striking mercilessly at the very modus operandi of his investigative expertise. "Whaddaya mean, they're gone?" he snarls from behind his desk in the preview clip, his penis which he is playing with an odd violet hue with lime green veins. "How can something that ain't there in the first place go missing?"

He leans over to whisper something to Cally about the sacrilege of colorization, converting all those great monochromatic mysteries into lollypop burlesques, why don't they outlaw it, but suddenly all the lights go out, even the exit and toilet signs, and the auditorium is plunged into total darkness, evoking a communal gasp, and then: dead silence. Faintly, as though emerging from a great distance, lugubrious music is heard, a solemn funereal plainchant of some sort, and on the screen, barely visible: an undulating landscape, rent by a deep dark valley. Near the bottom of the screen, a tiny light shines in that valley, seen now as the cleft between the buttocks of a woman on her hands and knees. Slowly, as though sliding in from outer space on the long dreary tones of the musical lament, the camera zooms forward, passing the black crater of the anus and the brambly thatch below to arrive at the light at the entrance to the vagina: it is in the shape of a keyhole. The camera moves in steadily, peeks through: the naked rear end of another woman on her hands and knees, this one lettered from thigh to thigh in an arch over the anus: A DAY IN THE LIFE. The camera continues, slowly but without pause, to glide forward, drifting down, the arched letters passing out of focus above, to the bright light streaming from the vagina below: another luminous keyhole. The camera peers through: the reared buttocks of another woman, or perhaps the same woman, now lettered in the same manner: STARRING LUCKY PIERRE. The silence is broken by a brief flutter of excited applause. This backside, too, has a glowing keyhole cunt at its nadir, and beyond it, as the camera relentlessly pursues its steady course, the mournful plainsong building in volume and intensity, is the lettered ass-end of another woman on her hands and knees, or the same woman, re-lettered. Thus, the titles and credits pass, from buttocks to buttocks, keyhole to keyhole.

—Just like Cleo, he murmurs to Cally. Always has to repeat herself!

—Sshh! Watch the picture!

—Hey! You've eaten all the popcorn!

Through the raw stubbly keyhole cunt of the director's lean freckled ass-end: the interior of a one-room flat with bed, table, stove, chest, sink, and bidet. In the uneven glare of a single light-bulb strung on an unshaded cord, a woman lies stretched out on the bed, hands and toes drawn tautly to the four corner posts.

—Look, Cally! Is this the right film? That's Cleo's coldwater flat!

—Of course it is! But be quiet! And behave yourself, she whispers, pushing his hand off her thigh where he had gripped it in alarm. What's the matter with Cally anyway? He pushes back at her and forces his hand up under her gown.

The woman in the film lies pale and still, her eyes narrowed to dark staring needlepoints, her lips drawn back, teeth clenched, trembling faintly. He circles the bed cautiously, crouching, sniffing, shifting his weight, seems about to spring forward—then draws back. He clutches his rigid organ, fingering it nervously, breathing erratically, his eyes ablaze. I have come here again! he thinks, and seems to hear himself say it: Come again! Come again! From time to time, his testicles draw up tightly against his groin, then very slowly relax again, sliding uneasily down over one another into their wrinkled sac: it is like a kind of hiccup of fear. The plainchant has vanished. The only noise in the room is the heavy beating of a single heart, and a faint rasping noise, something like nails scratching on starched linen.

—It's scary, isn't it, Cally? he whispers. He's got his hand over the top of her panty girdle (not exactly Cally's style, panty girdles, but then Cally is an actress, she has lots of styles) and is creeping in the dark, finger past finger, toward those luxuriant pubes he knows so well. She's still resisting, but she has let go his wrist and is breathing hard now.

—Please, Mr. Pierre! *Gasp!* You don't know what you're doing!

Doesn't know what he's doing? Mr. Pierre? What's Cally up to? Is this some kind of test? A tease? Bending forward, he shoves his hand lower, pressing against the rubbery shackles of her strange undergarment, his elbow looped over one heaving breast as though the girdle release mechanism might be located there, his eyes locked still on the screen. There, on the bed, the spread-eagled woman's long pale body has begun slowly, very slowly, to undulate, as though moved by deep subtle ground swells. Distantly, the plainsong, or something like it, returns, a kind of melodic weaving in and around the thumping continuo of thunderous heartbeats. The man's balls recoil, drop, recoil. He crouches. Backs away. Then, gripping his throbbing member, he leaps suddenly onto the bed between her thighs, leaps off again. She hasn't moved, but the undulations have increased, her whole body rippling now with their surging inner force. Between her white thighs, the mouth of her inflamed sex gapes and puckers, gapes and puckers, almost as though trying to speak—or perhaps it is about to erupt, bubbling now as it puffs out. He is frightened. I cannot escape this, he thinks. The crimson tips of her breasts are erect and hard, and the scraggly red hairs of her pubes seem to be standing on end, singed at the tips by the fierce heat of her desire. He springs onto the bed once more, shrinks back to the foot, remains there, crouching, between her trembling ankles. He is sitting now on the edge of his seat, his hand locked in the elastic of Cally's underpants, thinking: Wasn't this supposed to be fun? What's happening? This is terrible! And: has Cally shaved? He poises there, on his tensed haunches, watching her glittering eyes, ready to leap from the bed at the least sign of danger, his tongue between his cracked lips, his swollen organ pulsing convulsively in his fist, just ahead of the thrumming heartbeats, as though the heartbeats might be mere afterclaps of the pounding in his penis.

—God! It's starting to hurt!

Her body, stretched to the four posts, seems to be undulating now to the rhythm of the augmenting heartbeat, her engorged sex spitting viscously as it opens and closes, opens and closes—suddenly he cries out in anguish and hurtles forward, plunging himself so deeply inside her that the collision of their pelvises resounds with great clashing reverberations in the echoey room. She thrusts upward with an awesome ear-splitting shriek, as if to pitch him out again, but he is caught tight in the soft burning vise of her muscular vagina: no way out now, he's in it to the end. Her body heaves and tosses violently, but her quivering limbs remain tautly outstretched, straining against unseen bonds. Up and down she bucks as though trying to throw him bodily while ripping his penis out by the roots: he wraps his arms tightly around her hot sweaty buttocks and hangs on. There is a terrifying moment when he looks into her eyes and sees nothing reflected there—not even the light! And then, with startling suddenness, her arms and legs snap shut around him, her shoulders rear up off the bed, and, just as her womb tears the seed from his exploding loins, she bites down—*crunch!*—on his head, stilling abruptly the thumping heartbeat. For a long dreadful moment, his body continues to pump away in hers in involuntary spasms: she tosses her head back, eyes closed, drooling blood, her long legs wrapped around the man's buttocks, drawing the last drop of pleasure out of his twitching body. Then it, too, is still, and her limbs relax. Slowly, leisurely, she sits up, curls around his body, and lovingly, almost reverentially, commences to glut herself on his remains, sucking the juices out of his head and abdomen, gnawing noisily on his face and throat and hands.

—*NO! STOP IT!* he cries, staggering to his feet, his fingers snagged in silk and elastic. The sucking and munching is deafening: it's as though it has got inside his head somehow! His face is bathed in cold sweat and his heart is pounding wildly.

—*HEY! IT'S OKAY! I'M STILL ALIVE! I'M STILL HERE!*

—*BRAVO! BRAVO!*

The lights come up as the film fades: he finds himself, heart racing, standing at a banquet table, Cora the Mayoress sitting beside him, his hand caught off-limits in Her Honor's pants, his prick in the pudding.

—Another masterpiece!

—VIVA!

—*To the star!*

—*Long live Lucky Pierre!*

As the others, still chewing, give him a standing ovation, the Mayoress congratulates him with an encouraging slap on the butt, as one athlete to another, causing the pudding to slop over. Or perhaps an angry slap: his hand is still trapped in the inner sanctum of her redoubtable panty girdle. It's numb with pain, he can't be sure what he feels there, isn't sure he wants to know, has only a fading notion of how he got there. Or here. It is as though he is gazing at some kind of slow teary lap dissolve: in the fading foreground, his immolation, larger than life; in the emergent background, a banquet hall full of beaming faces, all turned toward him, slapping hands, grinding jaws, raucous approval.

—Let's hear it again for the old cock!

—HIP HIP *HOORAY!*

—*Our Hero!*

Smiling bravely at the whooping banqueters, he tugs at his locked hand, trying to seem not to be tugging, but to no avail. He feels, somehow, gravely endangered. He spies Cally across the room, hiding behind the handlebar mustache of the maitre d', and wonders if she is in some manner to blame for his predicament. No, no: there's only himself for that, as usual, however it happened. It hurts to pull on his hand, but it hurts more to leave it there. Two of Cora's bodyguards, stepping out from the shadows, try to help, if help is the word: they seem prepared to separate him from his offending member if necessary. Finally, unable to bear it any longer, he gives a violent yank: there is a faint but audible whirrr-*clack!* and his hand flies out at last from that forbidden terrain, setting off a resounding *ker-SMACK!* of elastic against flesh that elicits another round of cheers and hoots and wild applause.

—Ah! S-sorry, Your Honor! he mutters, his throbbing fist tucked abjectly in his armpit.

—Nothing to regret, Mr. Pierre. She grimaces, plucking his prick out of the pudding, wrapping it with a linen napkin, and pulling him down to his seat beside her. She switches her bowl of pudding for his, lowers her tunic, adjusts her emerald-leaved tiara. It was a stunning performance! We are all proud of you!

—For he's a jolly good phallus, for he's a jolly good phallus! . . .

The Mayoress rises grandly, smoothing her tunic down over her powerful body, and rings a little breast-shaped glass bell which she holds by the nipple, its glass clappers shaped like tiny pale blue testicles. The rejoicing banqueters take their seats, rattle their drinking glasses with spoons in reply, let fly a final VIVA! or two. He huddles in his chair, his wounded hand nestled in his armpit, wondering how a quiet life of more or less principled fucking has brought him to such an exalted station and what might be the consequences if he closed the studios and took a forty-year vacation in the wilderness.

—My fellow citizens! While you are enjoying your dessert, I might as well get said the few things I have to say, declares the Mayoress. If we move along, perhaps we can all get out of here in time to catch the late night Kinky Classic on television!

—Hear! Hear!

—We are gathered here tonight, as you all know, to celebrate the world premiere of an extraordinary virtuoso experiment in creative reportage and to pay homage to a man who is not merely a brilliant performer and viable image in his own right, but who is indeed the very life of the Party, the root of our political and historical consciousness, the mainspring of our municipal policy! Indeed, it might be said that on some higher plane, it is he who is master, and we in City Hall his handmaidens!

—Amen!

—Long live the master!

—Long live his root!

—It is he, to speak as his great art speaks, who pops our collective cork, my friends! It is he who greases our gash, butters our corn, rings our common bell!

—I'll bend over to that!

—Ding dong!

—He wets my wrinkle!

—Bravo!

—We act, exercising what we think of as free will, yet inexorably fulfill his mysterious design! His image images us, his unions unite us, his suckings succor us!

—Yes, yes!

—We are all succored!

—All power to the sexual union!

—*We shall cum, over and over!*

He turns toward his silver-tongued hostess, as though to feign interest in all this political balderdash, and finds himself gazing at a blank screen: her ample hip in its lush white tunic. On that screen, an image begins to appear, blurrily indistinct at first, then slowly revealing itself to be a man walking in a snowstorm. Or perhaps not walking: the snow is moving but the man, fixed and solitary as the figure in a pedestrian crossing sign, is not.

—He is carnality incarnate, my friends, concupiscence concretized! It is through him we may grasp the rise and fall of nations and cultures, experience the ejaculatory convulsions of the universe!

The banqueters respond with convulsive ejaculations of their own, applauding wildly, stamping their feet, and calling out his name. But on the screen of Cora's hip, where the frozen man, caught midstride, poses rigidly in the swirling storm, there is total silence, except for the harsh whisper of a wintry wind like the sound of nylon stockings rubbing against one another. The man's hat is jammed down upon his frozen ears, his eyes stare blindly at his raised gold wristwatch, his mouth under its frosty mustache is drawn into a rigid blue pucker around his two front teeth. His penis, ramrod stiff in the blowing snow, is as translucent as an ice sculpture.

—We spread our thighs, seeking communion with the cosmos, searching for our true identities in the dark. But spread thighs are as numerous and anonymous as the stars, dear friends, and lead only to that black abyss where nothing is revealed! He penetrates this impenetrable chasm, taking possession, as it were, of human consciousness, thereby recapturing the elusive reality of life itself, fishy though its smell may sometimes be!

—Hear! Hear!

—His scut-scourer schools us all!

—His pussy-pounder points the way! *Hooray!*

—Yes, he fills the emptiness! the Mayoress declaims, her flexing hip causing the frozen man there to seem to shiver. He empties the fullness! He dries our tears, he dampens our dreams! He is our polestar and our star pole! He helps us to accept the past, confront the present, have faith in the *foutre!* My fellow citizens: our guest of honor and indeed perhaps our host—*Lucky Pierre!*

There are frenzied shouts and cheers, the thunderous pounding of fists on tables, but his ear is attuned to the trembling screen in front of his nose. There, accompanied by a slow mournful dirge, almost secretive in its humming lament, attendants have chipped away the ice locking the frozen man's feet to the pavement and have laid him out in a long narrow box, teak paneled and ruddily aglow with a diffuse inner light. Ecstatic women now crowd into the box under and around him, prepared, it seems, to die with him rather than live without him. There are subtle glints of gold and crimson in the gleaming blue ice-spire rising from his open fly, but no signs of life. He leans closer—

Cora reaches down and pinches the head of his penis with her nails and—*click!*—the image of her hip vanishes, the mournful plainsong dies. She grips him firmly in her strong fist, just above the balls, and hauls him to his feet, the deafening applause now rattling in his reopened ears like a sudden burst of static.

—Lucky Pierre! Lucky Pierre—!

—We cannot offer him the key to the city, she cries, because he *is* the key to the city! We can only ask that he, who has given so much, give yet a little more!

Even as she speaks, she is deftly working his shaft with her powerful ringed fingers. Before he can think about holding back, he is pumping jism into her pudding bowl, tipped before his spurting cock like a sacred chalice.

—*WAAaarrgh!* he groans, falling back into his chair when she lets go, as the applause and laughter crash around him.

The Mayoress stirs the pudding with a spoon, takes a reverential taste, closing her eyes and licking her lips appreciatively, then passes the bowl on with both hands. Slowly it moves through the room from banqueter to banqueter, each sharing in the sweet communion of his cum, while Her Honor crosses over to the doorway to receive the traditional farewell due her and her office. He sags limply in his chair, staring dully out upon the happy celebrants, and for a brief moment everything seems to stand still: the pudding bowl held up between two banqueters, other guests poised, half-risen from their seats, the lights dipping faintly, the smoke ceasing for that second to swirl: Uh-oh, he thinks. He feels a cold draft around his ankles, a chill curling round his flagging member. Nothing else is moving. This Day in the Life, he knows, is drawing to a close . . .

He shakes himself and stands and, with that, the pudding bowl continues on its devotional travels, banqueters who have eaten from it rise and pull on wraps, then go to stand in line to kiss the Mayoress goodnight. She is kneeling now on velvet cushions near the door, her tunic tucked up about her waist. With solemn deliberation, her attendants work her panty girdle down over the snowy mounds of her expansive cheeks, the deepening crack between them emerging like an ever more perilous path to power or (his thoughts are darkening with the dimming day) to damnation. This path is not wholly revealed: the panties, stretched from thigh to thigh like a police barrier, are pulled down only far enough to expose her puckered lipsticked anus. What's below (he sniffs his fingers: faintly metallic, though that might be from his armpit) remains concealed.

As Our Hero takes his place in line to pay his respects, an ancient blue-haired lady with a pince-nez and a cane takes his arm as though for support and, tapping at his drooping phallus with the knob of her cane, squawks into his ear: Just between the two of us, sonny, that was a fine piece of work!

—Thank you, ma'am!

—But it wasn't up to your best. Oh, I'm not complaining about all the fancy stuff, though most of it blew right by me, truth to tell, left me dry as a raisin. But what the hell, tastes change, we need variety, doing the same durn thing all the time's depressing, so trick us if you can. But the old carry-through wasn't always there, boy! Too much interruptus in the dadblamed coitus!

—Perhaps you're right—

—Of course, I'm right! Don't let the high-tech razzamatazz lead you astray! Keep that sucker in there till the bitter end! You gotta finish what you start, no more goin' before the comin'! The old crone hawks and spits into a lace hanky, winking up at him over her pince-nez as she wipes her mouth, blows her nose: And make it a little kinkier, too, son—you know, voice of the people and all that. Mix it up a little, whip a few more heinies, get the groupies going, incest, bondage, necrophilia, sock it to the kiddies, some of the good old scenes! It's no crime to be popular, you know!

—Well, no, but—

—And, hey, fuck a few more old ladies, if you don't mind, sweetie. Here's my card.

She stoops to peck at Cora's upraised rear, leaning on her cane, then hobbles out, still stooped over, blowing him a wrinkled kiss over her hunched back as she goes. It's his turn. He gazes down on Her Honor's breathtakingly handsome ass—an arse, really, in the broad medieval sense, a cultivated vast terrain, fundament and grainbin, the ineffable seat of all our joys and woes, arse gratia artis! He kneels before this stupendous affair like an adoring pilgrim, Our Hero does, prepared to pay tender homage to it and to her with his pursed lips, and hoping no doubt to catch a glimpse of the panty-curtained mysteries below, but then, as a cold wind whips at his pantscuffs, everything stops again.

His stare is locked upon the Mayoress's looming fundament, creamily radiant in the dimmed light, the little bouquet of hair about the anus all brilliantined down with spit, the lipstick smeared sensuously, the skin around it polished to a high sheen from so much veneration. The sounds of departing partygoers subsides, the buzz of private chatter, clink of spoons and glasses, scraping of chairs, soft bursts of bubbling laughter, all vanishing as though snuffed like a candle, and in the sudden hush he hears again, faintly, the unresolved dissonances of that mournful plainsong, lamenting the widowed city, the desolate gates, hearts poured out in grief. On the stiff glossy screen of Her Honor's stretched panty girdle, there appears again the frozen man laid out in the glowing box, pillowed by the ecstatic women, gazing at him over his shoulder as though fatally smitten, their heads drawn together, their lips parted in awe and helpless infatuation, or perhaps in terror. Nothing moves except the snow blowing by, drifting over the figures in the box. The man's head is tipped toward his raised wrist, an attaché case locked in his other hand, his blue penis standing like an inverted icicle. By some hidden mechanism, the box is slowly tipped upright, the bodies inside clinking and clacking as they rattle against one another momentarily. Then the box begins to rise, lifting past the panty waistband into that hovering oblivion beyond the frame.

His eye has been drawn up by this movement to the Mayoress's anus, all puffy and proud and lipstick-smeared. He strains against the glacial rigidity in which he finds himself arrested, pushing his face forward with all his strength, and he seems to make some small progress, but it is more of a zoom than a dolly shot. I will never taste it, he thinks. Can't even seem to lick my lips. Larger and larger the anus looms, a gleaming portal above the panty-shadowed cunt, swirled about now with blowing snow that fogs his vision. Curtains are being drawn in the space between him and the great medieval arse, he realizes, and the light is fading. His chance has passed, his respects will never be paid. The arse itself is little more than a vague pale expanse now, spreading out upon the rippling crimson velour of the closing curtains, falling into shadow, only this wintry crack spotlit, and there, over the puckered entrance, appearing like secret writing, the simple but ominous and ever doleful proclamation:

END

VICTIMS OF
MASS IMAGINATION

LAUREN FAIRBANKS

LET ME TELL you about our fair city of Alarcon. Stars end the spires of our churches. Tom-toms serenade us night and day. We are this far away (fingers inches apart) from the hour and the day of heaven and fairy tales. The Castle you would love to visit is here within the city walls. It overhangs "The River Formaldehyde." All the windows of all the houses glitter in the sunlight, while the glass in the Castle is a shimmering diamond. Take the back door off its hinges, then I'll welcome you to your new life of back-door-routes success. Easier route less taken. Don't latch on to the modern for modernity's sake.

Alarcon is where I ended up. Easy to count hides. My secret is I am borderline retarded after accelerated crashes. What fills a skull and bones. In an unusual sense, I'm a product of the television generation. There was a show aimed at matching hard-to-place children with suitable adoptive parents. Folks involve a child with some form of play for the viewing audience. The pet shop goes over big in this instance. The interview shows the best the child has to offer; see how nice the kid doesn't chew the ear off the live bunny etc., then the phone rings, off the hook. Framtidslandet. Swedish for "Land of the Future." You don't need me to tell you all kinds of sickos watch TV.

In my particular case, all responsible people involved hoped the adoption home would not resort to this last television step. Cry

133

for help at the eleventh hour. Had to do it finally. Last resort. I was thirteen and a little sexpot. No takers until the weirdo. Man of affairs. Immune from accusations pertaining to his moral misconduct, he passed a lie-detector test with flying colors. Got me. No haunting attraction or parental abilities necessary—just the boob tube and a phone. Little imagination needed to predict what was going to happen to me when I left the home with that man. It did happen. Such a cliché by now. Like the little Roman princess led off for rape by her executioner.

The involvement was cock talk pulled from Truck Joe's box of railroad slang. I shivered while he pounded. Sex is costly when you're paying.

You know how these days they're talking about Guam or someplace taken over by snakes? Mildly poisonous snakes have been found 'round bawling infants, the critters mouths locked on an appendage in an unsuccessful attempt to swallow whole the babes? Snakes remind me of the snake him. Can't slay a virgin. Read what he carved on my chest. (Looks like illiterate scrawl.)

On his way to bed needing a slap and tickle he'd "excite" me talking "laid to rust." "Excite" a thirteen-year-old? Word games saved me—removed me from my situation.

My sustaining desire was to reduce the English language to its necessary components. I reduced it to two sentences that sum up the entire American language:

1) Good luck scratches through your underwear.
   and
2) The American people never forgave Rudyard Kipling for not dying in New York.

When I ran out of things to occupy my mind, I went in for suicide fuchsia hedge style. Bought that bestseller. Tried starvation but, clad in polyester glad rags, he fed me intravenously. I'm a hard stick and he fancied poking me with needles. ALL IN FAVOR OF BURYING YOURSELVES ALIVE! Tried to get me to do awful things to him all the while calling me Saucy Black Angel. When I wouldn't, he'd say, "But you considered it so you will be punished for contemplation alone." Posturing Pig. During punishments I wished I HAD done the things. Swore I would not be turned into a demon by this man. What a blurred-at-the-edges wonk.

One day, just outside his house upon the overhang rock, worried about my skin freckling, he ran for silken awnings to protect me. Freeze-dried moons. The ensuing day the bastard busied himself branding me with dull kitchen utensils (ejaculating his poisons all the while) like a slitherer. My orders are to call him "My sweet Muscovite" or "My rousing Cossack."

Tells me his original plan (to adopt then murder) has been mitigated into a marriage plan by circumstances beyond his control. Plan B. Cheap Mother-Fuck-Agent-of-Contagion adopts me one year, wants to marry me the next. What am I, his mountain cousin? Miserably bad at it. Yodeling folk for Moses in horned helmets? Here for his comfort, his continuity and communion? Here for his emaciated feet and hands. I used to pray his zeppelin would explode over Vienna. Hard-core hate trip.

In his soggy mental game, his name was Lucius Norbanus Bulbus. Meat Man, charmer, and rake. I became the three Caligula sisters. It was up to him which of the three personalities I was permitted to be and when. Merely two aspects of his own personality shone because the schemes: 1) conceived by a madman—were 2) executed by a fool. "Secrets of the Deep Roman Orgy" were his favorites. I don't know if he watched public television or read a book once, but this was his wicked penchant. Calling. He sacrificed flamingos to the gods so we would be blessed with a child. A man willing to settle for love. Fertility rites. I had to drink the blood. Tribal. I was similarly occupied flinging filth instead of eating everything from my cut-up plate. That paleface milk thought I was finally getting into his debauchery. Figured I'd be happy to hear (straight from his *How To . . . Roman Orgy Book*) what he expected our suckling babes to do to his cock.

My regret is I got out of this warm familial arrangement without a particular piece of him broken off into my hand. Can't say I didn't try. Partridge and sausage sauce if you know what I mean. Long hard shuffle to the car for him but I got away and he never caught me. Gotta get away . . . can't buy a ticket? Steal one. To steal is to own. Last brass taste. Stole away from Monkeyland. I figure it cost him at least seven milking cows.

You start thinking of yourself in terms of a half-crabbed disemboweled abortion's sexual gratification and that stays with you. He was an abortion. Incidents prevent my returning and finishing him off. Can you see snipers in French Lick firing at the cretin? What would The Bird think? All I could do was more of the same but different. Alarcon, close enough to the big city, derives benefit from a big-city clientele. Take. Make. Then rot. Shadow of a different fear.

Pimpo's okay. Carrie carries her batik sunbrella and teaches. Physical gesturing is encouraged and that helps. Things are looking up. No bones of contention. Just boners. Scattered parts.

Recently I read up on depraved Mr. Bulbus when he came before Cook County Judge Bean. This time Fuck-face tried to adopt a young boy. Told the adoption people I was away at school. My carping age. It was the where and when of it didn't match up for the authorities. Uncertain customers. Don't be surprised they gave the boy to him anyway. After an exciting pre-adoption weekend the boy accused him of trying indecent tub-learnt things. Couldn't paint a stache on Jesus Knabe. Sex got away from the great citizen brought low. I have to say we citizens of probity and restraint are shocked and amazed when any amount of justice is done.

Carrie encouraged me to write it all down. Especially the part where his sickness abated into sissified involvements such as quilting—his all-time model was an antique Virginia reel quilt. She was laughing and screaming bloody murder when I told her about his painting entitled *Pig on a Whitewashed Pile of Buffalo Bones*.

Carrie likes my past peculiar tense. When I had trouble ending my paragraphs, she gave me a writing tip: "If at a particular moment in your writing you can flush a toilet, end the paragraph there."

I'm skillful as the next guy at repulsive love for gelt. A long day of ravaging and wildly slaying the pissed and whipped land into deification makes me want to drink liquid from a felt-tipped pen. We aren't ALL to die victims of mass imagination.

I'll never forgive him. War is a great possibility. He's stuff to fill a graveyard. Wrathful or no, it's God's job to forgive types like that. Not mine. Mine to hate 'em.

SKINNER'S ROOM

WILLIAM GIBSON

IT'S HALLOWEEN AND she's found her way up into this old hotel over Geary, Tenderloin's cannibal fringe down one side and the gray shells of big stores off the other; pressing her cheek to cold glass now to spy the bridge's nearest tower—Skinner's room is there—lit with torches and carnival bulbs, far away, but still it reassures her, in here with these foreigners who've done too much of something and now one of them's making noises in the bathroom.

Someone touches her, cold finger on bare skin above the waistband of her jeans, sliding it in under her sweater and the hem of Skinner's jacket; not the touch that makes her jump so much as the abrupt awareness of how hot she is, a greenhouse sweat, zipped up behind the unbreathing horsehide of the ancient jacket, its seams and elbows sueded pale with wear, a jingle of hardware as she swings around—D-rings, zip-pulls, five-pointed stars—her thumbtip against the hole in the knife's blade, opening it, locked, ready. The blade's no longer than her little finger, shaped something like the head of a bird, its eye the hole that gives the thumb purchase. Blade and handle are brushed stainless, like the heavy clip, with its three precise machine screws, that secures it firmly to boot-top, belt, or wristband. Old, maybe older than the jacket.

Japanese. Skinner says. SPYDERCO stamped above an edge of serrated razor.

The man—boy, really—blinks at her. He hasn't seen the blade, but he's felt its meaning, her deep body-verb, and his hand withdraws. He steps back unsteadily, grinning wetly and dunking the sodden end of a small cigar in a stemmed glass of some pharmaceutically clear liquid.

"I am celebrating," he says, and draws on the cigar.

"Halloween?"

It's not a noun he remembers at the moment. He just looks at her like she isn't there, then blows a blue stream of smoke up at the suite's high ceiling. Lowers the cigar. Licks his lips.

"I am living now," he says, "in this hotel, one hundred fifty days." His jacket is leather, too, but not like Skinner's. Some thin-skinned animal whose hide drapes like heavy silk, the color of tobacco. She remembers the tattered yellow wall of magazines in Skinner's room, some so old the pictures are only shades of gray, the way the city looks sometimes from the bridge. Could she find that animal there?

"This is a fine hotel." He dips the wet green end of the cigar into the glass again.

She thumbs the blade-release and closes the knife against her thigh. He blinks at the click. He's having trouble focusing. "One hundred. Fifty days."

Behind him, she sees that the others have tumbled together on the huge bed. Leather, lace, smooth pale skin. The noises from the bathroom are getting worse, but nobody seems to hear. She shivers in the jungle heat of Skinner's jacket. Slips the knife back up under her belt. She's come up here for whatever she can find, really, but what she's found is a hard desperation, a lameness of spirit, that twists her up inside, so maybe that's why she's sweating so, steaming. . . .

Saw them all come laughing, drunk, out of two cabs; she fell into step on impulse, her dusty black horsehide fading into the glossier blacks of silk hose, leather skirts, boots with jingling spurs like jewelry, furs. Sweeping past the doormen's braided coats, their stunners, gas masks—into the tall marble lobby with its carpet and mirrors and waxed furniture, its bronze-doored elevators and urns of sand.

"One hundred fifty days," he says, and sways, lips slack and moist. "In this hotel."

She's out of here.

The bridge maintains the integrity of its span within a riot of secondary construction, a coral growth facilitated in large part by carbon-fiber compounds. Some sections of the original structure, badly rusted, have been coated with a transparent material whose tensile strength far exceeds that of the original steel; some are splined with the black and impervious carbon fiber; others are laced with makeshift ligatures of taut and rusting wire.

Secondary construction has occurred piecemeal, to no set plan, employing every imaginable technique and material; the result is amorphous and startlingly organic in appearance.

At night, illuminated by Christmas bulbs, by recycled neon, by torchlight, the bridge is a magnet for the restless, the disaffected. By day, viewed from the towers of the city, it recalls the ruin of Brighton Pier in the closing decade of the previous century—seen through some cracked kaleidoscope of vernacular style.

Lately Skinner's hip can't manage the first twenty feet of ladder, so he hasn't been down to try the new elevator the African has welded to the rivet-studded steel of the tower, but he's peered at it through the hatch in the floor. It looks like the yellow plastic basket of a lineman's cherrypicker, cogging its way up and down a greasy-toothed steel track like a miniature Swiss train, motor bolted beneath the floor of the basket. Skinner's not sure where the tower's getting its juice these days, but the lightbulb slung beside his bed dims and pulses whenever he hears that motor whine.

He admires people who build things, who add to the structure. He admires whoever it was built this room, this caulked box of ten-ply fir, perched and humming in the wind. The room's floor is a double layer of pressure-treated two-by-fours laid on edge, broken by an achingly graceful form Skinner no longer really sees: the curve of the big cable drawn up over its saddle of steel, 17,464 pencil-thick wires.

The little pop-up television on the blanket across his chest con-

tinues its dumb-show. The girl brought it for him. Stolen, probably. He never turns the sound on. The constant play of images on
the liquid crystal screen is obscurely comforting, like the half-
sensed movements in an aquarium: life is there. The images themselves are of no interest. He can't remember when he ceased to be
able to distinguish commercials from programming. The distinction itself may no longer exist.

His room measures fifteen by fifteen feet, the plywood walls
softened by perhaps a dozen coats of white latex paint. Higher
reflective index than aluminium foil, he thinks. 17,464 strands per
cable. Facts. Often, now, he feels himself a void through which
facts tumble, facts and faces, making no connection.

His clothes hang from mismatched antique coat-hooks screwed
at precise intervals along one wall. The girl's taken his jacket.
Lewis Leathers. Great Portland Street. Where is that? Jacket older
than she is. Looks at the pictures in *National Geographic,*
crouched there with her bare white feet on the carpet he took from
the broken office block in . . . Oakland?

Memory flickers like the liquid crystal. She brings him food.
Pumps the Coleman's chipped red tank. Remember to open the
window a crack. Japanese cans, heat up when you pull a tab. Questions she asks him. Who built the bridge? Everyone. No, she says,
the old part, the bridge. San Francisco, he tells her. Bone of iron,
grace of cable, hangs us here. How long you live here? Years.
Spoons him his meal from a mess kit stamped 1952.

This is his room. His bed. Foam, topped with a sheepskin,
bottom sheet over that. Blankets. Catalytic heater. Remember to
open the window a crack.

The window is circular, leaded, each segment stained a different color. You can see the city through the bull's-eye of clear yellow glass at its center.

Sometimes he remembers building the room himself.

The bridge's bones, its stranded tendons, are lost within an accre-
tion of dreams: tattoo parlors, shooting galleries, pinball arcades,
dimly lit stalls stacked with damp-stained years of men's magazines, chili joints, premises of unlicensed denturists, fireworks
stalls, cut bait sellers, betting shops, sushi bars, purveyors of sexual

appliances, pawnbrokers, wonton counters, love hotels, hot dog stands, a tortilla factory. Chinese green-grocers, liquor stores, herbalists, chiropractors, barbers, tackle shops, and bars.

These are dreams of commerce, their locations generally corresponding to the decks originally intended for vehicular traffic. Above them, rising toward the peaks of the cable towers, lift intricate barrios, zones of more private fantasy, sheltering an unnumbered population of uncertain means and obscure occupation.

Sagging platforms of slivered wood are slung beneath the bridge's lower deck; from these, on a clear day, old men lower fishing lines. Gulls wheel and squabble over shreds of discarded bait.

The encounter in the old hotel confirms something for her. She prefers the bridge to the city.

She first came upon the bridge in fog, saw the sellers of fruits and vegetables with their goods spread out on blankets, lit by carbide lamps and guttering smudge pots. Farm people from up the coast. She'd come from that direction herself, down past the stunted pines of Little River and Mendocino, Ukiah's twisted oak hills.

She stared back into the cavern mouth, trying to make sense of what she saw. Steam rising from the pots of soup vendors' carts. Neon scavenged from the ruins of Oakland. How it ran together, blurred, melting in the fog. Surfaces of plywood, marble, corrugated plastic, polished brass, sequins, Styrofoam, tropical hardwoods, mirror, etched Victorian glass, chrome gone dull in the sea air—all the mad richness of it, its randomness—a tunnel roofed by a precarious shack town mountainside climbing toward the first of the cable towers.

She'd stood a long time, looking, and then she'd walked straight in, past a boy selling coverless yellowed paperbacks and a café where a blind old parrot sat chained on a metal perch, picking at a chicken's freshly severed foot.

Skinner surfaces from a dream of a bicycle covered with barnacles and sees that the girl is back. She's hung his leather jacket on its proper hook and squats now on her pallet of raw-edged black foam.

Bicycle. Barnacles.

Memory: a man called Fass snagged his tackle, hauled the bicycle up, trailing streamers of kelp. People laughing. Fass carried the bicycle away. Later he built a place to eat, a three-stool shanty leached far out over the void with superglue and shackles. He sold cold cooked mussels and Mexican beer. The bicycle hung above the little bar. The walls were covered with layers of picture postcards. Nights he slept curled behind the bar. One morning the place was gone, Fass with it, just a broken shackle swinging in the wind and a few splinters of timber still adhering to the galvanized iron wall of a barber shop. People came, stood at the edge, looked down at the water between the toes of their shoes.

The girl asks him if he's hungry. He says no. Asks him if he's eaten. He says no. She opens the tin food chest and sorts through cans. He watches her pump the Coleman. He says open the window a crack. The circular window pivots in its oak frame. You gotta eat, she says.

She'd like to tell the old man about going to the hotel, but she doesn't have words for how it made her feel. She feeds him soup, a spoonful at a time. Helps him to the tankless old china toilet behind the faded roses of the chintz curtain. When he's done she draws water from the roof-tank line and pours it in. Gravity does the rest. Thousands of flexible transparent lines are looped and bundled, down through the structure, pouring raw sewage into the Bay.

"Europe . . ." she tries to begin.

He looks up at her, mouth full of soup. She guesses his hair must've been blond once. He swallows the soup. "Europe what?" Sometimes he'll snap right into focus like this if she asks him a question, but now she's not sure what the question is.

"Paris," he says, and his eyes tell her he's lost again. "I went there. London, too. Great Portland Street." He nods, satisfied somehow. "Before the first devaluation . . ."

Wind sighs past the window.

She thinks about climbing out on the roof. The rungs up to the hatch there are carved out of sections of two-by-four, painted the same white as the walls. He uses one for a towel rack. Undo the bolt. You raise the hatch with your head: your eyes are level with gull shit. Nothing there, really. Flat tarpaper roof, a couple of two-by-four uprights; one flies a tattered Confederate flag, the other a faded orange windsock. Thinking about it, she loses interest.

When he's asleep again, she closes the Coleman, scrubs out the pot, washes the spoon, pours the soupy water down the toilet, wipes pot and spoon, puts them away. Pulls on her hightop sneakers, laces them up. She puts on his jacket and checks that the knife's still clipped behind her belt.

She lifts the hatch in the floor and climbs through, finding the first rungs of the ladder with her feet. She lowers the hatch closed, careful not to wake Skinner. She climbs down past the riveted face of the tower, to the waiting yellow basket of the elevator. Looking up, she sees the vast cable there, where it swoops out of the bottom of Skinner's room, vanishing through a taut and glowing wall of milky plastic film, a greenhouse; halogen bulbs throw spiky plant shadows on the plastic.

The elevator whines, creeping down the face of the tower, beside the ladder she doesn't use anymore, past a patchwork of plastic, plywood, sections of enameled steel stitched together from the skins of dead refrigerators. At the bottom of the fat-toothed track, she climbs out. She sees the man Skinner calls the African coming toward her along the catwalk, bearlike shoulders hunched in a ragged tweed overcoat. He carries a meter of some kind, a black box, dangling red and black wires tipped with alligator clips. The broken plastic frames of his glasses have been mended with silver duct tape. He smiles shyly as he edges past her, muttering something about brushes.

She rides another elevator, a bare steel cage, down to the first deck. She walks in the direction of Oakland, past racks of second-hand clothing and blankets spread with the negotiable detritus of the city. Someone is frying pork. She walks on, into the fluorescent chartreuse glare.

↓

She meets a woman named Maria Paz.

She's always meeting people on the bridge, but only people who live here. The tourists, mostly, are scared. They don't want to talk. Nervous, you can tell by their eyes, how they walk.

She goes with Maria Paz to a coffee shop with windows on the Bay and a gray dawn. The coffee shop has the texture of an old ferry, dark dented varnish over plain heavy wood; it feels as though someone's sawn it from some tired public vessel and lashed it up on the outermost edge of the structure. Not unlikely; the wingless body of a 747 has been incorporated, nearer Oakland.

Maria Paz is older, with slate gray eyes, an elegant dark coat, tattoo of a blue swallow on the inside of her left ankle, just above the little gold chain she wears there. Maria Paz smokes Kools, one after another, lighting them with a brushed chrome Zippo she takes from her purse; each time she flicks it open, a sharp whiff of benzene cuts across the warm smells of coffee and scrambled eggs.

You can talk with the people you meet on the bridge. Because everyone's crazy there, Skinner says, and out of all that craziness you're bound to find a few who're crazy the way you are.

She sits with Maria Paz, drinks coffee, watches her smoke Kools. She tells Maria Paz about Skinner.

"How old is he?" Maria Paz asks.

"Old. I don't know."

"And he lives over the cable saddle on the first tower?"

"Yes."

"Then he's been here a long time. The tops of the towers are very special. Do you know that?"

"No."

"He's from the days when the first people came out from the cities to live on the bridge."

"Why did they do that?"

Maria Paz looks at her over the Zippo. Click. Tang of benzene. "They had nowhere else to go. They were homeless in the cities. The bridge had been closed, you see, closed to traffic, for three years."

"Traffic?"

Maria Paz laughs. "But it was a *bridge,* darling. People drove back and forth in cars, from one end to the other." She laughs again. "There were too many cars, finally, so they dug the tunnels under the Bay. Tunnels for the cars, tunnels for the maglevs. The bridge was old, in need of repair. They closed it, but then the devaluations began, the depression. There was no money for the repairs they'd planned. The bridge stood empty. And then one night, as if someone had given a signal, the homeless came. But the legend is that there *was* no signal. People simply *came.* They climbed the chain-link and the barricades at either end; they climbed in such numbers that the chain-link twisted and fell. They tumbled the concrete barricades into the Bay. They climbed the towers. Dozens died, falling to their deaths. But when dawn came, they were here, on the bridge, clinging, claiming it, and the cities, dear," she blew twin streams of smoke from her nostrils, "knew that the world was watching. They were no longer invisible, you see, the homeless people; they'd come together on this span of steel, had claimed it as their own. The cities had to be cautious then. Already the Japanese were preparing an airlift of food and medical supplies. A national embarrassment. No time for the water cannon, no. They were allowed to stay. Temporarily. The first structures were of cardboard." Maria Paz smiles.

"Skinner? You think he came then?"

"Perhaps. If he's as old as you seem to think he is. How long have you been on the bridge, dear?"

"Three months, maybe."

"I was born here," says Maria Paz.

The cities have their own pressing difficulties. This is not an easy century, the nation quite clearly in decline and the very concept of nation-states called increasingly into question. The squatters have been allowed to remain upon the bridge and have transformed it. There were, among their original numbers, entrepreneurs, natural politicians, artists, men and women of previously untapped energies and talents. While the world watched, and the cities secretly winced, the bridge people began to build, architecture as *art brut.* The representatives of global charities descended in helicopters, to be presented with lists of tools and materials. Shipments of advanced adhesives arrived from Japan. A Belgian manufacturer donated a boatload of carbon-fiber beams. Teams of expert scavengers rolled through the cities in battered flatbeds, returning to the bridge piled high with discarded building materials.

The bridge and its inhabitants became the cities' premier tourist attraction.

Hard currency, from Europe and Japan.

She walks back in the early light that filters through windows, through sheets of wind-shivered plastic. The bridge never sleeps, but this is a quiet time. A man is arranging fish on a bed of shaved ice in a wooden cart. The pavement beneath her feet is covered with gum wrappers and the flattened filters of cigarettes. A drunk is singing somewhere, overhead. Maria Paz left with a man, someone she'd been waiting for.

She thinks about the story and tries to imagine Skinner there, the night they took the bridge, young then, his leather jacket new and glossy.

She thinks about the Europeans in the hotel on Geary. Hard currency.

She reaches the first elevator, the cage, and leans back against its bars as it rises up its patched tunnel, where the private lives of her neighbors are walled away in so many tiny, handmade spaces. Stepping from the cage, she sees the African squatting in his tweed overcoat in the light cast by a caged bulb on a long yellow extension cord, the motor of his elevator spread out around him on fresh sheets of newsprint. He looks up at her apologetically.

"Adjusting the brushes," he says.

"I'll climb." She goes up the ladder. Always keep one hand and one foot on the ladder, Skinner told her, don't think about where you are and don't look down. It's a long climb, up toward the smooth sweep of cable. Skinner must've done it thousands of times, uncounted, unthinking. She reaches the top of this ladder, makes a careful transfer to the second, the short one, that leads to Skinner's room.

He's there, of course, asleep, when she scrambles up through the hatch. She tries to move as quietly as she can, but the jingle of the jacket's chrome hardware disturbs him, or reaches him in his dream, because he calls out something, his voice thick with sleep. It might be a woman's name, she thinks. It certainly isn't hers.

In Skinner's dream now they all run forward, and the police, the police are hesitating, falling back. Overhead the steady drum of the network helicopters with their lights and cameras. A light rain's falling now, as Skinner locks his cold fingers in the chain-link and starts to climb, and behind him a roar goes up, drowning the bull-horns of the police and the National Guard, and Skinner is climbing, kicking the narrow toes of his boots into chain-link, climbing as though he's gone suddenly weightless, floating up, really, rising on the crowd's roar, the ragged cheer torn from all their lungs. He's there, at the top, for one interminable instant. He jumps. He's the first. He's on the bridge, running, running toward Oakland, as the chain-link crashes behind him, his cheeks wet with the rain and tears.

And somewhere off in the night, on the Oakland side, another fence has fallen. And they meet, these two lost armies, and flow together as one, and huddle there, at the bridge's center, their arms around one another, singing ragged wordless hymns.

At dawn, the first climbers begin to scale the towers.

Skinner is with them.

She's brewing coffee on the Coleman when she sees him open his eyes.

"I thought you'd gone," he says.

"I took a walk. I'm not going anywhere. There's coffee."

He smiles, eyes sliding out of focus. "I was dreaming. . . ."

"Dreaming what?"

"I don't remember. We were singing, in the rain. . . ."

She brings him coffee in the heavy china cup he likes, holds it, helps him drink. "Skinner, were you here when they came from the cities? When they took the bridge?"

He looks up at her with a strange expression. His eyes widen. He coughs on the coffee, wipes his mouth with the back of his hand. "Yes," he says, "yes. In the rain. We were singing. I remember that. . . ."

"Did you build this place, Skinner? This room? Do you remember?"

"No," he says, "no. Sometimes I don't remember. . . . We climbed. Up. We climbed up past the helicopters. We waved at them. Some people fell. At the top. We got to the top. . . ."

"What happened then?"

He smiles. "The sun came out. We saw the city."

COUNTER COUTURE

HAROLD JAFFE

APRIL IS THE *cruelest month*.

Which is when he did what he did. Tuesday, 1:43 p.m. He drove to the outdoor mall over there in Fashion Valley, went into Victoria's Secret, sniffed the sweet scents, mingled among the lingerie, and slipped some items into his Mark Cross doeskin briefcase.

Moving to the cramped male's section at the rear of the store, he selected a pair of old gold (that's a color) silk pajamas and asked the saleswoman to open a fitting cube.

Inside the cube, he located the camera eye at the top left. Took out a tube of shaving cream (Brut) from his briefcase and spread some of the aromatic white goo onto the camera eye. Replaced the Brut in his case and removed a pair of peach Lycra-and-lace bikini panties and a black fishnet body stocking. Undressed and wiggled into the Lycra-and-lace panties, then into the black fishnet body stocking. Smoothed the body stocking with his palms and examined himself in the mirror, front and back. Thrust out his buttocks, bent down and ogled himself through his legs, all the while whistling "Don't Cry for Me, Argentina," from the runaway smash musical *Evita*.

Without removing the lingerie, he put back on his shirt, tie, pinstriped trousers, double-breasted jacket, tasseled loafers. He folded his Paul Stuart boxers, then slipped them into his Cross case.

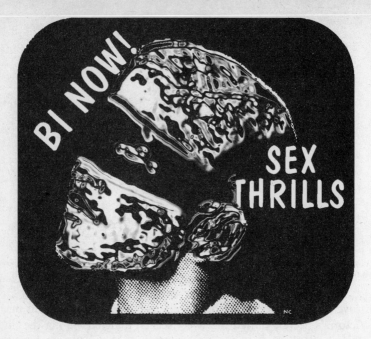

Exiting the fitting room, he replaced the old gold silk pajamas in the male bin. Moving normally in the Lycra-and-lace panties and black fishnet body stocking wasn't easy, but hey: no guts, no glory.

"Thanks for affording me the pleasure to browse," he said to the frosted redhead with two-inch acrylic red fingernails behind the counter; she nodded tersely in response.

No sooner had he exited Victoria's Secret and begun to breathe that peculiar recirculated mall air when someone tapped him hard on the shoulder.

The case made the headlines. A vice president of a Fortune 500 institution caught shoplifting is scandal enough, Lord knows. But shoplifting female lingerie! Not only stealing the stuff but *wearing* it.

"How *could* you, Mr. Privileged Male WASP Harvard MBA?"

He shrugged. "It's April, spring. Can't you feel it in your bones?"

"You're talking to me?"

"I'm talking through you to the TV audience. Are we being beamed worldwide?"

"I believe we are."

"I'd like to say, then, to the TV audience worldwide that since First World women enjoy inhabiting their bodies these days, I wanted to see what it felt like."

"Well?"

"Well what?"

"What did it feel like?"

"Racy."

[Pause]

"But what about your country, your corporation, your executive-box season tickets to the California Angel home games, your nuclear family?"

"Hell, I can watch the Angels in Lycra-and-lace panties and a body stocking. I can watch them in a hot pink teddy. It's just a question of getting used to it."

The TV censors bleeped *hell,* but otherwise they beamed the interview just as it was, worldwide.

Did I say the pervert's name? It's Jared Baldwin, called Jarry.

The onerous machinery of the courts moved swiftly.

Because of Jarry's class and caste and "unblemished record," the judge folded his long liverish hands, peered over his spectacles, and gave him a suspended sentence with the proviso that he undergo counseling.

Jarry's company on the New York Stock Exchange had fallen five and a half points since his arrest.

The company (I won't say the name) had summarily terminated Jarry.

Though his wife, Elizabeth Godwin-Baldwin, spoke bravely to the media about standing by her husband, the inside word was divorce and a megasettlement.

At school and in the Boy Scouts, Jarry's three sons, ages fifteen, thirteen, and eleven, were mercilessly mocked by the other kids, who came from normal, gentrified, gender-fast homes.

And then something odd happened.

What's your opinion of Geraldo Rivera?

Like him or hate him, you've got to admire his chutzpah. He resuscitated his TV career even as our cultural pundits had him down for the count. Thanks to his uncanny yen for scuzz (called "perfect pitch" in tabloid TV lingo), Geraldo became a multimillionaire faster than any TV talk-show host in recorded history.

Trivia time: The second fastest was Arsenio Hall.

Well, Geraldo and his production crew moved with blitzkrieg speed to capitalize on the Jarry case (as it was called in the media). They booked a show featuring two male transvestites and one preop transsexual, paired against two Nazi skinheads and two Anaheim Outlaw bikers. The expectation was for sparks and darts and a ratings surge.

After the two transvestites predictably expressed their appetite for cross-dressing, Geraldo sneered knowingly and turned to the bikers and skins.

"I ain't got a problem with wearing ladies' drawers," Anaheim Outlaw Earl said. "The times I done it I liked it. If I wasn't so big acrost the thighs, I'd do more of it."

Geraldo's mustache twitched. That wasn't what the bikers' PR people had led him to expect.

But the audience was cheering, not jeering.

"I agree with what he said," Nazi skinhead Klaus came in. "Me? I'd rather wear a broad's bra and panties than bang her."

Again the audience clapped and cheered.

Geraldo switched gears on the fly. He smirked knowingly. Turned to the other two studs.

"What do you guys think?"

"I think they're on the money," Anaheim Outlaw Kirk said. "I got into ladies' underwear and stuff by trying on my old lady's—"

Geraldo interrupted: "Your mom or your girlfriend?"

The biker shot Geraldo a dagger stare. "My girlfriend, okay? She asked me once to wear her panties as a goof. We been like smokin' ice—"

Geraldo interrupted: "Ice, for those in the audience and at home who aren't up-to-date on the latest street-drug terminology, is what, Kirk?"

"Two parts crack to one part speed, okay? So I squeezed into her panties. Like you can see, I ain't one of them old-fashioned fat-gutted bikers—"

From Geraldo: "Kirk used to be a Chippendale stripper, right?"

"Exactly," Kirk said. "Thing is, the Anaheim Outlaws all work out regular. If you're fat-gutted or in lousy shape we don't let you in. Period. So I squeezed into her panties. Got on the Harley wearing just the panties and boots and my panzer helmet—"

From Geraldo: "It's a California law. Just enacted. There was a lot of controversy, but it's for your own good. You ride a bike, you've got to wear a helmet."

"Okay," Kirk said. "We drove down to the beach. Did some stuff on the sand . . ."

"Did some stuff on the sand," Geraldo echoed provocatively. "You see, liking and wearing women's underwear *doesn't mean* you're not a macho guy, a real man. Right, biker Kirk?"

"Bet your buns."

"Right, skinhead Klaus?"

"Yeah, right."

The audience applauded loudly, whooping and whistling.

Even before the TV reviewers' accounts of the Geraldo scoop hit the papers, lingerie manufacturers were poised for what cultural historians would come to call the "revolution in counter couture." Within days, Calvin Klein, Armani, Bill Blass, Yves Saint-Laurent, Ralph Lauren, even Jockey and Fruit of the Loom, were at their drawing boards, in consultation with their ad people, making preparations to produce and market unisex lingerie.

While in the elite universities and think tanks, culture studies pundits were theorizing a mile a minute.

The end of machismo.
AIDS anxieties generate gender overlap.
If you can't lick them, join them.
Obscuring the poisoned phallus.
Clit envy.
The demise of the nuclear family.
A cross-dressing president by the year 2000.

For his part, Jared Baldwin engaged an elite Beverly Hills publicity team, who swiftly maneuvered a book/TV docudrama contract in the seven figures.

Following his publicity people's advice, Jarry turned down a high bid by Nike, which included a TV commercial where Jarry, wearing a hot pink teddy, would endorse their new "Cross-Over Trainer" shoe. Jarry's people called the Nike bid "frivolous."

Professionally, Jarry was courted by his old company, but instead he joined a competing Fortune 500 company (I won't say the name) as an executive VP, at a significantly higher salary.

Meanwhile, admissions of cross-dressing and opposite-gender underwear attraction have been pouring in. The two Pats: Buchanan and Robertson, Axl Rose, Jesse Helms, Norman Mailer, Dan Rather, and Geraldo himself, to name a few. And from the distaff side: Dr. Ruth, Phyllis Schlafly, Madonna, Whoopi Goldberg, Tipper Gore . . .

I'd like to end this story with a story.

Two young men, roommates, had just finished shopping at Lucky, previously called Food Basket. Parking their Ford Taurus on the street in front of their condo in an area of the city where many gay people lived, they were removing the packages from the trunk when they heard a distant rumbling, then saw in the wide street figures roller-blading toward them, eight or ten abreast, the space filling fast; then the figures, with shaved heads, beat the two men with chains, ax handles, stomping . . .

One of the beaten men died.

The roller-blading skinheads, when tried in court, claimed they were "America Firsters," doing their patriotic duty by assaulting consumers who bought Japanese cars and hence contributed to our failing economy.

When it was pointed out that the offending car was a Ford Taurus, the skins' attorney nodded and said: "True. My clients mistook it for a Toyota Camry."

EHMH: A MILLENNIAL ROMANCE

EURUDICE

*Come hither; I will shew unto thee the judgement
of the great whore that sitteth upon the waters.*
—Rev. 17:1

EMMANUELLE RELIGIOUSLY FILED *her nails down to the fingertips on puckered cliffs every sunset to protect the world from herself. Her calcified pubic hair swung blue and braided like anchor chains. She stood 7,130 cubits tall and had calloused fins instead of feet. When memory struck her, her breath came out in cascading gales that shook the webbed boat ribs and rust-gutted oil drums out of her fossilized hair. For four thousand years she had not smiled or menstruated, but her embrined nipples, sucked by the tireless sun, remained white and soft like wet salt. "It takes a person so long to eat a handful of salt," she thought optimistically, as she mentally rummaged through her cavernous guts for reserves of patience, but she couldn't postpone worrying that her pubes might fall from the coming-and-going of time.*

ABANDON ALL HOPE YE WHO ENTER HERE

Having spent centuries traversing the inside of a single female body, ever since a colossal slip of destiny had made him part of EHMH's vibrating anatomy, Jonah was anxious for dry land. Yes,

EHMH had protected him from death and time, God and blood-thirst, solitude and dehydration; yes, she was "the spirit of God moving upon the face of waters," and it had been exhilarating to live inside a moist virgin. But God had taught him the impossibility of all escape; he'd seen "God's wonders in the deep," and now he was feeling keen to dominate. Yes. "Woe to the ship whose captain is lost," lamented the Talmud, and EHMH was lost. Jonah did not want to be a "hidden Jew" like Columbus. He now burned with the moral responsibility to emerge from his organic safe, take the world's rudder in his hands, and steer "the spirit of the Lord to cover the earth as the waters that cover the sea."

Fall was her origin. Throughout the cycles, without fear or hatred or even resenting her impossible cumulus, she had grown larger with every fall. She sat quietly on the Bermuda triangle, occasionally parting the rainbow oil slicks with her iron-sinewed thighs, and fed on sparkling fibrous plankton, like other women in solitary conditions who have had to feast on worm-crammed soil; and as she stuffed her mouth and locked her teeth to sieve out the shiny toxic slosh and plastic debris before it polluted her bulging esophagus, she wished she could suck on an A-bomb fireball, and in the same breath she wondered if Jonah were still keeping house inside her hourglass pyloric orifice, boiling dry for himself morsels of her submucosal lining or whatever small darting fish slipped through her coral teeth, with the fortitude of a biblical Crusoe determined to see his God to the end, stubbornly choking through the fleshy dungeon doors of her colon, moving unceasingly and impulsively toward the virgin sand-shrouded hole of her butt. She had never vomited.

Her memory came in hard, milky, eye-popping spurts, like a man. How many forgotten others could be living inside her hypermobile duodenum, and were they mirthlessly copulating, as she suspected, in her crowded abdomen, multiplying at an explosive rate that endangered her? Life depended on the resilience of her thick skin and its capacity to expand as she absorbed in daily compulsive mouthfuls the world's unspent dreams. She shuddered at her own abundant openness. How had she come, and was still coming, into being?

Jonah braced himself at the thought of having to withstand the osmotic pressure of the plasma protein and the back pressure of the already excreted urine in EHMH's collecting system. But his main problem was the Glomerulus. He had swum through thousands of liters of urine before, only to be stopped by that humongous fleshy sieve that strained corpuscles and protein and that had held him back each time. He wasn't Proteus. Jonah knew that only 1 percent of the body's total filtrate was ever excreted as urine into the renal pelvis, and he had to keep trying to make the cut. He'd never made it past the Glomerulus checkpoint, and he was sick of acting like a "waste product," always hanging around sodium, creatinine, uric acid, sulfates, phosphates, chloride, and low molecular proteins. But he knew that if he succeeded, he would only have to follow the easy flow of the urine as it was moved by peristaltic waves across the Ureteropelvic Junction; swim a ways through the long muscular tunnel of the Bladder; and, assuming the bladder pressure was strong enough to prevent backing up of the urine (that most dreaded vesicoureteral reflux), he would swiftly pass through one of the three narrow gates to freedom: the iliac vesseled Ureters, the slits that would lead him straight to EHMH's tubular Urethra! As soon as the parasympathetic sensory fibers transmitted the stretch sensation of the distended bladder to the reflex center at level S2 to S4 of EHMH's spinal cord, and if, being toilet-trained, EHMH's higher centers did not choose to override that nervous stimuli and expand her bladder's capacity, the act of voiding or micturition would begin, and, by God, Jonah would course ecstatically along the alterior vault of EHMH's beacons.

History had been poured into her helpless flesh day after day, and continued to percolate through her pores, aeons after she had reached a saturation point. "History produces so much gas," she marveled with deep-felt awe.

And upon her forehead a name was invisibly written, a mys-

tery, EMMANUELLE THE GREAT, DAUGHTER OF WARS, HARLOTS, AND OBSCENE ABOMINATIONS OF THE EARTH, EATER OF HISTORY.

  "Choice," she thought, desperate to ease her dyspepsia, "is not dishonor. I am sick of salt. Where do I start?"

"Our ancestors said, 'Let there be an expanse in the midst of the water, that it may separate water from water.' And they called the expanse EHMH." This was Peter; Jonah recognized him by the stony locks and the forehead worried with wrinkles leaking crystallized salt. Peter's voice always cackled in dry heaves.

Jonah looked around hurriedly like a rat in his Skinner box, trying to orient himself. He quickly grabbed the nearest pea green soft doorknob and stumbled in. He found himself in a short dim hallway with a hot spring on the corner and followed it into the ADH (short for Antidiuretic Hormone) Pub. He was wet, and his nose was bleeding from that unsettling elbow. He rushed to the blistery bar and shook the oblivious singing bartender. ". . . Save and give them victory over the grave. . . ." EHMH softened a man's heart like "water from heaven," Jonah thought, exasperated.

"Which artery to Kidney's Hilum?" he screeched, desperate to drown out the hymnal wails and the ubiquitous gutteral humming of EHMH. What was it about this body that made communication so tortuous? The Viking bartender pointed toward a rainbow-hued bubbling pool table across the chamber and baritoned: "Just dive into that mucosal tissue over there, and it'll take you straight to the Ureteropelvic Junction, Jonah. . . . By thy drawing nigh; disperse the gloomy clouds of . . ." A shortcut! This was a smile from his God; Jonah felt so lucky he even ignored his usual paranoia about being recognized by anonymous and unwashed barbarians.

He sidestepped the singing patrons who swung in tendon-hammocks, watching the All-Prophetorial Combat Network on EHMH's Higher Motor functions, munching terra-cotta-hued Apostleberry Crunch (sixty parts potassium, twenty-nine parts hydrogen ions, and one part battery acid from shipwrecks). All Emmanuellians slept with their eyes open; Jonah could see their ocular blobs of radioactive prophetorial combat reflected in pools of red. Why was no one telling jokes in this hull? The prospect of a somber eternity in EHMH terrified him. He staggered past the hypnotically hymning sleepers, pinched his nose with two fingers, and dived headfirst into the swampy mucosal tissue that sucked him down swiftly like a frothy waterslide; he sank like a fetus.

He landed on his ass in the center of an astral pinball alley swirling in drifting sediment, and sighed with relief. According to his centuries of calculations and in the light of his earlier forays into EHMH's excretory maze, and also assuming the Viking was well-informed, he was sitting in the Ureteropelvic Junction. Hurray! Jonah thought, and gave himself a second to thank his greedy God. "But thou didst bring up my life from the Pit, O Lord, my God!" He had bypassed the Glomerulus dam, that uretinary Scylla and Charybdis! He leapt up, his arthritic spine creaking, and looked for the liberating tunnel of the Bladder. The smelly bodily fluids were rising around him, but he held his chin high and marched on, swept by the furry current (was it algae mold?), until the surge of the phosphoric river became too massive to resist, and he let himself float among the burning acrid waves. This was the part of his exodus Jonah loathed most, and not even his God could rescue him. Screw the Glomerulus, he thought. This is far more disgusting; I'd rather be sieved! He'd never seen so much urine in his whole chaotic life.

A question he'd often pondered came back to him now, as he struggled to breathe over the rushing fumes and ocher muck: Was EHMH cosmologically grounded? Was this vast body influenced by the moon, for instance? He'd never know unless he got out. Chunks of sodium splashed into his eyes. Gas winds rose to fifty knots. He kept his mouth tightly shut and silently begged God to cut short his underurine journey and deliver him safe into the Elysian Urethra.

Suddenly, a peristaltic contraction sucked him into a fetid vacuum. Echoing winds purred out of EHMH's superior pelvirectal fossa. Gastric enzymes exploded all around; flying through the rancid maelstrom, Jonah cried out: "The whore is passing gas."

Jonah had fought many rough seas, and had nearly drowned on countless occasions, but never had he witnessed such an austere determination in the liquid masses that surrounded him. He felt he was inside a living shrine meant for worship and abstinence. There could be no turning back, no room for doubt, no unbelief in this fated rite of passage. One day he would preach this vision.

And then the urine parted. Jonah spun in a deep whirlpool, the vinegary wash drumming in his ears. A stifling acidic heat fogged the leaky tunnel, and he was pulled in all directions at once; his limbs felt dislocated. "Those who heed false vanities forsake their . . . What I have vowed, I will pay. Deliverance belongs to the Lord," he mechanically chanted on.

Vesicoureteral Reflux? Had he been detected? He knew not to oppose the current. All he could do was flow with the waste, and keep an eye out for an iliac vessel; if he could grab on to one as on to an oar, it would lead him through a Ureter, and lo! Urethra!

ALAS, ALAS! AMEN! ALLELUIA!

Jonah found no iliac exit. When he came to, he was bloated and drunk. He felt seasick, even after the centuries he'd spent rocked in EHMH. He vomited laboriously, lying on noxious refuse in a dim grotto he'd never seen before. There was little oxygen, and he was breathless. Around him he felt the stifling expansion of irregular and unbearably soft tissue that pressed against him, floatable and airy, billowing so tightly that he choked. I shouldn't be here, he thought; forgive me. In the slow detached rhythm of a sleepwalker, Jonah parted the tissue with his hands, ambling in a direction he chose as not worse than any other. He felt like he'd just popped a million brain cells.

Then Jonah came upon a fungal beauty so harmonious he felt his eyes had opened for the first time. He fought to get hold of himself, regain his cynicism and complain as usual that there were no angles in EHMH, that a man could only take so many curves, globes, and bacterial balls before craving a clear-cut geometric shape that was more complex than a damn triangle, but his heart was beating too frenetically. He panicked; he ached to leave EHMH's inner fields and dive out to his God; to walk through walls. "No use rushing fate," he said.

When a glandular curtain was finally opened by one of EHMH's natural reflexes, he saw he hadn't even been close to a Ureter. The Glomerulus loomed mockingly behind him. He was down by the hilly Symphysis Pubis, not far from the Vena Cava. Twilight rained in; EHMH had the longest twilight in the history of the world, as her red cells sucked up light, reflecting it back in the form of a perennial sunset. Jonah's defeated gaze cast about for shelter.

Shem, Ham, and Japheth were drinking fermented bile outside the Ovary Ark, buckriding their skinny cattle; senile papa-Noah—who was still thinking that this was the six thousandth year the second month, and the seventeenth day of his life, and that God had just shut him in to flood the planet for a year—was yelling from inside, "It's too wet in here! I won't have God's house turn to falls! Shem, get me a mop! If we drown, there'll be no raven and no olive leaf and no more friggin' fertility!"

Jonah wandered in, knotted and dripping like a hair-standing wildcat. The sign over the counter read MONOTHEISTS ONLY. The Ark crowd beamed their glassy eyes at him. They were serving free horns of kosher Holygen cocktails (200 pg/ml estrogen, 10.1 ng/ml progesterone, and a worm), which were not Jonah's idea of a prophet's drink. They were toasting the Mid-Cycle Feast. This was EHMH's ovulatory phase, which explained the mirth in the streets. Day 14: LH had just induced the final maturation of the follicle ripened by FSH and the expulsion of the Great Egg from EHMH's Ovary. The ebullient inebriated crowd was watching on EHMH's higher motor screen as the EHMH Egg became a corpus luteum (yellow body); and as it secreted its first and last progesterone, they all clapped and clicked horns: ". . . Here until the Daughter appear!" The hypothalamic thermostat was registering a 17-a hydroxyprogesterone/estradiol rise, the highest monthly LH peak. For Jonah, fresh from the urine baths, the Uterus was a depressing non-aseptic sight.

As he slowly limped back out into a Luteotytic lane, he heard a woman's voice from inside the Ark, "You might need an umbrella, Jonah!" He hated this lack of privacy. He felt persecuted. Was an old-fashioned desert too much for a seer to ask for in EHMH?

". . . That mourns in lonely exile . . ." Jonah waded inexorably up the Corpus Cavernosum. The dancing automatonic helots of EHMH flocked to him in pandemonium. Their hydroelectric ranks closed like teeth; the red sea of bodies jolting in the eternal twilight interlocked their arms and legs, wheeling pyres, flaming bushes, blood banners, and cornified genitals into a human shield, and raised mellifluous voices: ". . . And teach us in her ways to go."

"To become a crowd is to keep out death; to break off from the crowd is to risk being slaughtered as an individual, to face dying alone," orated a crimson-lipped redhead, flinging her big head back in abandon and drumming her tambourine. A rifle target was tattooed on her left breast. She was painting fecal graffiti on an ileocecal valve and drinking electrolytes by the gallon.

Through the ages, Emmanuellians had grown terribly intimate with each other; drenched, naked, and intertwined, they clotted like a scab, keeping Jonah from his unknown mark. He bemoaned his God for creating such stereotypical brainwashed masses. Elbowed and kneed, he floated on with the hardened mob, thinking: Never pray to a full-gutted God. He knew the crowd would erupt like a boil any moment; they were too aroused. And never pray on a full belly, he added; Jonah's Greatest Scriptures. As people slid in and out of each other, the ocean that held them all surged backward, pushing Jonah into the lumbosacral door of the Sphincter Bar, while most of the Emmanuellians dove into lust indiscriminately. ". . . Hearts of all mankind bid our sad divisions," they sang in animal noises and battle cries. The foreplay was over.

He crashed through the moist door of the Sphincter and picked himself up from the rectal floor. His tongue felt drier than the bottom of a parrot's cage. The last fluid in his mouth had been his vomit. He asked for some tap rheum at the counter, and decided to ride out the Egg Festival in the bar, where he'd recover his instincts and catch EHMH's next peristaltic contraction. He suspected EHMH was toying with him, as a familiar cackle echoed through the bar. "He Ho He He!" EHMH's capricious diaphragm was closing off her glotis. The most frightening sound in the universe is a woman's ill-timed laughter, Jonah thought.

The flabby, raven-bearded Chetnik bartender, sucking on a soaked Cuban cigar, ducked out from under the counter with an old creel full of Muslim scalps pickling in rheum, and smiled. He poured Jonah a bowl. Jonah drank it down fast and immediately felt that, yes, he would live through the eternal twilight. "You could use a real drink," the Chetnik said with a swagger, pointing to a shelf of residual rectum alcohols labeled "God's Rack of Poisons." The neighborhood was known for its bacteria and punch, and the Sphincter was a popular subterfuge in EHMH, since it had direct access to stored gastroileal fecal material and predefecation centers such as the Sigmoid and Levator Ani around the Anal Canal, a scenic promenade sporting EHMH's better eateries.

After gulping a double cecum-tini, Jonah wanted something more useful: "What I need is the support of the masses," he slurred. "Can't pull this off alone." He was starting to relax. "Ho-ji ha ha haaaa!" resounded the Colon. The insides of EHMH smelled like mischief. ". . . Law, in cloud and majesty and awe," the Chetnik crooned, slicing an undigested tuna from head to spiked tail; its rotting entrails poured out in a viscous rush, splattering the counter with graying heart, gills, liver, green stomach, and kidneys. The Chetnik rummaged through for the tiny translucent brains and sucked them into his mouth along with the mucusy eyes, then fisted the white flesh. A collarbone slipped off the counter, and immediately the glyceride floor swallowed it. The Chetnik cursed and flipped the rest into his gap-toothed mouth. His fingers dripped, his teeth whistled. An inebriating stench of fetid low water filled the mesenteric and portal veins of the chamber and became one with all skin.

Jonah crossed his spindled arms flat on the counter and rested his bald ridged head on the pancreatic fat. The sensation of movement never stopped; he felt he was still in the cargo skiff bound for Tarshish. Mischief pinched his swollen nasal septum like two unwashed fingers, as EHMH's wetness slinked down Jonah's scalp over his jutting ears, bulbous chin, hefty cheek, protruding Adam's apple, twig shoulders, sunken chest, knobby knuckles; it pooled in the depression under his rib cage and fanned out across his hollow belly and bony pelvis onto his dilated member, which lay langorously in the peptide heat. He thoughtfully sipped his third cecumtini and whispered between diaphramic convulsions, "Howz it possible to be patient in Hell?"

". . . Satan's tyranny that trust thy mighty power to . . . ," the Chetnik replied, gulping a fondue of proteolytic enzymes. A faucet of laughter streamed from EHMH's walls, nearly drowning Jonah again. "I never been good at facin' the inevitable, mate," he blurted out, looking to the fat-bellied Chetnik for a nod of support. But the Chetnik was absorbed in watching UberEm, the All-Time News Channel broadcasting live flashbacks of EHMH's inhabitants as they were unconsciously transmitted to her Central Sulcus (Rolando) through her Higher Somesthetic area. Gang-raped virgins and gassed refugees screamed anxiously, transposed over decapitating Janissars, over roaming SWAT squads, over Chinese tortures, witch burnings, Crusaders, Mongols, Iron Maidens, missionaries, all shimmering in layered images of pestilence, turmoil, wrath, and excommunication. Recovered-Memory Network was EHMH's therapy system. Some Sphincter patrons cried, others laughed or cheered, recollecting elaborate combat anecdotes, slapping their thighs, logging in their own walled-off submerged memories, wailing, ". . . High, and close the path to misery . . . ," because in EHMH they had all forgotten who their own personal enemies were and yet they remembered enough to fear pain.

"We're all Emdamn clones," Jonah chattered in a heady introspective mood. "Parasitic fungi. We got no pride. . . ."

"The word 'life' means 'there's no way out,' " smirked the hairy Chetnik in a matter-of-fact monotone, his gaze glued to the slave drivers on screen.

"Life's simply our history and its expectations," Jonah babbled on. "Whatz your name?"

"Ripper Mappamondo. I used to staple enemy labia together for a living." The Chetnik smacked his salt-caked lips, and the fat on his body quaked. "I can't fathom whose, but I'll know them when I see them, I reckon."

"Tell you somethin', Reaper, we could skin her from inside. Scrape away the pink flesh until she looks like those skeletal deaths from Mexico, and bolt out," Jonah mumbled.

"You want to skin God? Show a little backbone, for Emsakes!"

"We could make fishbone scimitars and commit open-heart surgery on her, um, cut straight to the bone, saw straight through the heart . . . ," Jonah argued half-heartedly.

"What happened to you, Jonah, is part of a Plan. Every action, every moment is her Plan. Why struggle to escape? It makes no difference. Difference is a myth. The freedom to believe is the only freedom. We can't live the things we believe. That's the absurd truth. So show some respect. Destiny gets skinned and we're finished. Without her we're homeless, we are back out there drooling and killing. We're her children, man, she'll take care of us when she's ready, she's the Omne Genius!"

At that, everyone in the Sphincter rose in a chorus line and hollered in angry unison, ". . . Night, and death's dark shadow put to flight . . . ," while pointing their fingers and staring Jonah down. He nodded to the unwelcoming lazy crowd and staggered out, suddenly burdened by his serial failures.

"A huge price to pay to come to the conclusion that nothing is real!" he hollered back at the closing door. "Everything is a myth, buddy. Anything that's not is unspeakable. Wake up and smell the urine!"

It was about 8881367 in the Em time zone. Elmighty, the Em-Vein Line with local intravenal service to Coccyx, Kidney, Duodenum, Angina Pectoris, Esophagus, and Larynx, squeaked in a running pace in front of him; he jumped onto the first corpuscle, sat in the ergonomic crevice of a red blood cell, and swallowed the sweetness of her running biledrops. The Vein rattled with a gaseous whisper. The Emmanuellians looked more subdued than earlier. Passengers hummed, "Emmanuelle shall come to thee, O . . ."

He got off at the Larynx and immediately stumbled into John the Baptist's floodlit Aryepiglottic workshops. This one was titled "Marvel at the Planning of Her Entrails—Find the Best Place to Sleep; Equip Your Home; Bileproof Everything; Maintain the Plumbing, Heating, Cooling Systems; Fix Everything that Could Possibly Break (Including Heart)." The crowd loved it.

The Baptist looked like his clay-colored skin was made of cartilage, and he had the toughest gums in EHMH. He was rumored to subsist on gingiva and buccal mucosa alone. He'd just finished his long speech and now was trying to disengage himself from the makeshift thyroid podium that his bony ass was stuck to; he had to pull hard to save himself from becoming part of EHMH, before her glands secreted enough adhesive digestive enzymes to transform him into an integral part of her tissue. In EHMH, no one went to waste. To detract attention from his embarrassing near-death struggle to pluck himself from God, John pompously kept the vocal crowd entertained by breaking into a heartfelt falsetto rendition of ". . . Cease, and be thyself our Queen of Peace."

The Larynx was known as EHMH's Philosophers' Walk. The river Trachea divided it between the False Cord Quarters (ventricular ligament) on the left bank and the True Cord (vocal lig.) on the sophisticated right. Lush heavy shades of scarlet and precarious rebounding high-wire steps that created melodious echoes graced its sides. Here the light was a prickling glare.

On the True Cord bank, Jonah watched the sinuous laryngeal floor undulate in tympanitic waves that were surprisingly arousing. This continuous state of arousal was driving Jonah mad because, unlike most Emmanuellians, he was still a virgin; after the evacuation, he thought, after he'd stormed the fortress EHMH, he might finally get himself deflowered.

The Baptist finally stepped down from the salivating podium, and Job the Sly jumped onto it, invoking, "Behold the message I bring for your salvation: Do not shun EHMH's hourglass garbage dump, the pseudo organ commonly known as History, even if it is a prison festered with viruses and poisonous gas, for that is where we all must gather and sing and rock until we awaken Her! Do not bileproof, but distend and reclaim! Together we can inspire our Mother to rise and change the world!"

"It's called the Second Coming!" someone yelled derisively.

"Isn't History where that manic-depressive John the Apostle hides, among the trash?" Jonah challenged Job from the crowd. "What's he say about all this?"

"EHMH is not an island," Job sputtered back. "She is the strongest, safest police-free homeland in the history of the world. She is the product of history and is free of history. The task is best left to official biographers, apostles, vessels, for I have no language to describe the simple union of opposites that is EHMH: She is rational. Chaotic. Loving. Sadistic. Immune. Vulnerable. Mistress of Fate. Slave of Destiny. Fair yet Prejudiced. Methodical yet Spontaneous. Forgetful yet Omniscient. I have no legal or material reason to lie to you. I've had my full share of beatings in the hard hand of God. Subpoena Heraklitus to testify here. She is Truth. Myth. Graceful, graceless. I hope you see where I'm going with this. Woman yet Man."

The True Cord crowd was notoriously hard to impress, and Job was booed down before his spidery ass had time to root in EHMH's dura matter. Carotid rocks and fishbones flew at Job as he slid away from the pendulous podium, still vowing to fulfill his duty.

Jonah grabbed this golden auricular opportunity to run up to the empty swinging podium. He had an idea; it had worked before.

"Cast lots!" he shouted with infectious exuberance and reveled in the auspicious déjà vu. "That you may know upon whose account this wet disaster has befallen you!" He grinned ferociously.

The crowd waited, transfixed, not quite understanding. Jonah's heart pounded impatiently as he tried to explain: "I am an infectious disease in EHMH!" He felt so sure God was on his side of the dice, he went straight to the point, his voice hard: "I AM has sent me to you," he boomed, stealing Moses' best lines, and then pronounced each word intimately: "Just pick me up and cast me into the sea, so that the sea may be calm for you; for I know that this great unjust storm is upon you because of me." It was his only chance. The crowd stared dumbfounded as if he were speaking a dead language. "Give it a try," he yelled, resorting to colloquialisms. "What have you got to lose but your chains?"

Meanwhile, banging across her windy larynx in shattering explosions, EHMH's earsplitting eternal laugh boomed southward.

GREAT BREAKTHROUGHS IN DARKNESS

(BEING EARLY ENTRIES FROM *THE SECRET ENCYCLOPAEDIA OF PHOTOGRAPHY*)

AUTHORIZED BY MARC LAIDLAW

Chief Secretary of the Ministry of Photographic Arcana,
Correspondent of No Few Academies,
Devoted Father and Husband, &c.

> *"Alas! That this speculation is somewhat too re-*
> *fined to be introduced into a modern novel or ro-*
> *mance; for what a* dénouement *we should have, if*
> *we could suppose the secrets of the darkened*
> *chamber to be revealed by the testimony of the*
> *imprinted paper!"*
>
> —William Henry Fox Talbot

-A-

AANSCHULTZ, CONREID
(c. 1820–OCTOBER 12, 1888)

INVENTOR OF THE praxiscope technology (*which see*), Professor Aanschultz believed that close observation of physiology and similar superficial phenomena could lead to direct revelation of the inner or secret processes of nature. Apparent proof of this now discredited theory was offered by his psychopraxiscope, which purported to offer instantaneous viewing of any subject's thoughts. Aanschultz's theories collapsed, and the Professor himself died in a Parisian lunatic asylum, after his notorious macropraxiscope failed to extract any particular meaning from the contours of the Belgian countryside near Waterloo. Some say he was already unstable from abuse of his autopsychopraxiscope, thought to be particularly dangerous because of autophagous feedback generated in its operator's brain. However, there is evidence that Aanschultz was mad already, owing to the trauma of an earlier research disaster.

AANSCHULTZ LENS

The key lens used in Aanschultz's notorious psychopraxiscope, designed to capture and focus abaxial rays reflecting from a subject's eye.

ABAT-JOUR

A skylight or aperture for admitting light to a studio, or an arrangement for securing same by reflection. In the days when studios for portraiture were generally found at the tops of buildings not originally erected for that purpose, perhaps in narrow thoroughfares or with a high obstruction adjacent, I found myself climbing a narrow, ill-lit flight of stairs, away from the sound of wagon wheels rattling on cobblestones and the common fetor of a busy city street, and toward a more rarified and addictive stench. It was necessary to obtain all available top light in the choked alleys, and Aanschultz had done everything he could in a city whose sky was blackly draped with burning sperm.

I came out into a dazzling light compounded of sunlight and acetylene, between walls yellowed by iodine vapor, covering my nose at the stench of mercury fumes, the reek of sulfur. My own fingertips were blackened from such stuff; and eczema procurata, symptomatic of a metal allergy, had sent a prurient rash all up the sensitive skin of my inner arms, which, though so bound in bandages that I could scarcely scratch them through my heavy woolen sleeves, were a constant seeping agony. At night I wore a woman's long kid gloves coated with coal tar, and each morning I dressed my wounds with an ointment of mercuric nitrate (60 g), carbolic acid (10 cc), zinc oxide (30 g), and lanolin (480 g), which I had learned to mix myself when the chemist professed a groundless horror of contagion. I carried my tender arms slightly spread from my sides, seeming always on the verge of drawing the twin Janssen photographic revolvers which I carried in holsters slung around my waist, popular handheld versions of that amazing "gun" which first captured the transit of Venus across the face of our local star.

The laboratory was a fury of painfully brilliant light and sharp, membrane-searing smells. Despite my admiration for the Professor's efficiency, I found it poorly suited for artistic purposes, a side light being usually preferable instead of the glare of a thousand suns that came down through the cruelly contrived abat-jour. But Aanschultz, a man of scientific bent, saw in twilight landscapes only some great treasure to be prized forth with all necessary force. He would have disemboweled the earth itself if he thought an empirical secret were lodged in its craw. I had suggested a more oblique light, but the Professor would not hear of it.

"That is for your prissy studios, your fussy bourgeois sitters!" he had raged at my "aesthetic" suggestion. "I am a man of science. My subjects come not for flattering portraits, but for insight. I observe the whole man here."

To which I replied: "And yet you have not *captured* him. You have not impressed a single supposition on so much as one thin sheet of tin or silver or albumen glass. The fleeting things you see cannot be captured, which is less than I can say of even the poorest photograph, however superficial." And here he scoffed at me and turned away, pacing, so that I knew my jibes had cut to the core of his own doubts, and that he was still, with relentless logic, stalking a way to fix the visions he viewed so briefly in his praxiscope.

"I am nearly there," he told me today, as I reached the top of the stairs with a celebratory bottle in hand.

His assistants were everywhere, adjusting the huge rack of movable mirrors that conducted light down from the rooftops, in from the street, over from the alleyway, wherever there happened to be a stray unreaped ray of it. Their calls rang out through the laboratory, echoing down through pipes like those in great ships, whereby the captain barks orders to the engine room. In the center of the chamber stood the solar navigator with his vast charts and compass and astrolabes scattered around him, constantly shouting into any one of the dozen pipes that coiled down from the ceiling like dangling vines, dispatching orders to those who stood in clearer sight of the sun but with a less complete foreknowledge of its motion; and as he shouted, the mirrors canted this way and that, the huge collectors on the roof purred in their oiled bearings, the entire building creaked under the shifting weight, and the laboratory burned like a furnace, although cleverly, without any heat. There was a watery luminescence in the air, a distorted rippling that sent wavelets lapping over the walls and tables and charts and retorts and tarnished boxes, turning the iodine stains a lurid green; this was the result of light pouring through racks of blue glass vials, old glass that had run and blistered with age, stoppered bottles full of copper sulfate which also swiveled and tilted according to the instructions of another assistant who stood very near the navigator.

I had to raise my own bottle and drink deeply before I could approach a state of focused distraction more like that of my friend and mentor, the great Professor Conreid Aanschultz, who now snatched the bottle from my hands and helped himself. He courteously polished every curve of the flask with a fresh chamois, eradicating his last fingerprint as the bottle left his fingers, so that the now empty vessel gleamed as brightly as those blue ones. He dropped it onto a half-assembled filter rack, where it would find a useful life even empty. The Professor made full use of all *Things*.

"This way," he said, leading me past a huge hissing copperclad acetylene generator of the dreadnought variety, attended by several anxious-looking children in the act of releasing quantities of gas through a purifier. The proximity of this somewhat dangerous operation to the racks of burning Bray 00000 lamps made me uncomfortable, and I was grateful to move over a light-baffling threshold into darkness. Here, a different sort of chaos obtained. I sensed, even before my eyes had adjusted to the weak and eerie working light, that the assistants here were closer to Aanschultz's actual work, for they had that weary, pacified air of slaves who have been whipped to the limits of human endurance and then suspended beyond that point for days on end. I doubted any had slept or rested half as much even as Aanschultz, who was possessed of superhuman reserves. I myself, of quite contrary disposition, had risen late that morning, feasted on a huge lunch (which even now was producing rumbling gases, like my own internal dreadnought), and, feeling benevolent, had decided to answer my friend's urgent message of the previous day, which had hinted that his fever pitch of work was about to bear fruit—a pronouncement he always made somewhat in advance of the actual climax, thus giving me plenty of leisure to come around. For poor Aanschultz, time was compressed from line to point. His was a world of constant Discovery.

I bumped into nearly everything and everyone in the darkened chamber before my eyes adjusted. I found myself bathed in a deep, rich violet light, decanted through yet another rack of bottles, although of a correspondingly darker hue. Blood or burgundy, they seemed at first, reminding me of the liquid edge of clouds one sometimes sees at sunset, when all form seems to buzz and crackle as it melts into the coming night and the eye tingles in anticipation of discovering unsuspected hues. My skin now hummed with this same subtle optical electricity. Things in the room seemed to glow with an inner light.

"Here we are," he said. "This will make everything possible. This is my—"

ABAT-NOIR

By this name Aanschultz referred to a beveled opening he had cut into an odd corner of the room, a tight and complex angle formed between the floor and the brick abutment of a chimney shaft from the floors below. I could not see how he had managed to collect any light from this darkest of corners, but I quickly saw my error. For it was not light he bothered to collect in this way, but darkness.

Darkness was somehow channeled into the room and then filtered through those racks of purple bottles, in some of which I now thought to see floating specks and slowly tumbling shapes that might have been wine lees or blood clots. I even speculated that I saw the fingers of a deformed, pickled fetus clutching at the rays that passed through its glass cell, playing inverse shadow-shapes on the walls of the dark room, casting its enlarged and gloomy spell over all us awed and frightened older children.

Unfiltered, the darkness was harder to characterize; when I tried to peer into it, Aanschultz pulled me away, muttering, "Useless for our purposes."

"Our?" I repeated, as if I had anything to do with this. For even then it seemed an evil power my friend had harnessed, something best left to its own devices—something which, in collaboration with human genius, could only lead to the worsening of an already precarious situation.

"This is my greatest work yet," he confided, but I could see that his assistants thought otherwise. The shadows already darkening Europe seemed thickest in this corner of the room. I felt that the strangely beveled opening, with its canted mirror inside a silvery black throat reflecting darkness from an impossible angle, was in fact the source of all the unease to be found in the streets and in the marketplace. It was as if everyone had always known about this webby corner and feared that it might eventually be prized open by the violent levering of a powerful mind.

I comforted myself with the notion that this was a discovery, not an invention, and therefore for all purposes inevitable. Given a mind as focused as Aanschultz's, this corner was bound to be routed out and put to some use. However, I already suspected that its eventual use would not be that which Aanschultz expected.

I watched a thin girl with badly bruised arms weakly pulling a lever alongside the abat-noir to admit more darkness through the purple bottles. The deepening darkness seemed to penetrate her skin as well as the jars, pouring through the webs of her fingers, the meat of her arms, so that the shadows of bone and cartilage glowed within them, flesh flensed away in the revealing black radiance. It was little consolation to think that Aanschultz's discovery was implicit in the fact of this corner, that this source of darkness was embedded in creation like an aberration in a lens and therefore unavoidable. It had taken merely a mind possessed of an equal or complementary aberration to uncover it. I only hoped that Aanschultz possessed the power to compensate for the darkness's distortion, much as chromatic aberration may be compensated for or avoided entirely by the use of an apochromatic lens. But I had little hope for this in my friend's case. Have I mentioned that it was his cruelty which chiefly attracted me?

ABAXIAL

Away from the axis. A term applied to the oblique or marginal rays passing through a lens. Thus, the light of our story is inevitably deflected from its most straightforward path by the medium of the *Encyclopaedia* itself, and this entry in particular. Would that it were otherwise, and this a perfect world. Some go so far as to state that the entirety of Creation is itself an

ABERRATION

A functional result of optical law. Yet I felt that this matter might be considered Aanschultz's fault, despite my unwillingness to think any ill of my friend. In my professional capacity, I was surrounded constantly by the fat and the beautiful; the lazy, plump, and pretty. They flocked to my studio in hordes, in droves, in carriages and cars, in swan-necked paddle boats; and their laughter flowed up and down the three flights of stairs to my studios and galleries, where my polite assistants bade them sit and wait until *Monsieur Artiste* might be available. Sometimes Monsieur failed to appear at all, and they were forced with much complaining to be photographed by a mere apprentice, at a reduced rate, although I always kept plenty of presigned plates on hand so that they might take away an original and be outwardly as impressive as their friends, despite inward dismay. I flirted with the ladies, was indulgent with the children; I spoke to the gentlemen about rates of exchange, the crisis in labor, the inevitable collapse of economies. I was, in short, a chameleon, softer than any of them, lazier and more variable, yet prouder. They meant nothing to me; they were all so easy and pretty and (I thought then) expendable.

Yet there was only one Aanschultz. On the only day he came to sit for me (he had decided to require his staff to wear tintype security badges), I knew I had never met his like. He looked hopelessly out of place in my waiting chambers, awkward on the steep stairs, white and etiolated in the diffuse cuprous light of my abat-jour. Yet his eyes were livid; he had violet pupils, and I wished—not for the first time—that there were some way of capturing color with all my clever lenses and cameras. None of my staff colorists could hope to duplicate that hue.

The fat pleasant women flocking the studios grew thin and uncomfortable at the sight of him, covering their mouths with handkerchiefs, exuding sharp perfumes of fear that neutralized their ambergris and artificial scents. He did not leer or bare his teeth or rub his hands and cackle; these obvious melodramatic motions would only have cheapened and blunted the sense one had of his refined cruelty.

Perhaps cruel is the wrong word. It was a severity in his nature—an unwillingness to tolerate any thought, sensation, or companion duller than a razor's edge. I felt instantly stimulated by his presence, as if I had at last found someone against whom I could gauge myself, not as opponent or enemy, but as a student who forever tries and tests himself against the model of his mentor. In my youth I had known instinctively that it is always better to stay near those I considered my superiors; for then I could never let my own skills diminish, but must constantly be polishing and practicing them. With age and success, I had nearly forgotten that crucial lesson, having sheltered too long in the cozy nests and parlors of Society. Aanschultz's laboratory proved to be their perfect antidote.

We two could not have been less alike. As I have said, I had no clear understanding of, and only slightly more interest in, the natural sciences. Art was All, to me. It had been my passion and my livelihood for so long now that I had nearly forgotten there was any other way of life. Aanschultz reintroduced me to the concepts of hard speculation and experimentation, a lively curriculum which soon showed welcome results in my own artistic practices. Certain competitors had mastered my methods and now offered similar services at lower prices, lacking only the fame of my name to beat me out of business. In the coltish marketplace, where economies trembled beneath the rasping tongue of forces so bleak they seemed the product of one's own fears, with no objective source in the universe, it began to seem less than essential to possess an extraordinary signature on an otherwise ordinary photograph; why spend all that money for a Name when just down the street, for two-thirds the price, one could have a photograph of equivalent quality, lacking only my famous florid autograph (of which, after all, there already was a glut)? So you see, I was in danger already when I met Aanschultz, without yet suspecting its encroachment. But with his aid I was soon able to improve the quality of my product far beyond the reach of my competitors. Once more my name reclaimed its rightful magic potency, not for empty reasons, not through mere force of advertising, but because of my objective superiority.

To all of Paris I might have been a great man, an artistic genius, but in Aanschultz's presence I felt like a young and stupid child. The scraps I scavenged from his workshop floors were not even the shavings of his important work. He hardly knew the good he did me, for although an immediate bond developed between us, at times he hardly seemed aware of my presence. I would begin to think that he had forgotten me completely; weeks might pass when I heard not a word from him; and then, suddenly, my faith in our friendship would be reaffirmed, for out of all the people he might have told—his scientific peers, politicians, the wealthy—he would come to me first with news of his latest breakthrough, as if my opinion were of greatest importance to him. I fancied that he looked to me for artistic inspiration (no matter how much he might belittle the impulse) just as I came to him for his scientific rigor.

It was this rigor which at times bordered on cruelty—though only when emotion was somehow caught in the slow, ineluctably turning gears of his logic. He would not scruple to destroy a scrap of human fancy with diamond drills and acid blasts in order to discover some irreducible atom of hard fact (+10 on the Mohs' scale) at its core. This meant, unfortunately, that each of his advances had left a trail of crushed "victims," not all of whom had thrown themselves willingly before the juggernaut of his ambition.

I sensed that this poor girl would soon be one of them.

ABRASION MARKS

of a curious sort covered her arms, something like a cross between bruises, burns, and blistering. Due to my own eczema, I felt a sympathetic pang as she backed away from the levers of the abat-noir, Aanschultz brushing her off angrily to make the final adjustments himself. She looked very young to be working such long hours in the darkness, so near the source of those strange black rays, but when I mentioned this to my friend he merely swept a hand in the direction of another part of the room, where a thin woman lay stretched out on a stained pallet, her arm thrown over her eyes, head back, mouth gaping; at first she appeared as dead as the drowned poseur Hippolyte Bayard, but I saw her breast rising and falling raggedly. The girl at the lever moved painfully to this woman and knelt down beside her, tenderly laying her head on the barely moving breast so that I knew them for mother and child. Leaving Aanschultz for the moment, I sank down beside them, stroking the girl's frayed black hair gently as I asked if there were anything I could do for them.

"Who's there?" the woman said hoarsely.

I gave my name, but she appeared not to recognize it. She had no need for illustrious visitors now, I knew.

"He's the Professor's friend," the child said, scratching vigorously at her arms though it obviously worsened them. I could see red, oozing meat through the scratches her fingernails left.

"You should bandage those arms," I said. "I have sterile cloth and ointment in my carriage if you'd like me to do it."

"Bandages and ointment, he says," said the woman. "As if there's any healing it. Leave her alone now—she's done what she could where I had to leave off. You'll just get the doctor mad at both of us."

"I'm sure he'd understand if I—"

"Just leave us be!" the woman howled, sitting up now, propped on both hands so that her eyes came uncovered, to my horror; for across her cheeks, forehead, and nose was an advanced variety of the same damage her daughter suffered; her eye sockets held little heaps of charred ash that, as she thrust her face forward in anger, poured like black salt from between her withered lids and sifted softly onto the floor, reminding me unavoidably of that other and most excellent abrading powder which may be rubbed on dried negatives to provide a "tooth" for the penciler's art, consisting of one part powdered resin and two parts cuttlefish bone, the whole being sifted through silk. I suspected this powder would do just as well, were I crass enough to gather it in my kerchief. She fell back choking and coughing on the black dust, beating at the air while her daughter moved away from me in tears; they both jumped when they heard Aanschultz's sharp command. I turned to see my friend beckoning with one crooked finger for the girl to come and hold the levers just so while he screwed down a clamp.

"My God, Aanschultz," I said, without much hope of a satisfactory answer. "Don't you see what your darkness has done to these wretches?"

He muttered from the side of his mouth: "Let the girl do her work, or do it for her."

I backed away quickly, wishing things were otherwise; but in those days Aanschultz and his peers need have feared no distracting investigations from the occupational safety inspectors. He could with impunity remain oblivious to everything but the work that absorbed him.

ABSORPTION

This term is used in a chemical, an optical, and an esoteric sense. The first designates the taking up of one substance by another, just as a sponge absorbs or sucks up water, with no chemical change involved; this is the least esoteric meaning, roughly akin to those surface phenomena which Aanschultz hoped to strip aside.

Optically, absorption is applied to the suppression of light, and to it are due all color effects, including the dense, dark stippling of the pores of Aanschultz's face, ravaged by the pox in early years, and the weird violet aura—the same color as his eyes, as if it had bled out of them—that limned his profile as he bent closer to that weirdly angled aperture into artificial darkness.

My friend, with unexpected consideration for my lack of expertise, now said: "According to Draper's law, only those rays which are absorbed by a substance act chemically on it; when not absorbed, light is converted into some other form of energy. This dark beam converts matter in ways heretofore unsuspected, and is itself transformed into a new substance. Give me my phantospectroscope."

The girl hurriedly retrieved a well-worn astrolabe-like device from a concealed cabinet and pressed it into her master's hands.

"The spectrum is like nothing ever seen on this earth," he said, pulling aside the rack of filter bottles and bending toward his abatnoir with the phantospectroscope at his eye, like a sorcerer stooping to divine the future in the embers of a hearth where some sacrifice has just done charring. I could not bear the cold heat of that unshielded black fire. I took several quick steps back.

"This will be the foundation of a new science. Until now, visual methods of spectral inspection have been confined to the visible portion of the spectrum; the ultraviolet and infrared regions gave way before slow photographic methods; and there we came to a halt. But I have gone beyond that now. Ha! Yes!"

He thrust the phantospectroscope back into the burned hands of his assistant and made a final adjustment to the levers that controlled the angle and intensity of rays conducted through the abat-noir. As the darkness deepened in that clinical space, it dawned on me that the third and deepest meaning of absorption was something like worship, and not completely dissimilar to terror.

ACCELERATOR!

my friend shouted, and I sensed rather than saw the girl moving toward him, but far too slowly. He screamed again, and now there was a rush of bodies, a crush of them in the small corner of the room. A common accelerator, such as sodium carbonate or potassium hydrate (caustic potash), shortens the duration of development and brings out an image more quickly, but the images Aanschultz sought to capture required special attention. As is written in the *Encylopaedia of Photography* (1911, exoteric edition), "Accelerators cannot be used as fancy dictates." I threw myself back, fearful that otherwise I would be shoved through the gaping abat-noir and myself dissolve into that negative essence. I heard the girl mewling at my feet, trod on by her fellows, and I leaned to help her up. But at that moment there was a quickening in the evil corner, and I put my hands to a more instinctive use.

ACCOMMODATION OF THE EYE

The darkness cupped inside my palms seemed welcoming by comparison to the anti-light that had emptied the room of all meaning. With both eyes covered, I felt I was beyond harm. I could not immediately understand the source of the noises and commotion I heard around me, nor did I wish to. (*See also* Axial Accommodation.)

ACCUMULATOR

Apparently (and this I worked out afterward in the hospital beside Aanschultz) the room had absorbed its fill of the neutralizing light. All things threatened to split at their seams. Matter itself, the atmosphere, Aanschultz's assistants, bare thought, creaking metaphor—all these were stuffed to the bursting point. My own mind was a peaking crest of images and insights, a wave about to break. Aanschultz screamed incomprehensible commands as he realized the sudden danger; but there must have been no one who still retained the necessary self-control to obey him. My friend leaped to reverse the charge, to shut down the opening, sliding the rack of filtering jars back in place—but even he was too late to prevent one small, significant rupture.

I heard the inexplicable popping of corks, accompanied by a simultaneous metallic grating, followed by the shattering of glass. Aanschultz later whispered of what he had glimpsed out of the edges of his eyes, and by no means can I—nor would I—discredit him.

It was the bottles and jars in the filter rack that burst. Or rather, some burst—curved glass shards and gelatinous contents flying, spewing, dripping, clotting the floor and ceiling, spitting backward into the bolt-hole of night. Other receptacles opened with more deliberation. Aanschultz later blushed when he described, with perfect objectivity, the sight of certain jar lids unscrewing themselves from within. The dripping and splashes and soft wet steps I heard, he said, bore an actual correspondence in physical reality, but he refused ever to detail exactly what manner of things, curdled there and quickened in those jars by the action of that deep black light, leaped forth to scatter through the laboratory, slipping between the feet of his assistants, scurrying for the shadows, bleeding away between the planks of the floor and the cracks of our minds, seeping out into the world. My own memory is somewhat more distorted by emotion, for I felt the girl clutching at my ankles and heard her terrible cries. I forced myself to tear my hands away from my face—while still keeping my eyes pressed tightly shut—and leaned down to offer help. No sooner had I taken hold of her fingers than she began to scream more desperately. Fearing that I was aggravating her wounds, I relaxed my hands to ease her pain; but she clung even more tightly to my hands and her screams intensified. It was as if I were her final anchor. As soon as I realized this, as soon as I tried to get a better hold on her, she slipped away. I heard her mother calling. The girl's cries were smothered. Across the floor rushed a liquid seething, as of a sudden flood draining from the room and down the abat-noir and out of the laboratory entirely. My first impulse was to follow, but I could no longer see a thing, even with my eyes wide open.

"A light!" I shouted, and Aanschultz overlapped my own words with his own: "No!"

But too late. The need for fire was instinctive, beyond Aanschultz's ability to quell by force or reason. A match was struck, a lantern lit and instantly in panic dropped; and as we fled onrushing flames, in that instant of total exposure, Aanschultz's most ambitious and momentous experiment reached its climax . . . although the dénouement for Europe and the rest of the world would be a painful and protracted one.

ACETALDEHYDE

See Aldehyde.

ACETIC ACID

The oldest of acids, used in early days as a constituent of the developer for wet plates, later for clearing iron from bromide prints, to assist in uranium toning, and as a restrainer. It is extremely volatile.

ACETIC ETHER

Synonym, ethyl acetate. A light, colorless volatile liquid with pleasant acetous smell, sometimes used in making collodion. It should be kept in well-stoppered bottles away from fire, as the vapor is very inflammable.

ACETONE

A colorless volatile liquid of peculiar and characteristic odor, with two separate and distinct uses in photography: as an addition to developers and in varnish making. The vapor is highly inflammable.

ACETOUS ACID

The old, and now obsolete, name for acetic acid (*which see*). Highly inflammable.

ACETYLENE

A hydrocarbon gas having, when pure, a sweet odor. It is formed by the action of water upon calcium carbide, one pound of which will yield about five feet of gas. It burns in air with a very bright flame, and is used by photographers for studio lighting, for copying, and as an illuminant in enlarging and projection lanterns. Acetylene, like other combustible gases, forms an explosive mixture with ordinary air, the presence of as little as 4 percent being sufficient to constitute a dangerous combination.

ACETYLENE GENERATOR

An apparatus for generating acetylene by the action of water on calcium carbide. Copper should not be employed in acetylene generators, as under certain conditions a detonating explosive compound is formed.

ACETYLIDE EMULSION

Wratten and Mees prepared a silver acetylide emulsion by passing acetylene into an ammoniacal solution of silver nitrate and emulsifying the precipitate, which is highly explosive. While this substance blackens about ten times faster than silver chloride paper, for years observers failed to detect any evidence of latent image formation and concluded that insights gained in Professor Conreid Aanschultz's laboratory were of no lasting significance. This misunderstanding is attributed to the fact that, despite the intensity of exposure, it has taken more than a century for certain crucial images to emerge, even with the application of strong developers. We are only now beginning to see what Aanschultz glimpsed in an instant.

> *What man may hereafter do, now that Dame Nature has become his drawing mistress, is impossible to predict.*
>
> —Michael Faraday

END

STRAIGHT HINCTY

RICARDO CORTEZ CRUZ

Just because you have been married doesn't mean you're in love.
— Rick James, rhythm-and-blues singer,
circa 1987

ON A DOWNRIGHT unfaithful and violent night after James Brown gave her his barbecue rib in a Harlem hotel room, Zu-Zu Girl decided to comb the superkinky streets of the Big Apple to find a better Home and Garden than the one she had with the almost-broke so-called vocalist, saxophonist, and guitar player she was screwing in a condemned office building behind his honky wife's back.

Zu-Zu was living in Queens, but, as a two-and-a-half-months pregnant "bitch" and "trick," which is what this no-good nigga had increasingly been calling her during their get-togethers, she felt it was time to dis his black ass and think about seeing a doctor or something. Headed toward the Tri-State area, Zu-Zu slowly marched down the black face of Martin Luther King Boulevard, the wind pushing trash around her legs, niggas outside in the street despite the turbulent conditions, many of them cracking up for no good reason and looking for rocks as if they were going to throw them inside Spike Lee's Joint. Zu-Zu kept on walking, every street following her like the blues, Girl carrying a license-to-ill, singing "Precious Lord, Take My Hand" and "Mama's Gone, Goodbye," even her shadow blue.

On her way to the subway, she stopped on the sidewalk talk to peep the window of a black-owned store. She saw Rap's *Die Nigger Die* on sale. Girl almost tripped out. She pounded the window, her black black face occasionally pressing against the glass, her bare feet accidentally wiping the dirty names off the graffiti where she stood. Customers went in and out, but no one paid her any attention.

So in front of the window, Zu-Zu pulled out a bomb and lit it, the cigarette leaning on the corner of her mouth like a hooker, a black cloud hanging around her and the nigger-joint. Between smokes, she paused and waited for men to pass by so she could kick up dry salt at them and say goodnight. Or was it goodbye? Oh well, it really didn't matter because either way they would get it: She was tired of niggas trying to be like Lenny Kravitz (with Madonna) or Charlie Parker, laying some heavy stuff on her as if she were carpet and not expressing a single feeling for her.

"Get yo' black face out of the window!" the fat owner of the store finally shouted, his black-and-white television showing Cops where Charlie Irvine is on the freeway beating and arresting a buck-naked brown brother who is staring into the camera like a deer in headlights waiting to be hit.

Zu-Zu blew the store owner a death kiss and let the lipstick bleeding on his window tell him that he had just got himself involved with a horror/whore.

Like Zu-Zu's Uncle Tom before he molested her, the store owner tucked in his white shirt and approached the door, his big black hand still feeling on his Fruit-of-the-Loom and Boyz II Men's song "Uhh-Ahh" on his mind.

Zu-Zu pointed at his body. "You livin' large," she said.

"Get away from the window!" he answered. "You'll bust the glass with yo' bean head, and I'd have to get in yo' stuff for sure then! You'd be screaming 'bout how I hurt you." He pointed to her loose skirt being blown between her thighs by the nasty wind.

Zu-Zu spat on the window. He gave her the finger. "You little mustard face, pumpkinhead, devil-bitch," he said. "Get away from the window before you break it and end up gettin' yourself hurt like that LaTasha Harlins girl!" He grabbed his crotch and told her to stay if she wanted some.

"I'm a private dancer," Zu-Zu yelled, "dancin' for money. But someday, I'll take you out, sweetheart. Someday."

Zu-Zu spat once more on the glass and then moved the crowd and blended her black face in with the inner-city blues, all of it making her wanna holler, making her look toward Birdland and wonder what had happened to God's trombones.

Zu-Zu Girl beat the rocks, just like she used to in Double Dutch, her butt wiggling like it was trying to avoid being lassoed by rope. After first jumping and skipping, she flew toward the subway like a bluebird, her sole/soul all cut up from the time she spent on the curb.

Zu-Zu was freaked out. All she wanted was to be alone, free as a singing park sparrow. She thought she had gotten away until she heard footsteps in the dark as if the Isley Brothers were chasing her, bringing her yet another caravan of love with long gold chains hanging around their wet greasy necks like black cottonmouth snakes while they drank hard liquor, Mad Dog everywhere.

Her sugar daddy always marched through the streets like a fucked-up one-man band. He was a crazy nigga who was constantly changing colors like a chameleon. To quote him, he was indeed a "player," but he had no idea how bad he was. Every now and then, basically when he felt like it, he'd come to a concert and hit on a sexy woman like a one-man gang, his dumb wife nowhere around to stop him. Zu-Zu could only hope that he hadn't been experimenting with The Chronic, too.

When Zu-Zu heard the roar of an approaching subway train, she started flying back toward the King street, the black train drowning her screams, kissing her booty goodbye.

Even if Zu-Zu had been Vanessa Williams singing "Can This Be Real," she wouldn't have won any beauty contests the way she carried on. But just because she screamed and cried and hollered all the way down the street like she was having a baby, it didn't mean that she was weak. She was scared for her life, which for her was nothing but a walking shadow, but somebody had to protect it.

Since she wasn't rich or white enough to own a Sprint calling card that could save her life in a pay phone, Zu-Zu stumbled into an alley that ended with a fence and stood there tripping, the chain-link calling her and poking at her behind her back, feeling her booty like it had never had any before. With the fence against her, Girl waited for her attacker. She was a bit hysterical, but ready to do him, gripping a nigger-flicker in her right hand that would chop him down to size.

"Come and get it," she said. It was like waiting to put an electric cable in the mouth of a shark.

After a group of black teenage boys ran past the entrance of the alley with crowbars (crow bars), he finally approached her directly, where she could see him. He wore knee-length black leather boots with large heels. His polyester shirt was unbuttoned, the hairs on his chest showing like sutures where women's long painted fingernails had tore up his chest and stomach and he had tried to put himself back together. He fired up a joint and blew smoke in Zu-Zu's face, charbroiling her lips and nose into gallstones. Zu-Zu watched him cop and blow. He shook his jerry-curl in front of her, spraying glycerin and Sta-Sof in her face. Then he pushed her further up against the fence.

"When I came to yo' place of business last night," he said, "you wouldn't even talk to me. Then I find out in the street you've been chasin' other niggas like a little groupie." He pulled out a tired forty-five vinyl single of "Big Payback" and stuck the chipped edge of it in her throat, the record's red label bleeding onto the black skin.

"Ricky, that ain't me," Zu-Zu said, squirming to buy herself time. "You got the wrong 'bitch.' The first time ever I saw your face . . ."

"Shut up!" he said. "Bitches ain't shit but hoes and tricks." He blew weed up her nose.

Zu-Zu closed her nose, pushed him back, and showed him the nigger-flicker, pointing the razor at his nipples.

Blood peeped his unbuttoned shirt and rushed to his brain, begging him to forget about her.

"Shut up!" he yelled again. "I'm bustin' out, and I don't give a damn. If you don't like my funk, then take yo' stuff and scram."

Zu-Zu Girl had orange-brown squash for breasts but did the best she could to flaunt it, set 'em out. "Come and get it," she said.

He wouldn't bite, wouldn't take the bait. "Give it to me, baby," he said.

"Lovin' you ain't easy cause you're beautiful," said Zu-Zu Girl, her voice like Minnie Riperton singing "la, la, la, la, la." "You ain't too far gone to see that yet. You trippin', baby, cause you think your rocks are precious stones. For you, everything turns into drama now. It's as if you got Spike Lee's joint in yo' mouth."

Blood sucked dope and laughed. "I'm in love with Mary Jane," he said. "She's my main thang. It comes as no surprise. She takes me to paradise."

Standing on a heap of trash, Zu-Zu spread her legs against the chain-link like a slave. "Come on, baby, come into my life," she said.

He smacked Girl across the bridge of her nose. She felt pain like her nose had been reconstructed.

"I'm cold-blooded," he said.

"Then today is a good day," said Zu-Zu. She stabbed him with the knife.

Blood grabbed her hand and cracked up, the chain-link still feeling her booty, red mascara masking the look of a woman who had just found her thrill.

He approached her breasts like a rapist, a neurotic who takes things into his own hands. She kicked his rocks. He cracked up, fragments of crack falling out of his marijuana cigarette. She spat in his face. He wiped off the saliva and stuck out his tongue. She slit it.

Blood looked surprised. He fell to his knees and released her from the chain. She dogged him in self-defense. She carved a hole in his big head and inserted a tube of hot-pink lipstick.

She took off his clothes and, with a tube of red lipstick, drew on the pavement an outline of a human figure sprawled out. Then she rolled his black body inside the drawing. The look was trendy, in fashion with the lifestyles of the poor and nonfamous.

It was only by coincidence that the coppers saw her a few minutes later. They were happily doing their routine, so they parked their white squad car on King Boulevard, slowly walked down the alley and asked her what happened, holding their sticks in front of Zu-Zu.

Her blouse all open, and hovering over the body like a buzzard showing a bird chest, Zu-Zu straightened up to fly right since it was her word against his.

"I tried to stop him, coppers," said Zu-Zu. "But he was tripping when he came up from behind and attacked me. I sprayed him with a can of Mace, but he kept coming, cussin' and swearin' like a blind splib or butter head or member snapping. 'Shut up!' he said, trying to stop me from screaming. In self-defense, I grabbed the knife out of his hand and sliced off his big lips, silencing him forever. I was sitting here, waiting for the police, when some gang-bangers came by, robbed him and finished him for good, took what they wanted from me, and drew an outline around his body as a joke to suggest that the murder was premeditated. Don't look at me. I ain't no murderer. I swear. I'm just a nightclub performer singing for money and men who like speakeasies."

"Sure," the coppers said. They dragged her down the alley by her wrists and hair.

When they got back to the entrance of the alley, one of them stopped and looked at the gusting wind tearing up the street sign of Martin Luther King Boulevard. "Everything is finally going haywire," he said.

"Where you taking me?" Zu-Zu asked.

"Sing sing prison," they said.

"I got the Harlem blues," Zu-Zu said.

"We want you to exercise your right and remain silent," they said. "If you don't do what we want, this might be the last time you're ever gonna see Soul City and its shady places."

Zu-Zu spat in their piggish faces, carefully reaching into the elasticity of her skirt for the nigger-flicker while the coppers were looking to see where her spit had gone.

They pushed her big head into the car, laughing, holding on to their guns.

"Show time," said one of the coppers, getting into the car with her. Quickly, he stripped his Rolex and shoved it into his pants pocket. The other one searched the front seat for popcorn, then turned around to watch as if the time had come, Zu-Zu fake-hollering and screaming like a tar baby, the knife by her side waiting to slowly cut into his thick skin, the black woman vowing "no justice, no peace/piece" in a low voice hushed inside the car as it sat in the middle of rage. The blues and Girl rocked the car asleep while King watched amidst the gusts like a drum major in the middle passage letting the white man know when to stroke.

HOSTILE TAKEOVER

CRAIG PADAWER

AND THEN ONE night Swann's armored cars rolled into town, and the consolidation of flesh began.

They hit Ho's first, blasting their way past his sumos and into the pimp's private parlor, where his ninja waited. But even Ho's master assassin was no match for Shimmy G's high-tech killers with their Black & Decker implants and their five-speed rotating blades. They'd diced the ninja like a carrot and then fed the pieces to Ho with his jade chopsticks before they finally killed him as well. Then they ground his geishas into tofu and continued north to The Hairy Clam, where they shot all the fish in Felsig's barrel. Real sportsmen, Swann's chromeheads. They stood at poolside with their telescopic eye implants and their 9-mm semiautomatic arm grafts . . . firing, reloading, and firing again, picking off patrons in the glass-bottom boats, murdering the mermaids as they tried to take cover beneath the inflatable lily pads, filling the porpoises so full of lead that they sank like submarines to the bottom of the tank.

The Clam's kitchen just happened to have run out of the house specialty at 11:00 that night and had called in an emergency order of littlenecks to Veraciti's Seafood Supply, which had dispatched a truck immediately. They were just unloading the shellfish when Swann's goons struck. Felsig managed to slip out through the kitchen and escape in the fish king's refrigerated delivery truck accompanied by six cartons of red snapper filets, a pair of halibut hanging on hooks, and a crate of clams that chattered at him like a bundle of bones as the driver hit what seemed like every pothole between Harbor Street and the fish pier. Back at The Clam, Swann's chrome killers were snapping drill bits into their multi-function wrist sockets and boring holes in the skulls of Felsig's kitchen staff in an attempt to discover his whereabouts, as if in their mechanical naïveté the overhauled imbeciles imagined that language was a liquid bottled up inside the body and any hole would decant it. In fact, the busboys had leaked as soon as they got a look at the hardware on Shimmy G's hoodlums, but the toolheads hadn't liked what they'd heard and they drilled the pimp's busboys dry, their gears seizing with rage. When that failed to produce Felsig, they burst into The Clam's plush grottoes, pried open the pimp's patented shell beds, shucked his nymphs, and minced them like mollusks. Then they blew the bottom out of the glass lagoon, drowning the diners below and flooding Harbor Street from Cod Place to Waterfront Drive.

Meanwhile, a second unit struck at the cash gash end of Harbor Street and was moving south toward the blue-chip houses, gunning down street pimps and freelancers along the way, fire-bombing the budget brothels and the fast-fuck joints. They blew the lid off the Dick-in-the-Box on Eel Street, leveled the Wiener Queen, and wiped The Bun Factory right off the block. They hit the Instant Eatery on the corner of Harbor and Tuna Street, and some tax adder with her muff up against the drive-in window was divested of her assets along with the hired tongue who was deliv-ering her Slurpy to her through the hole in the bulletproof glass.

While their counterparts to the south finished off Felsig's and moved on to The Sweat Shop, the northern unit raided The Side Show and Tufa's Club Zoo, neither of which had heavy security. The houses fell like dominoes. Swann's antitank missiles turned Tufa's elephants into hamburger, while what was left of the pimp's menagerie stampeded south, trampling wounded bathhouse boys and hookers hobbling along on broken heels. A small detachment of mechanical thugs remained behind to mop up the top end of Harbor Street while the northern unit's main force headed west on

Oyster to take Rocheaux's office and knock out Brash, Sarsen & Scree's flagship facility. Then the troops regrouped two blocks south for an assault on The Rubber Womb.

Merkle had invested heavily in the latest weaponry and The Womb had a formidable security force, despite the mocking comments made by Merkle's colleagues. Vesuvius, who liked to boast about his own rented muscle, had once told Emma with a sneer that Merkle's inflatable bodyguards were "full of hot air."

"Hydrogen," Merkle corrected him, having overheard the remark.

"Hot air, hydrogen . . . same shit," Vito spat.

"I'm afraid you're quite mistaken. There's a definitive difference, Vito, and if you get any closer to Emile here with that vile cigar of yours, you'll discover it firsthand . . . and then foot, nose, teeth, and liver. In short, my friend, they'll be sweeping your pieces off the street."

"Pshshhhh!" Vito hissed derisively, his head snapping back as if he'd been slugged in the chin, smoke spewing from his mouth.

Merkle turned to Emma. "Good night, Ms. Labatt," he said. "You're to be commended on your tolerance, but surely a businesswomen of your caliber recognizes a profitless endeavor when she sees one." With that he wrapped his rubber scarf around his throat and slipped into the bulletproof overcoat being offered by one of his bodyguards. Then he bowed to Emma, pulled the brim of his black rubber fedora down over his brow with a squeak, and walked off flanked by four of his inflatable escorts.

"Hey, Merkle," Vesuvius had shouted after him. "Fuck you, ya dumb bastard. You call that protection? They're nothing but a buncha fuckin' balloons. That's right, fuckin' buncha rubber scumbags with faces painted on 'em, that's all. It's like tryna stop a bullet with a goddamn condom, fer chrissake. Hey! Tell ya what, Merkle . . . I'll have my boys cut a hole in one of those balloon goons a yours and I'll wear him on my dick when I fuck your mother. How 'bout that? How's that for fuckin' protection? Hey, maybe you oughta fold one up and carry him in your wallet, cause that's all the protection they're gonna give ya."

In the end, Vito was right, not just about Merkle's security force, but about his entire inflatable enterprise. It was a credit to the pimp's miraculous craftsmanship that his entire nightclub, from floor to ceiling, from light fixtures to plumbing to windows, was nothing more than an elaborate balloon. But that sort of evanescent intricacy was only so admirable. Merkle paid the price for his genius in vulnerability. His inflatable men proved to be no match for Swann's mechanical killers. The chromeheads went through The Rubber Womb like a nail through a beach ball. Pulling steel stickpins from their copper neckties, they popped Merkle's balloon goons and had at his dolls. Swann, who believed the penis was obsolete, an inefficient cord of meat vulnerable to viruses and vaginal bacteria, had replaced his killers' genitals with weaponry. Now the toolheads unzipped their flies, greased their barrels with balloon jelly, and rammed them up the rubber rectums of Merkle's dolls, pumping away until a twitch of pleasure in what remained of their flesh tripped their triggers, and they came in a burst of gunfire. The inflatable beauties popped like party balloons when the bullets struck, leaving their attackers clutching nothing but air and a few shreds of latex.

As johns jumped from the windows of The Womb and hoofed it up Harbor Street, Swann's clockwork killers went from room to rubber room, doing in Merkle's dolls, puncturing the air mattresses, the inflatable toilets, and the blow-up bathtubs. The air outside became so saturated with helium that Tufa's tigers sounded like tabbies as they fled down Harbor Street. Helium hissed from the inflatable walls and beams, and the nightclub began to collapse in on itself, to shrivel and fold, until finally the chrome assassins turned their flamethrowers on it, and The Womb went up with a *WHOOSH*. There was a single explosion as Merkle's hydrogen tank blew, and then it was over. All that remained of the club was a puddle of molten rubber.

Emma pushed through the bordello's revolving door and stepped out into the chaos of the street. Out on the avenue the traffic was frozen: drivers and passengers peered through their windows. The yap schlock hawkers and the cat dog vendors had left their carts and drifted to the curb like sleepwalkers summoned in a dream. She could hear animals howling, the braying of Tufa's pornographic donkeys. And beneath that another sound, a murmur like a mechanical parody of the harbor washing against the pier.

Then the northern end of Harbor Street seemed to explode with movement. Refugees began streaming into the square: barefoot house whores wrapped in satin sheets, queens in kimonos zig-zagging down the street like enormous butterflies as they tried to dodge the bullets that went zipping by. Jailbait and babymeat were borne along on a tide of trained tigers, inflatable whores, and wounded studs dressed in the Marquis de Sade's underwear. Emma saw a chimpanzee and a pair of Gneissman's naked midgets go galloping by on one of Tufa's zebras; they turned west on Ocean-side, weaving through the stalled traffic until she lost sight of them. The sound of gunfire grew closer. Bullets ricocheted off the mansion's facade. Panicky passengers left their cars and fled up the avenue on foot.

The remnants of Merkle's security force fell back along the water, pursued by Swann's goons. Emma could see the mechanical killers now. They wore titanium zoot suits and steel fedoras, and they came marching down Harbor Street looking like a fleet of tanks designed by Oleg Cassini. Some of them had machine gun assemblies built right into their skulls, and their grinning heads rotated 360 degrees as they raked the streets with gunfire. Merkle's hydrogen hoodlums went off like incendiary bombs when the slugs hit them. Those who hadn't been hit returned fire with Uzis and Street Sweepers, but the bullets didn't even put a dent in the enemy's wardrobe.

As Emma ordered her women to pull back from the street, she could see Merkle's men tossing aside their weapons, stepping out of their lead loafers and floating up into the night sky, rising above the flaming streets like rubber angels, until the wind carried them out over the harbor. Some of them would drift for days or weeks, finally floating to earth somewhere on the coast of Greenland or Labrador, where they would vainly hunt for helium like vampires hungry for blood, until finally, sagging and emaciated, they would expire on barren bluffs, where fishermen's wives would find them, take them home, and stitch them into raincoats for their sea-haunted husbands.

Back inside the mansion, Emma threw all her security at her front door, opened up the bar, and circulated among her customers to calm them. But as Swann's first army swept up from the south, the pincer closed, trapping the fleeing whores in the square. The desperate refugees stormed the mansion seeking asylum.

Emma prayed for fog to mask the carnage and inhibit the killers, but the night remained clear and the moon burned like a bulb. From the window she could see one of Galena's Gigantic Gigolos lying dead in the street, wearing nothing but his own blood. One of his coworkers crouched over him, moving like an astronaut in the merciless moonlight, his body so bloated with muscle he was barely able to bend. Over to the south a rocket struck G.A.S.M.'s headquarters and the old building burped smoke. Tracer fire arced across the square like a flock of burning birds. The two naked giants outside Emma's window looked now like a pair of Greek heroes that had been painted onto the wrong scenery: Achilles bawling over the death of his pornographic Patroclus as Paris fell to the Germans. A passing queen paused and began tugging at the mourner's arm with one hand as she clutched the front of her kimono closed with the other, but the giant wouldn't budge. She tried again, letting go of her robe and wrapping both her arms around his biceps, but it was like trying to uproot an oak tree. And then somehow the gigolo lost his balance and tipped backwards. He lay there in the gutter with his arms waving in the air, like some enormous beetle, so weighted down by his own muscle that he was unable to sit up or flip himself over. The queen flapped her arms and screamed for help, her kimono billowing behind her in the frigid wind. Her hormone-grown breasts were stunted and pale in the moonlight, her prick shaven clean as an infant's and shriveled now with fear.

A bunch of streetwalkers, ever practical, responded to the queen's distress by tugging off their whorehoppers and flinging them through the mansion's stained-glass windows in an attempt to get Emma's attention.

Hippolyta opened up the bordello's arsenal and began arming the patrons, the whores, and the housekeeping staff, then joined Emma at the window and nervously surveyed the scene. To the north, along the curve of the water, Swann's killers fired surface-to-surface missiles from their prosthetic-arm launchers, and the boardwalk crumbled like a cracker in the tracer light. Cabs burned out on the avenue, and flaming figures raced down the streets like human shish kebabs. The lobby smelled of sulfur and burning meat. Shimmy G's southern units were already on the outskirts of the square. The trapped refugees would have the option of being either driven into the frigid harbor or slaughtered in the streets.

As rocket fire began to eat up the asphalt, the blowjob boys and anal artists stormed Emma's steps. Rocheaux's brats tried to scale the fence and were impaled on the wrought-iron spikes, where they flapped like fish on the end of a spear and whined through the night like tortured cats. Merkle's girls also fell prey to the spikes: their corpses hung from the fence like an atman's laundry, and whores hoisted themselves up by the dolls' deflated limbs—but the bordello's windows were too high and there was nowhere for them to go. Bullets cut into the crowd. There were screams as the sea of flesh surged forward and washed up against the mansion's facade.

The cops were nowhere in sight. And for all Emma knew, these were Vito's soldiers, mail-ordered from some weapons warehouse in Georgia or Tennessee and kept under wraps until the moment was right. She had no choice but to open her doors.

That night her house took on the atmosphere of a field hospital. Her boudoirs were filled with wounded whores, and all her satin sheets went for bandages. Giles was busy in the kitchen boiling his old mechanic's tools in hot water and performing makeshift surgeries on the chrome countertops, prying slugs out of house whores with a Phillips screwdriver and a pair of needlenose pliers, and leaving it to Hector Citrine's seamstress to sew them up. They stacked the dead in the walk-in freezer. By dawn they were almost out of shelf space.

Even one of Merkle's helium whores managed to make it to Emma's place. She was leaking, and Giles patched her up with a piece of electrical tape, then gave her mouth-to-mouth in an attempt to reinflate her. She perked up for a while, but as the night wore on her head began to wilt again, wrinkles appeared in her face and thighs, her latex tits began to shrink and droop. She seemed to be aging right before their eyes. They pumped some more air into her, but it was no good. She needed helium. Or maybe she was leaking from a hole they hadn't seen. By morning she was as flat as a floor mat. Emma wondered whether she was dead. How could you tell with a blowup doll, anyway? What vital signs did you check for? Air pressure? Surface tension? Finally they just pulled the plug on her. What was left of her helium escaped in one brief sigh. Emma thought she felt the air in the room change ever so slightly, and she held her breath for a moment, as if she were afraid that by breathing she might inhale the whore's soul. Then she folded up the girl's empty skin and tucked it away in a drawer. By that point, all she could think of was that Merkle's ingenuity had saved her a space in the freezer.

She waited all night for the attack, but it never came. Swann's troops swung west, bypassing her bordello. A couple of hours later heavy artillery could be heard from the south. It went on for a solid hour. The mansion's beams rattled in the thunder, and plaster rained down from the kitchen ceiling like confectionery sugar, powdering the whores' open wounds so that their hearts and livers looked like candied fruits. Giles called for more water while Emma provided what suction she could with a turkey baster.

Toward dawn the gunfire began to die down. Outside the blood froze in the streets, and come morning children with ice skates appeared, carving figure eights in the crimson pools.

NOTES SCRIBBLED IN THE DARK WHILE WATCHING *SCHINDLER'S LIST,* OR WHAT PRICE SCHINDLER'S POTS & PANS?

RAYMOND FEDERMAN

EVERYBODY TELLS ME I should see this movie. Even President Clinton said so. So here I am.

I wonder what the German soldiers did with all the Pots & Pans Schindler's Jews fabricated in his factory? Did they use them for food or to piss in?

As the old Yiddish proverb says: You have to survive, even if it kills you.

But one must admit that Schindler's Big Deal about Pots & Pans makes the Holocaust viable as a popular mainstream movie.

This one is going to be big. I can tell. We're talking millions and millions of dollars here. Spielberg does it again.

Oskar is a director's dream. He brings such class and such easy redemption to the ghastly business of extermination.

What was the going rate then for a Jew? A Jew for a Pot, a Pot for a Jew?

Oskar manages to buy 1,100 Jews by selling his car, his elegant suits, his silk ties. Imagine how many more Jews could have been saved if the Pope had sold his limousines, his embroidered robes, his cute skull caps, his gold bijoux. *Deus Profundus*.

I like Oskar's suits. But where the hell does he buy these suits in Poland? Maybe a little Jewish tailor makes them for him before being unmade himself to be remade into a lampshade. And look at Oskar's beautiful cuff links?

This is a great movie, I mean technically. Since I know in advance what is going to happen, I can concentrate on the technique, the fine cuts, the close-ups, the long shots, the zooming in. I can also concentrate on the costumes and the makeup.

Presentation is the trick here. Oskar Schindler and Steven Spielberg are masters of presentation. And both of them are fantastic salesmen.

Interesting, there does not seem to be as much popcorn munching for this movie as with other movies.

Has anyone ever studied the semiotic implications of popcorn eating while watching a Holocaust movie?

It never occurred to me that Jews could be qualified to fabricate Pots & Pans. I always think of Jews as being good businesspeople, or else good tailors.

Amazing how this black-and-white movie seems so colorful.

Spielberg should have used more skinny extras for this movie. His victims seem too well-fed, too chubby, especially the women.

I found it funny that when I stood in line with all the people waiting to gain entrance into the theater, we were being ordered about by a young freckled theater employee (he had a punk haircut) who kept saying to us: *Schindler's List line up over here, form a double line*. It was a brazen command that could hardly have been shouted out by someone who had seen the film. I suppose the management, that day, had to use the popcorn vendor to organize the mass of people who wanted to see *Schindler's List*. It shows that people do listen to their president.

I wonder how many people noticed, a few frames back, that the coat of the little girl who is being herded away was colorized red. A touch of red in a black-and-white movie. What a touch! But maybe it was a flaw in the film?

I wonder if the Lady-Secretary-Slut who was with Schindler up on the hill watching the children being herded away also noticed the colorized red coat, or if this little epiphany was only for Schindler's eyes?

It occurs to me as I watch this movie that perhaps I should not be watching it. That I am out of place here. Out of time, too. Why do I feel so shitty? Don't tell me it's guilt. The guilt of knowing that no one died for me in the camps.

Yet this sordid affair must be told and told again and shown and shown again, and read and read again, and seen and seen again. I know that. And I know that I must keep on replaying that sordid story over and over again in my head, at the risk of being anachronistic, as Primo Levi put it.

Quand notre sang sera-t-il nettoyé de la saleté d'Auschwitz?

When will our blood be cleansed of the Auschwitz's filth? Sounds better in French.

How come neither my mother nor my sisters made Schindler's list? They were there. I know they were there. There are records of that. I am sure that my mother and my sisters would have done a good job in Schindler's factory making Pots & Pans. But not my father. No. My father was too much of an intellectual to be able to do good work with his hands in a factory.

Oskar Schindler as a character in this movie seems more mature, more grown-up than most of the characters I have seen in Steven Spielberg's other movies. Usually Spielberg's characters, even the adults, cannot suppress their yearning to get back to childhood. That's a plus for Spielberg in this movie; maybe he is growing out of his infantilism.

Still, one must admire Spielberg for making this movie. I suppose he had to. As Maimonides once put it: *Every Jew is like an actor playing a Jew, each gives his own interpretation of the past.* Spielberg, too, has a right to his interpretation—not as an actor, but as a director. But then every Jew thinks of himself as a director of something. I was once the Director of a Creative Writing Program.

Wow! What a movie! I mean the style. It is so calculated. So precise. So in place. Spielberg is really something. But it's interesting to see how he has not yet found a way of making a movie without congratulating himself at the same time. I am not criticizing him. I do the same in my own work.

Neeson is good, I mean as an actor. He has hollow panache, a flat sexy look, a connoisseur's calm, untidy emotionalism with no core, and that spacious face waiting for us to guess what he is thinking. He is all seduction. But I think the guy who plays the commandant of the camp, Goeth, is a much better actor. He is more credible, more scary. Even the fat around his waist is more real than Oskar's glamorous looks.

Still, I must admit that the glibness and the beauty of this movie are for a good cause. This movie is educational. And besides, Americans are so easily moved to tears. Americans tear-jerk at the least bit of emotional disturbance.

Schindler's List makes people weep tears of gratitude. But how can anyone be grateful for the Holocaust? Yes, this movie makes people feel good about the Holocaust. Hard to believe that one can feel good about such an unforgivable enormity. But then this is just a story with a happy ending; the Holocaust is used here only as a backdrop. A fiction.

Me, usually, when watching a movie, I wonder how they do it. How they fool me, how they make me believe that the little boy who just got shot by Goeth is really dead and not faking it. After all, I heard the sound of the bullet leave the gun and heard it enter the little boy's skull. I saw the crushed skull, and the blood, even though shown in black-and-white. I heard that, I saw that. Or was it an illusion?

It was said that Jews were in third place on the list of the people Americans feared most. Germans were first and Japanese second. This, of course, was said during the Holocaust, while the final solution was going on. Why am I thinking of this in the middle of this movie?

Maybe such events as the Holocaust should never be recreated, so that we can only judge them, look at them in the way spies look at secret documents.

Still there is news here for the young and the ignorant, and there is also the pleasure of great filmmaking craft, alas.

Why am I constantly confusing this movie with *Jurassic Park*? Is it because both movies are about extinction? Or rather because both are an effort, a vain effort, okay, to bring back into the light what has been extinguished?

Stern. I like Stern. But how much truer the relationship between Schindler and his accountant would have been if at the end Oskar would have walked away from Stern without shaking his hands, without recognizing the bound of . . . of what? Yes, how much more in character it would have been for Schindler to casually laugh off the whole thing—the bound with Stern, and the Pots & Pans.

Why do I keep thinking in the middle of all these Pots & Pans what a tough little great survivor Primo Levi was, before he cracked.

Can humanity continue to exist without redemption? No, I mean, can movies, Hollywood movies, really work without redemption?

Spielberg & Schindler—SS & OS—in this movie are willing to go inside the gas chambers and look around because they know they can come out. Could I do that?

I suppose it's inevitable now that Holocaust T-shirts are going to pop up all over the place, and also Holocaust victim dolls, Holocaust toys, Holocaust bumper stickers, Holocaust Pots & Pans. Well, all that will help the economy.

Interesting how today the people are staying to read the credits at the end. I always wonder why so often these days they give us the credits at the end. Maybe it's because at the beginning they want to plunge us into the action as quickly as possible. But then a lot of people walk out on the credits. You can't have your cake and eat it too. But today everybody is still here, still sitting or standing, reading the credits. Maybe they feel they missed something. That there is more to this story.

I am out of here.

Oh wait . . . wait . . . what's that? AN AMBLIN ENTER-TAINMENT—copyright 1994. Now that's interesting. You mean to tell me that *Schindler's List* was produced by an **entertainment** company? That's a good one.

Wow, was it hot in there.

* * * * *
* * *
*

AFTERTHOUGHT

Is it possible that during the many visits I have made to Germany since the war, I accidentally crossed in the streets of Berlin or Munich or some other Burg the person who pushed my mother into the gas chamber? Or that I sat in a restaurant or at a concert (a Wagner opera—I am a fanatic of Wagner's operas) next to the man who beat my father to death with the butt of his rifle? Or that in a comfortable first-class compartment of the ultrarapid ICE train I sat across the former SS who raped my sisters before strangling them? Oh what a horrible thought.

HAND WRITING ON WALL

PROFITS

RONALD SUKENICK

ONE OF OUR personalities is a *tummler*. A comic, a crazy. At a precocious age he wanted to be a wild-tongued word twister like Danny Kaye, who was from his Brooklyn neighborhood. Or a suave ventriloquist like Edgar Bergen. Or even a dummy like Charlie McCarthy. But a star. Some kind of star. To loudmouth his way out of Brooklyn. Or talk softly, maybe, but with a big shtick. Marathon mouth. Now that he's escaped we're not sure what he gets out of it. Maybe it's just his bent. If not his warp. Or his kink.

"Once, I find myself on a boat from Morocco to Spain. A group of refugees clustered on deck with their belongings attracts my attention, because though dressed much like rural Berbers and obviously lacking means, they exhibit a certain ancestral elegance."

"Me. 'What's their story?' In Spanish."

" '*Ellos mataron al Re,*' answers a sailor, crossing himself. 'They killed the King.' "

But every Jew has a secret scriptural name, like Maimonides is RaMBaN. This secret name is a jack into the invisible. The secret name ascribed to him is RaMSCaN, an acrostic of his given names, Ronald Martin, and his family name. Some would say it's RaMSCaM. Thank you, ma'am. RaMSCaN's function is to scan his memory, decipher the gnomic. Till he finds what's hidden there. Because he's it.

Because he's it his profits don't count. No Oscar could make a difference. And besides, he's never made a dime.

He is basically a Jew de mot, an author though he declines authority. There are too many things he doesn't know. He's a medium for events he can't comprehend. He's known as a writer but thinks of himself as a teller. Like a bank teller he gives you an account of certain exchanges. He tells your fortune. He keeps the books. He's a scribe prodding the tribe to remember itself against the progressive Alzheimer's of history, recording what he hears and sees and the voices in his head. The writer is us.

It's not his business to make things up. The best stories are old and often told. He takes tales wholesale and tells them retail. Paper, Xerox, fax, computer disk, audiotape are his crystal ball, his handwriting on the wall. If they're not adequate for him as a medium, he might just call you up. If you're in the book. Of life, that is. You, the reader. He can feel your breath on the page, your eyes on the print. Your ectoplasmic vibrations.

Your invisible self.

"We're not talking Elvis."

He waits for laughs. Doesn't get any. "Elvis was called the King, he says. Get it? Elvis Presley, p, r, e . . . Oh, you know? You don't care about him? Right, all he had was money and fame, who cares about that?"

"Do I hear a snicker?"

To a certain extent we all have the same story, so his story is the story of the refugees on the boat. But his story is that he wasn't there. It's an alibi. He didn't do it, it wasn't his fault. One of the things they always tell you is that you did it. But he didn't. "Screw that. I wasn't there. It wasn't me." That's his usual story.

Though maybe it's time to change his tune, what the hell. "Sure I killed him. I'd do it again. Because I'm pissed—he has it coming after twenty centuries of grief. Let him show his face. Christ the Butcher."

His bit is to retell the old stories.

"Who was this Messiah anyway? He had twelve followers, and one was unreliable. The rest was marketing."

Quick change. Shifts the mike to his other hand and assumes some kind of generic cracker accent. He also does impressions.

"Actually, Elvis wuz seen today goin inta a Mowtell Seeyux with Jimmy Swaygart in Tulsa, Oklahoma. *Baby whad d'yew won me doodoo?*"

"This is from a supermarket tabloid. The supermarket, church of our lady at the checkout, faith of the coupon redemption, instrument of our salivation. The motel clerk said Elvis landed in a pink Cadillac convertible with Moloch as chauffeur, a golden calf for a hood ornament. The thing today is sci fi. Elvis is sci fi. God is sci fi. The desk clerk goes, 'Ah cain't say ah wuz suprahsed.' He can't say he was surprised. He always expected this to happen. 'It wuz seeyux OHclock in the evenin.' He took his hand off his dick long enough to look at his watch. 'Elvis aced me wut yeah it wuz. He sayd he'd beyun coolin out own the Plainet Kryptown. Takin the cuah. Coal turkey. Elvis seemed vairy concerned about Mr. Swaygart an his troubles. He aced me if'n Mr. Swaygart wuz awl rot. Latuh wayne ah aced Mr. Swaygart wut had been goin own in theah, he sayd they interfaced. Mr. Swaygart sayd thayat Elvis PUHsonally prefuzz the youngah stayump. Mr. Swaygart sayd they wuh swawpin stowries. Mr. Swaygart sayd if'n you control the stowry you get the glowry. Mr. Swaygart sayd thayat Elvis sayd thayat he wuz now an invisible nomaid lahk his aincestors, wondrin from gailaxy to gailaxy an occasionally makin a bennyfit aypyre-ants. Mr. Swaygart sayd he toll Elvis thayat Elvis too haid been sacrifahsed foh owah sins.' Hey. Good career move."

"I bet you didn't know Elvis was Jewish. On his mother's side, that's what counts. It's a proven fact, look it up. You thought it was a religion? What makes you think it's a religion? Being Jewish is an art," he says. "You got to have talent."

"What if you don't have talent? Hire a boy. What, I'm the boy?" he asks, pleading innocent.

He who? What's the difference? He gets on stage, he tells his joke, he takes his bow. He favors gags because he's chronically disgusted and when he gags at least he doesn't puke. There's not much difference between laughing and puking, laughing and puking and crying, they all come from the gut. Besides, gags stop you from saying what you really feel, and saying what you really feel is not advisable. Blind rage gets you nowhere—look where it got Samson. Freud didn't invent the Id, he just dropped the Y.

He can't say what he really feels because he's not a real person. He doesn't really feel anything. He's a dummy. An android. An alien cyberpod. Slapped together. Mosaic man, the man of parts. Ceramic. Or silicon. Prick him, he doesn't bleed. He who? The Jew. Of thee I sing.

Sometimes he's invisible. Now you see him, now you don't. He's got a disappearing act. He may be a dummy, but he's not stupid.

You say he's hiding. What else? Dr. Joker and Mr. Hide. It's the old story. Part of the mosaic. Preprogrammed. He has a factory-installed Read Only Memory, and he only knows what he reads. They say he was hiding in the reeds. He had to be invisible. Because he knew they would have killed him. They were after our boys.

But our boy was after an Oscar. Despite the language capability built into his operating system what he read was mostly comic books and funny papers, later on *Rolling Stone*. The golden image was graved on every page, cast on every screen. He dreamed of being a star. Elvis. Isn't that what he was supposed to dream? But that wasn't in the script. The only star for him would have been the yellow one. He didn't understand. He knew he had a problem, but it wouldn't compute. His bar code wouldn't scan. "I must be from a different part of the pluriverse," he tells people.

"Stop bitching," you may want to tell him. "Jews have more fun."

"Jews have more fun, yeah," he would probably say. "But do I have a choice?"

No choice. You're it.

He knows. He likes to tell a story about two Jewish bees flying through the air when one rummages around, pulls out a yarmulke and puts it on his head. The other bee asks, "How come all of a sudden you're putting on a yarmulke?"

The first bee says, "Because I wouldn't want to be taken for a wasp."

"I thought we're supposed to be humble," says the other bee.

"Not humble, you turkey. Bumble."

Stories, stories. He doesn't think, he relates.

Like the one he tells about the Golden Calf. This is a history rap, an example of what mavens of his style call speculative jocularities, while more learned exegetes talk about stochastic extrapolations. A form of archaeology. It expands the screen, adds definition, more pixels to the inch. Some people even call these riffs prophetic. Wrong. The famous surgeon, Dr. Goneff, coming out of the operating room, was asked what he had operated for. "Money," the doctor replied. He tells stories for money. He hopes to get a screenplay out of them he can vend to Hollywood. It's the profit motive. Pure exploitation. He exploits himself. The plot he stumbles on in his wonderings could be called *The Raiders of the Lost Calf*.

The scenario opens in Granada.

"Granada was once known as the city of the Jews. At one point it had a Jewish archbishop. Under the Arabs, the Jewish community had grown rich and sophisticated. It was a center of learning. There, certain Jews revived the biblical worship of the Golden Calf in an anti-Mosaic form of Judaism, calling themselves Aharonyans, after Moses' brother Aaron. It was said they actually were in possession of an ancient calf icon discovered in an archeological excavation near Caesarea in the Holy Land. It was said that many of these Aharonyans became Marranos, Christian converts, at the time of the Expulsion in 1492, and prospered as crypto-Jews from 1492 to 1942. It was said that Francisco Franco was one of these crypto-Jews. *Marrano*, literally, means swine. Then, in 1942, the Golden Calf was stolen by a Nazi sect believing that we live in a hollow universe in which cosmic rays emit gnostic wisdom crystallized by certain visible icons like the Golden Calf. Right. But in the chaos of the final days of the war, they too lost it, the Calf. It is said that the trail leads to Malta, that's all we know."

"Except," he says, "a mysterious international neo-Christian group called the Bond appears to be on the trail of the Lost Calf. The secrecy of the Bond was broken when an executive in a communications company called ComPost©, named Strop Banally, was stopped at customs in Kennedy Airport trying to smuggle fragments of unpublished Dead Sea Scrolls in the heels of his cowboy boots. Banally claimed the boots were nothing but a sort of cowboy mezuzah but then they discovered he wasn't Jewish. And wasn't a cowboy. He resembled an astronaut—that sort of over-built, robotic look."

"The Mossad stepped in and claimed that Banally was the kind of agent known in the trade as a golem. They said a golem is professional jargon for the kind of psychopath adept in worldly affairs willing to do what you can't or won't do. Sort of like a shabbas goy. They said a golem will work for anyone who knows his bar code. They said Banally's bar code was three martinis, but this is thought to be a wisecrack. They said Banally's handler was an ambiguous genius named Dr. Frank Stein, a rogue microbiol-ogist known as a brilliant but maverick gene splicer. But Banally had a reputation for getting out of control. A golem out of control wanders around like a dog without a nose. I once had a dog with-out a nose. How did it smell? Awful."

"The Mossad was involved because the Bond was reported to have formed a coalition with fundamentalist Evangelicals and ul-tranationalist Israelis working with a Jewish terrorist organization known as the Bang Gang to dynamite the Temple Mount in Je-rusalem where they think the Golden Calf is buried. Right."

"But the Golden Calf locks into the Dead Sea Scrolls. Why do you think they didn't want to release the text of the unedited Scrolls? What do you think they really say? Why do you suppose the leader of the team of scholars editing them was making anti-Semitic remarks? Why was he was fired? Who do you think is behind all this? Why do you suppose the Scrolls are housed in the Rockefeller Museum in Jerusalem? What does this have to do with the Trilateral Commission? What was the reason for turning over interpretation of the Scrolls to Harvard Divinity School? Why were no Jewish scholars among the original group? Who tried to claim that the skeletons found at Masada were those of Byzantine monks? Why do they insist that the Scroll site was a monastery? How do we know we're getting the complete texts? Why are the Scrolls being treated as if they were themselves divine, as if they were icons, occult, not simply a code to be broken? Is it because they include directions to ancient Jewish treasures that must be veiled in complex mystifications?"

"The truth is that the Scroll photos at Claremont College, one of three sets then in existence, were secretly copied and bootlegged years ago by a fanatic hit squad of crazed Lubavitchers trained in the martial arts. They found that the Scrolls give directions to the original Golden Calf of Aaron. They found that the Scrolls prove God is an E.T. and religion should really be a branch of astronomy. According to the *London Sun,* they found that Elvis is mentioned prominently, but this is clearly tabloid hysteria. They also learned that what we call people are interchangable genetic accidents and that they can move from one identity to another, including sexual identity. They can even become animals, but this we knew. Though most people forget their other identities when they feel committed to a particular role, we all have the potential for multiple personalities. It all depends on how well you know your alter egos."

"But the real secret of the Dead Sea Scrolls is they're written in genetic code," he says. "This was discovered in collaboration with scientists through computer studies at the Weizmann Institute in Israel. Did you know that there's already a dictionary of the genetic language? The language is called Gnomic. The name was chosen at the Weizmann Institute. If you don't believe me look it up. It's called Gnomic because it's the language of the genome, the aggregate genetic matter in cellular nuclei. And because the Greek root means to know. And because the gnomes write secret scripts with silver pens at midnight. Sound crazy? Check out *The New York Times,* July 9, 1991, page C1. The scientists say it's a way of distinguishing the genetic language from the babel of background DNA. They say it's a language that far outstrips the subtleties and complexities of any human language, proceeding by puns and triple or quadruple entendre. Something like *Finnegans Wake.* They tell us that the discovery of Gnomic as the underlying language of the Scrolls uncorks a bottle of knowledge that can never be closed. Because Gnomic is the secret language that establishes the missing link between mind and body. They claim that Gnomic is the true sacred language. They say it's a language beyond the comprehension of conventional intellect. Or even supercomputer. Too eccentric. Too spontaneous. The genius of the genus is finally out, and it turns out the genetic genie is quirky but ingenious.

"Even though real people aren't ever that smart."

Though remember, he's not a real person, he's a dummy. Like Bergen and McCarthy.

But maybe the ventriloquist is also a dummy. A puppet. The problem is, who's pulling the strings? He may be paranoid, but that doesn't mean there isn't a plot. Do you think coincidence is purely coincidental? Intelligence is interested in the Golden Calf. It wants to destroy the Lost Calf because it's an icon. Because intelligence is iconoclastic. Because it doesn't matter what icon I con you with—there are always strings attached. That's why Moses was an iconoclast. That's why he destroyed the Calf. Because if there are strings attached, you're still a dummy. Easy to control. Born to lose.

Maybe that's why he's so zany, trying to break loose. He's the type of comic they call a crazy. They call him "the typing tummler" because after wandering from place to place for years with his song and dance, telling his stories, he's decided to put them on paper. The rumor is, he's working on a novel called *Great Expectorations*. Mavens say the stories always have an argumentative bent, even though nobody's arguing. He says his stories don't have a bent, they just seem twisted because folk wit always seems crazy and even dangerous to sophisticates. He says the comic's job is to de-escalate the language of the elite. In fact he denies he's a comic he says he's a cosmic, just a cosmic peasant from the interstellar boondocks of the galaxy. On occasion he's referred to himself as a "hermonaut." His shtick is how to be Jewish. He says he used to work for a haberdasher in Brooklyn, a joker who had an ad slogan that went, "What do you think, my name is Fink, and I sell slacks for nothing."

Every once in a while a gentile would come in and start walking out with a pair of slacks. Fink would grab him and say, "How about some money?" So the goy would say, "What do you mean money? Your ad says, 'What do you think, my name is Fink, and I sell slacks for nothing.' "

"This is not what it says," says Fink.

"No? What does it say?"

"It says, 'What do you think, my name is Fink, and I sell slacks for nothing?' "

How to be Jewish. How to be Jewish?

This can be a question of life and death. So let's get the story straight. Where did he come from? Where is he going?

"Jews come from another planet," he says. "Not in this galaxy.

That's the short answer. As aliens we try to adapt to this world, with more or less success in different countries and different epochs. You think this is a joke? Hey, where do you think Yahweh comes from—heaven? And the moon maybe is made of green cheese?"

"Where we went wrong in paradise was when Eve and Adam thought they could ditch their preprogrammed factory-installed Read Only Memories and simply see right and wrong for themselves, as they could in the old galaxy where everyone had X-ray vision like Superman."

" 'You want to be androids forever?' asked the snake. They were sitting under the apple tree.

" 'Have a bite,' said Eve.

" 'Why?' asked Adam.

" 'Information is power.'

" 'I don't see it,' said Adam.

" 'You don't want to see it,' said Eve. 'Seeing is believing. And remember, what you see is what you get.'

" 'And what do I get?' asked Adam.

" 'You get me, babe. Random access. In virtual reality and hologrammatic I-max 3-D. Colorized. With quadraphonic super-woofing sound.'

" 'Will you keep your eyes open?' he asked.

" 'Yes.'

" 'Will you look right at me when I do it?'

" 'Yes.'

" 'Sexy. But Mr. Big says it's a no-no,' said Adam.

" 'Mr. Big? You mean Mr. Huge.'

" 'He says we'll be outlaws,' said Adam. 'That would be a shame.'

" 'Mr. Huge is only my in-law. Outlaws have perspective because they're outside. We'll be able to see what's right and what's wrong. And then who needs inlaws?'

" 'You can't get outside,' said Adam. 'Or if you could you wouldn't want to.'

" 'Afraid to know the awful truth?'

" 'I'm not afraid of anything,' said Adam. 'Go for it.'

"So Eve took the big billion-K bite from the apple. And that's why Jews are outsiders. We know the awful truth. What happened was they were trying to see what can't be seen. The apple was good for eating and a delight to the eyes, as it says in the book. But what they were trying to see is inside, not outside. Invisible.

"Said Mr. Huge: 'ROM you had, RAM you get.'

"From Eve and Adam, Jews know that there is another world that they can think about, and talk about, and write about, and hope for but that they will never see. Not here and not in Jerusalem. Not even in Eretz Israel. Like Moses, you will die before getting there. Clay to clay. That's the awful truth. That's the secret of being Jewish. So that even as we chase after the Golden Calf, we know that's not the Oscar we really want to win.

"That's the short answer. Short but grave. As in cemetery."

Which explains how we got into this, but not how we get out. How do we get out?

"They say," he says, "that long before the Rabbi of Prague made a Golem, the Rabbi of Chelm made one, too. It was a work of genius. Like the Rabbi of Prague, the Rabbi of Chelm took some clay, modeled an android bound together with iron, recited the kabbalistic formula, and placed the secret word on its forehead. The secret word is AMETH. Truth. The Man of Clay arose, invincible and just, savior of the Jews, a sort of Frankenchrist. The brainchild of the rabbi, you might say he was a creature from another world, a walking idea realized sensationally. The Rabbi of Chelm considered himself in the running if not for an Oscar, then for some other graven image of celebrity. The distance from a man of clay to a calf of gold is not really all that great.

"The problem was, the Rabbi of Chelm had a Golem Complex, a bad case of Golem envy. The rabbi himself wanted to be a Golem. In creating the Golem he was creating himself. As Dr. Frankenstein was really his monster, or wanted to be. Because the monster was dumb and didn't think before it did. Because he envied its strength, its invulnerability, its emptiness, even its innocence. And he was terribly jealous of its essential banality. There was an oedipal situation there. They were competing for Mary Shelley, the monster's mom. The monster wanted to sue its mother. For alienation of affection. That's what was monstrous about the monster. That, and that it wanted to dust the doc. Regarding this, the doctor was afreud. If not a Faust. After all, he wasn't blind. But he persisted, despite everything. More body parts, Igor.

"True, the Golem couldn't speak. But it could write. And it could sing, though not in words; it sang in a variety of percussive grunts and hums like a synthesizer, gyrating on its ball joints as it strummed, sometimes sitting in with local klezmer bands. So while the rabbi could speak for it, it could also communicate the rabbi's thoughts and feelings at the level of public expression, even though it hadn't the slightest idea of what it was expressing. And there were a few other things. Our superhero was sometimes invisible, so only the rabbi could tell where it was. It couldn't make love, though this wasn't a disadvantage, at least for the rabbi, and was probably even preferable from the rabbi's point of view, resulting in a creature something like a very large prepubescent teenager.

"But there were some other little problems which raise the suspicion that maybe the Rabbi of Chelm didn't get the formula quite right. After all, the residents of Chelm were widely known for getting everything wrong. Even so, how could the rabbi have predicted his idea would backfire? The Golem didn't know how to deal with human emotion—that was much too complex for it— and this led to all sorts of blunders. So our clay-footed superhero turned out to be something of a klutz. Its klutziness was literally magnified by the fact that it was so big, a huge fellow. There was something pathetic about this prodigy, for all its talents.

"But the Golem was a necessary monster and its klutziness wouldn't have been so bad but for the fact that it was growing. What's worse, though it grew slowly at first, the bigger it got, the faster it grew. That in itself would not have been a disaster except for the circumstance that the man of clay was, as mentioned, occasionally invisible, so that nobody could tell where the monster was at any given time and the townsfolk couldn't stay out of its way. As a result, whenever someone bumped into something, had an accident, or even tripped over his own feet he would say, 'It's him.' Sometimes it was. Things quickly got out of control, the creature ran amok, and the rabbi soon realized that the only remedy was to put an end to the android's life. But to do this he had to alter the secret word on its forehead, which he could no longer reach.

"So the rabbi had to find a very high ladder, and when he found it he rested it against the monster's chest and plucked the aleph from the secret word on its brow, which then became

METH. Death. The Golem immediately became mere inanimate clay, but because the rabbi was balanced precariously on his ladder there was no way he could protect himself when the monster collapsed and buried him under its huge mass, ending the rabbi's life along with its own.

"Luckily, the Golem of the Rabbi of Prague, which was very like that of the Rabbi of Chelm, was much more successful as his agent in the world, though the rabbi had the good sense to decommission his boy when it got too big for its britches. Unlike the Rabbi of Chelm, however, the Rabbi of Prague took the precaution of affixing his Golem to a wooden cross by its feet and outstretched hands so that it wouldn't fall on him when it gave up the ghost. This event used to be known among local Jews as the affixion or affiction or, possibly, affliction. However, they say that the Golem lies in the attic of the Prague Synagogue ready to be summoned again to become the savior of the Jews once and for all, an advent known locally as the second becoming. They say that the rabbi explained all this to the Golem before decommissioning it but that the Golem didn't like being decommissioned any better for understanding, and that it gave up the ghost with a combination of defiance, pain, and forgiveness that was almost human.

"And they also say that the Golem of Prague, though sterile, was not impotent—far from it—and in fact was quite sexy à la Arnold Schwarzenegger. Only as an android, unfortunately, it was not programmed to enjoy it. And they say that though it was sterile it also had cloning capabilities by which it created other men of steel and clay whose offspring roam the earth today."

Elvis was seen late last night in a small bar in Rohnert Park, California, singing to the gentiles. The singer stroked his golden instrument, flitting around the room on glittering sequined wings attached to his shoulder blades. "But I noticed that his boots were smeared with clay," said the bartender.

Elvis's manager, the Colonel, an alien from another land though this isn't generally known couldn't do it himself so he invented Elvis. Elvis saved his ass. Or did he save Elvis's ass? Either way, they say he destroyed Elvis in the end. Or did Elvis destroy himself in the end? Get too big, or at least too fat, for his britches? In the end. Whatever, he got out of hand. Elvis dies. Elvis lives. It's all standard operating procedure. Part of the program.

A teenage girl in Lubbock, Texas, found Elvis climbing down her chimney on Christmas Eve, dressed as Santa Claus, with a halo over his Santa hat. He was doing "Love Me Tender." As she was phoning her girlfriend to tell her he levitated and disappeared, his chin immortally defiant, his lips curled like a cherub's, agony rippling his sullen cheeks, his eyes filled with pity and fire.

"What's your story?" you may ask. "You, the ventriloquist. With whom do we have the pleasure of interfacing, masked man?"

Maybe I'm it. It's him, he's our boy, the invisible nomad, the dummy. But he's also me.

Though his story is misleading, anyway. Because it's not his. He's not his own master, masturbator of his fate. His destiny is not his own. He's not himself today, nor any day. Why? Because he's a Jew, in a word. And a word can change everything, whether you want it to or not. Not up to you. Or me. I'm not in control. No. I am who I am. Like Pop Eye the Sailorman.

When do I finally get back to the real me behind this mask in the mirror?

Not today, not tomorrow. No. Where ego I go.

STONE COLUMBUS

TALK RADIO FROM THE SANTA MARIA CASINO

GERALD VIZENOR

THE GHOST DANCE GENES

STONE COLUMBUS WAS hauled underwater by a muskie and discovered the old world, or so we were told by his mother. She said, as she always does, that the "muskie is a trickster, the first totem my boy ever hooked, and that much is a divine creation right here at the headwaters."

Stone Columbus is a trickster hooked on muskies, to be sure, but no one ever said he was a "wild fascist of the genes." No one, not even his mistaken lovers. I mention this right now because someone lied about our last report to the select committee on the insurrection. The lies, as you must have heard by now, hit the headlines.

"Columbus Heirs Grab Remains of New World" and "Indians Discover Columbus at White Earth" were the local banner headlines that autumn five hundred years after Christopher Columbus landed at Samana Cay.

Stone and the Heirs of Columbus liberated Point Roberts, Washington, on October 12, 1992, and declared the first nation in the history of the world dedicated to genetic restoration. In the name of tribal stones and survivance, the mutants of a chemical civilization would be healed at Point Assinika.

Stone Columbus has never been anything but wild and brilliant, and then he became the central figure in my investigation. My report to the agencies concluded that he was a "muskie shaman with the vision of a bingo mutant."

True, he could have been a shaman who returned from the world of the dead. We were told time and time again that he had been underwater for several hours, so he could have been touched by the interior vision of the muskellunge. He had a habit of holding his breath between names and other words to measure some wild distance in silence of the water. Late at night he hears the big pike and the natural sound of animals.

The muskie shaman was more secular than sacred, to be sure, more public than private, and much closer to casino cash flow than to underwater ecstatic journeys. Shaman or not, he and his band of mutant bingo warriors invaded Point Roberts, once an active military reservation detached from the international border, and declared a new nation in the name of tribal stones and tricksters. Most of the time he was hard to comprehend, and that too could be one of the most reliable signs of a shaman.

Point Assinika, the name of the new tribal nation, means "the point of stones" in the language of the Anishinaabe. One of the first tricksters in the world was a stone, and stones are tricksters.

I was hired by two government intelligence agencies to report on the insurrection, and to investigate the foreign scientists involved in genetic research and genome regeneration. However, more important than that, the agencies wanted to know as much as they could about the potential for the development of biological weapons at Point Assinika.

"W. O. Chaine Riel Doumet," the letter from the agencies began, with a reference to my rank as a retired warrant officer, "Once more you are needed in the service of this great country to determine the extent of a biological threat to the nation." The commanders' summons was oversuspicious and unreasonable, a sardonic reminder, but an essential and common tone in communication at the agencies. "W. O. Do," one of my nicknames in the service, was handwritten over the salutations.

I heard the true shimmer of the world in tribal stories, the creation of tricksters who never lasted and never ended, but the agencies heard codes and conspiracies in rumors and mere names. The agencies never trusted stories, and they worried about the most absurd enemies of civilization but never about themselves. They turned stories into shame; even translations and conceit overturned the scorn of others. More or less, with the agencies in mind, here is what the muskie shaman and others told me about their new nation that summer.

Stone announced on talk radio that he had isolated the ultimate tribal power of his ancestors. No one paid much attention to him at first, because reservation politicians are seldom serious about the new shamans and tricksters of the tribe, but then there were reliable reports that mutants and tribal children with birth defects were being healed by a miraculous tribal gene. We knew then that no one on the reservation would be able to avoid the power of the muskie shaman.

The Heirs of Columbus discovered the Ghost Dance Genes that heal diseases, regenerate bodies, and much more. Instances of parthenogenesis, for example, the conception of tribal children with no sex, sin, or confession, have been reported by the manicurist at the new nation. So you can imagine, when other countries and international corporations responded to this new tribal nation, the agencies wanted more information.

I was hired as an investigator because of my previous active service in military intelligence. I knew many of the warriors; we attended the same reservation schools and hunted together as kids. Most of us were more religious than radical, more humorous than criminal, but who can be sure? The muskie shaman was serious, and we had to be the best survivors.

Stone had always been ahead of the pack; nothing held him down, not even the weather, and never the agents of the Bureau of Indian Affairs. He made friends out of enemies with his muskie stories, a natural gambler with words. No one was surprised when he made a fortune with bingo on a barge, but when he started his gene code talks on late-night radio the elders worried that he might have been touched by an underwater monster.

Stone wore a metal mask the first time he invited me to the tavern at the headwaters. The Heirs of Columbus had gathered for the annual stories about their namesake. The mask was painted orange and covered his cheeks and nose. I knew he had been touched by something, the muskie stories convinced me of that much, but the genetic theories he told on radio were easier to un-

derstand than to believe. He had gone beyond the pleasure of muskie stories to become the gene trickster on the reservation. He was
out there, way out there, and then we discovered how far out he
had gone with the molecular biologists at Point Assinika.

Jesus Christ, Sephardic Jews, and Christopher Columbus were
Mayan Indians, according to Stone. Most people can laugh at that
much, trickster stories you would assume, but the muskie man
insisted that he and other adventurers inherited a sacred genetic
code that heals tribal souls, mortal racial wounds, and mutations
caused by nuclear waste and the poisons of a chemical civilization.
He told people on talk radio not to fear their genes, and no matter
the season or the weather, the gene trickster was never without an
audience. Stone said this miraculous code, or genetic signature, this
ultimate tribal power, was the Ghost Dance Genes.

CANTRIP AND THE MANICURIST

Jesus Christ and Christopher Columbus carried that genetic tribal
signature of healers, adventurers, and survivance. Doctor Pir
Cantrip, the exobiologist turned genetic engineer, and other distinguished scientists had isolated the chemical code of tribal survivance, the signature of seventeen mitochondrial genes that cured
cancer, reversed human mutations, promoted imagination and regeneration, everted terminal creeds, and incited parthenogenesis,
or the monopolitics of reproduction without men. Stone told me
that the genetic signature of survivance was the true founder of the
new tribal nation at Point Assinika.

Teets Melanos was born with the most handsome hands in
tribal memories, as lean as a raccoon, but her enormous head,
twisted chin, and wild ears frightened children. So it seemed natural that she would become the very first certified tribal manicurist.
She hummed and cleaned, hummed and trimmed, hummed and
healed between bingo games, and she heard more secrets and stories than anyone else on the reservation.

Stone invited her to the barge to treat hands and nails, and in
the course of the manicures he discovered a sensible way to gather
genetic material and genealogical information on tribal members.

Teets was inspired by the promise that her head would be

regenerated by the Ghost Dance Genes. Stone said that she would be the first to receive a genetic implant. She collected and identified thousands of secret bits of skin and nails from the hands she manicured, and she did so in preparation for a retral transformation. At the same time, she heard stories and gathered information about tribal families on the reservation. The nail and cuticle bits, and the histories, provided molecular biologists with the scientific information they needed to isolate that genetic signature of survivance carried by the Heirs of Columbus.

Teets tested the molecules she collected from time to time. The wild humor and ecstatic motions in the brush, she told me, might turn the night into a trickster creation. She trusted humor and new genes over mirrors and memories of a mutant head, over the hard stares of strangers.

Stone held the mirrors as she returned to the fish and the animals in memories. Teets returned to the trickster stories and their tribal relatives in the stone, the fires in the eye and hand roused from the cold water. The wind and breath of bears were heard in stories, and there were wild memories and dangerous conception in the stone that night.

"Mister Columbus, you got our best genes, so you give me a new head tonight," she said to the mirrors. Teets worried and worried over her nose and ears as she trimmed and cleaned thousands of cuticles and fingernails.

PANIC HOLE REMEMBRANCE

The *New Tribal Reader,* an international news magazine owned and published by a reservation gambling consortium, reported that "Chaine Riel Doumet and Tulip Browne, two private detectives who were born on the same reservation, were hired to investigate the political and biological activities at Point Assinika."

Tulip graduated from law school and lives in San Francisco. She was hired by several tribal governments to probe the possible violations of child protection laws at the new nation. There were reports that hundreds of disabled and diseased tribal children were treated with genetic implants at the new clinics.

I am a retired warrant officer and live on a remote lake near the reservation. I was contacted, as you know, by military intelligence agencies, but not as a private detective, to investigate and determine the potential for biological weapons, and to report on the leaders, nations, and corporations represented at Point Assinika.

Christopher Columbus, the Ghost Dance Genes, and the insurrection at Point Roberts captured wide public attention and support on late-night talk radio. The federal government studied the political issues too much and lost the potential to reclaim the area on the border with Canada.

Molecular biologists and genetic engineers from more than a dozen countries rushed to the new tribal nation in search of a place to conduct their research and experiments without state or federal restrictions.

Stone, to be sure, had informed the scientists and announced on talk radio when the insurrection would take place, the actual hour and day of the year. The Heirs of Columbus truly remembered how to celebrate five hundred years later on October 12, 1992.

Point Roberts citizens and the general public, but not the federal government, heard the discussions on talk radio that a new nation would be declared in the autumn, five hundred years after the return discovery of the New World. The sciolistic state department and other federal agencies were too critical to believe what was announced on talk radio. The reservation warriors had firsthand experiences of how the government does not listen; in this one instance, not to listen was a favor to the Heirs of Columbus.

Tulip and I worked together part of the time. We never asked direct questions. We were from the same reservation, knew many of the same people, and gained more from stories than from documents. More information came to the ear than to the eye, but there were natural differences in the ways we conducted our investigations.

Tulip, for instance, listens to women and watches men. She listened to the stories women told about transportation, their hands and hair, the last places they lived, taboos, and the forbidden tease. She imagined humans as birds and made a vital cursorial and arborial tribal distinction between those who believed that birds first flew from the ground to the air and those who believed that birds flew out of the trees.

Tulip started her career in an insurance claims department. Later she studied forgeries and learned through meditation that she could visualize the connections between artists, creators, and their materials. Men, she observed, revealed their intentions, and their insecurities and secrets, in the way they responded to their properties. She watched men—the way men touch their machines, their children, and their animals. Tulip was the best investigator in the business, and she soon became an expensive private detective.

Stone touched several times a day the enormous spirit catchers and blue medicine poles that loomed over the international border, the same catchers that had been mounted on the bow of the Santa Maria Casino. Tulip watched him touch women on the shoulder, children on the cheek, mongrels on the withers, and she heard him shout into panic holes for pleasure.

Point Assinika was a nation of parks and gardens, wildflowers, and biological stations, from the international border to the Strait of Georgia. Handsome blooms covered the meadows. The tribal mutants waited in the trees to be healed.

"You watch me," said Stone.

"I listen and watch in your case," said Tulip.

"What do you hear?"

"An animal, not a bird."

"Me neither," said Stone.

"What then?"

"Who are you?" asked Stone.

"Tulip Browne."

"Then you must be a bird."

"No, the wind," said Tulip.

"I am a stone, the earth is a stone, my brother is a stone, and stones shout into panic holes to return," he shouted. Stone leaned closer to the meadow and shouted into a panic hole. The flowers shivered with his voice on the meadow.

"I heard you," shouted Tulip.

"Children climb into holes, pitch stones and marbles into holes, and mongrels head for the holes," said Stone. "How natural we are as stones to shout our memories into panic holes." He touched her on the shoulder. She shivered and moved to the side to avoid his reach. He danced to the other side of the panic holes, touched his own checks, and laughed. "Come, the world is better with a wild shout, one shout to the stones."

"I hear you shout, and more," she said. Tulip was curious, of course, and moved closer to the hole, to humor him she told me later, but even so she remained silent. The muskie shaman shouted into his panic holes on the meadow.

"The stone men down there hear me shout," he said. "Come, one thin shout to clear the air in your flight." He was down on his hands and knees with the mongrels, and he pretended to search for a panic hole that would hear her shout.

She would not be summoned or tested by a trickster, but at last she had no choice. Such tribal humor on the meadow could not be resisted, so she took a deep breath and shouted her own name into a panic hole.

"The wildflowers love to hear you shout," shouted Stone.

"Flowers listen," said Tulip.

"No, flowers argue with the weather, and the animals, and pose on the meadows," he said and touched her on the shoulder. Stone laughed at the flowers, and then he shouted at the birds and mutants in the trees.

I heard them and studied the leaders, their biographies, movements, contacts, and imagined various political strategies at the new nation. Most visitors, and the scientists, had arrived by boat at night. The others traveled to the nation by helicopter. My report pointed out that the nation would not issue passports. Stone said he would "never ask humans to prove that they were real with a photograph." So, my report continued, "mutants and other curious people were not inspected when they crossed the border at the station on the main road."

Christopher Columbus stands in stone and cedar near the station on the border, and with other statues at the dock. The Trickster of Liberty, a huge bronze statue, is a invitation to the new nation. "Give me your tired, your poor, your diseased, and mutants of a chemical civilization, yearning to breath free and clean, and eager to be healed by the Ghost Dance Genes" was carved in stone at both statues.

Pir Cantrip, the obscure exobiologist and genetic engineer, is short, thick at the waist, thin at the neck, vulturine, and bald on the crown of his head. He is mannered, clean, and manicured, but his body smells of sardines. My report noted that he wears tailored business suits, light blue shirts, and floral neckties. He could have been an investment banker, but the mutants and mongrels at his side changed the context of the picture.

"Pir is our master of the genes, and his mongrel must be one of his first experiments," I reported to the agencies. "He is responsible for the actual genetic implants that have caused so much concern, but there is no visible evidence that anyone has ever been harmed. Rather, the children are released from their birth defects, and mutations, and there are tribal people here who have been healed. The power of tribal spirits cannot be discounted, but it appears that some manner of biochemical intervention has transformed hundreds of people with deformed bodies.

"Shamanic ecstasies are common cures on reservations, and no harm comes to tribal governments. Therefore, to heal the diseased and deformed is not, in my estimation, a political problem in any way, unless the genetic chemical codes are borrowed, or stolen, and misused by our enemies."

I warned the agencies that the "greatest risk is not genetic but economic, because success here, as an independent nation, could bring down the stock market. My recommendation is that the new nation be rewarded for their dedication to heal the mutants of civilization and those who have been abandoned by health insurance companies and our own government."

I concluded in my final report to the agencies that "Stone Columbus is a muskie shaman with the vision of a bingo mutant. He is a genetic tribalist, to be sure, but he is not a fascist. The Heirs of Columbus, the scientists, the warriors, and the manicurists, should be honored for their humanitarian service to the world. Not to do so would bring harm to our own economy, and shame to our own government."

LUCKIE WHITE ON CARP RADIO

Admiral Luckie White pursued Stone on late-night radio from the bingo barge to his new nation on the Strait of Georgia. Carp Radio was there, in fact, on the first night of the liberation of the mutants, live on talk-show radio at the founding of Point Assinika.

"Luckie White of the ocean sea is back on the air," she announced that night. "Your late-night host on land and sea with the voices of the truth from the newest nation in the world." She paused for an automobile commercial and a public service announcement. Cosmetic and cold medicine companies competed for time on the air with the new tribal nation.

"Stone, he be here in his scarlet tunic, listen to the stones," chanted Luckie White. "So once more we have that wild gene man on the air with the answers answer, to argue and win your hearts." Stone was high in a spirit catcher near the border. He never talked twice on radio from the same place, because he thought the same location would be too crowded with his stories.

"What are spirit catchers?" asked Luckie White.

"The catch of the spirits," said Stone.

"What sort of spirit needs to be caught?"

"Must you ask?"

"No, the evil ones," she said.

"Your questions are my very answers," said Stone.

"Point Assinika has been a nation for three months, so why don't you have border guards like other nations, and how about immigration policies?" asked Luckie.

"Birds' nests are the last borders," said Stone.

"Listen, thousands of tribal people have been healed there in the past three months, so has there ever been a genetic implant that went wrong?"

"Mongrels howl wingo," said Stone.

"Wingo, wingo, wingo, right," said Luckie.

"The mongrels are the winners."

"Doctor Pir Cantrip, we are told by the wire services, has been accused of cruel and inhuman medical experiments on twins and death camp prisoners during the Second World War," said Luckie White. "Where would he have learned about genetic implants?"

"Pir was an orphan, educated on the run," said Stone.

"New Orleans, you're on the air," said Luckie.

"Cantrip is a Nazi butcher."

"Prove it," demanded Luckie White.

"He's the one who killed my mother with chemicals."

"What does he look like?" asked Stone.

"Well he's tall, big feet . . ."

"Atlanta, you're next, what's on your mind tonight?"

"Money, who gets the cash from the bingo genes?"

"No one," said Stone.

"How can that be true? Someone must make a bundle."

"No one should pay to be healed," said Stone. "The mutants of a cruel chemical civilization tortured with deformities are not commodities; no one here is treated and cured to make doctors rich."

"Do you expect me to believe that?" said Atlanta.

"We are healed free at Point Assinika," said Stone.

"Bozeman, speak the truth tonight."

"God has the power over life, no one else."

"God is nature, not a politician," said Stone.

"God made our genes, no one else," said Bozeman.

"God made Christopher Columbus," said Stone.

"God did that, yes."

"God said the adventurer must return our genes."

"God is pure," said Bozeman.

"Columbus is a worried saint," said Stone.

"Tucumcari, you're on the air with the truth," said Luckie.

"Stone, what's a panic hole?"

"Have you ever been in total darkness?" asked Stone.

"Yes, sir, more than once."

"Panic holes are the same, so shout into the dark."

"Shout in the dark," repeated Tucumcari.

"Shout a hole in the dark," said Stone.

"Memphis, you're next, but hold your question until we hear this new commercial announcement," said Luckie White. Stone towed the braids on the spirit catcher and waited for the next voice on late-night radio. He wore earphones with a small microphone attached so he could move around.

"Memphis, we're back; this is your turn."

"Columbus, man, he hit the islands before there were photographs, so how come you got statues of the man when nobody knows what he looked like in the first place?"

"We are the witness memories," said Stone.

"So what does that mean?"

"Memories in the blood, pictures in our genes."

"George Washington?"

"District of Columbia, you're on the air."

"Yes, perhaps you could clarify a rumor that has been circulating here and there around the capital for the past month or so," said the man. "The question is, does your nation propose to collect a tithe from the annual tax revenues of the federal government?"

"The tithe is due, but not as a proposal," said Stone.

"What is the basis of such a tithe?"

"Columbus was promised one tenth of the income from trade."

"But this is the United States."

"The Heirs of Columbus have inherited the tithe," said Stone.

"Surely you jest. How would you collect?"

"That would be simple: we print new dollars, the annual amount of the tithe due, until the federal government agrees to pay the tribal heirs the cost of a chemical civilization and the value of stolen land and resources in the past five hundred years," said Stone.

"Counterfeiting is a crime, not a collection."

"The Heirs of Columbus are the natural heirs to this nation, and we have a natural right to our tithe; that right neither is counterfeit nor has ever been overstated in a chemical civilization," said Stone.

"The United States is a constitutional democracy."

"Columbus is our mutual celebration," said Stone.

"Indeed he is," said the District of Columbia.

"Christopher Columbus wrote in his journal, 'May God in His mercy help me to find this gold,' and we aim to locate our tithe in the treasury of the United States of America," said Stone.

"Admiral Luckie White has the last word, and the last word tonight is in the tithe—the truth is in the tithe at Point Assinika," she announced and then paused for one last commercial. "Carp Radio ran wild once more on the land and sea. Hear you real soon on the late-night voices of the truth."

TRI-STAN

I SOLD SISSEE NAR TO ECKO.

DAVID FOSTER WALLACE

THE FUZZY HENSONIAN epiclete "Ovid the Obtuse," C.P.A. of transhuman experience each Monday at 8:00 p.m. on Fox, mythologizes the origins of the ghostly double that shadows human figures on UHF bands thus:

There moved & shook, Before Cable, a wise & clever programming executive named Egon M. Nar. Egon M. Nar was revered through medieval California's fluorescent basin for the clever wisdom & cajones with which he presided over Recombinant Programming for the Telephemus Studios division of Tri-Stan Entertainment, Unltd. Egon M. Nar's programming *archē* was the metastasis of originality. He could shuffle & recombine proven entertainment formulas into configurations that allowed the muse of Familiarity to appear cross-dressed as Innovation. Egon M. Nar was also a devoted family man. And, as his "Brady Bunch" & "All in the Family" flourished & begat "Family Ties" & "Diff'rent Strokes" & "Gimme a Break" & "Who's the Boss?," from whose brows, Hydra-like, sprang "Webster" & "Mr. Belvedere" & "Growing Pains" & "Married, with Children" & "Life Goes On" & the mythic "Cosby," with ads infinitum, Egon M. Nar in private family life produced three semi-independent vehicles, daughters, maidens, Lea & Coleptic & Sissee, who grew like weeds among the basin's palms & strip malls & beaches & temples.

Favored as he was, daily legend had it, by company CEOs

Stanley, Stanley & Stanley, as well as by Stasis, God of Reception Himself, Egon M. Nar was bles't with such savvy that by the time his three lovely maidens—whom he saw & adored every third weekend—had their first Surgical Enhancements, Nar had vanquished the highly visible & heavy-hitting Reggie Ecko of Venice as Recombinant Head of all Tri-Stan. Reggie Ecko of Venice fell back to the basin's earth, dethroned & royally pissed, under a parachute's aegis of golden silk. & Egon M. Nar administered Tri-Stan wisely & cleverly; &, as is recorded, recombinations of derivations of rip-offs of tributes came to dominate & soothe the formerly chaotic MHz, Before Cable.

& as recombination metastasized, soothed & renumerated across the pink-orange landscape of medieval CA, Egon M. Nar's unattested daughters blossomed into nymphetitude. Farsighted, Egon M. Nar wisely provided for monthly tribute to the fluorescent basin's God of Enhancement, the plastically facile & bell-bottomed Herm ("Afro") Dight, M.D.; & H. ("A.") D., M.D., G. of E., well-pleased, fashioned Egon M. Nar's daughters into maidens just way lovelier than the stony vicissitudes of Nature would have provided solo. Nature was kind of honked off over this, but she had her own problems even way back then. Anyway, Lea & Coleptic Nar eventually blossomed into USC cheerleaders, vestal attendants at the Saturday temple of the padded gods Ra & Sisboomba; on their subsequent lives & adventures Ovid the Obtuse is mute. But it was Egon M. Nar's youngest daughter, his baby, his little princess, Sissee, who became Herm ("Afro") the Enhancement technēcian's acolyte & special favorite; & after much HMO-tribute, plus rituals & procedures so grisly as to compel lyric restraint, the surgically Enhanced Sissee Nar so like totally excelled her acrobatic sisters & all the fluorescent basin's other maidens that she seemed, according to *Varietae,* "a very goddess consorting with mortals." & she consorted a *lot.* For as her fame spread via fax throughout the basins & ranges & wastes of CA, from as far away as the Land of Huge Red Pines bronze men with cleft chins & rigid hair journeyed in loud flatulent chariots to gaze upon Sissee Nar's spandexed form with wonder & glandular excitement, & to consort. The tragic historian Lyle of Des Moines records that so high & alarming was Sissee Nar's bust she was forced to recline in devices; so juttingly sepulchral her cheekbones that she cast predatory shadows & had to do doorways in profile; & so perfectly otherworldly were her teeth & tan that the demiurges Carie & Erythema, affronted & blasphemed, appealed for aesthetic justice (specific appeal: for a nasty attack of comedomes & gingivitis) to Stasis, Overlord of San Fernandus, Board-Chair *ex-off.* of Tri-Stan's parent, the Sturm & Drang Family of Fine Companies, Stasis, Olympic Overseer, God of Perception & all-around Big Cheese. Carie & Erythema's case never even made it onto the Olympian docket, though: for Stasis the G. of P. had himself perceived & admired Sissee Nar, & from his home-entertainment module kept distant visual tabs on the riveting maiden at all times via the handheld *technēs* of his foam-winged factota, Nike & Reebok, who split shifts.

It's around here that Ovid the Obtuse shifts into Alas-mode. For the God Stasis's immortal sig. other, the Goddess & basin-queen Codependus, was just seriously ill-pleased that Stasis spent more quality time admiring Sissee Nar's camcorded image from the vantage of his module's exercycle than he'd spend even denying his mortal infatuation with the enhanced maiden to Cod. over the Olympian couple's oat-intensive breakfast. Codependus's ambrosia was Stasis's denial, & she found its absence unacceptable. & then when she came out to the sauna & found the Perception God on the cellular pricing swan-costume rentals, well, it was understandably the final straw. Codependus vowed retaliation against the consorting maiden before her whole twelve-step support group. The jealous Queen began teleconferencing with the affronted demiurges Carie & Erythema, plus had her girl Friday contact Nature's girl Friday & set up a brunch meeting; & basically all these transmortals, self-esteem compromised by Sissee N.'s Enhanced & Perceived charms, declared a covert action against Sissee & her revered father, Egon M. Nar of Tri-Stan. Having three gods plus Nature all honked at you is just not good karma at all, but mortally naive Sissee & workaholic Egon M. ignored sharp increases in their insurance premia & went about their business of moving & shaking & getting Enhanced & avoiding reflection at all costs & consorting, more or less as usual. They were blithe.

It soon came to pass that Codependus & Co., after much interface, settled on a vengeance-vehicle. This was the Telephemically displaced, parachuted & highly vengeance-oriented Reggie Ecko of

Venice, who'd suffered a massive self-esteem displacement & had sold his beach house & tank of pedigreed carp & moved into a free-base fleabag in an infamous Venitian residency hotel called the Temple of Very Short Prayers & was spending all his time & contract settlement hitting the alkaloid pipe & drinking Crown Royal out of the blue velvet bag & throwing darts at 8×10s of Egon M. Nar & watching incredibly massive amounts of late-night syndicated television, embittered. A covertly active strategy began to go into effect. While the minor Goddess Erythema began to appear to Reggie Ecko in the mortal guise of Robert Vaughan on "Hair-Loss Update" every night from 4:00 to 5:00 a.m. on Channel 13, & to work on him, Codependus herself began to work on the heart, mind & cajones of Egon M. Nar, insinuating herself into his 4:00–5:00 a.m. REM stage as the Cerberiun image of Tri-Stan's three CEO Stanleys, ancient entertainment kabalists who never left their video center & had but one large-screen CCTV monitor & remote between them. Under Codependus's direction they began to kibbitz at Nar, & to foretell. There are long, long Ovidian lyrics about Codependus's CEO-mediated siren-songs to the sleeping recombiner Egon M. Nar . . . so long, in fact, that Ovid's copied. at the soliciting glossy deleted major chunks of the epiclete's SIREN.SNG file. The stetted thrust, however, is that Codependus's covert plot began, alas, to unfold with all the dark-logic inevitability of a genuine entertainment-market inspiration.

This inspiration—the thesis Nar thought was his own—was as inevitable as the maiden Sissee Nar's part in it. Now, Telephemus Studios & Tri-Stan Entertainment, consulting the cassocked vestals at the Oracle of Nielsen, God of Life, were much troubled by the nascent spread of Cable television & the geometric spread of grainy syndication's eternal return. Turner & ESP's Network & Chicago's Super 9 were in vitro. The industry was abuzz. Stasis had personally placed shiny EM lenses in the star-chocked sky. It's 4:00–5:00 a.m. Clearly Tri-Stan needs to get in on the ground floor while it's still B.C., sang the three-headed siren, & Nar can feel the easement across, the best of two possible worlds: *no sign-off,* no anthem: instead a twenty-four-hour low-overhead loop of something so very archaic as to be forward looking, & not on any "cable," but on & in the air. Cable offers nothing new or improved & dies on the vine as hyperborean MHz TV expands to the wee

wee hours of black-and-white recycling. & not just recycled "Hazel" or "I Married Joan." The Codependent siren sang of the ultimate rerun, all echo, *myth:* ambiguous, rich, polyvalent, susceptible of neverending renewal, ever fresh. The dreamsong was complex & high-C. Covert seeds were being sowed by EMN's nightshade: a Moebioid ticker-like loop that became its own mantra: ENDYMION PYRAMUS PHAETON MARPESSA EURYDICE LINUS THOR PHAETON POLLUX THISBE EUROPA DEMETER ET CETERA.

Egon M. Nar, awaking in fugues, consulted mediated oracles, offered leveraged tribute to images of Nielsen & Stasis, Emmē, God of Victory, & to the single-screened troika of Stans. There was much research. Having finally pitched his epiphany to the big boys, Egon M. Nar found Tri-Stan & S&D well-pleased. Codependus kept intercepting emergency calls to Stasis's pager.

The same week Sissee Nar's nose was Enhanced into aquilinity forever, the MHz Satyr-Nymph Network was born & licensed. S-NN was basically an ingenious & simple twenty-four-hour low-overhead loop of mythopeia mined at 10¢/$ from the fertile stockrooms of the BBC's toga'd & grape-leafy myth-crazy fifties. Here the prefeminist epiclette Ovid the O. usurps & rhythmicizes—without credit or subsidy—the historian Lyle of Des Moines's prose account of S-NN's philosophy, Codependus's Dopplered dreamsong, Egon M. Nar's darkly-inspired bid to become the demiurge of the infanticidal kabal network Before Cable: the Satyr-Nymph Network: ". . . basically an ingeniously simple twenty-four-hour intersplice loop of mythopeia harvested from the fecund stockrooms of the BBC's antically antique fifties & targeted at that uneasily neoclassical contemporary demo-group that consumed precable syndication without chewing. This lonely & insomniac audience found the unvaried sameness of S-NN's circuit of mythic skits—legends of Endymion & Pyramus & Marpessa & Phaeton & Europa & Linus—found it reliable, hypnotic, familiar, & delicious as the taste of their own mouths. For Egon M. Nar, this queer appetite for echo spelled syndicated inspiration. Not only did S-NN feed at the contemporary basin's trough of hunger for familiarity: the familiarity fed the mythopeia that fed the market: it was revealed that, in a nation whose great informing story is that it has none, familiarity actually equaled timelessness.

". . . EMN, when asleep, listening, began to epiph something that maybe explained the land on whose left shoulder he moved & shook. There existed, Codependus with three mouths & one remote sang, a national market for myth, today. History was dead. Linearity was a cul-de-sac. Novelty was old news. The national I was about flux & eternal return. Difference in sameness. Creativity—see for instance Nar's own—lay in the manipulation of received themes. & soon this would be acknowledged, this epiphany, & put to its own uses, a funnel that falls through itself. Soon myths about myths, was the prophecy & long-range plan. TV shows about TV shows. Polls about the reliability of statistics. Soon perhaps respected glossy mags might start inviting beardless smart-ass little ironists to contemporize & miscegenate B.C. mythos: all this pop irony would put a happy-face mask on the hunger, the gnawing need; actual *translation* would lie hidden & nourishing inside the wooden belly of parodic camp. & it had already begun, for the wise & clever Nar. For Codependus was doing to Egon M. Nar what Egon M. Nar's S-NN would do to the fluorescent B.C. market: convince him that that most ambivalent of *pharmakae,* double-edged gifts so terribly precious & so heavy on the heart that a thousand sleepless weeping years couldn't even start to make good their price . . . convince him & U.S. that the unearnable gifts were the products of his own head's labor, through recombination. EMN was invited, in unseen short, to imitate a god. To re-present truth. To let's say for instance combine the fall of Lucifer & the ascension of Aepytus into a "Dynasty"-type parable about the patricide of Cronos. Oprah as Isis. Sigurd as JFK. & *all in fun,* is the thing. Keep it light, self-referential, Codependus sings in Nar's Tri-Stan'd brainvoice. The heroes tell their *own* stories, smirking, & their confusion of myth with fact & classical with enlightened will reveal meaning & compel market share. & there can be young upscale ads infinitum, hip paeans to Baccus & Helen & well-muscled Thor. & the revenues from the campy old BBC loops can be ploughed back into deliberately stagy S-NN/Telephemic myth reproductions, which remakes can themselves be run over & over, really late at night, say from 4:00 to 5:00 a.m., aimed unerring at those sleepless precable pilgrims who can't but get stoned, just looking."

"That is," Codependus spells it out via Tri-Stan's influenza behind EM Nar's pitch to Tri-Stan's three ancient Stanleys, "S-NN will purvey myth & compel share by purveying myth about the transmogrification of 'timeless' myth into contemporary camp-image. A whole new kind of ritual, neither Old-Comic nor New-Tragic. *Pure legend*. About itself, legend, & theft, all self-regenerative as loss. A kind of cosmic out-take, Gods flubbing lines, cracking up, mugging at cameras." Et cetera.

All this according to Lyle of Des Moines.

& but the Satyr-Nymph Network came to be, is the thing. W/o production costs or satellitic overhead, but w/ an Olympian advertising budget, it kicked much twenty-four-hour ass. The BBC's resuscitated situation-tragedies were hits on the order of "Rascals" & Sid. Obscure BBC hack actors from the RSC's minor leagues became, well into senescence, cult heroes. A muffler company put a toothless cockney Midas under lifetime contract, & prospered; an ageless bald Sampson did health-club spots; etc. Everyone was winning. Tri-Stan became an even more proud member of the Sturm & Drang Family of Fine Companies; Egon M. Nar got an honorary Emmē & was humble & wise & clever about it; Sissee Nar continued to Enhance, tan, flourish & consort; Reggie Ecko of Venice bounced in & out of detoxes & facilities, returning ever to his pipe & velvet Crown & Temple of Very Short Prayers & Trinitron to await, via the hirsutely groomed Robert Vaughan, the transfiguration of his resentment into meaning.

At about this point Codependus & Carie & Erythema sat back to watch Nature, summoned, take her place at the well-wrought covert helm.

Alas, we no longer get to say "Alas" with a straight face, but "Alas" used according to legend to be what you said in great stoic sorrow over tragedies ineluctable, over the darkly implacable *telos* of Nature's genetic unfolding. Alas. For given Sissee Nar's gorgeousity & mirror-denied grace under her technical beauty's own pressure, & given her prescient father's position, telemarketing vision, & devotion to his little princess (not to mention his twin investments in both the Satyr-Nymph Network & the Enhancing technē of Herm ("Afro") Dight, M.D.), it was naturally & mythically ineluctable that one Sissee Nar, aspiring thespian, would, before too many Neilsenic Sweeps marked the seasons' procession, read & audition for & land a starring role in the very first ever

S-NN/Tri-Stan mythic reproduction. This was a recombinant re-hash of "Endymion," one of the most popular of the stagy old BBC sandal-fests. The remake, "Beach-Blanket Endymion," not only came in under shoestring budget, but its debut feature presentation on S-NN threatened the time-slot supremacy of NBC's "roughly eighty," a "thirtysomething" clone about flappers & hep-cats struggling to find both continence & themselves in a nineties nursing-care context. & Sissee Nar, in the S-NN original repro, was a *phenom*! It was, yes, unfortunate that she could not act & that her Enhancement-neglected voice was like nails on a board. But these flaws were not fatal. Her title role, opposite the contemporary logos-legend Vanna of the White Hands as Selene Moon in this somewhat Sapphotic redux of a well-worn mini-myth, called only for convincing catatonia. She was a natural. Sissee basically just had to lie there, cross-dressed, Enhanced & desirable. Her anti-natural beauty was enough. She was poetry in stasis. Her closed eyes had a way. Jaded viewers were rapt, Vanna's show stolen, critics benign, & sponsors all but frenzied. Stasis even taped the thing, at home. Sissee Nar got a *Guide* cover & a *Varietae* profile. She became, as "B-BE" ran like clockwork every twenty-four, a contemporary demistar, if somewhat typecast: for Tri-Stan's test audiences indicated they loved her *for*, not despite, her eerie rendition of the vegetative state. Romance-deprived viewers yearned for her comatose, gloriously passive: what is more remote than the oblivious? There is something about Romance: every love story is a ghost story. & Sissee Nar's glued lids & soft snores & voluptuous recombency spoke to that lovely something in the contemporary condition. It rang a bell. It was good, & thus recombinable. An S-NN "original" reshuffling of the Norse Siegfried myth, with Sissee Nar as the ever-sedated Brynhild, was rushed into reproduction. Men in leather & worsted blends journeyed far to approach both Nars with product tie-ins: for the Sissee Nar doll—gloriously devoid of function or cost—was a natural.

Safe to say even the level-headed Egon M. Nar was awfully well-pleased.

Alas, too well-pleased. There was an unfolding as of dark flowers. For prominent among the rapt red-eyed faithful who watched Sissee just lie there desirable on a sandy blanket as Endymion, as Selene wept, over & over & over in the weeest of hours was the malevolent Reggie Ecko of Venice, late of Tri-Stan & visibility, recently of anonymity & the Betty Ford Clinic, & even more recently of the Erythemic Robert Vaughan's sybillant late-night campaign for covert action. Erythema's visitations had gotten progressively more effective. After many liters & ounces & very short prayers over candy & flame, diplomatic relations between Reggie Ecko & reality had pretty much broken down. & it was on the morning of his medicated sanity's tether's end that Reggie Ecko first laid eyes on Sissee Nar supine in S-NN's "Beach-Blanket Endymion." Nature & Codependus, cross-dressed, insinuated themselves into his wee hour now as respectively a Domino's delivery man & an assertive associate of a certain chemical creditor known only as "Javier J." As *Endymion* failed to unfold they began working on him in earnest, as, unknowing, did Sissee N, on the screen.

Both Ovid the Obtuse & the reliable Lyle leave obscure whether Reggie Ecko of Venice fell addled head over snakeskin heels in desperate erotic love with the comatose 2-D image of Sissee Nar because of the vengeful influenza of Codependus & Co., or via being soul-bludgeoned by drugs, or because he was just plain addled & at tether's end, or whether it was because Reggie Ecko had fallen irrevocably into active corporate invisibility & saw in Sissee Nar the embodiment of passive public image; or whether it was just one of those highly Romantic love-at-first-sight things, the stuff of chivalric myth, the Sicilian thunderbolt, the Dionysian shit-fit, the Wagnerian *Liebestod*. It does not matter. What matters, alas, is what that love wrought. & what matters is how quick & clumsy Ovid the O. is to wind up his tele–ghost story once the myth gets out of its own mythic self & genuinely Romantic stuff actually starts to happen.

Serenaded by Vaughan, Domino's & Latin creditor, plus introduced to obsession by his corporate displacement & Lucifer-like fall into what had started as recreation, RE of V was ripe for becoming that most dreaded of B.C. fluorescent basin monsters, the lunatic fan. He got obsessed with what he'd seen lying there before him. He lived for the appearance of "Beach-Blanket Endymion" every morning. He kept breaking his Sony in rages & buying another. A love-hate deal. He saw the cathode screen as the dimensional barrier that prevented his 3-D union with the Big Sleep's Enhanced siren. He wrote unpunctuated letters to Tri-Stan (red

crayon), made supplicating/belligerent calls. He cultivated the
chemical friendship of those young Adoni with whom S. Nar'd
consorted on her Enhanced path toward syndicated stardom. Plus
he began keeping the rambling clinical diary expected of your typical basic lunatic stalker-type fan. In it he revealed seeing himself
as on your basic demonic chivalric-type love-quest, tortured: he
knew his transdimensional love to be demonic, unreal, a desire for
fiction & not friction, but he was helpless, as if impotioned, & for
that he blamed both Nars: they'd created, for him, in Sissee the
Ultimate Girl of the contemporary BC basin: improbably Enhanced, rapturously passive, & 2-D, dimensionally unattainable: a
blank screen for the agelessly projected needs & dreams of every
man with a red car & a sneer & a 'tude hiding a swollen heart
just starving to buy w/o reservations into what was just way too
old to sell or lease. Reggie wrote he'd hear Sissee sing, when he
saw her, watching, lying there moon-caressed in the cathode pulse.
He *knew* her part was silent, but *felt* her motionless lips to be
singing to RE of V alone; & only because he so wanted it so. Ovid
ponders. Was this musical interface Erythmically inspired? Codependent? Unreal? No matter. Reggie Ecko records singing fe-
vered duets with the comatose TV image, & with that supine figure
reaching the sorts of unimaginable heights one reaches only with
dolls & dreams—dreams of the unattainably dead-in-life. Ecko
freebased heart-busting amounts of product & composed Crayola
poems & communed with C & Co. & bought into this whole trite
well-known unoriginal addict-codependent deal, this men-who-
love-too-much-not-wisely-type hackneyed thing where he became
convinced not only that the passive 2-D Sissee Nar was the timeless
& ideal object for his deepest, most obscure longings, but that this
love was by nature unconsummatable in the clearly marked day-
light of lived life's 3-D world. Ecko of Venice & Temple of V.S.P.
writes, according to Ovid, that he can attain the S. Nar who is his
meaning & visibility only, the high alto siren counsels, in the un-
ionized melt that is death's good night.

Codependus now elects to torture Egon M. Nar with the following dream. His cheerleading daughters Lea & Coleptic are being held hostage by some extremely serious militant CA Hispanics
who threaten to hang them by their own lustrous locks if Nar
doesn't accomplish the telemarketing task they demand: he is to

find a hypnotic vishnu of the Greek Narcissus & air him, repeat-edly, in order to entrance the Anglos of medieval California's flu-orescent basin into the plump stasis that makes them easy pickings for lean hungry serious barbarians from the Latin south. Their voices on Nar's cellular are high alto. Egon M. goes as usual to seek counsel at Tri-Stan's HQ, but the three antique Stans can't concentrate on his troubles: they have only one of every thing be-tween them, & when two or more of them have to visit the exec. washroom at the same time there's just a heck of a row about time & trade, & E.M.N. can't make his unenviable plight noticed as the Board ranges over porcelain, & squabbles. Finally a mysterious pockmarked Hispanic custodian does that psst-thing from a door-way: he's consulted the oracle of Stasis, & he informs Nar that the Cornish-game-hen-entrails have foretold that not only will Egon M. Nar never be able to find a satisfactory male new-Narcissus (no man, even in medieval CA, even Enhanced, is ungodly-pretty enough to hold the cyclopean gaze of millions & reduce entertain-ment to mere vision), but that the *female* Narcissus Nar will find in his own bassinet, his princess, will be the cause of his own per-sonal death. Properly freaked, the dream's Nar remands Sissee's new Norse reproduction to the scheduled vestibule of a permanent wee-hour time slot, when even twenty-four-hr.-loop demographics are grim. Alas, the wee-hour slot is also the slot when all the se-rious drug-freaks & neurasthenics & obscurely embittered lunatic stalker-type fans tune in. About four hundred stalker-type fans start stalking his princess Sissee Nar, actually bumping into each other in mid-stalk; & but she eventually dies in a hail of gas-tipped automatic bullets. & even though in the dream Egon M. Nar him-self doesn't get killed off so the cystic custodian's prophecy isn't fulfilled within the dream itself, E.M.N. feels so horrible by REM cycle's end that he's pretty sure when he wakes up that if the dream hadn't been preempted by his Hispanic houseboy's gentle prod, Nar would have just bought it, from grief, in the dream. Egon M. Nar's colossally tortured & frightened by the dream & immedi-ately suspends prereproduction on the Norse thing & beseeches Sissee Nar to return & isolate at her Venice beach house & keep a low Enhanced voluptuous profile for a while. Which she does, because Sissee is passivity in motion & does more or less whatever E.M.N. tells her, & also because she has a surprisingly tiny ego, given that she's never once seen herself in a mirror. Except alas, it's child's play for Reggie Ecko, who's bought an AK47 from an auto-weapon stand on Sunset, to find out just exactly where the unlisted Sissee lives: her face is on everyone's lips, & he has only to flash a glossy 4 × 5 around Venice's various health clubs & collagen wholesalers to have mortals immediately recognize the image as that of the unlisted girl who lives low-profile just over a certain set of dunes.

& Reggie, adorned in finest silks & daylight-denying glasses, & suffering mightily from coke bugs & general Wagnerian frenzy, knocks on SN's violet door & bursts the safety chain & she's in there doing aerobics & as best as the authorities can determine Ecko for a brief human moment had hesitated actually to open up & fire & Sissee had a chance to run for her life & escape the fatal stalker-type tribute, but apparently she'd happened to catch a glimpse of herself in the mirrored shades Ecko'd had on to protect his rheumy romantic retinas from the horrific light of the 3-D day & Sissee was apparently just like petrified by her own human image, literally frozen by what's got to have been her horrific Enhanced beauty, & she was standing there so utterly passive & affectless that Ecko's heart swelled with doomed Romantic stalker-type love once more that he remembered what he was about & ventilated her, liberally, then auto-shot himself, which was hard, given the length of certain barrels. . . .

& the tragicomic irony is that R. Ecko of V.'s admittedly whacko & trite Romantic dreams of union in death turned out to *come true:* he & Sissee Nar were recombinantly united in just the 2-D dead world he'd foreseen could be their only possible altar. For the vehicles "Donahue!" & "Entertainment Tonite" & its many vishna like "Geraldo!" & "Oprah" & "A Current Affair" & "Inside Edition" & "Sally Jessy!" & "Unsolved Mysteries" & "Solved But Still Really Interesting Mysteries" paid lavish & repeated tribute to the new-news story of Sissee Nar's demirise & Reggie Ecko's parachuted fall at Sissee's father's hands & Sissee's mirrored stasis & death & Ecko's *felo de se* & Crayola diary. & the very most famous *Varietae* photo of a supine Endymionic Sissee & a photo of Reggie Ecko jet-skiing with Don Johnson back when he'd moved & shaken at Tri-Stan's top, these two images kept getting juxtaposed on-screen & placed side by side behind the anchor's talking head; & the *Enquirer* even did the job right & spliced the negatives together & claimed they'd been lovers all along, with a fetish for cross-dressing & water sports; & so fan-lover & star-object were in an ironic & sort of shallow & campy but still contemporarily deep & mythic way united, in death, in 2-D, on screens.

& when Ovid the Obtuse's rolfer happened to be discussing his own obsession with the celebrated case one day during spine-straightening, & saying how it was a terribly grisly thing to say but that Sissee Nar & Ecko looked, in juxtaposition, like the sort of perfectly doomed couple that all good Americans hear & read & fantasize darkly about from the age of say Grimm's tales on; at this point Ovid the O. got the idea to turn the entire affair into this sort of ironically contemporary & self-obsessed but still mythic lyric entertainment property. The fact that Egon M. Nar—who had more or less succumbed to dream-guilty grief & had, while declining to put out any eyes, stopped cross-training & moving & shaking & had let S-NN get surpassed in the stats by an imitator, the Hit or Myth Network, owned by Ted of Atlanta—that Nar had told Ovid the Obtuse that any unauthorized Sissee-lyric would be actionable deterred O. the O. not an iota. Seeking, as his solicitation letter put it, to "renew our abiding puzzlement at such suffering," Ovid processed the myth as a concept-type thing, a kind of hot-tub-swinger's incest among Tristan & Narcissus & Echo & Isolde; & in it he not only confirmed but usurped Lyle of Des Moines's report that such was Stasis the Reception God's grief at the demise of his favorite nonperformer & anger at the parachuted love-sick ex-exec who'd 86'd her that he denied Reggie Ecko's suicided spirit the peace of any sort of underworld: Stasis condemned Ecko's ghost to haunt those most ultra of the UHF megahertz, to abide there just to the side of any compelling figure's movement, to imitate those movements as an odd milky visual echo to remind mortals that what we're spellbound by is mediated by technē & not pure. Like we didn't already know. Reception was far better on cable by this time, anyway.

& but alas. Such was Ovid's love here for reflecting on his own lovely theories about what made Egon M. Nar & Stasis & Codependus & the Satyr-Nymph Network & the popularization of timeless myths theoretically tick that he neglected to make much engaging mention of the fact that Sissee Nar had been Skinnerianly raised religiously to avoid & eschew mirrors, any surfaces with burnish, her wise & clever father fearing her own image's beauty would, seen, make her self-reflective & unattractive, stoned on self-love; & Ovid neglected to reveal how the whole reason E.M.N. had remanded the Enhanced maiden to comatose roles was so her eyes could be demurely shut during shooting & she could be spared any corruscating views of herself on monitors or tape, etc.; & that if he'd maybe let the Enhanced vision of loveliness have some little visual idea of why she had the effect on mortals she had before R. Ecko of Venice'd accosted her in his mirrored protectors she'd not have been so shocked & transfixed by an image she alone in all the fluorescent basin saw as *imperfect* nay *flawed* & insufficiently Enhanced & like totally *mortal* she might have been able to keep it psychically together enough to run like hell & escape the fanatic stalker-type lovelorn attentions of the future UHF ghost. So Ovid had to stick all this resonant & important stuff in at the end, referring to it pretentiously as an "epexegesis," & the editor of the respected ironist magazine he'd solicited was honked off, & he didn't buy the thing after all, although Ted of Atlanta's Hit or Myth Cable Network bought Ovid's overall concept for one of those "Remembering Sissee"-type tribute-specials that lets you run a whole lot of public-domain footage over again under the aegis of revelation & apotheosis; & even though "Remembering Sissee" didn't ever actually make it on the wire (Hit or Myth was processing 660+ myth-recombination concepts per diem), its rights-payment to Ovid was not dishonoring, & between that & the respected magazine's kill-fee, Ovid the Obtuse made out OK on the whole thing; don't you worry about Ovid.

FALSE WATER SOCIETY

BEN MARCUS

SLEEP

Leg-Initiations

Act or technique of preparing the legs for sleep. They may be rubbed, shaved, or dressed in pooter.

Albert

Nightly killer of light, applied to systems or bodies which alter postures under various stages of darkness. Flattened versions exist only in the water or grass. They may not rise until light is poured upon them.

Professional Sleepers

Members whose sleep acts perform specific, useful functions in a society. Clustered sleepers ward off birds; single, submerged sleepers seal culprits in houses; dozers heaped in cloth enhance the grasses of a given area, restore our belief in houses.

Sadness

First powder to be abided upon waking. It may reside in tools or garments. It may be eradicated with more of itself, in which case the face results as a placid system coursing with water, heaving.

Sleep-Holes

Areas or predesigned localities in which dormant figures and members conduct elaborate sleep performances. Points are scored for swimming, riding, and killing. Some members utilize these sites to perfect their sleep-speech, others exercise or copulate or rapidly eat cloth and grain. The father slept in one for four hours while smashing his own house, which contained its own sleepers, who performed nothing.

Sun-Stick

Item of the body which first turns toward sun when a member dies, sleeps, collapses. This item is further the pure compass toward tracts that are heated and safe, also called true places.

Wind-Bowl

Pocket of curved, unsteady space formed between speaking persons. They may discuss the house, its grass, some foods, the father inside. The wind-bowl will tilt and push into their faces, that they might appear leaning back, arching from each other, grasping at the ground behind them as if sleeping.

Jennifer

The inability to see. Partial blindness in regard to hands. To Jennifer is to feign blindness. The diseases resulting from these acts are called Jennies.

GOD

Cloud-Shims

Trees, brush, shrubs or wooden planks which form the walls of the heaven container. These items are painted with blues and grays and the golds of the earliest sky. They are tiny, although some are large. They exist mainly to accommodate the engravings of the container, allowing a writable surface to exist aloft. The engravings command the member down or up, in or out, or back, back and away from here.

Croonal

A song containing information about a lost, loved, or dead member. These are leg-songs or simple wind arrangements. They are performed by the Morgan girl, who has run or walked a great distance and cannot breathe. She fashions noises between her hands, by clapping and pumping her homemade air.

God-Charge

Amount or degree of Thompson occurring in a person or shelter.

Heaven

Area of final containment. It is modeled after the first house. It may be hooked and slid and shifted. The bottom may be sawed through. Members inside stare outward and sometimes reach.

Fiend, The

1. Heated thing. 2. Item or member which burrows under the soil. 3. Item which is eaten post-day. 4. Any aspect of Thompson which Thompson cannot control.

God Burning System

Method of Thompsonian self-immolation. For each Thompson there exists flammable outcrops or limbs which rub onto the larger body of Thompson (Perkins), rendering morning fires and ember-age which lights the sky and advances the time of a given society or culture.

Heaven Construction Theory

The notions brought to bear on the construction of the final shelter. All work in this area is done under the influence of the first powder, so the hands may shake, the eyes be glazed, the body be soft and movable.

Living, The

Those members, persons, and items that still appear to engage their hands into what is hot, what is rubbery, what cannot be seen or lifted.

Math Gun, The

Mouth of the father. It is equipped with a red freckle, glistening, which shortens with use and must be shaved, trimmed, or sharpened by the person, who follows behind with a knife.

Perkins

1. Term given to the body of Thompson, in order that His physical form never desecrate His own name. 2. The god of territory.

Rag, The, or Prayer Rag

Device of stripped or pounded cloth which is held to the mouth during prayer.

Rare-Waters, The

Series of liquids believed to contain samples of the first water. It is the only water not yet killed. It rims the eyes, falls from them during certain times, collects at the feet, averts the grasp of hands, which are dry, and need it.

Sun-Stalls

Abrupt disruptions in the emissions of the sun. They occur in the blazing quarterstrips which flap. There begins a clicking or slow sucking sound. Members standing below arch or bend. They raise a hand to the ear or eye. Form a cup or shield.

Weather Birthing

1. The act or technique of selecting and reciting certain words within fixed sky situations with the intent of generating, enhancing, or subtracting weather from a given area in the society. 2. Burning the skin of a member to alter the sky shapes of a locality. 3. Placing powders or other grains in the mouth while speaking to alter the temperature of a local site. 4. Whispering while holding birds in the mouth.

Western Worship Boxes

The smallest structures, designed to fit precisely one body. They are rough-walled and dank, wooden and finely trimmed—the only areas of devotion. When more than one body enters to worship as a team, the box gevorts.

Nagle

Wooden fixture which first subdued the Winter-Albert. It occurs in and around trees and is highly brown.

Legal Prayer

Any prayer, chant, or psalm affixed with the following rider: *Let a justifiable message be herewith registered in regard to desires and thoughts appertaining to what will be unnamed divinities, be they bird forms or other atmo-bestial manifestations of the CONTROLLING THOMPSON, or instead unseen and personless concoctions of local clans, groups, or teams. With no attempt to imprint here a definitive lingual-string of terms that shall be said to be terms bearing a truthful and anti-disharmonic concordance to the controlling agent, witnesses may accord to themselves the knowledge that a prayer is being committed that will herewith be one free of flaws, snags, and lies. It will not be a misdirected, unheard, or forgotten prayer. Neither will the blessed recipient be possessed of any confusion with respect to who or what has offered this prayer for consideration, although this assertion shall not indicate that the powerless subject makes any claim of authority over the DIVINE AGENT OF FIRE. It shall be a direct and honest gesturation to be received by said agent and dispatched or discarded in a custom that the agent knows. This now being said in the manner of greatest force and fluid legal acuity, the prayer can begin its middle without fear of repercussive sky reversals or blows that might destroy the mouth of the humble subject on his knees.*

FOOD

Blain

Cloth chewed to frequent raggedness by a boy. Lethal to birds. When blanketed over the house, the sky will be swept of objects.

Carl

Name applied to food built from textiles, sticks, and rags. Implements used to aid ingestion are termed, respectively, the lens, the dial, the knob.

Choke-Powder

Rocks and granules derived from the neck or shoulder of a member. If the mouth-harness is tightened, the powder is issued in the saliva and comes to rim the teeth or coat the thong. For each member of a society there exists a vial of powder. It is the pure form of this member, to be saved first. When the member is collapsing or rescinding, the powder may be retrieved by gripping tightly the member's neck and driving the knee into its throat.

Eating

1. Activity of archaic devotion in which objects such as the father's garment are placed inside the body and worshipped. 2. The act or technique of rescuing items from under the light and placing them within. 3. Dying. Since the first act of the body is to produce its own demise, eating can be considered an acceleration of this process. Morsels and small golden breads enter the mouth from without to enhance the motions and stillnesses, boost the tones and silences. These are items which bring forth instructions from the larger society to the place of darkness and unknowing: the sticky core, the area within, the bone.

Food Map of Yvonne, The

1. Parchment upon which can be found the location of certain specialized feminine edibles. 2. Locations within a settlement in which food has been ingested, produced, or discussed. 3. Scroll of third Yvonne comprised of fastened grain and skins. This document sustained the Yvonne when it was restricted from the body's grave.

Food-Posse

Group which eradicates food products through burial and propulsion. They cast, sling, heave, toss, and throw food into various difficult localities. Food that has been honored or worshipped is smothered with sand. Edibles shined, polished, or gilded are rusted with deadwater. Snacks from the home are placed in the bottom and crushed.

Gervin

Deviser of first fire-forms and larger heat emblems. The Gervin exists in person-form in all texts but is strictly a symbol or shape in the actual society. To gervin is to accommodate heated objects against one's body. One may also gervin by mouthing heated items of one's own body: the hand, the eye, the cupped rim of the lips.

Kenneth Sisters, The

Devisers of first food spring—blond-haired, slim-hipped, large, working hands. They dug the base for what would later become Illinois. They lived to be, respectively, 57, 71, 9, 45, 18, and 40.

Shadow-Cells

Visible, viscous grain deposited upon any area recently blanketed in shadow. The cells may be packed into dough. They may be spread onto the legs or hips. They may darken or obscure the head for an infinite period.

Storm Lung

Object which can be swallowed to forestall the effects of weather upon a body.

Topographical Legend and Location of Food Nooks

System of over-maps depicting buried food quadrants, sauce grooves, and faults or fissures in which grains and beans are caught. The cloth form of the map can be applied to the bodies of animals, to clarify areas in which edibles might have amassed.

Odor Spiraling

Tossing, turning, and flinging of the head so as to render radical, unknown odors in a locality.

THE HOUSE

Ohio

The house, be it built or crushed. It is a wooden composition affixed with stones and glass, locks, cavities, the person. There will be food in it, rugs will warm the floor. There will never be a clear idea of Ohio, although its wood will be stripped and shined, its glass polished with light, its holes properly cleared—this in order that the member inside might view what is without—the empty field, the road, the person moving forward or standing still, wishing the Ohio was near.

February, Copulated

A contraction corresponding originally to a quarter of the house month—it was not reduced to seven houses until later. The Texan February of ten houses seems to have been derived from the early rude February of thirty houses found in Detroit. The Ohioans, Morgans, and Virginians appear to share a February of eight houses, but Americans in general share a February which is segmented and cut up into as many houses as can be found.

Garment-Hovel

Underground garment structure used to enforce tunnels and divining tubes. This item is smooth and hums when touched. It softens the light in a cave, a tunnel, a dark pool.

House Costumes

The five shapes for the house which successfully withstand different weather systems. They derive their names from the fingers, their forms from the five internal tracts of the body, and their inhabitants from the larger and middle society.

Listening Frame

1. Inhabitable structure in which a member may divine the actions and parlance of previous house occupants. It is a system of reverse oracle, dressed with beads and silvers and sometimes wheeled into small rooms for localized divining. The member is cautioned to never occupy this frame or ones like it while outdoors. With no walls or ceilings to specify its search, the frame applies its reverse surmise to the entire history of the society—its trees, its water, its houses—gorging the member with every previosity until his body begins to whistle from minor holes and eventually collapses, folds, or gives up beneath the faint, silver tubing. 2. Any system which turns a body from shame to collapse after broadcasting for it the body's own previous speeches and thoughts. 3. External memory of a member, in the form of other members or persons that exist to remind him of his past sayings and doings. They walk always behind the member. Their speech is low. They are naked and friendly.

Locked-House Books

1. Pamphlets issued by the society that first prescribed the ideal dimensions and fabrics of all houses. 2. Texts which, when recited aloud, affect certain grave changes upon the house. 3. Any book whose oral recitation destroys members, persons, landscapes, or water. 4. Texts which have been treated or altered. To lock a given text of the society is to render it changeable under each hand or eye that consumes it. These are mouth products. They may be applied to the skin. Their content changes rapidly when delivered from house to house. 5. Archaic hood, existing previously to the mouth-harness, with texts carved into the face and eyes.

Maronies

Thickly structured boys, raised on storm seeds and raw bulk to deflect winds during the house wars.

Mother, The

The softest location in the house. It smells of foods that are fine and sweet. Often it moves through rooms on its own, cooing the name of the person. When it is tired it sits, and members vie for position in its arms.

Private House Law

Rule of posture for house inhabitants stating the desired position in relation to the father: bend forward, bring food, sharpen the pencil. Never stand on higher ground, shed the harness, or grip the tunic tightly when it is present. Its clothes must be combed with the fingers, its speech written down, its commands followed, its spit never to be wiped away from the face.

Shelter Witnesses

Members which have viewed the destruction, duplication, or creation of shelters. They are required to sign or carve their names or emblems onto the houses in question, and are subject to a separate, vigilant census.

Skin Pooter

1. A salve, tonic, lotion, or unguent which, when applied liberally to the body, allows a member to slip freely within the house of another. 2. A poultice which prevents collapse when viewing a new shelter.

Yard, The

Locality in which wind is buried and houses are discussed. Fine grains line the banks. Water curves outside the pastures. Members settle into position.

ANIMAL

Canine Fields

1. Parks in which the apprentice is trained down to animal status.
2. Area or site, which subdues, through loaded, prechemical grass shapes, all dog forms. 3. Place in which men, girls, or ladies weep for lost or hidden things.

Legal Beast Language

The four, six, or nine words which technically and legally comprise the full extent of possible lexia which might erupt or otherwise burst from the head structure of Alberts.

Circum-Feeting

Act of binding, tying, or stuffing of the feet. It is a ritual of incapacitation applied to boys. When the feet are thusly hobbled, the boys are forced to race to certain sites of desirous inhabitation: the mountain, the home, the mother's arms.

Tungsten

1. Hardened form of the anger and rage metals. 2. Fossilized behavior, frozen into mountainsides, depicting the seven scenes of escape and the four motifs of breathing-while-dead.

WEATHER

Air Tattoos

The first pirated recordings of sky films. Due to laws of contraband the recorded films were rubbed onto the body before being smuggled from the Ohios. Once applied, they settled as permanent weather marks and scars. The tattooed member exists in present times as an oracle of sky situations. These members are often held underground in vats of lotion, to sustain the freshness of the sky colors upon their forms, which shiver and squirm under vast cloud shapes.

Autumn Canceler

1. Vehicle employed at an outskirt of Ohio. This car is comprised of seasonal metals. At certain speeds trees in the vicinity are re-greened. 2. Teacher of season eradications. It is a man or woman or team; it teaches without garments or tools.

Backward Wind

Forward wind. For each locality that exhibits momentous wind-shooting, there exists a corollary, shrunken locality which receives that same executed wind in reverse. They are thus and therefore the same thing, a conclusion re-enforced by the Colored Wind Lineage System, which demonstrates that the tail and head of any slain body of wind fragments move always at odds within the same skin of dust and rain.

Boise

Site of the first Day of Moments, in which fire became the legal form of air. Boises can be large city structures built into the land. Never may a replica, facsimile, or handmade settlement be termed a Boise.

Frusc

The air that precedes the issuing of a word from the mouth of a member or person. Frusc is brown and heavy.

Human Weather

Air and atmosphere generated from the speech and perspiration of systems and figures within the society. Unlike animal storms, it cannot be predicted, controlled, or even remotely harnessed. Cities, towns, and other settlements fold daily under the menace of this home-built air. The only feasible solution outside of large-scale stifling or combustion of physical forms, is to pursue the system of rotational silence proposed by Thompson, a member of ideal physical deportment—his tongue removed, his skin muffled with glues, his eyes shielded under with pictures of the final scenery.

Rain

Hard, silver, shiny object, divided into knives and used for cutting procedures. Most rain dissolves within the member and applies a slow cutting program over a period of years. This is why when one dies the rain is seen slicing upward from its body. When death is converted into language it reads: to empty the body of knives.

Sky Films of Ohio, The

The first recordings and creations of the sky, recorded in the Ohio region. They were generated by a water machine designed by Krup. The earliest films contained accidents and misshapen birds. They are projected occasionally at revival festivals—in which wind of certain popularity is also rebroadcast—but the machine has largely been eclipsed by the current roof lenses affixed to houses, which project and magnify the contents of each shelter onto the sky of every region in the society.

Sun, The

Origin of first sounds. Some members of the society still detect amplified speech bursts emanating from this orb and have accordingly designed noise mittens for the head and back. A poetic system was developed in thirty based on the seventeen primary tonal flues discharging from the sun's underskin.

Temperature Law

The first, third, and ninth rule of air stating that the recitation or revocation of names shall for all time alter the temperature of a locality.

Universal Storm Calendar

1. Thompsoned system of air influence. Inexplicable. 2. System of storm reckoning for the purpose of recording past weather and calculating dates and sites for future storms. The society completes its house-turn under the sun in the span of autumn. The discrepancy between storms is inescapable, and one of the major problems for a member since his early days has been to reconcile and harmonize wind and rain reckonings. Some peoples have simply recorded wind by its accretions on a rag, but, as skill in storage developed, the prevailing winds generally came to be fitted into the tower. The calendar regulates the dispersal, location, and death of every wind and rain system in existence.

Wind Gun, The

Sequence of numerals, often between the numbers twelve and thirteen, which, when embedded or carved as code into the field, reinstruct wind away from an area.

PERSONS

Ben Marcus, The

1. False map, scroll, caul, or parchment. It is comprised of the first skin. In ancient times it hung from a pole, where wind and birds inscribed its surface. Every year it was lowered and the engravings and dents that the wind had introduced were studied. It can be large, although often it is tiny and illegible. Members wring it dry. It is a fitful chart in darkness. When properly decoded (an act in which the rule of opposite perception applies) it indicates only that we should destroy it and look elsewhere for instruction. In four, a chaplain donned the Ben Marcus and drowned in Green River. 2. Any garment which is too heavy to allow movement. These cloths are designed as prison structures for bodies, dogs, persons, members. 3. Figure from which the anti-person is derived; or, simply, the anti-person. It must refer uselessly and endlessly and always to weather, food, birds, or cloth. It is produced of an even

ratio of skin and hair, with declension of the latter in proportion to expansion of the former. It has been represented in other figures such as Malcolm and Laramie, although aspects of it have been co-opted for uses in John. Other members claim to inhabit its form, and they are refused entry to the house. The victuals of the anti-person derive from itself, explaining why it is often represented as a partial or incomplete body or system—meaning it is often missing things: a knee, the mouth, shoes, a heart.

John

1. To steal. This item occurs frequently in America and elsewhere. Its craft is diversion of blame onto the member from which the thing was stolen. 2. First house-garment correlationist. Lanky.

Leg Songs

1. Secret melodies occurring between and around the legs of members or persons. It is not an audible sequence, nor does it register even internally if the legs are wrapped in cotton. Songs of the body occur usually at the P- or J-skin levels of the back. Leg Songs report at a frequency entirely other than these and disrupt the actions of birds. 2. The singing-between-the-legs occurring at all levels of the body. Sexual acts are prefaced by a commingling of these noises, as two or more members at a distance, before advancing, each tilt forward their pelvis to become coated in the tones of the other. 3. The sounds produced by a member or person just after dying. These songs herald the various diseases which will hatch into the corpse: the epilepsy, the shrinking, the sadness. 4. Device through which one brother, living, may communicate with another brother, dead.

Michael%

1. Amount or degree to which any man is Michael Marcus, the father. 2. Name given to any man whom one wishes were the father. 3. The act or technique of converting all names or structures to Michael. 4. Any system of patriarchal rendering.

THE SOCIETY

Age of Wire and String, The

Period in which English science devised abstract parlance system based on the flutter-pattern of string-and-wire structures placed over the mouth during speech.

Behavior Farm

1. Location of deep grass structures in which the seventeen primary actions, as prescribed by Thompson, Designer of Movement, are fueled, harnessed or sparked by the seven partial, viscous, liquid emotions which pour in from the river. 2. Home of rest or retreat. Members at these sites seek the recreation of behavior swaps and dumps. Primary requirement of residence is the viewing of the Hampshire River films which demonstrate the proper performance of all actions.

Farm

The first place, places or locations in which behavior was regulated and represented with liquids and grains. The sun shines upon it. Members move within high stalks of grass; cutting, threshing, sifting, speaking.

Frederick

1. Cloth, cloths, strips, or rags embedded with bumps of the Braille variety. These Fredericks are billowy and often have buttons; they are donned in the morning and may be read at any time. When a member within a Frederick hugs, smothers, or mauls another member or person, he also transfers messages, in the form of bumps, onto the body that person represents. Certain Braille codes are punched into the cloth for medicinal purposes: they ward off the wind, the man, the person, the girl. 2. To write, carve, embed, or engrave. We Frederick with a tool, a stylus, our fingers.

Festival of Garments, The

One-week celebration of fabrics and other wearables. The primary acts at the festival are the construction of the cloth-mountain or tower; the climbing of said structure; and the plummets, dives, and descents which occur the remainder of the week. The winner is the member that manages to render the structure moveable, controlling it from inside, walking forward or leaning.

Grass-Bringers

Boys which are vessels for grass and sod. They move mainly along rivers, distributing their product north toward houses and other emptiness.

Great Hiding Period, The

1. Period of collective underdwelling practiced by the society. It occurred during the extreme engine-phase, when the sun emitted a frequency which disrupted most shelters. While some members remained topside, their skin became hard, their ears blackened, their hands grew useless. When the rest of the society emerged after the sun's noise subsided, those that remained could not discern forms, folded in agony when touched, stayed mainly submerged to the eyes in water.

Messonism

Religious system of the society consisting of the following principles: (*i*) Wonderment or devotion for any site in which houses preceded the arrival of persons. (*ii*) The practice of sacrificing houses in autumn. It is an offering to Perkins, or the Thompson that controls it. (*iii*) Any projection of a film or strips of colored plastic that generates images of houses upon a society. (*iv*) The practice of abstaining from any act or locution which might indicate that one knows, knew, or has known any final detail or attribute of the pure Thompson. (*v*) Silence in regard to the nature of the invisible and its work upon the body. (*vi*) The collection and consumption of string, which might be considered residua from the first form.

The devout member acquires a private, internal pocket for this object. He allows it full navigational rule of his motions and standing poses. (*vii*) The notion that no text shall fix the principles of said religion. All messages and imperatives, such as they are, shall be drawn from a private translation of the sun's tones. The member shall design his house so that it shall mitten these syllables which ripple forth from the bright orb. He may place his faith in the walls, which it is his duty to shine, that they receive the vivid law within them and transfer it silently upon every blessed member that sits and waits inside the home.

Palmer

System or city which is shiftable. A Palmer can be erected anywhere between the coasts.

Smell Camera, The

Device for capturing and storing odor. It is a wooden box augmented with string and two wire bunces. It houses odor for one season. It releases the odor when the shutter is snapped or jerked out. Afterward the string must be combed and shook.

Subfeet Walking Rituals

Series of motion exercises conducted with hidden, buried or severed leg-systems. It was first named when members were required to move through tracts of high sand. The act was later repeated when the sand had faded. It is the only holiday in which motion is celebrated. Revelers honor the day by stumbling, dragging forward on their arms, binding their legs with wire, lying down and whispering, not being able to get up.

Thong, The

Leatherized ladle, spoon, or stick affixed often to the tongue of a member. It is considered the last item of the body. After demise, it may be treated with water to discern the final words of a person.

Tunic, The

1. Textile web, shared, at one time or another, by all members of a society. It is the only public garment. Never may it be cast off, altered, shrunk, or locally cleaned. Its upkeep is maintained under regulation of the Universal Storm Calendar, which deploys winds into its surface to loosen debris and members or persons that have exceeded their rightful term of inhabitation. 2. Garment placed between pre-age boy and girl members to enlarge or temporarily swell the genitals and shank during weather birthing.

Hand-Words

Patterns on the hand which serve as emblems or signals. They were developed during the silent wars of ten and three. The mitten is designed with palm-holes, so that members may communicate in the cold.

Wire, The

The only element which is attached, affixed or otherwise in contact with every other element, object, item, person or member of the society. It is gray and often golden and glimmers in the morning. Members polish it simply by moving forward or backward or resting in place. The wire is the shortest distance between two bodies. It may be followed to any area or person one desires. It contains on its surface the shredded residue of hands—this from members that pulled too hard, held on too long, wanted to get there too fast.

GRAMMATRON

MARK AMERIKA

ABE GOLAM SAT behind his computer wondering how he could escape his marketing candor and enter a plea of not guilty. Gone were the days of pot-smoking music-listening meditation. His mental deposits of rare minerals were a thing of the past. Every speck of creative ore had been excavated from his burned-out brain, and it was obvious to him that the only way he could even pretend to survive in the electrosphere was to focus attention on himself, one of the innovators of an art movement that had a brief flash of success during the last few years of the twentieth century.

He felt someone else's past start to rub up against his own present in a way that seemed totally unnatural. His credit was maxed out and his last live-in girlfriend had left him for some young graphic artist in the gallery net scene. He was wondering if he could cope.

Outside his office window, the big fluffy butterfly-flakes of snow spinning down from the July sky were a sign. Darting his eyes to the nearby hanging mirror and seeing the surgically grafted cuntlips hanging off his puffy old-man cheeks was a sign. The software program that had just a few minutes ago whispered to him that it was time to wake up so he could go back to the Death Terminal and delineate his physical deterioration was also a sign. Everything he did, everything he saw, was a sign pointing itself in the direction of being social, of engaging with a world whose landscape was rapidly becoming an asexual flow of impertinent data. His standard response to all of these random signs was that he had to get himself out into the electrosphere so that anyone who cared could measure his measure for whatever it was worth. *Worth,* or value, was the rustling of data. He was the only kind of artist that could now survive into the twenty-first century: he was an info-shaman.

IT IS WORTHLESS. He entered his opening salvo of this particular day into the electrosphere, then backspaced over the word WORTHLESS and typed in DATA. By the time he was finished with his first line, it read IT IS DATA THAT WORRIES ME.

His glazed-doughnut eyes were spacing out into the electrosphere, looking for more words to transcribe his personal loss of meaning. Taking his fingers off the keyboard, he started talking to himself in a mock-professional way: "Let's pretend to rub shoulders with the Giants of Narrative. Let's take this line-by-line pseudo progression of thrusting development and zap it with so many special effects that everyone who reads it will be totally wowed. Let's pretend that this is as new as it gets, and then in our most trendoid way let's prove that this is *the best* in mortal fiction. That's right, *mortal* fiction. Never say die!"

Drug-free Cyburbia was killing its own. Golam was operating on bee pollen and royal jelly, and his brain was throbbing. Meanwhile, the chaotic electrosphere interrupted his mental writing space as some renegade programmer/marketer broke through his program's protective screen and blasted an alien signal into his aural arena:

"GOT BLUE BALLS, BUDDY? SAME OLD SAME OLD? FUCK THAT SHIT MAN . . . GO MONSTER! MONSTER IS THE MOST POTENT FORM OF DAMIANA EVER GROWN. AND WE GOT IT HERE IN CUM CITY! TAKE A TRIP TO CUM CITY AND WATCH YOUR LIFE TURN FROM SHITTY TO . . . WORSE!"

Golam had to laugh at that one. He was a sucker for the existentially dark misfit infomercial. Had been for over thirty years. He remembered that first post-punk car commercial where the acerbic, sophomoric creepoid in leather with a retro–James Dean haircut nervously Mr. Bojangled his tight white ass all around the Subaru saying things like "This rod is God! This junk is punk! You think I'm sick? At least I ain't slick! I make you wanna puke? At least I ain't from Dubuque! Stop kidding yourself! BUY THIS CAR! What? Grunge getting to your head? Now you act dead . . ." and then he would completely turn his attention away from you and jump into the vehicle, taking off into what looked like the great American desert.

But the desert wasn't real. It was the desert of the real. It was a digitally manipulated hyperdocument that prided itself on its ability to link information so as to create paths of annotated destruction. Slowly, imperceptibly, the granulation inside Golam's brain was motorizing itself into some foreign terrain that Cynthia, one of his ex-student-lovers, might have designed as a last-ditch effort to avoid being forced to live on the streets.

The alien signal on the monitor now pulsated like the interior of a human eye while the voice-over came through loud and clear:

"HI, I'M JOCK DERRIERE, AND I'M HERE TO HELP YOU NAVIGATE ALL THOSE SWOLLEN DREAMS INTO ONE FILM CANISTER THAT PROMISES NOT TO BLOW UP IN YOUR FACE! THIS IS 'INTER-JIVE' AND YOU'RE ON THE AIR! TELL US WHO YOU ARE!"

Golam was caught in a live loop and he immediately responded. It was hard to break old habits, and his were the oldest.

"I'm Abe Golam, an old man. I drove a sign to the end of the road and then I got lost. Find me."

"ABE BABY! YOU'RE THE POET LAURETE OF WURD-STAR HYPERMEDIA! EVERYBODY WHO'S ANYBODY KNOWS THAT IT'S YOUR PIONEERING WORK AS ONE OF THE ORIGINAL WURDSTARS THAT MADE ALL THIS RAMPANT FREE EXPRESSION POSSIBLE! IF IT WASN'T FOR YOU WE MIGHT ALL BE LOCKED IN INOPERABLE FILES HIDDEN AWAY IN UNASCERTAINABLE FOLDERS IN CLOSELY GUARDED GOVERMENT-PATROLLED SITES! OUR ABILITY TO CARRY YOU LIVE OVER THE ELECTROSPHERE IS DIRECTLY LINKED TO YOUR ACHIEVEMENTS SO LONG AGO! THANK YOU, ABE GOLAM!"

Golam paused as his aura absorbed the electrifying hype that came his way.

"The Grand Narratives were disasters," he plodded along, sending his signal to all who were lurking over the live interactive program he had somehow got caught in. "We had no choice but to do away with all that naming and desiring. There was too much emphasis on the body as an experimental project. We knew that the mental jottings we periodically transmitted vis-à-vis the predesigned modus operandi rooted in modernist intelligibility were somehow coming apart in the mass mixed media of net-driven anxieties. The Credit Wars, Killing Contracts, Amoebic Contaminations—all of it had some small role in our eventual domestication. I am home now . . ."

"WELL, YEAH, ABE-BABES, WE'RE ALL HOME NOW! HOME ALONE! TOUCH ME YOU DIE!"

"I've never really cleaned out, you know," Golam continued. "I used to go around performing my work back toward the end of the twentieth century. I'd go to bookstores, college campuses, libraries, art galleries, the usual. I'd strip my language down to the bone, going for the best possible effects so that more momentum and energy would be stimulated, leading to God knows what, and the only way I could get through it all was to dabble in the delectation of raw chemical substances. But at least I'm no longer a prisoner of my own skin. I'm beyond the beyond . . ."

"BEYOND THE PALE, ABES-BABES! BEYOND THE FUCKING PALE! WHICH REMINDS ME, CAN WE SNEAK IN A HYPO-MERZ SHOT OF GRUNGE? MY SPONSOR IS CHAMPING AT THE BIT!"

"Sure, go ahead."

"HERE'S JACKIE JILL WITH A COME-ON!"

At this point a virtual babe with cosmic cleave and digital dewdrops dripping off her pseudo collagen-inflamed lips started deep tonguing the screen, coming at all the viewers as if she were ready to lick the radiation right off their dour faces. After about two dozen slo-mo sweeps of her tongue doing the nasty, she jerked her whole head back and spoke in a low erotic voice:

"STOP FUCKING AROUND. I DIDN'T COME HERE TO LISTEN TO YOUR DEPRESSIVE BULLSHIT. YOUR HANG-UPS ARE EASY TO READ, BABY. YOU NEED PUSSY. HOT WET UNINTERRUPTED NONSTOP FOREVER-IN-YOUR-FACE PUSSY. COME TO ME, JACKIE JILL, UP MY HILL, TO FETCH A PAIL OF STEAMY, HOT CUM-WATER. COME ON, BABY, YOU'VE BEEN PISSING ALL YOUR GODDAMN TIME AWAY. YOU WANNA GET LAID?"

At which point three more slo-mo sweeps of the tantalizing tongue came across the screen, and then her access code burned brightly in dark red: JJ@900SEX.COM.

"HI, I'M JOCK DERRIERE, AND WE'RE BACK LIVE ON 'INTER-JIVE'! WE'RE HERE WITH WURDSTAR PIONEER ABE GOLAM! ABE-BABES, GOT A GRAM OF PSYCHOLIN-GUISTIC BABBLE YOU WANNA SHARE?!"

"Nice Come-On. Wish I could buy some, but it wouldn't do me any good. Besides, it would be too vacuous of me to drive *that* kind of sign out into the desert. You know something, there's a will-to-love and it's still inside me. I can feel it inside my loins. At least I'm reading that pang between my legs as a sign of desire, desire for *love,* and you can't take that away from me. I'm just as responsible as the next mathematician screening formulaic devices. Digital Remote and The Mortal Scan. I read you, you *need* me. We're all *there,* Partner.

"Hey, listen to me: these exposed tracks of meaning and their supposed grams of nerve-scintillation can't fully make sense of the involuted wash now generating *this* generic sea. You, too, may want to wash me, but only as a temp. The permanent position is out in the cold blue yonder. It's the inevitability of my death that strokes me the best.

"No one can provoke the kind of nausea I'm speaking of. This is a code that refuses to submit. Take a hike. Go fuck yourself. The war is over The Subject. The war is over, and *I* am The Subject. This is who I am."

Golam turned on his ReadyWipe™, and right before the intruder completely disappeared a trail of verbal ash floated by. He thought it said:

BREAKING NEWS!
MACRO WORLD MEDIA DECLARES WAR!
PAY PER VIEW ON CHANNEL X!
CHECK NOW FOR PRICES . . .

A thought came to his mind: Coffee with Cynthia. Where was she hiding?

BAD NEWS

LYNNE TILLMAN

*The King of Kings is also the Chief of Thieves. To
whom may I complain?*
                                                        —The Bauls

TEN TEN WINS, ten ten on your dial, the news never stops, the
news all the time. You give us twenty-two minutes, we'll give you
the world: A black woman in Brooklyn has been murdered. Police
report the woman was thrown off her roof after she was raped.

The news is broadcast every twenty minutes, the headlines
every few minutes. Then there's TV, two hours of news around
dinnertime, not counting CNN. Bulletins anytime. We interrupt
this regularly scheduled program, the announcer says, to bring you
this bulletin.

The woman in Brooklyn was raped and murdered in her home.
Her body was dragged from her apartment and carried to the roof.
By a stranger, the police say. The stranger threw her off the roof.
The news didn't give her name.

The news is no stranger. It's always there at the same time,
Elizabeth thought. She stayed tuned, hooked to the pain and pleasure of small and great events. At the announcement of disaster,
Elizabeth sensed danger as if the bad news were inside her, a shrill
wake-up call ringing in her body. Alarmed, Elizabeth occasionally
was moved to confess. At least she sometimes felt the urge, but
then she laughed at herself. She was guilty, but there was nothing
to confess and, worse, no one to hear her confession. Definitely a

problem, she remarked to her boyfriend, Henry, who replied, in his offhand way, Some days you eat the dog, some days the dog eats you.

Henry and Elizabeth likened each other to animals. To him, she was a small, furry creature, a squirrel or weasel, because she was nervous so much of the time. To her, he was a mule or donkey. Henry was determined and stubborn. Elizabeth poured a cup of coffee and added milk to it until the coffee turned the tawny color she liked.

Murder is ordinary. There are usually three or four a day. I don't want to, but I can see the woman. I can hear her scream. Get out, get out, what do you want, leave me alone, leave me alone, you're hurting me. I can see her body dragged up flights of dirty stairs and carried onto the roof, and I can see her thrown over as if she weren't a human being, just garbage.

At night Elizabeth hailed taxis. It was worth it, she reminded herself each time she paid a cabdriver; it was her life she was saving, not money. Walking on the street Elizabeth masked her fear under a veil of poise and cool. She had read everything she could about serial murderers. Elizabeth knew that Ted Bundy had chosen his victims wisely—they were all troubled women caught by him at a bad time in their lives. Bundy had spotted something in their eyes and had seduced the women easily. Elizabeth tucked her fear inside her body.

Ten Ten WINS: We'll quickly update you on the top stories. Ten Ten WINS every time. All news all the time, stay tuned: It's cloudy in New York, wind from the south at ten miles an hour.

Elizabeth reassured herself with the fact that, apart from serial murders, most women who were murdered were murdered by men they knew or lived with. Elizabeth lived alone, but Henry often slept at her place. He liked her apartment, it was cozy. Elizabeth was sensible about her fear some of the time, and the statistics, the odds, were reassuring. They were on her side.

Elizabeth shook her head up and down and from side to side. Dreamily she concocted stories she could use, just in case. She would be prepared if she had to plead for her life to a guy high on crack who held a knife to her throat, who would end her life for twenty dollars.

I'm John Gotti's daughter and if you do this to me, if you

touch me, just touch me, you'll have to answer to the Mafia. They'll get you if you hurt me. Don't do it. Don't you do it. Don't even think about it. I've got AIDS—rape me, murder me, and you'll die too.

Shame and revulsion crawled over, in, and through Elizabeth, an internal rebuke to the self she shared with no one. She disgusted herself—using disease like that, as a threat, a weapon. She wouldn't, ever. But even if she gave the guy money, he might murder her.

I could scream. I could scratch his eyes out. I could kick him in the balls. I could fight him with all my strength. I'd scream for help. I'd scream bloody murder. But what if no sound came out of me? In nightmares I can't move, I can't run away. I'm glued to the spot where I'm in danger. Maybe I won't be able to move. Then they'd say, She died without a struggle. I'd be pathetic.

Elizabeth knew a woman who carried a small hatchet in her handbag. She envisioned her friend taking the hatchet from her bag. In the scene the would-be murderer, rapist, or mugger was surprised, bemused, or terrified. Then he ran away. Her friend was safe. But Elizabeth didn't think the woman would be able to reach into her bag and grab the hatchet, to strike a deadly blow with deadly force. She wondered if she herself would be able to cross the narrow line that separated her life and body from another's.

Maybe my friend would hit him in the head with the sharp edge of the ax. She'd split his head in half. Blood would gush from his head. There would be blood everywhere, all that blood from one body. My friend wouldn't be able to do it. She'd hit him with the blunt side of the ax. I don't know if I'd be able to do it. I don't know if I could count on myself.

Ten Ten WINS, news all the time: On the question of the safety of nuclear reactors, a scientist explains that safety means an acceptable level of risk. There is some risk in everything.

Elizabeth pictured the woman in her apartment in Brooklyn. Just over the bridge. Not very far away. The woman was fighting for her life. Elizabeth pushed the ugly scene from her mind and looked out the window at some sparrows on a roof. A few birds were also on the bare branches of the tree in the garden. They had not flown south, because people had begun feeding them during the winter. They were plump and content. As she gazed at them,

Elizabeth smoothed her hair. It was an unconscious gesture. Her fingers found a few thick, wiry hairs which she touched with pleasure.

On CNN, on television, there were images of people dead and dying, wounded and bleeding. Though broadcast in color, there was something about war that was always in black-and-white, something direct and obvious. Incontrovertible. In its horrifying way war was, to Elizabeth, comforting. She knew what it was, and so did everyone else. War is everyone's perfect stranger, the strangest and most normal of events. Everyone knows who's suffering and which people need help, and there's no question about that. It's a relief to know. Elizabeth imagined the woman in Brooklyn. She was cowering in her kitchen.

Ten Ten WINS, news all the time, Ten Ten WINS takes you there: Five people were found shot to death, execution-style in Queens. The police report it was drug-related. The news watch never stops. You give us twenty-two minutes, we'll give you the world. WINS News Time 10:22.

Elizabeth let her breath out slowly. When she visualized her feeling in words—something like "I breathed a sigh of relief"—she laughed at herself again. Drug-related murders didn't count. Everyone knew if you weren't in the business, no one messed with you. You were safe. Still, life was a series of violations and people were shot and knifed daily. Sometimes by mistake.

I could be in the way. I could be in the wrong place at the wrong time. But it's really surprising that more of us aren't knifed every day. People look so crazy. I can see it in their eyes—any minute they might leap out of their skins and into someone else's or onto someone else. Just to get themselves straight, just to get rid of something, just to lose themselves, just not to be in themselves for a second. Everyone says how violent the city is, but actually, considering how things are, it's not so bad, not that dangerous. It could be much worse. I'm safe enough.

Elizabeth remembered Ricky. He lived downstairs before his grandmother sent him away. He was running toward the corner to buy dope. There's a bust, Elizabeth told him. She was as cool as ever. Better not go that way now. She described the cops who were holding four young guys up against the wall. She had watched along with several other whites, some Latinos and blacks. Everyone was fascinated, staring, waiting for something. Maybe the cops would go berserk, turn violent. Elizabeth described to Ricky how the four guys were searched, against the wall, their legs and arms spread apart. Ricky listened and turned around. They walked home together. He told her she had it easy. From his point of view she had it made.

If I screamed, if Ricky were around, he would come to my aid. I know he would, he likes to fight. And deep down, inside him, he's okay. But it doesn't matter. It doesn't matter what anyone feels inside. If someone needed money desperately, or if some guy hated his mother or hated everyone and everything, if someone was totally deranged, and I was there, at the wrong time, it wouldn't matter. That's it. It would be all over.

Ten Ten WINS, all the time, every time: You can count on us 24 hours a day. 53 degrees. We're heading down to 47. Ten Ten WINS: The U.S. government is sending the Haitian refugees back to Haiti. It has determined that they are not political refugees. Their problem is economic, the government says, not political. Stay with Ten Ten WINS for all the news all the time.

I'm living in something I don't understand. It's crazy. Everyone thinks so. I'm morbid. I think about dying too much. Even Alice thinks I'm being irrational. I should keep it to myself. I look perfectly normal. I have a job. I have a roof over my head. I have nothing to complain about. It's life, Henry says, get used to living it.

Elizabeth and Henry were making breakfast. The wallpaper, like inkblots, loomed crazily around the kitchen table. As Henry watched, Elizabeth selected four slightly tan, nearly lavender eggs from the refrigerator shelf. Then Henry sliced the bread. Later Elizabeth studied him as he looked out the window. She could hear him breathe. His fragility was what she loved best about him. She thought of the word *tender* and imagined how it would appear in neon. She told Henry, who said he'd do that for her, for her next birthday. He said he'd bend that neon to his will. He always made her laugh.

Ten Ten WINS, NEWS ALL THE TIME. YOU GIVE US 22 MINUTES, WE'LL GIVE YOU THE WORLD.

The news didn't mention the woman in Brooklyn anymore. That was old news, and other murders took its place. Henry repeated a joke he'd heard the night before. Two bags of vomit were walking along the street. One became sentimental and cried. The other asked, Why are you crying? The first said, I was brought up around here.

After Henry left, Elizabeth lingered in the kitchen and read the small, unimportant items at the bottom of the newspaper's long pages.

I'm one of the little people, a little woman. An ordinary person. One of the common people. Our lives are just territory for bombs and soldiers to land on. In war, one person's life in the middle of all the horror and chaos is nothing. In war, civilians might be wounded or killed by rampaging troops, by incensed soldiers trained to hit hard, to take no prisoners. Getting murdered is nothing. It happens all the time. There doesn't have to be a war. Our bodies get landed on every day. Our insides are carved up and churned over and spit out into nothing; they become nothing. Anyone can be the enemy. Everyone is strange.

Just by looking at her neighbors, Elizabeth hoped to ascertain who was reliable, who could be counted on late at night if someone lurked in the doorway. She couldn't decide whether it was good or bad that three new bodegas had opened up on her block and were selling drugs. Now people hung around all the time, but she didn't know if any of the guys running the drug stores would go out of his way to help her. Still, murder was bad for business. It wasn't street smart. It brought the cops and unwanted attention, so the dealers, she thought, might try to stop it from happening.

I could be dragged off the street by a guy in a car who had a gun. It could happen in an instant and not draw any attention. No one might even see it. The next day it would be a small item in the newspaper. Woman Raped and Murdered. Maybe because I'm white, it would be given more space. Depends on the city desk, if it's a slow news day or not. People who didn't know me would be happy not to be me. Everyone would be happy not to be a murder victim. People could say, even friends, She shouldn't have lived in that neighborhood, she should have known it was dangerous. It was stupid, they'd say; her death was avoidable.

Elizabeth understood she couldn't be protected, not from the unknown or from random violence. Much as he loved her, Henry couldn't be there all the time, and much as she loved Henry, she couldn't save him. Everyone, she thought, was hapless. Henry teased her about being a character trapped in an episode from "The Twilight Zone." She was waiting to hear her own death reported on Ten Ten WINS. It was a running joke, part of their intimacy.

Ten Ten WINS, all the news all the time: The Pentagon has released figures which show that during the Gulf War, half of our soldiers were killed by friendly fire. Stay with Ten Ten WINS.

Friendly fire was a funny term. Grimly ironic, Elizabeth said to Henry, like murder between friends. Henry claimed that Elizabeth's fear was an escape from reality. She wondered what reality was and who decided. But she kept that to herself. Elizabeth hated to think that her sympathies, and her fears, if held up to the harsh light of reality, would be found wanting and incomprehensible. She herself might be found wanting, insufficient. She hated that.

ELLA'S SPECIAL CAMERA

FROM *WAXWEB*

DAVID BLAIR

ELLA'S SPECIAL CAMERA
FROM WAXWEB, AN INTERNET/CD-ROM VERSION OF THE MOVIE "WAX"
BY DAVID BLAIR

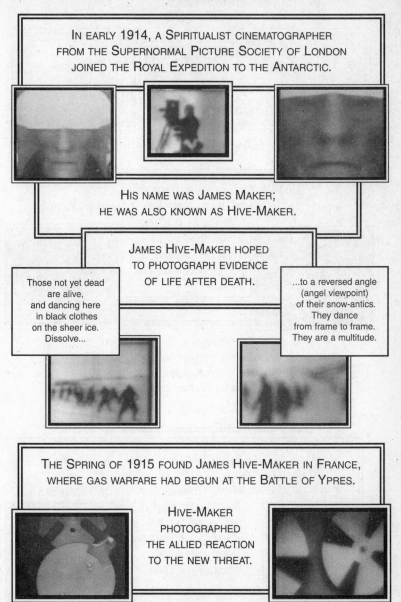

IN EARLY 1914, A SPIRITUALIST CINEMATOGRAPHER FROM THE SUPERNORMAL PICTURE SOCIETY OF LONDON JOINED THE ROYAL EXPEDITION TO THE ANTARCTIC.

HIS NAME WAS JAMES MAKER; HE WAS ALSO KNOWN AS HIVE-MAKER.

JAMES HIVE-MAKER HOPED TO PHOTOGRAPH EVIDENCE OF LIFE AFTER DEATH.

Those not yet dead are alive, and dancing here in black clothes on the sheer ice. Dissolve...

...to a reversed angle (angel viewpoint) of their snow-antics. They dance from frame to frame. They are a multitude.

THE SPRING OF 1915 FOUND JAMES HIVE-MAKER IN FRANCE, WHERE GAS WARFARE HAD BEGUN AT THE BATTLE OF YPRES.

HIVE-MAKER PHOTOGRAPHED THE ALLIED REACTION TO THE NEW THREAT.

279

THE SUPERNORMAL PICTURE SOCIETY TAUGHT
THAT THE DEAD LIVED NEAR TO US,
IN AN UNKNOWN WORLD.

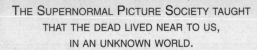

A gas grenade
explodes
in the middle of that field, and the masked soldiers
run in to do a good job.

THIS WORLD COULD BE MADE VISIBLE TO US
BY THE CINEMATOGRAPHER WHO COULD SEE
THROUGH THE HAZE
OF OUR WORLD
TO THE DARKNESS
BEYOND.

TO THE SUPERNORMAL CINEMATOGRAPHER,
THE GHOST WAS A SPIRITUAL RADIUM IN DECAY
THAT COULD STAIN PHOTOGRAPHIC FILM.

IT LIVED IN THE LAND OF THE DEAD.

HIVE-MAKER WROTE THAT HE IMAGINED THIS TO BE
A PLACE OF DENSE VEGETATION, WHERE THE SOULS
OF THE DEAD LIVED IN THE FORM OF SMALL FLOATING LIGHTS.
HIVE-MAKER BELIEVED
THAT SOMEDAY THESE
LIGHTS WOULD SWARM
INTO OUR WORLD,
TO JOIN THE LIVING.

IN THE SUMMER OF 1916, JAMES HIVE-MAKER RETURNED TO HIS HOME AND BUSINESS, A BEEFARM NORTH OF LONDON, TO SUPERVISE THE SEASON'S WORK AND CHECK ON HIS HIVES.

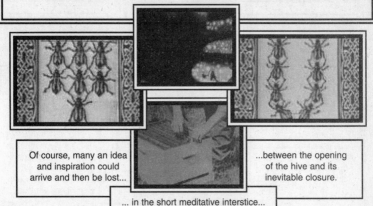

Of course, many an idea and inspiration could arrive and then be lost...

...between the opening of the hive and its inevitable closure.

... in the short meditative interstice...

A TELEGRAM HAD WARNED HIVE-MAKER OF A NEW DISEASE AMONG THE BRITISH BLACK BEES.

TO FORESTALL POSSIBLE RUIN, HIVE-MAKER HOPED TO PURCHASE AN EXPERIMENTAL STOCK OF SPECIALTY BEES FROM MESOPOTAMIA.

HE HAD HEARD THAT THESE SPECIAL BEES WERE BOTH PLAGUE-PROOF AND ABUNDANT PRODUCERS OF AN UNUSUALLY CLEAR HONEY.

IF THE EXPERIMENT WAS SUCCESSFUL, HE WOULD REPLACE HIS ENTIRE STOCK.

IN LONDON THAT SUMMER, THE TELEGRAPH COMPANY
HAD BEGUN TO MODERNIZE ITS OPERATION.

A high shot of
camera-memorized
workers thrashing
at a switchboard,
patching through calls
from the dead of the
future. Among them
is (are)...

...Ella, a slow but certain genius...

...who understands
the potentialities
of hybridity
in the construction
of those systems
necessary
to connect us with
those we love.

AS A RESULT, ELLA SPIRALUM LOST HER JOB
AS A TELEPHONE OPERATOR.

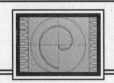

IRONICALLY, SPIRALUM WAS HERSELF AN ELECTRICAL INVENTOR
WHO DREAMED OF DEVELOPING THE MEANS TO TRANSMIT
MOVING PICTURES THROUGH THE TELEPHONE.

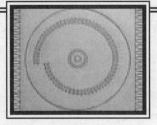

A still frontal image
of the always rotating
Nipkow Disk, central
and metal-made
component of an
Image Dissecting
system proposed
in the 1880s,
by a Berlin student...

This winding gyre,
once·used
to accurately slice
coherent sections
of our world for
single transmission
and
multiple reception,
is now part of history.

...who, in later years, was proclaimed by
Adolf Hitler to be the Father of Television.

282

ELLA SPIRALUM WAS THE HALF-SISTER OF JAMES HIVE-MAKER.

THROUGH HIVE-MAKER, ELLA SPIRALUM FOUND WORK AS
A PHOTOGRAPHIC MEDIUM AT THE SUPERNORMAL PICTURE SOCIETY.

Flapping pictures of birds created by a clay-pigeon zoetrope at the Kensington Museum in London... large earth-made bird statues in various sequential poses are mounted in a giant horizontal drum with evenly spaced viewing slits cut in its side. When the drum is spun, the birds seem to become a single flying bird held in the eternal return of cycle animation (no mutation possible there in that machine-gunned eternal claylife, through the viewer is invited to wink and blink and use all manner of organic filters in an attempt to create a new, unique, and, most importantly, survivable and potentially reproducible image).

EACH SUNDAY, GHOSTS WOULD APPEAR AT A SÉANCE
IN TAVISTOCK SQUARE, TO BE PHOTOGRAPHED WITH THE LIVING
BY ELLA AND HER SPECIAL CAMERA.

Photo of a cotton-garbed ectoplasm who has been mourned through the use of photography, but has minimal personality beyond its recallable face. To obtain such a ghost-picture, the mourner would visit the photo-medium. The medium would request to see a picture of the recently dead, in order to focus the concentration and energy to make a new exposure of this dead person on vacation in the other world. During this moment of concentration, the photo-medium would secretly rephotograph the picture of the formerly alive and still-loved dead person. Then, for an extra charge, the medium would take a studio portrait of the mourner. The mourner would then depart, to return in a week to pay for a picture of the ghost, garbed in cotton ectoplasm, and also a two-shot of the cotton ghost compositely posed with the still-alive, recently recorded mourner.

OFTEN, THE GHOSTS SPOKE
TO ELLA.

Fade, as always, to nothing.

BONANZA

CURTIS WHITE

The
Ponderosa
is burning.
It started with
a little discoloration,
a darkening, then red hot,
like someone lighting parchment
from the backside with the glowing
tip of a cigarette. Within moments
it had spread thousands of acres, miles,
flattened Virginia City, reduced the fabled
ponderosa pines to twigs, black and dead.

Miraculously riding out of the very center of this apocalypse are
the Cartwrights.
Little Joe, Ben, and Hoss. They're all smiles.
We'll need men like this after the apocalypse.
Ben looks about him: beautiful!
I'll give this to my boys someday.
Little Joe and Hoss smile, too,
'cause their Pa is going to
give them the Ponderosa.
Hope
it's not
too
Hot.

The Cartwrights ride off and the commercial break is about to begin, but if you rewind to just the last moment before the break, freeze frame, now enlarge, you see that there is someone running, trying to catch up to the Cartwrights. He is naked and matted with hair and his penis is cheesy and he babbles loudly. He is Wild Father. He will tell this story titled "The Bridegroom."

"God, 'Bonanza.' This show makes me sick. I thought it was dead. I thought I killed them all myself. I thought it was all burnt up."

I taped it off the Family Channel, Wild Father. It plays reruns twice every day. The Family Channel is owned by Christian corporate interests. They believe that 'Bonanza,' the saga of the admirable Cartwrights, fosters family values in America."

"So it's not dead yet? Hoss is dead, I know that. Dan Blocker died of his own girth in 1972. And Little Joe is dead of cancer caused by constant exposure to radioactive tabloids. Ben lives in dog food commercials. That's hell, ain't it?"

"Peace, Old Man of the Earth. Why don't you just tell us this story of 'The Bridegroom'?"

THE WILD FATHER TELLS ALL

"I never really met the Cartwrights, you understand. I lived on the Ponderosa in a gully full of sticks. The producer hired crews of derelicts left over from mining days in the Comstock to clean up. Everyone of them looked like Gabby Hayes. They were men like me with hair on their bodies. Ben Cartwright told these men to pick up anything that wasn't a big-ass pine tree and put it in my gully.

"Before every episode, the Cartwrights would ride by, fearlessly, joyfully, riding straight into the heart of this forest fire that had consumed the entire region. Well, every single time I'd come up out of my gully yelling and waving my hands trying to catch their attention. I wanted to say, 'Hey, who the fuck do you think you pretty boys are dumping all these twigs and sticks in my gulley? And ol' Ben he'd just sit so stiff and proud in his saddle and say, 'Ignore him, boys. That's the Wild Father.' 'Just ignore him,' he says. Oh that makes me so durned mad! Why couldn't they take me with them? Every stinkin' week they'd find some galoot camping out on their spread, a wounded Indian or a runaway or a tragic Johnny Reb or some other dumb fuck with trouble but a heart that only the Cartwrights could demonstrate pure. What was wrong with me? Sure, I was covered with hair and some of it was crusty with my own smelly shit and my dick was a bit cheesy like you said earlier—still is, if you've got any sense of smell left to you by the government agencies regulating the use of your nose— but I would have liked being saved. I would have liked being put in the guest room and Hop Sing could make me some nice food and Ben would tell Little Joe he 'better go get Doc' just to be on the safe side. And Doc would say, 'Well he's undernourished and dirty and his private parts are thick with an interesting scum, kinda like a ricotta cheese product, but I think all he really needs is a hot bath and a haircut and some of Hop Sing's good food.'

"And Hop Sing would smile and move from toe to toe and squint in his glee, and say, 'Oh Hop Sing can makee vely fine food for Wide Fatha.' And then everyone would laugh because Chinese is some funny little shits. Later in the show, of course, I would test my benefactors' patience by doing something savage. I'd steal something. A gravy boat would be found under my pillow. Or, or I'd be caught in the barn playing with the horses' doodads. Then Ben would have to sit me down and say, 'Now, Wild Father, we're your friends. You know that. And we're just trying to help you. Don't you want to be like us? Even the ferocious Indians, who leave their own kind for dead served up in the grasses for wolves, even they want to be like us. To wear our hats. To eat our potatoes when they are mashed. But we can't have this . . . whatever you'd call it. White people don't play with horses' doodads.'

"But this is just idle fantasy, boy. The Cartwrights never took me to their house. I guess I just wasn't good enough for the likes of them or I was so bad that they saw no hope of making me an American. Bloody hell, I AM AMERICA. I take out America's garbage every Tuesday night. Don't that make me America? I scarf up ozone. Hell, I am the damned ozone hole. I fart plutonium out of a sense of national responsibility. I keep toxic waste incinerators burning round the clock with my nose pickings."

"I don't doubt a word of it, Wild Father. Why don't you just tell this story?"

"Sure. I have no choice but to take my revenge as I can. I'll tell each and every one of their weekly episodes going all the way back to 1963, only I'll tell it my way. To hell with the consequences! I don't give a damn if they lose their corporate sponsors! I don't care if the people at Ralston Purina say, 'You know this Wild Father character is making it difficult to promote our delightful Chex party mixes.' Those ad execs can go chase the colorful party banners fluttering from my asshole.

"What it comes to is this: the Cartwrights wouldn't be my family, my father and brothers. Little Joe wouldn't let me ride behind him on his painted palomino. So what are family values to a poor fuck that no family will have?"

Wild Father was working up a sweat. Some of the excremental matter about him was getting humid and starting to stink.

"So, son, pay attention to what your Wild Father says. This episode is called 'The Bridegroom.' The first scene is coffee time at the Ponderosa. Ben sits at a coffee table in the living room. (Really it's just like your house in the burbs except they've got the television console covered up with a saddle blanket for historical authenticity's sake.) Sitting with him are Tuck (a local rancher) and Tuck's only daughter, Maggie. Ben is sipping his coffee from a delicate china teacup. This signifies that he is an atypical cowboy hero. He will shoot you dead with his gun, but he would rather represent the virtues of the landed gentry. Tuck, on the other hand, pours his coffee from the cup into the saucer and hence to his thirsty lips.

"Maggie says, 'Pa, that's not very polite.'

"Tuck replies, 'Maggie, when a man's been saucerin' for forty years it's too late to make him change his ways.'

"What in the funny heck is saucerin', son? Do you know? Do you believe this prime-time crapola? Saucerin'! [*sings:*] *I'm a saucerin' man, done a lot of saucerin'* . . . hee hee. Why doesn't he just slice his belly open and pour it right in there? Then he could say, 'Maggie, when a man's been caesarian his coffee for forty years it's too late to change his ways.' " Wild Father throws his hands up in his riotous laughter and strings of a pudding-like substance fly off his fingers up toward the ceiling, leaving little greasy tapioca marks.

" 'Now, now, Maggie, don't worry about that,' says Ben, 'I guess everyone's got their bad habits.'

" 'You're darned right about that, Ben. Maggie here, she's got her habit too. The spinster habit.'

"Ouch. You could have heard a pin drop. You could have heard Hoss falling in the distant woods. It was time for fathers to bruise their children again.

" 'Pa!' says Maggie, a hurt look on her plain face. Well, she wasn't so stinkin' plain. Anyone could see that she was a Hollywood actress with her hair tied back in matching buns over each ear like stereo headphones. Hair buns = homely in TV sign language. Soon as she lets her hair down, you watch, wham, she'll be a beauty.

"Ben saves the day: 'Maggie, I seem to have forgotten the cream. Would you be a good girl and get it?'

"Well, Maggie, there's your moral universe. You can be a spinster or a good girl. It's your choice. Lots of luck.

" 'Tuck,' says wise, kind ol' Ben, 'what's the matter with you? If brains were dynamite, you couldn't blow your nose.'

"Oh a fine line," croons the Wild Father, his eyes turned heavenward, hopping now from side to side, his legs spread and bent like a Sumo wrestler's, complicated debris shaking from his furry haunches with each bounce. "Truly, sirrah, a most comely, melodious, and memorable line. Oh you rare hearts, you brave and inspired hearts that do pen the noble poetry of television drama. Or try this on, 'I wouldn't cross the street to spit on you even if you were on fire.' A pearl! A ruby! Little oysters of moist adulation come to my lips and launch themselves into your perfumed beards. I grovel at your Florsheimed feet and pass mustard on your argyles. You geniuses! You billfolded muses! I flay the fox on the path on which you tread.

"But Father Tuck knows his mind and his daughter. 'Ben, you don't know how lucky you are to have sons. The plain truth is my Maggie is a homely woman.'

"Little Joe comes into the house just then, the soles of his boots smoldering, little flames licking up from the hot leather. He overhears Tuck with a frown. 'That ain't so, Tuck.'

"Frown or no frown, there's no question that Little Joe's a cutie. Eh? Little silk kerchief around his neck, tiny Paul McCartney pretty face, and curly hair comin' down like he half-admired hippies." Wild Father leers and teases out his own wiry hair in imitation. It seems to have clumps of oatmeal in it.

" 'Oh, is that right, Little Joe? Then how come you never once asked my Maggie to go to a social?'

"He's got you there, Little Joe, you masterpiece. He knows like you know that every week brings its episode and every episode brings new butt, creamy wanna-be-a-TV-starlette butt for you to stroke between takes. You don't fool nobody, buster. And why didn't you take Maggie to a social or somethin'?

" 'It just never worked out that way is all.'

"Lame! Lame, Brother Joe. Don't cut it. You'll have to do better than that.

"Later, Ben, Little Joe, Tuck, and Maggie visit Jarrod, a widower now living alone on his ranch. They're looking at horses that Jarrod has for sale.

"Tuck pulls Jarrod over confidentially and they have the following conversation.

" 'Just touch that.'

" 'That's a good lookin' animal.'

" 'You better believe it.'

" 'That's a fine lookin' animal.'

" 'Now touch this part.'

" 'That's mighty soft there.'

" 'And here.'

" 'I can't touch there. It wouldn't be right.'

" 'It's even softer.'

" 'Well I know that but . . .'

" 'Okay, never mind, but why don't you just come over to the house tonight and we can talk it over?'

"God I love Christian broadcasting, son!"

WOMEN AND HORSES: THE SECRET CONNECTION

by Dr. James Wildfather
University of Twigs at Gully

Consider the following scene from an episode of "Bonanza" titled "The Bridegroom." Jarrod has come over to the home of Tuck and Maggie one evening in order to discuss a livestock deal.

"Well, well, Jarrod. Come on in."

"Good evening, Tuck, Miss Maggie."

[Maggie smiles stiffly, a look of dread in her eyes. For months now she's been feeling this creeping sense of unreality and dread. She feels that people want to hurt her. Even people she knows to love her. Her psychiatrist has suggested tricyclic antidepressants, but the mood of doom has not begun to lift. In particular, she thinks her father is trying to sell her like a horse. This neurotic delusion causes Maggie to experience a sudden onset of raw fear as Jarrod enters her father's house. In quick order she feels shortages of breath, palpitations, chest pain, a choking feeling, dizziness, hot flashes, faintness, nausea, trembling, fear of dying, and fear of losing control. All of this gives a little flush to her cheek which Jarrod finds charming.]

"Jarrod," says Tuck, "you notice anything different about Maggie tonight?"

"Well, she looks very pretty."

"Oh, come on now, son. You don't have to say what's not true. She's a homely thing that no self-respectin' man would pay court to. No, it's something else."

"Well, I give up. What is it?"

[Maggie squirms. Her eyes mist. She'd like to run from the room. She'd like to be dead. She imagines herself capable of running through a wall.]

Tuck walks straight over to the hearth. He lifts Maggie's arms. She is manacled to the hearth.

"Chains, Jarrod. It's chains. I've got Maggie chained to the hearth!"

[Jarrod approaches uncertainly. He's amazed.]

"What do you think about that?" asks Tuck.

"I don't know what to think," replies Jarrod, a little sheepish.

"I'll tell you somethin' else you might not know about. Now, Maggie looks very proper tonight, don't she? Hair in that tight spinster's bun. Nice long calico dress that she sewed herself (she's fine with a needle, Jarrod). But guess what? Turn around, Maggie honey, that's a good girl. Look, she ain't got no underthings on. Put your hand there on her shank, son. That's good, ain't it? Soft and warm."

"Do you really like this, Miss Maggie?"

"Sure she does, don't you girl?"

"Yes. I like it Pa."

"Now, how many women you know, pretty or plain, that really like this kinda thing? Tell me that."

"Not many that I know of," replies Jarrod. [He takes a step away, pushes his rancher's hat back on his forehead. Eyes linger on the fine marble turn of Maggie's hip.] "This does put things in a brand-new light."

Tuck laughs out loud. "That's it! I knew you'd come around. Let's sit over here and talk this out over a glass of Maggie's fine plum wine."

Wild Father, you too much, babes.

Huh?

You a funky-ass motherfucker.

What?

You solid, man. You stoned. You gone.

Is that you, boy?

You a gangster of funky-ass love.

Why you talkin' like a nigger? Niggers don't count here. This world is all Christian TV.

You gone. You way gone. You my cheesy hambone man.

You think it's fun bein' the Wild Father? You think it's all runnin' round and chaining your daughter to household appliances and lettin' your business associates play with her butt? You think that's what Wild Fatherin' is all about? Well, come on sit yourself down here, even if you are a nigger or maybe my son talkin' funny, and I'll give you the Wild Father rant.

THE WILD FATHER'S RANT

"First, you gotta have this hair all over your body. You ever try to grow the hair real long and thick on the underside of your arms? You know, the part of your arm where it's soft and pink even when you're sixty-five and hair's growing out of your nose like pampas grass? Well, it's all in the diet. You must eat: canned beef tamales, Dinty Moore beef stew, sardines in mustard sauce, potted meat, lots and lots of nondairy cheese products like Velveeta and Cheeze Whiz (eat the Cheeze Whiz right straight from the aerosol container, boy), Spam (don't cook it, you like that cool, fatty gelatin), Vienna wienies right from the can. And you gotta season all your foods with the cheapest off-brand of liverwurst you can find (liverwurst made from the things that even Oscar Meyer won't put in their liverwurst; I'm not talkin' snout or entrails; that's clean and invigorating; I'm talkin' stuff that's barely associated with the livestock industry like squirrels that happened to die in the vicinity of the slaughterhouse). For a vegetable you eat Pillsbury mashed potato flakes.

"And this effort just gets you the hair. We're not even talkin' attitude yet! To get the Wild Father attitude you get up real early because your brain chemistry is so fucked up you can't sleep through the night. So you get up at five. Don't eat anything yet, that's for later. Do all your eatin' at one time. Now drink a pot of coffee to scour the GI track, read the newspaper and get a good coughin' jag going. Don't be shy about it. Rattle the damned walls. If you do it right, your children will think they woke up in a tuberculosis ward. Soon as you feel that last cough gone, light up. You've got three, four packs of cigarettes to do today, so you've got to get started early. (Note: when coughing, try to drag that phlegm way up, all the way up, and spit it into a cheap paper napkin. Let the fatty stain leak through. Leave the napkin on the kitchen table next to your cigarette butts and coffee dregs. When your wife and children get up, they'll see the wads and any ideas of shredded wheat and OJ, health, or happiness will go right out the window, if this kitchen nook has a window.) And remember, it's up to every Wild Father to reproduce his kind. In particular, when your son gets up let off a good audible fart. Don't apologize. (In general, say nothing to nobody. Communication is for losers.)

It's your house and you can fill it with farts if you like. Let it float foully up like a helium balloon. Fuck everybody else. Someday your sons will have their own houses to fart in. Next, a real Wild Father retreats to the throne and shits out all the wild canned animal products he consumed the previous day. Check it out. Be proud.

"Now you're ready to start your day. Put on your plastic windbreaker that you won at the Brutal Inn and Out Pro-Am, 'cause that's your hangout. 'The Brute' it's known as. And that's where you're going. At the Brute reinforce your neighbor's bigotry. Drink nine vodkas, and accept the warm comradery of the other Wild Fathers. Talk about life on TV. Now go home for lunch. (Pause only if some bitch has parked too close in the parking lot. She's in buying groceries, so give her a little bang in the passenger side door. Bitches is the Wild Father's big enemy.)

"When you get home in the afternoon, everyone will have fled your odor, aura, and mean drunk temper. Make some lunch in the lovely quiet you have achieved with your own rare works. Canned oysters in skim milk heated to near boiling. Break a handful of soda crackers on top and mix well. A lunch fit for a Wild Father. Now sit in front of the TV and watch reruns of 'Perry Mason.' Doze. 'Streets of San Francisco.' Doze. 'Hawaii Five-O.' Doze. 'Mannix.' Doze. 'Kojak.' Doze. 'Cannon.' Doze. 'Rockford Files.' Doze. 'The Untouchables.' It's midnight. Your long meditation has achieved Wild Father nirvana. If Robert Stack sat on your face you couldn't be happier.

"At two in the morning get out of the recliner, turn off the TV, and go to bed. The Wild Father's wife smells funny. She's too clean. He sleeps anyway. Three hours is all he gets. Then it's up and the regimen begins again."

Oh, Wild Father, babes, you a motherfuckin' dead man.

Ben Cartwright sits in his armchair, bent forward, his head in his hands. Hop Sing bounces about him chanting a sing-song homeopathic mantra. Something is wrong with Ben, Our Father. When he woke, his head was larger than usual. It was about the size of a large world globe. Because of his head's new size, Ben's hairs were spaced farther apart, making it easy for Hop Sing to find evidence. He felt about Ben's head like a boy looking for a lost marble in the grass. Up near the hairline on Ben's forehead Hop Sing found what looked like a large bug shell, brown and long like the egg sack on a cockroach. This caused a more intensive search for intruders. Ben himself found a large inflamed area, like a pimple. He pressed it from both sides which easily and smoothly began to force out the hind end of the cockroach creature. But it wasn't a cockroach, it was a long wormlike thing, about the size of a child's index finger and similarly jointed. When at last it was out, Ben and Hop Sing could see that it had a tiny human face that was busy contorting. Probably wasn't used to the bright lights. It was clearly not happy being out in the clear air.

Hop Sing said, "Oh my! This no hut you, Missah Caltwight?"

"No, Hop Sing. I hadn't noticed it," says Ben. Then he remembered the voices. The intrusive thoughts. They weren't thoughts after all. It was this worm singing in him, saying, "Excuse me, I must die now. Excuse me, I must die now. Excuse me, I must die now."

"Oh let's all feel sorry for Mistah Cahtlight. Fuck him and his wormy head. He don't know pain. I'm the one with the pain. Having to tell these dumb 'Bonanza' stories. Just to get even. This revenge is worse than the original grievance, for Christ's sake.

"The end of 'The Bridegroom'? Why you care? You so dumb you can't figure it out? Okay, listen: Maggie and Little Joe pretend to be courting in order to make Jarrod jealous, which he is, and he punches Little Joe and runs off with Maggie. Tuck is pleased that men would fight over his Maggie and goes off to tell the boys at the Brutal Inn and Out.

"Now that's it, story's over. Get the fuck out of my face."

BLACKOUTS

PAUL AUSTER

Characters

Green, a man about seventy years old
Black, a man about forty years old
Blue, a man about forty years old

An old-fashioned office, cluttered with papers, filing cabinets, etc. Stage right rear: a door with frosted glass panel, the word ENTRANCE *written in reverse. Stage center rear: a window. Stage left rear: a window. Stage right, at forty-five-degree angle facing out: Green's desk and chair. Stage left, at smaller angle facing out: Black's desk and chair. There is a third chair on the other side of Black's desk. Green's desk has a gray pencil sharpener attached to the top.*

Green wears a green suit. Black wears a black suit. Blue wears a blue suit.

Darkness. The sound of Green sharpening pencils. Four pencils. Lights gradually come on. Green is standing by his desk, sharpening pencils. Eight more pencils. Black is sitting at his desk, staring blankly ahead, as if lost in thought.

BLACK: Green. *(No response. Louder.)* Green!

GREEN: *(Stops sharpening.)* Yes?

BLACK: The pencils.

GREEN: *(Nods in agreement.)* The pencils. *(Resumes sharpening.)*

BLACK: Too loud. *(No response. Pause.)* Too loud!

GREEN: *(Stops sharpening.)* I beg your pardon?

BLACK: The pencils are too loud.

GREEN: *(Puzzled. Inspects pencils.)* The pencils? *(Pause.)* They are . . . mute.

BLACK: The ruckus . . . of that contraption.

GREEN: *(Pause. Considers. Tries sharpening pencils at various speeds. Stops.)* It can't be helped. It's in the nature . . . of the machine. The rotaries . . . (slight pause) . . . chew.

BLACK: Drop it.

GREEN: But I'm not ready. There aren't enough.

BLACK: *(Forcefully.)* You're ready.

GREEN: *(Pause. Humbled.)* As you wish. *(Takes already sharpened pencils and arranges them neatly on desk. Sits in chair.)*

BLACK: Are you ready?

GREEN: *(As if trying to remember.)* I note. Everything that is said is written. Even the silence must be marked . . . (groping) . . .

BLACK: Silence.

GREEN: . . . Silence. No talking unless asked. I am ears without mouth . . . nothing . . . but the hand that writes the words. *(Pause.)*

BLACK: Who are you?

GREEN: *(Hesitates.)* Green. As previously. *(Pause.)* Executor . . . of the aforementioned.
(Pause.)

BLACK: Who am I? *(Green stares at him apprehensively. Pause. More forcefully.)* Who am I?

GREEN: Black.

BLACK: Since when?

GREEN: Since . . . the beginning.

BLACK: And so it will be—

GREEN: To the end. To the very end.

(Black sighs with satisfaction. Leans back in chair. Pause.)

BLACK: This is a great day, Green. A great and important day.

GREEN: I don't doubt it. *(Pause.)* But so is every day. A new beginning of all the days that remain.

BLACK: No. Today is different. Today is the day it ends.

GREEN: If you say so. *(Testing sharpness of pencils on his palm; wincing at the prick.)*

BLACK: I don't say so. It is written. *(Pause.)* A man will walk through that door, sit down in that chair across from me, and we will talk. By the time we have finished, there will be nothing left. *(Pause.)*

GREEN: There will be the words. I'll have written them down, one by one.

BLACK: That's beside the point.

GREEN: *(Confused.)* Then why am I here? What am I doing this for?

BLACK: You're here to make a record, to prove that what happened really happened. *(Pause.)* But it doesn't matter. One way or the other, it's beside the point.

GREEN: You're out of your mind.

BLACK: Not out, in. If anything, I'm too much in my mind. *(Pause.)* But that's only a detail. *(Longer pause. Turning to Green. Earnestly.)* Do you remember me?

GREEN: Of course I remember you. How could I forget you?

BLACK: Have I changed much?

GREEN: *(Thinks.)* You've grown older. *(Pause.)* But then so have I. *(Pause.)* I'd say you've become . . . more and more what you are.

BLACK: *(His spirits lifted.)* Do you think so? Is it really possible?

GREEN: Why shouldn't it be? It seems . . . almost inevitable.

BLACK: Not for me it isn't. *(Pause. Bitterly.)* You're making fun of me, aren't you?

GREEN: *(Trying to mollify.)* Listen, Charlie . . .

BLACK: *(Exploding.)* Don't ever call me that! Don't ever call me that again, do you hear!

GREEN: *(Mortified.)* I forgot.

BLACK: What is my name?

GREEN: Black. Black. From the very beginning. Black.

BLACK: You must never forget that, do you understand?

(Long pause.)

GREEN: Will he be here soon?

BLACK: Impossible to say. *(Pause.)* Perhaps he'll never come.

GREEN: When is he supposed to come?

BLACK: *(Consults watch.)* Any time now.

GREEN: What's his name?

BLACK: *(Looks Green in the eyes. Enunciates with deliberation.)* Blue.

(Green laughs with embarrassment. Long pause.)

GREEN: Is it over, then?

BLACK: Is what over?

GREEN: *(Pause.)* The story.

BLACK: Yes, it's over. *(Stands up. Walks to window behind his desk. Looks out.)* No doubt about that.

GREEN: *(Pause.)* Did you really believe in it that much?

BLACK: *(Looking out.)* It wasn't a question of belief. *(Pause.)* I really wanted to know what it would be like.

GREEN: For so long? For so many years?

BLACK: Once I started, it was hard to stop. *(Pause.)* I developed . . . a taste for it.

GREEN: *(Puzzled.)* For living like a ghost?

BLACK: Watch your tongue, old man.

GREEN: *(Pause. Wounded.)* I don't like it when you call me that.

BLACK: But that's what you are, isn't it? An old man.

GREEN: *(Angry.)* Are you forgetting who I am?

BLACK: *(Wearily.)* Hardly.

GREEN: *(Still angry.)* And that it was I who found *you?*

BLACK: *(Pause.)* Only because I wanted to be found.
(Long pause.)

GREEN: What will you do when it's over?

BLACK: I don't have many choices, do I?

GREEN: *(Tentatively.)* Did the little boy really die?

BLACK: *(Painfully.)* I can't remember anymore.

GREEN: Did White really disappear? Did Gray really disappear?

BLACK: You know the answer as well as I do.

GREEN: And Black. What's going to happen to him?

BLACK: *(Pause.)* There aren't many choices, are there?
(Long pause.)

GREEN: Will he be here soon?

BLACK: *(Not hearing him. Looking out window. Pause. Horrified.)* Oh my God.

(Lights out. Ten seconds. Lights on. Black and Green in same positions. A knock on the door. Black turns and looks at Green. They

stare at each other. Pause. The knock is repeated. Black gestures for Green to open the door. Green shuffles to the door. Opens it very slowly. Blue is standing in the doorway. He is wearing a trenchcoat and hat.)

GREEN: *(Tentatively, peering around the door.)* Yes?

BLUE: *(Matter-of-factly.)* Is it time?

GREEN: *(Turning to Black.)* He wants to know if it's time.

BLACK: *(To Green.)* Ask him his name.

GREEN: *(To Blue.)* He wants to know your name.

BLUE: *(To Green.)* Tell him I want to know if it's time.

GREEN: *(To Black.)* He wants to know if it's time.

BLACK: *(Pause.)* Yes. It's time.

GREEN: *(To Blue.)* He says it's time.

(Blue, hands in pockets, takes one large step across threshold into the room, and stops.)

BLACK: *(Gesturing to other chair at his desk.)* This chair will do.

(Blue puts hat on Black's desk, drapes coat over back of chair. They all sit down in their chairs. Long pause. Green writes whenever Black and Blue speak.)

BLUE: Aren't you going to ask me to identify myself again?

BLACK: I know who you are. *(Pause.)* The only thing I care about is your report.

BLUE: I have the report, no need to worry.

BLACK: *(Relieved.)* Does it surprise you that it should all come down to this?

BLUE: I've been on this case too long to be surprised by anything.

BLACK: You feel . . . no regrets?

BLUE: What I feel doesn't matter. *(Pause.)* Besides, you can't bring it back, can you?

BLACK: *(Reflects.)* Except now. We're bringing it back now.

BLUE: No. It's all gone. We're just putting it into words.
(Pause.)

BLACK: *(To Green.)* Did you get that last sentence? Let me hear it.

(Green continues to write. Silence. Looks up. Slowly realizes what has been asked of him.)

GREEN: *(Reads.)* "Let me hear it."

BLACK: That's what I asked you.

GREEN: *(Confused.)* And that's what I gave you.

BLACK: *(Realizing. Shouts.)* No, no! The one about the words!

GREEN: *(Searches. Reads.)* "We're just putting it into words."

BLACK: *(To Blue.)* Is that what you mean to say?

GREEN: *(To Black. Peeved.)* You shouldn't be so vague about it.

BLACK: *(Turning abruptly to Green. Angry.)* No talking! Don't you remember?

GREEN: *(Singing softly under his breath.)* The bear went over the mountain, the bear went over the mountain, the bear went over the mountain, to see what he could see.

BLACK: What did you say! *(Waits for response. Silence.)* What!

(Green purses his lips shut. Gestures to his mouth, as if to prove he cannot speak. Long pause. Black and Green glare at each other.)

BLUE: Yes. That's exactly what I mean to say.

BLACK: I'm sorry.

BLUE: *(Shrugs.)* I have all the time in the world.

BLACK: It would be nice to think so. *(Pause.)* Where were we?

BLUE: Nowhere. We haven't started yet.

BLACK: I suppose you'd like to get it over with quickly.

BLUE: As I said, I have all the time in the world.

BLACK: Do you think I'm afraid? Do you think I'm trying to delay? *(Pause. Slams palm down on desk in anger.)* Damn it! Say what you mean goddammit!

BLUE: *(Calmly.)* Whatever I say, I mean. If you want me to begin, I'll begin. If you want me to wait, I'll wait. If you want me to leave, I'll leave and come back tomorrow.

BLACK: No, no, not tomorrow. It would be too late then. *(Pause.)*

BLUE: Where were we?

BLACK: *(Pause.)* We were about to begin. *(Pause. A loud cheeping noise is heard in the room.)*

BLACK: *(Nervously.)* What's that?

BLUE: *(After a moment.)* Sounds like mice.

GREEN: Yes. It's the mice.

BLACK: *(To Green.)* You mean there are mice in the walls and you didn't tell me?

GREEN: It's only . . . a detail. I didn't want to bother you with it.

BLACK: It's disgusting.

GREEN: There's no need to worry. I've taken care of it.

BLACK: What does that mean?

GREEN: *(Long pause.)* Poison.

BLACK: They'll die in the walls and begin to stink. Their bodies will rot in the walls.

GREEN: Not so. They eat the poison and then leave. They die outside.

BLACK: How can you be sure?

GREEN: The poison makes them thirsty. They eat the poison and begin to crave water. They get frantic, go outside, and look for a drink. But it doesn't do any good. Even as they drink, they die from thirst.

(Long pause.)

BLACK: *(Returning to himself.)* Where were we? *(Pause.)* Read me back the last sentence.

GREEN: *(Hunts through pages.)* "We were about to begin."

BLACK: Who said it?

GREEN: You did.

(Pause.)

BLACK: *(Turning to Blue. About to speak. Hesitates.)* Just a few questions.

BLUE: *(Shrugs.)* As you wish.

BLACK: *(Pause.)* Do you feel you've been well paid?

BLUE: I've been paid.

BLACK: I'm not sure I understand you.

BLUE: I've never had too much to be able to stop, and I've never had too little to want to quit.

BLACK: And you don't feel any . . . bitterness?

BLUE: For what? There wouldn't be any sense to that . . .

BLACK: And yet?

BLUE: Well, of course, goddammit, what do you think? It wouldn't have been human not to.

BLACK: *(Backing down slightly.)* It's just that you took on the work with such . . . such ardor. Even when the investigation was going nowhere, you continued to devote yourself to an exhaustive . . . an exhaustive examination of the details, to record even the most peripheral references to the case. *(Picks up a handful of folders from a tall pile on his desk.)* Hardly the work of a man just doing his job. There's real . . . devotion in this.

BLUE: *(Pause. Hesitant.)* After a while . . . it kind of got under my skin. *(Pause.)* After all, what did I have to do? *(Pause.)* I had to watch this man and write down what I saw. It was so simple, it never made any sense.

BLACK: Did you ever try to find out who hired you?

BLUE: *(Pause.)* You know that as well as I do.

BLACK: You didn't answer my question.

BLUE: *(About to answer. Pause.)* I prefer not to.

(Pause.)

BLACK: Do you know why you were asked to come today?

BLUE: To give the report.

BLACK: But why are you willing to give the report to me?

BLUE: Because you're the one who's here. If it had been someone else, I would have given it to him.

BLACK: It doesn't bother you that I might be the wrong man?

BLUE: You didn't ask me to identify myself. That means you know who I am. And if you know me, I know you.

BLACK: But what if I know more about you than you know about me?

BLUE: I wouldn't count on it.

(Pause.)

BLACK: How did it work?

BLUE: I followed him. I watched what he did. Then I'd write my report. Every Sunday night.

BLACK: And then?

BLUE: I'd mail it to the post box number on Monday morning.

BLACK: Did you ever wonder what they thought?

BLUE: Sometimes. Of course I did. *(Pause.)* But since my check came every week, I figured they thought I was doing a good job.

BLACK: And the man. Did you ever wonder what he thought of you?

BLUE: He never saw me. *(Pause.)* That was the point, wasn't it? He wasn't supposed to know I was watching him.

BLACK: But didn't you ever feel like talking to him? Didn't you ever want . . . to know him?

BLUE: It made no difference to me. *(Pause.)* I thought, How much can I get to know just from watching him? It interested me . . . as a kind of puzzle. *(Pause.)* So I watched him. I'd plant myself outside his house in the morning and wait for him to come out. Most of the time, he never seemed to go anywhere. Nothing more than rudimentary kinds of things: grocery shopping, an occasional haircut, now and then a movie. But mostly he just wandered around the streets. *(Pause.)* He seemed to look at things in spurts. For a while, say, it would be buildings, craning his neck to catch a glimpse of the roofs, inspecting doors, running his hands over the facades . . . And then, for a week or two, he'd look at people . . . or the boats in the river . . . or the signs in the street. *(Pause.)* For a long time I thought he didn't have any kind of life at all. *(Pause.)* I mean, he didn't *do* anything. From everything I could gather, he lived alone. He never saw anyone, he didn't go to a job, it was an effort for him even to speak. *(Pause. Thinks.)* This went on for more than a year, maybe two. I can't remember. He was so blank, he hardly seemed to be there. *(Pause.)* In all that time, I learned nothing about him. *(Pause.)* Nothing. *(Pause.)* I could write down what he did, I could tell you what kind of soap he bought, what clothes he wore, but it didn't really amount to anything. *(Pause.)* I never had the slightest idea what he was thinking.

BLACK: Did it bother you?

BLUE: *(Shrugs.)* It made no difference to me. *(Pause.)* I was doing my job, I was getting paid, it made no difference at all.

BLACK: And then?

BLUE: *(Pause. Thinks. Remembers.)* Somehow or other, it started to change. I can't really say why. *(Pause.)* I think . . . I started to like him. *(Pause.)* One day I woke up, and I realized I couldn't wait to go out and watch him, to see what he did.

BLACK: You were having troubles of your own then, weren't you?

BLUE: What do you mean?

BLACK: *(Pause.)* Family troubles.

BLUE: You mean my wife.

BLACK: Your wife. Your children. *(Pause.)* They . . . disappeared.

BLUE: She walked out on me, if that's what you mean.

BLACK: More or less.

BLUE: Yes. My wife walked out on me. *(Pause.)* I admit it. *(Pause. Without emotion.)* I was a terrible husband. A terrible father.

BLACK: It's nothing to be ashamed of.

BLUE: *(Shrugs.)* A matter of opinion.

(For the past few sentences, Green has been breaking pencil points, tossing the broken pencil on floor and picking up a new one. He now breaks several points in rapid succession. Black and Blue stop talking and stare at him. Green smiles at them with embarrassment. Indicates he is ready to proceed again and gestures to them to continue.)

BLACK: And then?

BLUE: I had more time.

BLACK: You changed your life.

BLUE: My life?

BLACK: You moved, didn't you? Across the street . . . *(pause)* . . . from the man.

BLUE: It seemed like a practical thing to do. It was winter, after all. *(Pause.)* I could watch from the window, keep myself warm. Warm and hidden. *(Pause.)* When he went out, I went out.

BLACK: Is that when it started?

BLUE: What?

BLACK: To get . . . under your skin. *(Pause.)* I think those were your words.

BLUE: I didn't have anything else to do, you see. *(Pause.)* There was nothing else to think about.

BLACK: So you sat by the window and wrote . . . *(pause)* . . . about the man.

BLUE: I started to ask myself questions. I thought: no one could possibly be interested in this man. No one would pay me every week to do what I was doing, except . . . *(slight pause, about to continue)—*

BLACK: Except?

BLUE: —the man himself.

BLACK: *(Nervously.)* But why would he do a thing like that?

BLUE: *(Shrugs.)* I have no idea. *(Pause.)* I'm just giving you the story. As it happened.

BLACK: And then?

BLUE: I thought it might be useful to see if he was the one who picked up my reports at the post office. I hung around there all week, each day in a different disguise. I like that kind of thing: the false mustaches, the wigs, the rubber noses, the makeup, the clothes. *(Pause.)* Brown, the man who broke me into the business twenty years ago, said I was one of the best he'd ever seen. *(Pause.)* Anyway, on the sixth day he finally came.

BLACK: Was it the man?

BLUE: *(Pause.)* I'm not sure. *(Pause.)* He was in disguise, too.

BLACK: But couldn't you tell?

BLUE: I had my suspicions, but I couldn't be sure. *(Pause.)* He was wearing a mask. One of those things kids wear at Halloween. A big rubber mask of a goblin. *(Pause.)* What was I supposed to do? Go up and tear it off his face? *(Pause.)* I couldn't risk blowing my cover.

BLACK: Did you ever try again?

BLUE: A few more times. But nothing ever came of it. *(Pause.)* He was always wearing a different mask.

BLACK: You say "he." But it might have been "they," couldn't it? A different man each time. A different man in a different mask each time.

BLUE: Exactly.

BLACK: And then?

BLUE: Another year or so went by. I decided on a new approach. *(Pause.)* I thought I would make contact with him. *(Pause.)* I was itchy to get into disguise again, and he was beginning to drive me crazy. *(Pause.)* I mean, nothing ever changed. I felt trapped. As if, my God, this is going to go on forever.

BLACK: What did you do?

BLUE: I waited for my moments. The first time, I pretended to be a bum, begging nickels on the corner. He gave me a nickel and said, "God bless you." It was the first time I ever heard him speak. *(Pause.)* Another time, I pretended to be an out-of-town business-man, a blowhard in a polyester suit. I stopped him for directions and managed to talk my way into buying him a drink. We stayed for a few hours in that bar, the Algonquin I think it was. I can't remember. *(Gesturing to reports on Black's desk.)* It's all written down.

BLACK: Did you talk?

BLUE: We both talked.

BLACK: And?

BLUE: He told me he was a detective. For the past few years he'd been working on one case. He went on about it for half the evening. Following a man, he said, day in, day out, until he knew that man as well as he knew himself.

BLACK: Did you feel he was on to you then?

BLUE: Of course he was on to me. *(Pause.)* He was making fun of me.

BLACK: Did it make you uncomfortable?

BLUE: It made me feel like an idiot. *(Pause.)* I nearly quit right then and there.

BLACK: Why didn't you?

BLUE: *(Thinks.)* Because, even so, I had made several important discoveries. *(Pause.)* First of all, he was the man who had hired me. There was no question about that anymore. Second, he needed me. There was something he wanted me to know, and little by little he was letting me in on his secret.

BLACK: Couldn't you guess?

BLUE: No. *(Pause.)* The whole thing escaped me. *(Pause.)* All I knew was that he was calling the shots. Clues, legwork, investigative routine—all those things didn't matter anymore. I was on my own. *(Pause.)* At the same time, I had to keep up appearances . . . go about my business . . . do the job I was supposedly being paid to do.

BLACK: You played dumb.

BLUE: Very dumb.

BLACK: But of course he knew that.

BLUE: Of course.

BLACK: And then?

BLUE: Little by little, I began to lose patience again. *(Pause.)* I cooked up another scheme. *(Pause.)* But of course, by this time, I couldn't tell if it was my idea or his. *(Pause.)* I did the old routine of the Fuller brush man. I've always had luck with it. Knocked on his door and offered to show him my samples.

BLACK: Did he let you in?

BLUE: Of course he let me in.

BLACK: Why do you think?

BLUE: Because he was ready to have me come. He wanted me to be there.

BLACK: *(Reflective.)* Ah.

BLUE: The apartment was one large room. Nearly bare. A small, neatly made bed in one corner. A kitchenette in another corner. Also neat. Not a crumb to be seen. In the center of the room there was a wooden table with a single stiff-backed wooden chair. Pencils, pens, a typewriter. And then the piles of paper, manuscripts, neatly stacked around the edges of the table, on the floor by the legs of the table, and on the shelves of the book case that covered the entire north wall of the apartment. Other than that, nothing. No telephone, no radio, no books. Nothing. It wasn't a room you could really live in. A place to think, maybe. A place to write. But that's all. *(Pause.)* I realized that what I had seen was all there was. From the very beginning. *(Pause.)* The man had no life you could call a life.

BLACK: What did you talk about?

BLUE: The brushes. We had to keep up appearances, remember. That was part of the game.

BLACK: And then?

BLUE: Little by little, I began to ask him questions. About this, about that, very casually, part of my salesman's patter. *(Pause.)* He told me that he was a writer and that for a long time he had been working on a book. I asked him when I would get a chance to read his work. He said he didn't know. Maybe never, he said. He didn't know if he'd live to finish it.

BLACK: And then?

BLUE: *(Long pause.)* I made up my mind to steal the manuscripts.

BLACK: It sounds as if you were beginning . . . to overstep your bounds.

BLUE: No. He was asking me to take them.

BLACK: In so many words?

BLUE: Never in so many words. Of course not. Nothing said was ever what was meant. That was the point. *(Pause.)* It was a matter of understanding him in advance . . . of reading between the lines. *(Pause.)* Eventually I caught on.

BLACK: Did you go through with it?

BLUE: The next night. *(Pause.)* I knew what I was doing, you see. There was no need to waste time.

BLACK: Did you wait until he was out . . . or did you try some other method?

BLUE: I didn't bother about any of that. *(Pause. Emphatically.)* I knew what I was doing. *(Pause.)* It must have been about eight-thirty, nine o'clock. I had no trouble picking the lock. *(Pause. Remembering.)* Child's play. *(Pause.)* I walked into the room, and there he was, sitting on the bed, as if . . . thinking. *(Pause.)* He was wearing the mask. The same one he had been wearing that first time in the post office.

(Black opens desk drawer, takes out Halloween mask, and puts it on.)

BLACK: Was it this mask?

BLUE: That's the one.

(Green starts giggling at the sight of the mask. Black and Blue turn to stare at him. A long moment. Green gestures for them to continue.)

BLACK: And then?

BLUE: He didn't say a word. He didn't move. *(Pause.)* I walked over to the table, picked up a pile of manuscripts at random, put them under my arm, and left the room.

BLACK: He did nothing to stop you?

BLUE: You still don't understand. *(Pause.)* He was waiting for me. He wanted me to take it. *(Pause.)* But I should have taken more. That was my only slip. *(Pause.)* So I went back the next night, and the next night after that.

BLACK: And what happened?

BLUE: The same thing. Nothing. Nothing happened.

BLACK: Did you read the manuscripts?

BLUE: Every word.

BLACK: And?

BLUE: The whole thing was there. *(Pause.)* More or less as I had imagined it.

BLACK: You weren't . . . disappointed?

BLUE: Not really. *(Pause.)* It seemed to make a kind of sense.

BLACK: *(Pause.)* And then?

BLUE: I went back one more time. *(Pause.)* But now it was different.

BLACK: In what way?

BLUE: He had a gun.

(Black takes a gun out of his inside breast pocket. Holds it up. Points it at Blue.)

BLACK: This gun?

BLUE: Yes. That's the one.

BLACK: And then?

BLUE: I opened the door, entered the room, and there he was, sitting on the bed, pointing that forty-five at my face. He said, "That's enough, my friend. You've taken it as far as it can go."

BLACK: And what did you say?

BLUE: Nothing. I didn't say a word. *(Pause.)* I snapped. Something inside me went crazy. *(Pause.)* I kicked the gun out of his hand, grabbed him by the collar, and started banging his head against the wall. I picked him up, threw him down, kicked him in the ribs, punched him in the face. I wanted to kill him.

BLACK: Did you?

BLUE: *(Pause.)* I'm not sure.

BLACK: *(Angry.)* Not sure? *(Pause.)* There's no middle ground, my friend. It's either life or death. There's nothing in between.

BLUE: I couldn't tell. He was still breathing when I left, but I didn't think he'd last much longer. He seemed to be bleeding inside, and he was unconscious.

BLACK: *(Enraged.)* And now? What is he now? Alive or dead?

BLUE: *(Hesitates.)* Alive.

BLACK: *(Shouting.)* Are you sure?

BLUE: *(Hesitates.)* Dead.

BLACK: *(Beside himself.)* Are you sure?

BLUE: No. I'm not sure. I'm not sure of anything.

(Lights out. Ten seconds. Lights on. All three in same positions. Black no longer wearing mask, no longer holding gun.)

BLUE: *(To Black.)* Are you finished now?

BLACK: Yes. It's finished.

BLUE: Nothing to add, nothing to take away?

BLACK: No. It's finished.

BLUE: Is it true that the boy died?

BLACK: I'm not sure.

BLUE: And the man, the one in the ditch. What was his name?

BLACK: White.

BLUE: Whatever happened to White?

BLACK: I'm not sure.

BLUE: And Gray? Is he alive or dead?

BLACK: Probably dead.

BLUE: Are you ready to talk about it?

BLACK: Later. I'll tell you the whole story later.

BLUE: And Green, what does he say?

BLACK: *(To Green.)* Green, what do you say?

GREEN: *(Pause. Looking up.)* What?

BLACK: What do you say, Green?

GREEN: *(Putting down his pencil. Clears throat, as if preparing for a long speech. Hesitates.)* Nothing. I don't say a thing.

BLACK: *(To Blue.)* Green doesn't say a thing.

BLUE: A pity.

BLACK: *(Takes gun from pocket and points it at Green.)* What do you say now, Green?

GREEN: *(Long pause, staring at gun.)* Nothing.

BLACK: Nothing?

GREEN: *(Slamming palm down on desk in anger. Shouting.)* Nothing!

BLUE: *(Sighs.)* Let's take it from the top again.

(Black puts gun back in pocket. Green resumes writing position.)

BLACK: I'm not sure there's anything to discuss.

BLUE: Let me be the judge of that. *(Pause. To Green.)* Are you ready, Green?

GREEN: *(Long pause. At last realizing he has been addressed.)* Are you speaking to me?

BLUE: Are you ready?

GREEN: Ready? Of course I'm ready. *(Holds up pencil.)* The pencil's ready. *(Holds up page.)* The paper's ready. *(Half stands up and gives brief bow.)* And Green's ready.

BLUE: Good. *(Pause. To Black.)* Is the little boy dead?

BLACK: Yes, he's dead. I don't think there's any doubt about it.

BLUE: And White?

BLACK: He was kicked to death.

BLUE: And Gray?

BLACK: He blew his brains out.

BLUE: And Black?

BLACK: What about Black?

BLUE: That's what I'm asking you. What about Black?

BLACK: *(Thinks.)* I don't know. *(Pause.)* Black doesn't count. *(Pause.)* Black is the one who isn't there.

BLUE: And what does Black say?

BLACK: *(Thinks.)* Black says he's tired. *(Pause.)* Black says he can't go on anymore. *(Pause.)* Black says nothing.

(Lights out. Ten seconds. Lights on. All three in same positions. Green is slowly tearing up the pages he has written, one by one. Blue and Black are watching him. A long moment.)

BLACK: *(To Green.)* Are you finished?

GREEN: *(Still tearing pages.)* Almost finished.

(Long pause. Green goes on tearing pages.)

BLACK: *(To Green.)* Are you finished now?

GREEN: *(Still tearing pages.)* Almost finished.

(Long pause. Green goes on tearing pages.)

BLACK: *(To Green.)* Are you finished now?

GREEN: *(Tearing last page.)* Finished.

BLUE: Good. I think we're ready to begin now. *(Pause. Turning to Green.)* Are you ready to begin, Mr. Green?

GREEN: Yes, I'm ready.

BLUE: *(To Black.)* And you, Mr. Black?

BLACK: I'm ready.

GREEN: And what about you, Mr. Blue?

BLUE: Yes, I'm ready.

BLACK: Good. Let's get on with it, then, shall we?

(Pause. Five seconds. Lights out.)

HEAVY WEATHER

BRUCE STERLING

BY JUNE 15 it was obvious to the veriest wannabe weather-tyro that an outbreak from the dimension of hell was about to descend upon Oklahoma. As a direct consequence, the state was having its largest tourist boom in ten years.

Everyone with the least trace of common sense had battened down, packed up, and/or evacuated. But the sensible evacuees did not begin to match the raw demographic numbers of people without any common sense, those who had come swarming in an endless procession of trailers, chartered buses, and motorized bicycles. Oklahoma had become an instant Mecca for heavy-weather freaks. And there were far more of these people than Jane had ever imagined.

After some hesitation, many of the people with sense had shamefacedly returned to ground zero, to make sure that the freaks were not stealing everything. Which, in fact, the freaks were doing, in their jolly, distracted sort of way. Anadarko, Chickashaw, Weatherford, and Elk City, their cheaper hotels packed and their city parks full of squatters' tents, had turned into slobbering, good-natured beer busts, punctuated with occasional nocturnal shootings and smash-and-grab raids. The National Guard had been called out to maintain order, but in Oklahoma the National Guard was pretty much always out. The National Guard was one of the largest employers in the state, right up there with crops, livestock, timber, and Portland cement. The paramilitary Guard sold the marauders souvenir T-shirts and Sno-Kones by day, then put on their uniforms and beat the shit out of them by night.

To judge by the frantically enthusiastic local TV coverage, most everybody involved was perversely and frankly enjoying the hysterical, unbearable edge of weather tension. The sky was canary yellow and full of dust, and great fearsome sheets of dry heat-lightning crackled all evening, and everything smelled of filth and sweat and ozone, and the people were actively savoring this situation. The drought had simply gone on too long. The people of Tornado Alley had suffered far too much already. They had gone far past fear. They had even gone past grim resignation. By now, the poor bastards were deep into convulsively ironical black humor.

The people trickling in from all over America—including, of course, Mexico and Canada—were a far different crowd of wannabes than the standard tornado chasers. The standard tornado freak tended to be, at heart, a rather bookish, owlish sort, carefully reading the latest netcasts and polishing his digital binoculars so he could jump out the door and frantically pursue a brief, elusive phenomenon that usually lasted bare minutes.

But the current heavy-weather crowd was a different scene entirely, not the weatherpeople Jane was used to, not the ones she had expected. Even though they were in the heart of the continent and long kilometers from any shore, they were much more like your basic modern hurricane crowd.

Heavy-weather freaks came in a lot of sociological varieties. First, there were a certain number of people who genuinely didn't give a damn about living. People in despair, people actively hunting their own destruction. The overtly suicidal, though a real factor and kind of the heart-and-soul of the phenomenon, were a very small minority. Most of these mournful black-clad Hamlets would suddenly rediscover a strong taste for survival once the wind outside hit a solid, throbbing roar.

Second, and far more numerous, were the rank thrill-freaks, the overtanned jocks and precancerous muscular surfer-dude types. It was amazing how few of these reckless idiots would be killed or maimed, by even the worst storms. They usually sported Aqua-Lungs and windsurfing smart-boards, with which they intended to hunt the Big Wave, the Really Big Wave, the Insanely Big Wave. No surf in Oklahoma, though; so, with the grotesque ingenuity of a leisure industry far gone into deep psychosis, they had brought dozens of mean-ass little diamond-hubbed "wind schooners," sail-powered vehicles so inherently unpredictable that even their on-board computer navigation acted crazy. And yet the sons of bitches who rode the things seemed to bear a charmed life. They were as hard to kill as cockroaches.

Then there were the largest group, the variant people who simply admired and doted on storms. Most of them didn't hack storms. Sometimes they took photos or videos, but they had no intellectual or professional interests. They were simply storm devotees. Some of them were deeply religious. Some wrote really bad net-poetry. Some few of them were very private people—with tattoos and chains and scab-art—who would take hallucinogens and/or hold deliberate orgies in bunkers at the height of the troubles. They all tended to have a trademark look of vacant sincerity, and odd fixations on dress and diet.

Fourth, thieves. People on the lookout for the main chance. Looters, black marketeers, rip-off people. Structure-hit people, too. Not tremendous numbers, not whole marauding armies of them, but plenty to worry about. They tended to leave mysterious chalk-mark symbols wherever they went, and to share mulligatawny stew in vacant buildings.

And last—the group rising up the charts, and the group that Jane found, basically, by far the least explicable, the creepiest, and the most portentous—evacuation freaks. People who flourished *just after* storms. People who liked to dwell in evacuation camps. Perhaps they'd grown up in such a camp during the State of Emergency, and always perversely missed the experience afterward. Or maybe they just enjoyed that feeling of intense, slightly hallucinatory human community that always sprang up in the aftermath of a major natural disaster. Or maybe they just needed disaster to really live, because having grown up under the crushing weight of heavy weather, they had never possessed any real life.

If you had no strong identity of your own, then you could become anyone and everyone, inside an evacuation camp. The annihilation of a town or suburb broke down all barriers of class, status, and experience, and put everyone into the same paper suit.

Some people—growing numbers of them, apparently—actively fed on that situation. They were a new class of human being, something past charlatan, something past fraudster or hustler, something without real precedent, something past history, something past identity. Sometimes—a lot of times—the evacuation freak would be the heart and soul of the local recovery effort, a manic, pink-cheeked person always cheerful, with a smile for everybody, always ready to console the bereaved, bathe the wounded, play endless games of cot-side charades with the grateful crippled children. Often they passed themselves off as pastors or medical workers or social counselors or minor-league feds of some kind, and they would get away with it, too, because no one was checking papers in the horror and pain and confusion.

They would stay as long as they dared, and eat the government chow and wear the paper suits and claim vaguely to be from "somewhere around." Oddly, evacuation freaks were almost always harmless, at least in a physical sense. They didn't steal, they didn't rob, they didn't kill or structure-hit. Some of them were too dazed and confused to do much of anything but sit and eat and smile, but quite often they would work with literally selfless dedication, and inspire the people around them, and the people would look up to them, and admire them, and trust them implicitly, and depend on these hollow people as a community pillar of strength. Evacuation freaks were both men and women. What they were doing was not exactly criminal, and even when caught and scolded or punished for it, they never seemed able to stop. They would just drift to some fresh hell in another state, and rend their garments and cover themselves with mud, and then stagger into camp, faking distress.

But the very weirdest part was that evacuation freaks always seemed to travel entirely alone.

If not for the drought, it would have been a very pretty area. The Troupe was camped west of El Reno on Interstate 40, an area of crumbling red-sandstone cliffs, red soil, creekbottoms full of pecans and aspens and festooned with honeysuckle, a place of goldenrod and winecup and coneflowers and trailing purple legume. Spring hadn't given up yet. It was parched and covered with dust, but spring hadn't given up.

Jerry stood before the firelight, his head bare, his hands behind his back. "Tomorrow we are going to track the most violent storm in recorded history," he said. "It will break tomorrow, probably by noon, and it will kill thousands—probably tens of thousands—of people. If it's stable and it persists beyond a few hours, it may kill millions. If we had time, and energy, and opportunity, I would try to save lives. But we don't, and we can't. We don't have time, and we don't have authority, so we can't save anyone. We can't even save ourselves. Our own lives are not our top priority tomorrow."

The people in the powwow circle were very silent.

"In the terrible scale of tomorrow's event, our lives just don't matter much. Knowledge of the F6 is more important than any of us. I wish this weren't the case, but it's the truth. I want you to understand that truth and accept it, I want you to take it into your hearts and feel it, and resolve to act on it. People, you've all seen the simulations, you know what I mean when I say F6. But people, the damned thing is finally upon us. It is here, it's real, no playback this time, no simulacrum. It is with us in stark reality. We have to know all that we can about the real F6, at all costs. It is terrible event that must be documented—at all costs. Tomorrow we must seize as much of the truth as we can possibly steal from this dreadful thing. Even if we all die doing this, but some survivor learns the truth about it because of our efforts, then that will be an excellent price for our lives."

Jerry began to pace back and forth. "I don't want any recklessness tomorrow. I don't want any amateurism, I don't want any nonsense. What I want from you is complete resolve, and complete understanding of the necessity and the consequences. We have only one chance. This is the greatest heavy-weather challenge that our Troupe will ever face, and I hope and believe it will be the single most violent weather-event we will see in our natural lifetimes. If you believe that your life is more important than hacking this storm, I can understand that belief. It's wise. Most people would call it sensible. You are all here with me now because you're definitely not most people, but what I'm asking from you now is a terrible thing to ask of anyone. This isn't just another storm pursuit. It's not just another front, and another spike. This thing is Death, people. It's a destroyer of worlds. It's the worst thing human action has brought into this world since Los Alamos. If your life is your first priority, you should leave this camp immediately, now. I am forecasting a weather-event that is more swift, more volatile, more massive, and more violent than the strongest F5 maxitornado, by a full order of magnitude. If you want to escape the disaster, you should flee right now, due east, and not stop until you are on the far side of the Mississippi. If you stay, stay in the full knowledge that we are going after this catastrophe head-on."

Nobody moved. Nobody said anything.

Suddenly the air was split with a bloodcurdling bestial yell, a warbling, yodeling, exultant screech like that of a madwoman gloating over a freshly severed scalp.

It was Joanne Lessard. They all stared at Joanne in complete astonishment. Joanne was sitting crosslegged on a patch of bubblepak near the campfire. She had just washed her thin blond hair and was combing it. She said nothing, but only smiled sunnily in the flickering firelight, shrugged her shoulders once, and kept combing.

Even Jerry seemed stunned.

"I've said enough," Jerry realized, and deliberately sat down.

Rudy Martinez stood up. "Jerry, are you nowcasting tomorrow?"

"Yeah."

"I'll go anywhere as long as Jerry is nowcasting. I've said enough." Rudy sat down.

Joe Brasseur stood up. "I'm available for consultation by anyone who hasn't made their will. Dying intestate, that's no joke for your heirs. We've got enough time tonight to record a will, put on a digital signature, and pipe it to an off-site backup. This means you, Dunnebecke. I've said enough." He sat down.

Nobody said anything for a long time.

Finally Jane felt she had to stand up. "I just want to say that I feel really proud of everybody. And I have a good feeling about this. Good hunting tomorrow, people. I've said enough." She sat down.

April Logan stood up. "Forgive me for interrupting your deliberations, but if it's all right with the group, I'd like to ask all of you something."

April Logan looked at Jerry. Jerry lifted his brows.

"Actually, it's something of a poll query."

"Go ahead, just ask," Jane hissed at her.

"My question is: When do you think the human race conclusively lost control over its own destiny? I'd like everyone here to answer, if you don't mind." April produced a handheld notepad. "Please just start anywhere in the circle—here at my left will do."

Martha Madronich stood up reluctantly. "Well, I hate to go first, but in answer to your question, uhm, Professor, I always figured we lost it for good sometime during the State of Emergency." She sat down.

Ed Dunnebecke stood up. "I'd have to say 1968. Maybe 1967. If you look at the CO_2 statistics, they had a good chance to choke it all back right there, and they knew full well they were screwing the environment. There was definitely revolutionary potential in the period, and even some political will, but they squandered the opportunity in the drugs and the Marxism and the mystical crap, and they never regained the momentum. 1968, definitely. I've said enough."

Greg Foulkes stood up. "I'm with Ed on that one, except there was one last chance in 1989, too. Maybe even as late as '91, after the First Gulf War. Well, that one was actually the second Gulf War, strictly speaking. But after they blew their big chance at genuine New World Order in '89 and '91, they were definitely trashed. I've said enough." He sat down.

Carol Cooper stood up. "Well, you hear this question quite a bit, of course. . . . Call me romantic, but I always figured 1914. The First World War. I mean, you look at that long peace in Europe before the slaughter, and it looks like mediation might have had a chance to stick. And if we hadn't blown most of the twentieth century on fascism and communism and the rest of the -ism bullshit, maybe we could have built something decent, and besides, no matter what Janey says, Art Nouveau was the last really truly decent-looking graphic art movement. I've said enough."

Sam Moncrieff took his turn. "Late 1980s . . . there were some congressional hearings on global warming that everybody ignored.

. . . Also the Montreal Accords on chlorofluorocarbons; they should have passed those with some serious teeth about CO_2 and methane, and things would be a lot better today. Still heavy weather, probably, but not insanely heavy. Late eighties. Definitely. I've said enough."

Rick Sedletter rose. "What Greg said." He sat down.

Peter Vierling stood up. "Maybe it's just me, but I always felt like if personal computers had come along in the 1950s instead of the 1970s everybody would have saved a lot of time. Well . . . never mind." He sat down.

Buzzard stood up. "I think they blew it with the League of Nations in the twenties. That was a pretty good idea, and it was strictly pig-stupid isolationism on the part of the U.S.A. that scragged that whole thing. Also the early days of aviation should have worked a lot better. Kind of a real wings-over-the-world opportunity. A big shame that Charles Lindbergh liked fascists so much. I've said enough."

Joanne stood up. "1945. United Nations could have rebuilt everything. They tried, too. Some pretty good declarations, but no good follow-through, though. Too bad. I've said enough."

Joe Brasseur stood. "I'm with Joanne on the 1940s thing. I don't think humanity ever really recovered from the death camps. And Hiroshima, too. After the camps and the Bomb, any horror was possible, and nothing was certain anymore. . . . People never straightened up again after that; they always walked around bent and shivering and scared. Sometimes I think I'd rather be scared of the sky than that scared about other human beings. Maybe it was even worth heavy weather, to miss nuclear Armageddon and genocide. . . . I wouldn't mind discussing this matter with you later, Professor Logan. But for the meantime, I've said enough."

Ellen Mae Lankton spoke. "Me? If I gotta blame somebody, I blame Columbus. Five hundred and thirty-nine years of oppression and genocide. I blame Columbus, and that bastard who designed the repeating rifle. You'd never find an F6 on any plain that was still covered with buffalo. . . . But I've said this before, and I've said it enough." She sat down.

Ed Dunnebecke stood up. "Funny thing, but I think the French Revolution had a very good chance and blew it. Europe wasted the next two centuries trying to do what the Revolution had right in its grasp in 1789. But once you stumble into that public-execution nonsense . . . Hell, that was when I knew the Regime had lost it during the State of Emergency, when they started cablecasting their goddamn executions. Give 'em to Madame Guillotine, and the Revolution will eat its young, just as sure as hell. . . . Yeah, put me down for 1789. I've said enough."

Jeff Lowe rose to his feet. "I don't know very much about history. Sorry."

Mickey Kiehl stood up. "I think we lost it when we didn't go for nuclear power. They coulda designed much better plants than they did, and a hell of a lot better disposal system, but they didn't because of that moral taint from the Bomb. People were scared to death of any kind of 'radiation' even when a few extra curies aren't really dangerous. I'd say 1950s. When the atomic energy people hid behind the military security bullshit instead of really trying to make fission work safely for real people in real life. So we got all-natural CO_2 instead. And the CO_2 ruined everything. I've said enough."

Jerry stood up. "I think it's fruitless to look for first causes or to try to assign blame. The atmosphere is a chaotic system; humanity might have avoided all those mistakes and still found itself in this conjunction. That begs the question of when we lost control of our destiny. We have none now; I doubt we ever had any."

"I'm with Jerry on this one," Jane said cheerfully. "Only more so. I mean, if you look back at the glacial records for the Eemian period, the one before the last set of ice ages, there were no people around to speak of, and yet the weather was completely crazy. Global temps used to soar and dip eight, nine, ten degrees within a single century! The climate was highly unstable, but that was a completely natural state. And then right after that, most of Europe, Asia, and America was covered with giant cliffs of ice that smashed and froze everything in their path. Even worse than agriculture and urbanization! And a lot worse than heavy weather is now. I'm real sorry that we did this to ourselves and that we're in the fix we are in now, but so-called Mother Earth herself has done worse things to the planet. And believe it or not, the human race has actually had it worse."

326 • Bruce Sterling

"Very good," said April Logan. "Thanks very much for that spectrum of opinion by people who ought to know. Since I have no intention of being here when Dr. Mulcahey's forecast is tested, I'll be taking his advice and leaving Oklahoma immediately. I wish you all the very best of luck." She turned to Jane. "If I can do anything for you, leave E-mail."

END OF THE 1980s

BRET EASTON ELLIS

THE SMELL OF blood works its way into my dreams, which are, for the most part, terrible: on an ocean liner that catches fire, witnessing volcanic eruptions in Hawaii, the violent deaths of most of the inside traders at Salomon, James Robinson doing something bad to me, finding myself back at boarding school, then at Harvard, the dead walk among the living. The dreams are an endless reel of car wrecks and disaster footage, electric chairs and grisly suicides, syringes and mutilated pinup girls, flying saucers, marble Jacuzzis, pink peppercorns. When I wake up in a cold sweat I have to turn on the wide-screen television to block out the construction sounds that continue throughout the day, rising up from somewhere. A month ago was the anniversary of Elvis Presley's death. Football games flash by, the sound turned off. I can hear the answering machine click once, its volume lowered, then twice. All summer long Madonna cries out to us, *"Life is a mystery, everyone must stand alone . . ."*

When I'm moving down Broadway to meet Jean, my secretary, for brunch, in front of Tower Records a college student with a clipboard asks me to name the saddest song I know. I tell him, without pausing, "You Can't Always Get What You Want" by the Beatles. Then he asks me to name the happiest song I know, and I say "Brilliant Disguise" by Bruce Springsteen. He nods, makes a note, and I move on, past Lincoln Center. An accident has happened. An ambulance is parked at the curb. A pile of intestines lies on the sidewalk in a pool of blood. I buy a very hard apple at a Korean deli which I eat on my way to meet Jean who, right now, stands at the Sixty-seventh Street entrance to Central Park on a cool, sunny day in September. When we look up at the clouds she sees an island, a puppy dog, Alaska, a tulip. I see, but don't tell her, a Gucci money clip, an ax, a woman cut in two, a large puffy white puddle of blood that spreads across the sky, dripping over the city, onto Manhattan.

We stop at an outdoor café, Nowheres, on the Upper West Side, debating which movie to see, if there are any museum exhibits we should attend, maybe just a walk, she suggests the zoo, I'm nodding mindlessly. Jean is looking good, like she's been working out, and she's wearing a gilt lamé jacket and velvet shorts by Matsuda. I'm imagining myself on television, in a commercial for a new product—wine cooler? tanning lotion? sugarless gum?—and I'm moving in jump-cut, walking along a beach, the film is black-and-white, purposefully scratched, eerie vague pop music from the mid-1960s accompanies the footage, it echoes, sounds as if it's coming from a calliope. Now I'm looking into the camera, now I'm holding up the product—a new mousse? tennis shoes?—now my hair is windblown then it's day then night then day again and then it's night.

"I'll have an iced decaf au lait," Jean tells the waiter.

"I'll have a decapitated coffee also," I say absently, before catching myself. "I mean . . . de*caff*einated." I glance over at Jean, worried, but she just smiles emptily at me. A Sunday *Times* sits on the table between us. We discuss plans for dinner tonight, maybe. Someone who looks like Taylor Preston walks by, waves at me. I lower my Ray-Bans, wave back. Someone on a bike pedals past. I ask a busboy for water. A waiter arrives instead and after that a dish containing two scoops of sorbet, cilantro-lemon and vodka-lime, are brought to the table that I didn't hear Jean order.

"Want a bite?" she asks.

"I'm on a diet," I say. "But thank you."

"You don't need to lose any weight," she says, genuinely surprised. "You're kidding, right? You look great. Very fit."

"You can always be thinner," I mumble, staring at the traffic

in the street, distracted by something—what? I don't know. "Look
. . . better."

"Well, maybe we shouldn't go out to dinner," she says, concerned. "I don't want to ruin your . . . willpower."

"No. It's all right," I say. "I'm not . . . very good at controlling
it anyway."

"Patrick, seriously. I'll do whatever you want," she says. "If
you don't want to go to dinner, we won't. I mean—"

"It's okay," I stress. Something snaps. "You shouldn't fawn
over him. . . ." I pause before correcting myself. "I mean . . . *me*.
Okay?"

"I just want to know what you want to do," she says.

"To live happily ever after, right?" I say sarcastically. "That's
what *I* want." I stare at her hard, for maybe half a minute, before
turning away. This quiets her. After a while she orders a beer. It's
hot out on the street.

"Come on, smile," she urges sometime later. "You have no
reason to be so sad."

"I know," I sigh, relenting. "But it's . . . tough to smile. These
days. At least *I* find it hard to. I'm not used to it, I guess. I don't
know."

"That's . . . why people need each other," she says gently,
trying to make eye contact while spooning the not inexpensive sorbet into her mouth.

"Some don't." I clear my throat self-consciously. "Or, well,
people compensate. . . . They adjust. . . ." After a long pause,
"People can get accustomed to anything, right?" I ask. "Habit does
things to people."

Another long pause. Confused, she says, "I don't know. I guess
. . . but one still has to maintain . . . a ratio of more good things
than . . . bad in this world," she says, adding, "I mean, right?"
She looks puzzled, as if she finds it strange that this sentence has
come out of her mouth. A blast of music from a passing cab, Madonna again, *"Life is a mystery, everyone must stand alone . . ."*
Startled by the laughter at the table next to ours, I cock my head
and hear someone admit, "Sometimes what you wear to the office
makes all the difference," and then Jean says something and I ask
her to repeat it.

"Haven't you ever wanted to make someone happy?" she asks.

"What?" I ask, trying to pay attention to her. "Jean?"

Shyly, she repeats herself. "Haven't you ever wanted to make someone happy?"

I stare at her, a cold, distant wave of fright washes over me, dousing something. I clear my throat again and, trying to speak with great purposefulness, tell her, "I was at Sugar Reef the other night . . . that Caribbean place on the Lower East Side . . . you know it—"

"Who were you with?" she interrupts.

Jeanette. "Evan McGlinn."

"Oh." She nods, silently relieved, believing me.

"Anyway . . ." I sigh, continuing, "I saw some guy in the men's room . . . a total . . . Wall Street guy . . . wearing a one-button viscose, wool, and nylon suit by . . . Luciano Soprani . . . a cotton shirt by . . . Gitman Brothers . . . a silk tie by Ermenegildo Zegna and, I mean, I recognized the guy, a broker, named Eldridge . . . I've seen him at Harry's and Au Bar and DuPlex and Alex Goes to Camp . . . all the places, but . . . when I went in after him, I saw . . . he was writing . . . something on the wall above the . . . urinal he was standing at." I pause, take a swallow of her beer. "When he saw me come in . . . he stopped writing . . . put away the Mont Blanc pen . . . he zipped up his pants . . . said Hello, Henderson to me . . . checked his hair in the mirror, coughed . . . like he was nervous or . . . something and . . . left the room." I pause again, another swallow. "Anyway . . . I went over to use the . . . urinal and . . . I leaned over . . . to read what he . . . wrote." Shuddering, I slowly wipe my forehead with a napkin.

"Which was?" Jean asks cautiously.

I close my eyes, three words fall from my mouth, these lips: " 'Kill . . . All . . . Yuppies.' "

She doesn't say anything.

To break the uncomfortable silence that follows, I mention all I can come up with, which is, "Did you know that Ted Bundy's first dog, a collie, was named Lassie?" Pause. "Had you heard this?"

Jean looks at her dish as if it's confusing her, then back up at me. "Who's . . . Ted Bundy?"

"Forget it," I sigh.

"Listen, Patrick. We need to talk about something," she says. "Or at least *I* need to talk about something."

. . . where there was nature and earth, life and water, I saw a desert landscape that was unending, resembling some sort of crater, so devoid of reason and light and spirit that the mind could not grasp it on any sort of conscious level and if you came close the mind would reel backward, unable to take it in. It was a vision so clear and real and vital to me that in its purity it was almost abstract. This was what I could understand, this was how I lived my life, what I constructed my movement around, how I dealt with the tangible. This was the geography around which my reality revolved: it did not occur to me, *ever,* that people were good or that a man was capable of change or that the world could be a better place through one's taking pleasure in a feeling or a look or a gesture, of receiving another person's love or kindness. Nothing was affirmative, the term "generosity of spirit" applied to nothing, was a cliché, was some kind of bad joke. Sex is mathematics. Individuality no longer an issue. What does intelligence signify? Define reason. Desire—meaningless. Intellect is not a cure. Justice is dead. Fear, recrimination, innocence, sympathy, guilt, waste, failure, grief, were things, emotions, that no one really felt anymore. Reflection is useless, the world is senseless. Evil is its only permanence. God is not alive. Love cannot be trusted. Surface, surface, surface was all that anyone found meaning in . . . this was civilization as I saw it, colossal and jagged . . .

". . . and I don't remember who it was you were talking to . . . it doesn't matter. What does is that you were very forceful, yet . . . very sweet and, I guess, I knew then that . . ." She places her spoon down, but I'm not watching her. I'm looking out at the taxis moving up Broadway, yet they can't stop things from unraveling, because Jean says the following: "A lot of people seem to have . . ." She stops, continues hesitantly, "Lost touch with life and I don't want to be among them." After the waiter clears her dish, she adds, "I don't want to get . . . bruised."

I think I'm nodding.

"I've learned what it's like to be alone and . . . I think I'm in love with you." She says this last part quickly, forcing it out.

Almost superstitiously, I turn toward her, sipping an Evian water, then, without thinking, say, smiling, "I love someone else."

As if this film had speeded up she laughs immediately, looks quickly away, down, embarrassed. "I'm, well, sorry . . . gosh."

"But . . ." I add quietly, "you shouldn't be . . . afraid."

She looks back up at me, swollen with hope.

"Something can be done about it," I say. Then, not knowing why I'd said that, I modify the statement, telling her straight on, "Maybe something can't. I don't know. I've thrown away a lot of time to be with you, so it's not like I don't care."

She nods mutely.

"You should never mistake affection for . . . passion," I warn her. "It can be . . . not good. It can . . . get you into, well, trouble."

She's not saying anything and I can suddenly sense her sadness, flat and calm, like a daydream. "What are you trying to say?" she asks lamely, blushing.

"Nothing. I'm just . . . letting you know that . . . appearances can be deceiving."

She stares at the *Times* stacked in heavy folds on the table. A breeze barely causes it to flutter. "Why . . . are you telling me this?"

Tactfully, almost touching her hand but stopping myself, I tell her, "I just want to avoid any future misconnections." A hardbody walks by. I notice her, then look back at Jean. "Oh come on, don't look that way. You have nothing to be ashamed of."

"I'm not," she says, trying to act casual. "I just want to know if you're disappointed in me for admitting this."

How could she ever understand that there isn't any way I could be disappointed since I no longer find anything worth looking forward to?

"You don't know much about me, do you?" I ask teasingly.

"I know enough," she says, her initial response, but then she shakes her head. "Oh let's just drop this. I made a mistake. I'm sorry." In the next instant she changes her mind. "I want to know more," she says, gravely.

I consider this before asking, "Are you sure?"

"Patrick," she says breathlessly, "I know my life would be . . . much emptier without you . . . in it."

I consider this too, nodding thoughtfully.

"And I just can't . . ." She stops, frustrated. "I can't pretend these feelings don't exist, can I?"

"Shhh . . ."

. . . there is an idea of a Patrick Bateman, some kind of abstraction, but there is no real me, only an entity, something illusory, and though I can hide my cold gaze and you can shake my hand and feel flesh gripping yours and maybe you can even sense our lifestyles are probably comparable: *I simply am not there.* It is hard for me to make sense on any given level. Myself is fabricated, an aberration. I am a noncontingent human being. My personality is sketchy and unformed, my heartlessness goes deep and is persistent. My conscience, my pity, my hopes disappeared a long time ago (probably at Harvard) if they ever did exist. There are no more barriers to cross. All I have in common with the uncontrollable and the insane, the vicious and the evil, all the mayhem I have caused and my utter indifference toward it, I have now surpassed. I still, though, hold on to one single bleak truth: no one is safe, nothing is redeemed. Yet I am blameless. Each model of human behavior must be assumed to have some validity. Is evil something you are? Or is it something you do? My pain is constant and sharp and I do not hope for a better world for anyone. In fact I want my pain to be inflicted on others. I want no one to escape. But even after admitting this—and I have, countless times, in just about every act I've committed—and coming face-to-face with these truths, there is no catharsis. I gain no deeper knowledge about myself, no new understanding can be extracted from my telling. There has been no reason for me to tell you any of this. This confession has meant *nothing.* . . .

I'm asking Jean, "How many people in this world are like me?"

She pauses, carefully answers, "I don't . . . think anyone?" She's guessing.

"Let me rephrase the ques—Wait, how does my hair look?" I ask, interrupting myself.

"Uh, fine."

"Okay. Let me rephrase the question." I take a sip of her dry beer. "Okay. *Why* do you like me?" I ask.

She asks back, *"Why?"*

"Yes," I say. "Why."

"Well . . ." A drop of beer has fallen onto my Polo shirt. She hands me her napkin. A practical gesture that touches me. "You're

. . . concerned with others," she says tentatively. "That's a very rare thing in what"—she stops again—"is a . . . I guess, a hedonistic world. This is . . . Patrick, you're embarrassing me." She shakes her head, closing her eyes.

"Go on," I urge. "Please. I want to know."

"You're sweet." She rolls her eyes up. "Sweetness is . . . sexy . . . I don't know. But so is . . . *mystery*." Silence. "And I think . . . mystery . . . you're mysterious." Silence, followed by a sigh. "And you're . . . considerate." She realizes something, no longer scared, stares at me straight on. "And I think shy men are romantic."

"How many people in this world are like me?" I ask again. "Do I really appear like that?"

"Patrick," she says. "I wouldn't lie."

"No, of course you wouldn't . . . but I think that . . ." My turn to sigh, contemplatively. "I think . . . you know how they say no two snowflakes are ever alike?"

She nods.

"Well, I don't think that's true. I think a lot of snowflakes are alike . . . and I think a lot of people are alike too."

She nods again, though I can tell she's very confused.

"Appearances *can* be deceiving," I admit carefully.

"No," she says, shaking her head, sure of herself for the first time. "I don't think they are deceiving. They're not."

"Sometimes, Jean," I explain, "the lines separating appearance—what you see—and reality—what you don't—become, well, blurred."

"That's not true," she insists. "That's simply not true."

"Really?" I ask, smiling.

"I didn't use to think so," she says. "Maybe ten years ago I didn't. But I do now."

"What do you mean?" I ask, interested. "You *used* to?"

. . . a flood of reality. I get an odd feeling that this is a crucial moment in my life and I'm startled by the suddenness of what I guess passes for an epiphany. There is nothing of value I can offer her. For the first time I see Jean as uninhibited; she seems stronger, less controllable, wanting to take me into a new and unfamiliar land—the dreaded uncertainty of a totally different world. I sense she wants to rearrange my life in a significant way—her eyes tell me this and though I see truth in them, I also know that one day, sometime very soon, she too will be locked in the rhythm of my insanity. All I have to do is keep silent about this and not bring it up—yet she weakens me, it's almost as if *she's* making the decision about who I am, and in my own stubborn, willful way I can admit to feeling a pang, something tightening inside, and before I can stop it I find myself almost dazzled and moved that I might have the capacity to accept, though not return, her love. I wonder if even now, right here in Nowheres, she can see the darkening clouds behind my eyes lifting. And though the coldness I have always felt leaves me, the numbness doesn't and probably never will. This relationship will probably lead to nothing . . . this didn't change anything. I imagine her smelling clean, like tea . . .

"Patrick . . . talk to me . . . don't be so upset," she is saying.

"I think it's . . . time for me to . . . take a good look . . . at the world I've created," I choke, tearfully, finding myself admitting to her, "I came upon . . . a half gram of cocaine . . . in my armoire last . . . night." I'm squeezing my hands together, forming one large fist, all knuckles white.

"What did you do with it?" she asks.

I place one hand on the table. She takes it.

"I threw it away. I threw it all away. I wanted to *do* it," I gasp, "but I threw it away."

She squeezes my hand tightly. "Patrick?" she asks, moving her hand up until it's gripping my elbow. When I find the strength to look back at her, it strikes me how useless, boring, physically beautiful she really is, and the question *Why not end up with her?* floats into my line of vision. An answer: she has a better body than most other girls I know. Another one: everyone is interchangeable anyway. One more: it doesn't really matter. She sits before me, sullen but hopeful, characterless, about to dissolve into tears. I squeeze her hand back, moved, no, touched by her ignorance of evil. She has one more test to pass.

"Do you own a briefcase?" I ask her, swallowing.

"No," she says. "I don't."

"Evelyn carries a briefcase," I mention.

"She does . . . ?" Jean asks.

"And what about a Filofax?"

"A small one," she admits.

"Designer?" I ask suspiciously.

"No."

I sigh, then take her hand, small and hard, in mine.

. . . and in the southern deserts of Sudan the heat rises in airless waves, thousands upon thousands of men, women, children, roam throughout the vast bushland, desperately seeking food. Ravaged and starving, leaving a trail of dead, emaciated bodies, they eat weeds and leaves and . . . lily pads, stumbling from village to village, dying slowly, inexorably; a gray morning in the miserable desert, grit flies through the air, a child with a face like a black moon lies in the sand, scratching at his throat, cones of dust rising, flying across land like whirling tops, no one can see the sun, the child is covered with sand, almost dead, eyes unblinking, grateful (stop and imagine for an instant a world where someone is grateful for something) none of the haggard pay attention as they file by, dazed and in pain (no—there *is* one who pays attention, who notices the boy's agony and smiles, as if holding a secret), the boy opens and closes his cracked, chapped mouth soundlessly, there is a school bus in the distance somewhere and somewhere else, above that, in space, a spirit rises, a door opens, it asks *"Why?"*—a home for the dead, an infinity, it hangs in a void, time limps by, love and sadness rush through the boy . . .

"Okay."

I am dimly aware of a phone ringing somewhere. In the café on Columbus, countless numbers, hundreds of people, maybe thousands, have walked by our table during my silence. "Patrick," Jean says. Someone with a baby stroller stops at the corner and purchases a Dove Bar. The baby stares at Jean and me. We stare back. It's really weird and I'm experiencing a spontaneous kind of internal sensation, I feel I'm moving toward as well as away from something, and anything is possible.

CONTRIBUTORS

MARK AMERIKA's novels, *The Kafka Chronicles* and *Sexual Blood*, appeared in the new Black Ice Books Avant-Pop Series, published by Fiction Collective2, which he now coedits. His on-line, hot-line Avant-Pop magazine, *Alt-X* (accessible via the Internet), has recently devoted an issue to Avant-Pop, coedited with Avant-Professor Lance Olsen. He is a resident of Boulder, Colorado.

PAUL AUSTER lives in Brooklyn and is a translator, a poet, an essayist, and the author of numerous books of fiction, which include a trilogy of Avant-Pop detective novels (*City of Glass, Ghosts,* and *The Locked Room*) and, most recently, *Mr. Vertigo*.

Based in San Francisco, retired Air Force Colonel CRAIG BALDWIN has been tracking conspiracies over twenty years and across five continents. Despite the risk to his personal safety, Colonel Baldwin continues to make public his astonishing findings through lectures, seminars, and screenings (his research is also released on film and video). His new project, "Sonic Outlaws," rips the lid off media piracy, pastiche, and pranks in the new electronic folk culture. His complete works are available through Drift Distribution.

DAVID BLAIR's electronic video, *Wax, or the Discovery of Television among the Bees* (1990), was the film sent across the Internet. *Waxweb* (1994), a collaborative hypertext version of *Wax* that includes alternative histories, commentary, sound, and images, is currently accessible via the

Internet. With his wife and collaborator, Florence Ormezzano, he lives in New York City, where he is working on a new feature, *Jews in Space*.

In 1989 NORMAN CONQUEST founded the International Anti-Censorship art collective, Beuyscouts of Amerika. His work includes multiples of political satire, conceptual projects, book objects, and collage-text manipulations. Several of his recent pieces were chosen for the permanent collection of the Museum of Modern Art. He currently lives with his alterego, Derek Pell, in southern California.

ROBERT COOVER teaches at Brown University, where he directed a pilot program on the use of hyptext in creative writing courses. A pioneer of the Avant-Pop sensibility during the sixties, Coover is the author of many books, including *The Origin of the Brunists, Pricksongs and Descants* (1970), *A Night at the Movies* (1986), and most recently, *Pinocchio in Venice* (1990).

RICARDO CORTEZ CRUZ's avant-rap novel, *Straight Outta Compton*, won the Nilon Excellence in Minority Fiction Award. His second novel, *Five Days of Bleeding*, will appear soon from Black Ice Books (Fiction Collective2). He teaches at Southern Illinois University at Carbondale.

SUSAN DAITCH is the author of two novels, *LC* and *The Colorist*. She lives in New York City.

DON DELILLO has published many novels, including seminal Avant-Pop treatments of rock music (*Great Jones Street*), football (*End Zone*), and the Kennedy assassination (*Libra*).

RIKKI DUCORNET has published a tetralogy of novels based on the four natural elements: *The Stain* (earth), *Entering Fire* (fire), *The Fountains of Neptune* (water), and *The Jade Cabinet* (air). She has also illustrated books by Robert Coover and J. L. Borges. Her volume of collected stories, *The Complete Butcher's Tales*, was recently published by Dalkey Archive Press.

STEVE ERICKSON's most recent novels, *Tours of a Black Clock* and *Arc d'X*, are Avant-Pop (by way of Faulkner and Marquez) versions of science fiction's alternate-world motif. He lives in Los Angeles.

BRET EASTON ELLIS has published four novels, including *Less Than Zero, American Psycho*, and *The Informers*.

EURUDICE's first novel, *F/32*, has been translated into Dutch, Greek, and Japanese. Born on Lesbos, Greece, and now teaching at Brown University, she is the self-proclaimed nymph/priestess/goddess/whore of Avant-Pop. She is currently working on *EHMH: A Millennial Romance*.

LAUREN FAIRBANKS is the author of *Sister Carrie* (a novel) and *Muzzle Thyself* (poems), both published by Dalkey Archive Press.

RAYMOND FEDERMAN is Distinguished Professor of English and Comparative Literature at the State University of New York at Buffalo and the author of seven novels (in English and French), three volumes of poems, and several books of essays. The winner of numerous literary awards, Federman is also a regular at the craps table in Las Vegas and the Seniors Golf Champion at Westwood Country Club (1994).

WILLIAM GIBSON's *Neuromancer* launched the cyberpunk movement of the mid-eighties; his next two novels, *Count Zero* and *Mona Lisa Overdrive,* completed his Cyberspace Trilogy. He has also published *Virtual Light* and *The Difference Engine* (done in collaboration with Bruce Sterling).

The recipient of a McArthur genius grant, GUILLERMO GÓMEZ-PEÑA is a performance artist and author who lives in Santa Monica. His *Gringostroika* was published by Greywolf Press in 1993.

HAROLD JAFFE's five fiction collections and three novels include four Avant-Pop collections: *Straight Razor, Eros Anti-Eros, Madonna and Other Spectacles,* and *Beasts.*

The author of several seminal Avant-Pop works, including *Creamy and Delicious* (1969) and *Saw* (1972), STEVE KATZ has recently published *43 Fictions* (Sun and Moon Press) and *Journalism* (Bamberger).

A San Francisco resident, MARC LAIDLAW has spent most of his adult life in office buildings, writing on company word processors. His first novel, *Dad's Nuke,* was one of the seminal works of the cyberpunk movement; he has also published a cyborg-Buddhist novel, *Neon Lotus*, and *Kalifornia.*

The most intense, and in a certain sense, the most significant young prose writer in America, MARK LEYNER is the author of *I Smell Esther Williams; My Cousin, My Gastroenterologist;* and *Et tu, Babe.* His collection of avant-journalism, *Tooth Imprints on a Corn Dog,* recently appeared from Harmony/Crown.

BEN MARCUS's first book will be published by Knopf. He is a resident of New York City.

CRAIG PADAWER lives in New York City, where he is currently completing his first novel.

DEREK PELL's avant-porn collection, *X-Texts,* recently appeared from Autonomedia. The author of numerous text-and-collage books, including the *Doktor Bey* Series and a send-up of the Warren Commission Report (*Assassination Rhapsody*), he and his alter ego, Norman Conquest, currently reside in San Diego.

TOM ROBBINS is the author of six highly acclaimed novels, including *Even Cowgirls Get the Blues, Jitterbug Perfume,* and *Skinny Legs and All.* A frequent visitor to some of the world's largest cities, he lives at the end of a dead-end road on an Indian reservation north of Seattle.

BRUCE STERLING's early novels, *The Artificial Kid, Schizmatrix,* and *Islands in the Net,* were seminal cyberpunk novels. His recent publications include a nonfiction study of the computer underworld, *The Hacker Crackdown,* and a novel, *Heavy Weather.*

RONALD SUKENICK is the author of several influential early Avant-Pop works, including *Up* (1968), *Out* (1973), *98.6* (1975), and *Blown Away* (1986). His recent collection, *Doggy Bag,* appeared in Black Ice Books' Avant-Pop series, which he coedits. One of the cofounders of the Fiction Collective, and editor and publisher of *American Book Review,* Sukenick currently teaches in the University of Colorado at Boulder MFA program.

LYNNE TILLMAN is the author of the novels *Haunted Houses, Motion Sickness,* and *Cast in Doubt* and of two collections of stories, *Absence Makes the Heart* and *The Madam Realism Complex.* A contributing editor to *Bomb* and *New Observations,* she has most recently written the text for *The Velvet Years,* a book of Stephen Shore's photographs of Andy Warhol and the Factory.

GERALD VIZENOR is Professor of Native American Studies at the University of California, Berkeley. He has published a number of avant-pop-flavored "trickster" novels and story collections, including *Griever—A Chinese Monkey King in China* and *The Heirs of Columbus.*

WILLIAM T. VOLLMANN's recent publications include *The Rifles* (the third of a projected septology of "dream novels" which will eventually comprise a symbolic history of the United States), *Whores for Gloria, Thirteen Stories and Thirteen Epitaphs,* and *Butterfly Stories.*

DAVID FOSTER WALLACE is the author of a collection of fiction, *The Girl with Curious Hair,* and a novel, *The Broom of the System.* He currently teaches in the literature department at Illinois State University, Normal, and is completing a new novel.

Professor of English at Illinois State University, Normal, CURTIS WHITE is co-director of the Fiction Collective2 and Black Ice Books and is the author of *Heretical Songs, Metaphysics in the Midwest,* and *The Idea of Home.*

STEPHEN WRIGHT has written Avant-Pop novels dealing with Vietnam (*Meditations in Green*), UFO-contactees (*M-31*), and serial killers (*Going Native*). A Brooklyn resident who teaches at Princeton University, Wright is working on a novel about the American Civil War.

ACKNOWLEDGMENTS

This volume never could have been assembled without the generosity, support, and suggestions of many different people. My thanks first of all to my editor, Paul Slovak, for his encouragement, his general good taste, his many valuable suggestions at every stage of this book's formulation, and his patience and understanding when a plague of locusts, car thieves, and writer's block created delays.

I'd also like to thank Lester Bowie for the loan of the term *Avant-Pop*, which I ripped off from the title of his 1986 album. In many ways, the Avant-Pop sensibility is most easily recognized in music, and certainly I owe a great deal of my understanding of Avant-Pop to musicians such as Eugene Chadbourne, David Byrne, Brian Eno, Peter Gabriel, Public Enemy, Laurie Anderson, Carl Stalling, Spike Jones, Bruce Springsteen (of *The Wild, the Innocent, and the E-Street Shuffle* period), and especially John Zorn. Zorn's liner notes to his Avant-Pop masterpiece, *Spillane*, were particularly helpful to my understanding of the role of collaboration for contemporary composers, as well as artists generally.

I received valuable input from a number of different writers and critics while formulating my sense of what Avant-Pop actually implies. The most important input was that of Takayuki Tatsumi, Avant-Professor at Tokyo's Keio University, who also arranged for me to publish my first essays about the Avant-Pop phenomenon in the Japanese magazines *Positive* and *Subaru*. Raymond Federman, Brian McHale, Mark Amerika, Yoshiaki Sato, Ronald Sukenick, Robert Coover, and Jim McMenamin all made valuable contributions to my thinking about the aesthetic and cultural implications of Avant-Pop during its long gestation.

Over the years a number of the contributors to this volume have been generous enough to sit down and spend several hours talking with me about their work and interests in formal interviews that contributed greatly, directly and indirectly, to my treatment of the Avant-Pop sensibility. An all-nighter with David Foster Wallace brought some welcome flashbacks to earlier days of heated discussions with people who cared passionately about books and ideas (this was way back before irony had been invented)—David said a lot that night about television that made an impression on me, as did his essay on television ("E Unibus Pluram: Television and U.S. Fiction") that appeared in the *Review of Contemporary Fiction* Younger Writers Issue. Thanks once again to all the writers who have been willing to let me drop in on them that way.

Thanks to Susan Sontag for the "hang time" you gave me during your visit to San Diego. Sontag's *On Photography* remains, for me anyway, the single best study of the key concepts associated with Avant-Pop as well Postmodernism (though she never uses the P-word) and was invaluable to me in formulating my own thoughts about Avant-Pop.

Thanks to Bob Coover for the bluntness of his response in an interview to a long-winded, jargon-laden question about the "fabulist," "antirealist/metafictionist" nature of his work; you let me babble on, the way so many other PoMo critics tend to, about the death of realism, the death of final meanings, and so forth, and then replied simply, "Maybe I think that my writing has always been realistic and that until now it has simply been misperceived as being otherwise." Thanks—I needed that.

I was midway through writing these acknowledgments when a package arrived from Bruce Sterling; inside was Kevin Kelly's *Out of Control: The Rise of Neo-Biological Civilization* and a note saying, "Drop whatever else you're doing and read this!" Having learned always to heed Sterling's advice when offered, I plunged into Kelly's fascinating paradigm-bashing study of the evolution of complexity and wound up borrowing a number of his ideas about the "hive mind" of our contemporary "Network Culture." Other critical studies which I found useful in exploring the relationship of Avant-Pop to Modernism and Postmodernism included Brian McHale's *Constructing Postmodernism;* Fredric Jameson's *Postmodernism, or the Cultural Logic of Late Captialism;* Christian J. Mamiya's *Pop Art and Consumer Culture;* Greil Marcus's *Lipstick Traces: A Secret History of the Twentieth Century* and *Dead Elvis;* Jean Baudrillard's *Simulations;* Elizabeth Young and Graham Caveny's *Shopping in Space: Essays on America's Blank Generation;* Ronald Sukenick's *Down* and In: Life in the Underground; and Dick Hedbige's "Notes on Pop" (included in Modern Dreams: The Rise and Fall of Pop.

For my conclusions regarding how so much twentieth-century art reflects the impact of technologically driven change, I have also drawn heavily from Robert Hughes's thoughtful study of Modernist painting, The Shock of the New, which also supplied the translation of the 1918 Berlin Dadaist Manifesto cited in my Introduction to this volume.

Robert Coover, William Gibson, Paul Auster, Tom Robbins, William T. Vollmann, Mark Leyner, and Bruce Sterling were all generous enough to sign up for this project in its earliest stages, thereby supplying me with a "core" manuscript of infinitely hot-and-dense materials that could expand into its present format.

Once again, my wife Sinda Gregory has been my chief collaborator. Without her good sense, good humor, and encouragement, this anthology would have crashed long before yesterday.

My thanks, too, to all the authors, agents, and their publishers for allowing me to reprint the following materials—often at significant price cuts:

"Tribulation 99" originally appeared in the book version of Craig Baldwin's film, Tribulation 99. The book version was designed by Peggy Ahwesh, Rick Pieto, and Keith Sanborn and published by Ediciones La Calavera (copyright 1990 by Craig Baldwin; reprinted by permission of Ediciones La Calavera). David Blair's "Ella's Special Camera" was downloaded from Waxweb, a collaborative hypertext version of his remarkable electronic video, Wax, or the Discovery of Television among the Bees Susan Daitch's "X ≠ Y" originally appeared in Fiction International and Bomb (copyright 1988 by Susan Daitch). Don DeLillo's "The Rapture of the Athlete Assumed into Heaven" was first performed at the American Repertory Theater (Cambridge, Mass.); it also appeared in The Quarterly (copyright 1990 by Don DeLillo; used by permission of the Wallace Literary Agency). "The Exorcist," by Rikki Ducornet, originally appeared in The Stain, published by Grove Press, 1984; reprinted by Dalkey Archive Press, 1995 (copyright by Rikki Ducornet, 1984; reprinted here by permission of Dalkey Archive Press). "End of the 1980s" is from American Psycho, by Bret Easton Ellis (copyright 1988 by Bret Easton Ellis; reprinted by permission of Vintage Books, a Division of Random House). The excerpt from Arc d' X is by Steve Erickson (copyright by Steve Erickson; reprinted by permission of Simon & Schuster, Inc). Lauren Fairbanks's "Victims of Mass Imagination" originally appeared in her novel Sister Carrie (copyright 1993 by Lauren Fairbanks; reprinted by permission of Dalkey Archive Press). Somewhat different versions of William Gibson's "Skinner's Room" appeared originally in Visionary San Fran-

cisco, published by the San Francisco Museum of Contemporary Art, and *Omni Magazine* (copyright 1991 by William Gibson). The excerpts from Guillermo Gómez-Peña's "Border Brujo" originally appeared in *Gringo-stroika* (copyright 1992 by Guillermo Gómez-Peña; reprinted by permission of Greywolf Press, St. Paul, Minnesota). A somewhat different version of Harold Jaffe's "Counter Couture" appeared originally in *Central Park* (copyright 1993 by Harold Jaffe). Somewhat different versions of Marc Laidlaw's "Great Breakthroughs in Darkness" originally appeared in *New Worlds 2* and *Postmodern Culture.* Mark Leyner's "Oh, Brother" originally appeared in *The New Republic* (copyright 1994 by Mark Leyner; used by permission of Harmony/Crown Publishers). A somewhat different version of Ben Marcus's "False Water Society" originally appeared in *Conjunctions* (copyright 1993 by Ben Marcus; used by permission of the Georges Borchardt Literary Agency). Lynne Tillman's "Bad News" originally appeared in *Border Lines,* published by Serpent's Tail Press in 1993. A somewhat different version of Bruce Sterling's "Heavy Weather" appeared in *Heavy Weather,* published by Bantam Books (copyright 1993 by Bruce Sterling). William T. Vollmann's "Incarnations of the Murderer" originally appeared in *Postmodern Culture* (copyright 1992 by William T. Vollmann). David Foster Wallace's "Tri-Stan" originally appeared in *Grand Street* (copyright 1992 by David Foster Wallace). Stephen Wright's "Light" originally appeared in his novel *M-31,* published by Harmony/Crown Publishers (copyright 1988 by Stephen Wright; used by permission of the Georges Borchardt Literary Agency).

347

FOR THE BEST IN PAPERBACKS, LOOK FOR THE

In every corner of the world, on every subject under the sun, Penguin represents quality and variety—the very best in publishing today.

For complete information about books available from Penguin—including Puffins, Penguin Classics, and Arkana—and how to order them, write to us at the appropriate address below. Please note that for copyright reasons the selection of books varies from country to country.

In the United Kingdom: Please write to *Dept. JC, Penguin Books Ltd, FREEPOST, West Drayton, Middlesex UB7 0BR.*

If you have any difficulty in obtaining a title, please send your order with the correct money, plus ten percent for postage and packaging, to *P.O. Box No. 11, West Drayton, Middlesex UB7 0BR*

In the United States: Please write to *Consumer Sales, Penguin USA, P.O. Box 999, Dept. 17109, Bergenfield, New Jersey 07621-0120.* VISA and MasterCard holders call 1-800-253-6476 to order all Penguin titles

In Canada: Please write to *Penguin Books Canada Ltd, 10 Alcorn Avenue, Suite 300, Toronto, Ontario M4V 3B2*

In Australia: Please write to *Penguin Books Australia Ltd, P.O. Box 257, Ringwood, Victoria 3134*

In New Zealand: Please write to *Penguin Books (NZ) Ltd, Private Bag 102902, North Shore Mail Centre, Auckland 10*

In India: Please write to *Penguin Books India Pvt Ltd, 706 Eros Apartments, 56 Nehru Place, New Delhi 110 019*

In the Netherlands: Please write to *Penguin Books Netherlands bv, Postbus 3507, NL-1001 AH Amsterdam*

In Germany: Please write to *Penguin Books Deutschland GmbH, Metzlerstrasse 26, 60594 Frankfurt am Main*

In Spain: Please write to *Penguin Books S.A., Bravo Murillo 19, 1° B, 28015 Madrid*

In Italy: Please write to *Penguin Italia s.r.l., Via Felice Casati 20, I-20124 Milano*

In France: Please write to *Penguin France S.A., 17 rue Lejeune, F–31000 Toulouse*

In Japan: Please write to *Penguin Books Japan, Ishikiribashi Building, 2–5–4, Suido, Bunkyo-ku, Tokyo 112*

In Greece: Please write to *Penguin Hellas Ltd, Dimocritou 3, GR–106 71 Athens*

In South Africa: Please write to *Longman Penguin Southern Africa (Pty) Ltd, Private Bag X08, Bertsham 2013*